D1047414

The Shining Shining Path

Also by Carroll Dale Short

I Left My Heart in Shanghi, Alabama (essays)

The Shining Shining Path

CARROLL DALE SHORT

Black Belt Press
Montgomery

The Black Belt Press
P.O. Box 551
Montgomery, AL 36101

This is a work of fiction. The characters, names, incidents, dialogue and plots are the product of the author's imagination or are used fictitiously. Any resemblance to actual persons or events is purely coincidental.

 Published in the United States by the Black Belt Press, a division of the Black Belt Communications Group, Inc., Montgomery, Alabama.

Design by Randall Williams

Printed in the United States of America

95 96 97 5 4 3 2 1

The Black Belt, defined by its dark, rich soil, stretches across central Alabama. It was the heart of the cotton belt. It was and is a place of great beauty, of extreme wealth and grinding poverty, of pain and joy. Here we take our stand, listening to the past, looking to the future.

This book is dedicated to Mary,
in appreciation for my new life;

To my mother, for reading me stories;

To my son Donovan, my father B.J., my grandparents,
and all my kin, for believing;

To Jesse Hill Ford, novelist and teacher extraordinaire;

To Alan Rinzler, story coach without equal;

To Randall Williams, publisher and human being
of rare faith and substance;

To Laurie Fox and Linda Chester, agents of my dreams;

And to the amazing Ray Bradbury,
whose gift of language and worlds lighted my way
through the dark halls of childhood.

Evil is a true thing. It goes about on its own legs.
Maybe some day it will come to visit you.
Maybe it already has.

—Cormac McCarthy

Some day, beyond the reach
Of mortal kin
Some day, God only knows
Just where or when
The wheels of earthly life
Will all stand still
And we shall go to dwell
On Zion's hill …

—Old Southern hymn

Caveat Emptor

This story is not to be construed as a reliable guide to the contemporary practice of Buddhism or of mathematics, nor to the actual monks of Drepung, for whom I have the utmost love and respect.

—C.D.S.

The Shining Shining Path

1

BY THE TIME THE blue Chrysler van carrying the six Tibetan monks finally got around the jackknifed poultry truck on Interstate 80 and found the exit to Kennesaw College, the program chairman at the Pride of the Prairie was in such a state of agitation that she had to go to the bathroom and splash cold water on her face and, moreover, take the last two Midol she had been saving for Intro to Volleyball at three o'clock that afternoon.

A willowy, severe-faced girl in a poplin sun dress, she met the monks' road manager at the door of the auditorium, wringing her hands. "Oh, thank God," she said. "I don't know how much longer I could have held them."

Turner looked past her at the collective student bodies sprawled in various attitudes of repose, loudly eating and drinking in spite of the huge signs forbidding it. A cherry-colored boom box on somebody's shoulder squealed out a distorted heavy-metal guitar solo.

"The guys dressed on the way, to save time," Turner explained to her. "Just give us about five minutes to unload the instruments." Actually, Chai Lo had given him hell the whole way for taking the interstate instead of the meandering two-lane with the brilliant corn rows so close on its shoulders you could almost grab an ear through the window. *The fast way takes so long you die*, was how the axiom roughly translated into English. Sure enough, if Turner had gone the scenic route through Bodine and LaSalle and East Jesus they'd have been here an hour ago. Monks loved being right better than birthdays.

The day now having been saved, though, the girl in the sun dress pressed her advantage. "Was there, like, some mistake? Didn't the contract say eleven-thirty?" The telltale print of a green Student Government Association check extended from the bundle of papers she held defensively against her bosom.

Turner leaned in close and looked placidly into the depths of her eyes for a count of ten, then slowly extended his palm as if feeling an unseen wall. "Here is truth," he said. "The fast way takes so long you die."

The girl's face was transfigured by wonder. "Wow! Neat!" she said, letting her papers sink gradually to waist level, where a gust of wind from the open door whisked up the check and let it sift lazily to the carpet. Turner retrieved it and held it out to her, but she only stared.

"Neat," she said.

Turner glanced to see the amount was right and slipped the check in his pocket.

Back at the van, Chai Lo—having already ventured out to find the college's vending machines—sat on the grass in the sun drinking a Coke. Bah Tow, Wah So, and Se Hon had put on their ceremonial saffron headdresses and brocaded temple gowns and were un-telescoping the sacred brass horns to their full eight-foot length.

Except for the fact that Bah Tow stood a good head-and-a-half taller than the other two, the trio looked enough alike to be brothers. They had seemed vaguely offended when Turner first pointed this out—though not nearly as offended as when, in an ill-considered moment, he had asked Wah So and Se Hon if they would mind wearing name badges to help him tell them apart.

Beh Vah, the youngest and most athletic of the monks, turned ecstatic cartwheels across the sloping lawn, his robe falling at the apex of each handstand to flash his bony brown legs. Across the way the college track team leaned against the chain link fence, transfixed by the spectacle.

Lu Weh was nowhere to be seen.

"Shy! Where's Louie?"

Chai Lo took an unhurried sip of his Coke and looked up at Turner with skeptical interest. Like the other monks, he had the broad golden face and heavy-lidded eyes of his race. He also looked disconcertingly like Jack Webb in the old *Dragnet.*

Chai Lo shrugged. "Sid," he said.

"Look, Shy, I don't need this. *Where* is he hid?"

The sitting monk looked east, west, then sipped his Coke and shrugged again. "Knoll sings," he said. "Spear it."

Turner felt the first tentative tremors of a headache destined to tip the Richter Scale. He made himself breathe deeply. "I *know* his spirit is in all things, but I need his butt on the stage in five minutes. Please, Shy. Please."

Turner grabbed up the fiberboard trunk with the ceremonial table adornments and hustled it down the sidewalk toward the backstage entrance, motioning for the others to follow him. In the air-conditioned dimness behind the closed stage curtains he extended the legs of the card table, spread it with the crimson cloth, and meticulously arranged the display—a task for which he'd had to get special dispensation from the Lama back at the Drepung monastery, since it was usually performed only by regular initiates of the order.

First, in the center, went the gold-framed watercolor of the Dalai Lama, the Great One; then on either side the brass candleholders and dishes of incense which Turner lit with his Bic in clockwise motion, careful not to feel haste or urgency. Simple as the arrangement looked, he had been nearly six months into his stay at Drepung before he'd performed it to the monks' satisfaction.

The first five months, he had arranged and unarranged the implements for a couple of hours daily while the head Lama (who appeared to be reading rather than watching) glanced up occasionally to cluck his tongue in pity, although offering no guidance on why the result had fallen short. Then, toward the middle of the sixth month, when Turner was frustrated and ready to chuck the whole idea, he was overcome one morning with a fit of aggravation and threw the table accouterments together in slapdash fashion, rattling and banging as he went. Before the noise had echoed away he was already remorseful, fully expecting the Lama to fail him on the exercise permanently and perhaps even ask him to leave.

But to his surprise the old spiritual master, whose name was Won Se, looked up from his text at the haphazard table setting and leaped into the air with a cry of rapture, falling on Turner's neck and smothering him with hugs. Won Se raced out of the room and rounded up a crowd of monks to come see. Each one who arrived repeated Won Se's delighted shout and praised Turner's accomplishment profusely, slapping his shoulders and hugging each other with abandon. The bare stone chamber took on the air of a locker room after a championship football game, and his months of frustration became lighter than nothing, became fragrance, became a shining path. His eyes misted over with relief and joy.

"Does it please you?" Won Se shouted, in Tibetan, above the clamor, "Does it please you so?" And Turner, dabbing at his eyes, had said, "Yes. Yes, very much."

At which point Won Se fixed him with a look that was cosmic in its coldness. All the monks, as one, turned away and left him in the room alone. That afternoon and night when the initiates gathered for meals nobody spoke to Turner or even acknowledged his presence. The next morning at the appointed hour he went to the room where his training took place, half expecting to find that the table and implements had been taken away.

But they were there. He knelt and began going through the familiar motions again: packing and folding, unpacking and unfolding, arranging with an eye toward symmetry and an eye toward economy of motion, packing and folding and trying again. Won Se never showed up to supervise that day. Or the next, or the next.

On the fourth morning Won Se happened by and stuck his head in the door, with an elaborate show of surprise at finding Turner still at work. Turner asked politely, in his best Tibetan, for an explanation of how he'd messed up. Won Se answered with the most exasperating of Tibetan expressions, a slurred one-syllable grunt that translates loosely as *Tell yourself, I'll listen.*

"Losing my cool?" Turner guessed. "Was that it?"

Won Se stayed impassive.

"Pride, then. Being proud when you all bragged on me?"

No expression from Won Se.

"Damn it, it's human. As hard as I tried? Crucify me. There's no way I can set this table to your satisfaction."

A sign of life in Won Se. One slightly raised eyebrow. When he replied, it was with the second most dreaded phrase in the Tibetan language—one generally delivered, as now, with an expression of cherubic innocence. Crudely oversimplified, it means, "Oh. Is *that* what we're doing?"

Turner said, "Then I *don't* have to set it to your satisfaction?"

Won Se shrugged. "The fish in the sea is not thirsty."

From that day, whenever Turner was around and a formal occasion arose, they asked him to lay the implements. For the sacred dances, for the festivals. Once for a funeral.

Meanwhile the students' dull roar continued to sift through the stage curtains as Bah Tow and Se Hon and Wah So trotted up the steps with the sacred horns on their shoulders, long as fishing poles. Right behind them came Beh Vah, his short black hair speckled with grass clippings from the cartwheeling, and old Lu Weh, freshly back from invisibility, both carrying their tri-cornered celestial cymbals.

Chai Lo, patient as a sheep herder, brought up the rear with his stubby mountain flute under his arm. As he walked he drained the last precious drop of his Coke and crushed the can in his fist, an exercise taught him by a one-eyed truck driver in Duluth and which he had come to enjoy above most earthly things.

Turner followed a glow back into the stage-right wing and found a boy in gym clothes, with a massive neck and shoulders, dozing at the control panel. He shook him awake and asked that the house lights be brought down in preparation. As the dimming lever was pulled, screams and catcalls erupted from out in the auditorium.

Since they were running late Turner decided to dispense with his usual fifteen-minute speech introducing the monks and their practices by way of a cultural and political overview of the region, a talk in which he answered the obvious question of how a butcher's son from Birmingham, Alabama, had come nose to eyeball with the sublime beauty of the mystic arts in a fog-roped mountain pass at the farthest reaches of the planet. Or how he had thus forsaken an extraordinary career at its very height (the baddest impresario of rock-show tours east of the Mississippi: cover of *Rolling Stone*, cover of *People*, commander of LearJets, buddy to Keith and Mick, the entire nine yards) in order to break off a small piece of that mystical sublimity and set it moving in ever-widening circles across the land of the free and the home of the brave with a message for our time which we ignore at our peril.

The monks were in their places, instruments at the ready. The comforting fragrances of incense and candle oil layered the air. Chai Lo gave Turner a slow-motion half nod, his signal to begin. Turner took a series of deep breaths, licked his palms, slicked his unruly hair straight back, and pushed apart the gap in the curtains to get to the soft blue footlights and the waiting microphone. The pandemonium of the audience subsided by several decibels. There was a sprinkling of sarcastic applause.

"Ladies and gentlemen," Turner said, "the sacred music and dance of Tibet."

This next was his favorite part, the moment he never got tired of—being in the wings as the curtains parted, shaping himself a small peephole through which to watch the rows of bland, self-possessed, self-pleasuring Western faces come suddenly upon an outrageous bump of an idea smack in the middle of the smooth, complacent highway of their existence: a race of people whose artists and athletes, saints and scientists and warriors are one and the same in intent; a civilization whose single transcendent striving is the painstaking eradication of self. The Self, our pampered pet, our yin and yang, be-all and end-all, namesake of magazines, theology of television advertising, sweet ringing gloss of exterior life that almost, almost screens out the insistent siren of contradiction and wonder wailing from the delicate underbelly of the universe like a million expiring Met tenors.

Like nearly every crowd they'd played to, this one responded with an inrush of breath that filtered to long seconds of absolute silence as the curtains opened fully and the tableau was revealed in all its glorious intractability: a sunburst of regal reds and golds and burnished brass, throwing metallic catchlights across the monks' impassive faces as free of intent or hurry as some deep substratum of clay, faces that even eye-blinked in slow motion, betraying no tics or tension, no nervous glances, faces prepared to wait millennia for what came next.

What came next was the first low note from the telescoping brass horns, a sound that began below the range of sound and slowly swelled to fill the world, a full two octaves below thunder, a note that made a tuba sound like a piccolo by comparison. With no seeming effort from the mouths of the three players, the initial tone, which conjured up the distant foghorn of a ferry departing for a slower and more sublime universe, grew in amplification and resonance until it contained all the chaos of existence and then went beyond even that, the sound an entire galaxy would make if it could harness the energy of its infinite whirlings and machinations for the sole purpose of breaking wind.

There is but a single appropriate human response to a sound of such magnitude, and the crowd responded appropriately, just as Turner himself had done the first time he heard the sacred music.

They giggled.

The hoarse, chaotic blatting of the big horns sustained and sustained and kept sustaining to the point of absurdity, of impossibility, until the two pairs of cymbals awakened with the agility of a conscience and began to insert a frantic tap-dance of accountability and order into the stagnant air above the abyss the horns had created. The cymbals clanged and clattered out short rings, long rings, *p-ding-rang, p-ding-ding-rang,* metallic pirouettes with endless variability of attack and decay, until sufficient balance had been struck between form and formlessness that Chai Lo's small flute felt moved to address the implications of it all, calling out in a voice as piercing and plaintive as a human child lost in darkness from its mother.

The flute took as its whole theme a single note, the same value as the low note of the big horns but an eon of octaves higher. In counterpoint to the fading low blasts Chai Lo insinuated the same note again and again in different lengths and questionings, sometimes flexing it the least bit as if it were considering becoming a half tone higher or lower but couldn't bring itself to commit. A voice condemned to cry out its one song forever between the chaos of the depths and the celestial wind-chime of the unattainable.

The spectacle of which lulled the once-rowdy audience into a bemused sort of waking dream, the state that results when your thinking brain smacks head-on into something it can't explain or categorize and so in frustration shuts down, handing over the reins to your contemplative brain and enjoying the ride.

Except.

Except for a small but annoying disturbance in the front row: a smug-faced boy with movie star looks and designer sunshades who had not progressed beyond the initial giggling and was putting on a show of his own, directing witty, smirking commentaries on the scene to his compatriots on either side, all while chugging ice from a soft drink cup and grinding it in his molars with a noise like coal falling down a chute.

Turner's nervous system went immediately on high alert, remembering Won Se's warning that pesky sub-demons in the hire of the evil realm might begin to bedevil the monks' mission long before the ultimate confrontation. He worked at quietening his spirit sufficiently to hold an image of the disruptive boy in his mind's eye without shimmer or waver and there perform on it the classic Five Tests of Origin for identifying malevolent beings. And though his concentration flagged for a moment midway through the fifth test, introducing a small possibility of error, the other four were so crystallinely negative he felt safe in assuming that the annoyance was benignly, if misguidedly, mortal and could be merely ignored.

Which Turner tried to do for several minutes, hoping that at least the supply of ice would run out, but the cup seemed inexhaustible. Finally the racket scraped his nerves so raw he was forced to act.

After all, he thought, as he negotiated the cords and pulleys of the darkened wings and crept out to the auditorium floor, this is some important shit. Probably the most important thing these kids will see in their whole lives, and he'd be hard-pressed to forgive himself if he let one thoughtless jerk ruin it for the bunch of them.

Trotting in a fluid crouch the way the infantry had taught him in Vietnam, torso nearly parallel to the ground but head-up and alert, he quickly cleared the distance to the aisle seat of the row immediately behind the offender and proceeded to crawl between the rows of chairs, mumbling apologies to the people whose knees he scrubbed.

By now the pretty-boy was producing a loud, off-key warbling sound in his nasal cavity, making fun of Chai Lo's flute, while vigorously shaking his drink cup to loosen more ice. With surgical precision Turner thrust his arm over the back of the seat and snatched the cup away.

The speed of the maneuver paralyzed the boy with perplexity for several seconds. He raised his sunglasses to his forehead and stared at his empty hand as if at a completed magic trick. Just as Turner was changing direction and beginning his crawl back down the row, the boy regained his composure and whirled to look behind him.

"What the fuh—?" he said, and made a feeble grab for the cup, his grip landing instead on Turner's shoulder. The spirit of the Great One counseled Turner to continue his quiet retreat, content with having been for an instant a tool for truth and justice, but the spirit of Turner couldn't rest until he turned back around and pinched the boy's ear hard enough to raise a blood blister.

His immediate remorse obliged him to deliver some constructive teaching in the wake of his departure. He leaned close into the boy's astonished face and whispered the same advice, albeit in exceedingly abbreviated form, that he himself had received so often at the feet of Won Se on the moist, cool mornings amid the swirling fog of the Drepung gardens:

"Grow up, dickhead."

The message resonated sufficiently in the silence between notes that many of the surrounding listeners were moved to applaud its applicability. But as Turner retreated backstage he heard the rhythm of the leftmost cymbal falter momentarily, signaling the fact that Beh Vah thought the applause was for him and was having to visualize for all he was worth to prevent his ego cutting him off from the universal song in deference to one of his own making, a prideful song, one regaling in temporality, alienation, and lust.

The kind of song, in fact, that had so captivated Beh Vah their first night off the plane in Los Angeles, when Lu Weh had twirled the dial of the motel's cable channel and it brought to the screen, with Ouija-like efficacy, the troubled societal dream of MTV.

The monks gave rock video mixed reviews. One of them responded with a laughing fit, another with a sad shake of his head and a prayer, and another by asking Turner, in Tibetan, "Criminals?" Two others had the presence of mind to turn the sound off and kneel with their eyes almost touching the screen, so as to enjoy childlike the endless play of colors and patterns divorced from any literal meaning, the way the network's far-sighted inventor originally intended.

As for Beh Vah, though . . . ah, Lord.

Beh Vah went as rigid where he stood as somebody receiving a vision. Head cocked lovingly to one side, eyes afire with a glimpsed new truth, he raptly absorbed the garish performance of the Wizened Lizards as if the fate of the world depended on it. As chance had it, the Lizards' guitar virtuoso was bald as an egg, vaguely Oriental, and cavorted atop his sarcophagus-shaped amplifier in a brown, loose-fitting monk's tunic tied at the waist with a rope.

When he bounded down from his perch and duck-walked the length of the stage, coaxing layer on layer of feedback from his instrument in a futile attempt to outsqueal the frantic fans, the smoky air thick with the steam of lust from ten thousand agitated pubescent torsos, Beh Vah's joy was complete.

While the other monks drifted away one by one to their baths or nightly reading, Beh Vah sat faithfully in front of the screen with the patience of a comet watcher, waiting for the Lizards to come around again. Sometime after midnight when Turner got up to use the bathroom he came upon Beh Vah in the dark, bobbing and weaving in front of the mirror, naked as a fawn, hands bunched at his navel doing the unmistakable work of playing an invisible electric guitar.

Turner's footsteps startled him, and Beh Vah went into an energetic pantomime of scratching his stomach to show that was what he'd been doing the whole time. After a few vigorous clawings, as if his midsection was visited by hell's own rash, he began yawning profusely and scampered off to bed.

Since then Beh Vah had spent a lot more time than usual in prayer.

Back in the sanctity of the stage's dim wings, Turner discarded the confiscated ice. Beh Vah's wayward cymbal reasserted its familiar brittle cadence; he had shaken his demon and refound the universal song.

Now it was almost time for the dance. The music thinned to a skeleton of itself as Wah So and Se Hon laid down their long horns, Lu Weh laid down his cymbal, and Chai Lo his flute. One by one they walked offstage, near where Turner was, and stood deep-breathing and shaking the tension out of their arms. At some inaudible signal in the rhythms of the remaining horn and cymbal the four dancers formed into a line and progressed toward the stage in unhurried synchrony.

They walked with arms spread, eyes forward, pacing methodically heel to toe, heel to toe, as if crossing some great tightrope, afraid to look down. But when they reached the center of the stage the staid geometry of their regimentation lifted like a cloud and the motions became joyful ones, fluid ones, arms as pliant as willows in a wind, hands cupped into vessels for catching some precious commodity from above, raindrops or grace, and then windmilling to cast out their contents with an awesome profligacy and wait for more. All while their feet, clad in woolen gym socks the color of daffodils, kept to their careful tightrope pace, seemingly oblivious to the flashing delight of the dancers' upper halves.

The subject of footwear had occupied a large portion of their time during the first weeks of the tour. Barefoot was the monks' method of choice for performing the sacred dances—and, in fact, for locomotion in general. Back at the monastery, dancing was done either on smooth stone floors or the sandy soil of the courtyard. The constant mild abrasion not only kept off calluses and corns but had the pleasant side effect of polishing the initiates' golden-tan feet to the consistency of fine teakwood, so that at the end of the day when they would rake the soles of their feet with their fingernails, the sound was not ordinary flesh-scratching but the crisp satiny scritch-scritch of a woodcarver fashioning a ship's prow or a carpenter planing the lintel of a cathedral doorway.

The delicate rice-cloth slippers they wore for more formal occasions had lasted less than a week after their plane first touched down on the west coast. The rigors of broken sidewalks, parking lot gravel, and alleyway trash reduced the frail cloth to tatters in no time, and when the crate of replacements Turner ordered from Drepung got lost twice en route he threw up his hands, unholstered his weary Visa card, and carted the monks off to a local shopping mall. To a man, they showed no interest in the bewildering array of ethnic and international shops with their handmade clothing and footwear, but instead made a beeline to a sporting goods store and chose the exact model of white Reebok that Turner wore.

At first they reserved the running shoes for outdoor travel and continued to dance barefoot. But they underestimated the degree to which the new podiatric environment was softening their soles, and when the dancers shuffled across a rickety stage floor one evening at the Pomona Beach community center and Se Hon impaled the tender pad of his foot on a two-inch splinter of oak, destroying his concentration as well as the symmetry of the whole Mountain Fennel movement of the closing section, new measures were clearly called for.

On the way to the emergency room they decided to try the next performance in Reeboks. Which they did, but with unexpected results. The moment the row of dancers shuffled sacredly into view on the stage, the crowd erupted in applause and hoots of laughter. It was several days before Turner understood exactly why.

In his ten-month absence from the American scene he was unaware that monks had become all the rage in corporate advertising. There were commercials starring winemaking monks, package-delivering monks, photocopying monks, and more, and the one thing they had in common was that they all wore white jogging shoes.

Turner wasn't sure why the concept was considered so hugely humorous, unless it was an outcropping of some repressed cultural imperialism—comforting evidence that even the most devout of spiritual pilgrims are secretly suckers for a well-marketed chunk of temporal matter. In any event, the preconception helped perpetuate the disturbing notion that the path of spirit required the stern renouncing of all possessions and pleasures. Little wonder, Turner thought, that people weren't exactly jostling in line to sign up. It was so gratifying to have the chance to explain the truth on this tour. And so maddening to watch the truth enter a listener's left ear and immediately exit at high velocity through the right where it attached itself to the nearest wall like a carelessly flung booger.

"I understand that monks are celibate, is that correct?" a student in a discussion group had asked just the day before—a gaunt, earnest boy with a prominent Adam's apple and ferocious acne.

Correct, Turner acknowledged. Whereupon the boy wanted to know, "So, like, is it because they think sex is evil, or what?"

Turner translated the question into Tibetan for Chai Lo, who shared the microphone with him. The monk gave Turner a beseeching glance and, out of view of the audience, rolled his eyes toward the heavens. Then, after careful deliberation, he elucidated a long and complex reply that Turner reconstituted into English.

"What he's saying, in effect," Turner told the questioner, "is that sex is a sacrament, one of the most sublime aspects of creation."

He was interrupted by scattered lewd applause, but the rowdies were quickly glared into silence by the more intellectually serious of the crowd.

"However," Turner went on, "the shining shining path is difficult enough to walk solo . . . er, unencumbered . . . without the added, uh, *contortion* of being responsible for another human being along the way." He looked to Chai Lo for confirmation and got a nod.

"Likewise for other blessings," Turner continued. "Cars and houses and land and blue-chip stock and good drugs and fine whiskey." Here the monks looked at each other quizzically, a sign to Turner that he might be editorializing a bit too freely.

"Each of these," he said, "is just another splendid flowering of the universe, but each is also capable of becoming a woeful encumbrance to a devoted seeker of truth. A millstone around your neck, say, rather than wings for your feet, on the path." This metaphor suited the monks better; they nodded enthusiastically.

"But calling insensate things evil," Turner began wrapping up, "is the mark of a sad schizophrenia which wrongly ascribes the battleground to the outer dimension rather than the inner dimension, and cuts one off from experiencing the blessed duality, the sacred totality, the entire gorgeous waterfall of ardent bliss that buoys up the unencumbered faithful at the very instant all is lost."

A long burst of silence from the crowd. "Does that mean, like, 'No?'" a girl in the back row asked. "I mean, you're not saying they're, like, gay or anything."

So, to make a long story short, the choice of the yellow wool gym socks for dancing had been, like so much of life, a compromise. The socks weren't the freedom of bare feet, nor the arch support and stylishness of Reeboks, but on the plus side they were an exact color match for the fringe of the ceremonial headdress and the saffron embroidery that graced the waist and shoulders of the monks' ceremonial robes. They were thick enough to provide protection from all but the most outrageous splinters and, best of all, were available at K-Marts from coast to coast in packs of exactly six.

(An added benefit, for Turner, from a purely ego-indulgent point of view, was the priceless pleasure of studying the range of expressions on the faces of a row of monks standing in line at K-Mart, not to mention the expressions on the faces of their fellow shoppers. Now, whenever a police car passed the van in pursuit of a speeder, the monks would shout joyously, "Brew right! K-Mart!" They were skeptical of Turner's patient explanation that the police were not agents of K-Mart even though their system of halting motorists was identical to the store's blue-light specials.)

Out on stage, the dancers reached a point of graceful stasis, heads bowed forward and arms encircling the air above them, as the music shuddered and galumphed to a halt like a car engine running after the switch is shut off.

Turner signaled the brawny boy at the control panel to bring down the footlights and close the curtains. After several seconds of silence, the audience erupted into fervent and sustained applause. Even the iceman clapped, though apparently more from peer pressure than aesthetic contentment.

▼

INTERLUDE: THE REALM

Of the twenty-eight known varieties of darkness, all can be found occurring simultaneously in only one place: an unknown region which lies just between the seams of existing star charts. It is thus invisible at most times to the untrained heart, even on occasions of great historical significance, such as this moment.

Over time, the fabric of undifferentiated darknesses occasionally takes on the appearance of a vast empty shelf, or a slightly convex wall, or a truncated lake. Now, though, the void stirs to become faintly theater-shaped; the darker broad stripe at its center becomes, with only minimal imagination, a throne of onyx, and the presences that congeal on it begin to speak.

They have chosen one, then? the foremost presence demands.

Affirmations around.

Let me see him.

The barest perceptible whir and whine, as the void within becomes enghosted with a moving image. Silence, for the longest time, around the throne.

Suddenly comes the beginnings of laughter, tentative at first as an oar-slap in brackish water, then deepening and broadening to include all the presences present until the void rumbles and rings with laughter, which echoes away only when breath seems incapable of sustaining it longer.

This is the world's best hope? Said incredulously, from the throne.

Silence, until a lesser presence ventures, *He is said to be fearless in battle.*

A huff of disbelief. *Look at his heart. What threat can he be to us, when he fears himself?*

Uncertain silence.

Should we study him further, lord, or enter his frame now?

Sole laughter. *Now, by all means. I have been too long without entertainment.*

Done, lord.

They disperse.

It begins.

▲

WHEN THE NOISE OF the crowd subsided, Turner made his way through the split in the curtain and announced that the T-shirt stand would be set up in the foyer in five minutes. He invited everyone to stop by and meet the monks, and to ask any questions they had.

Turner's friends had scoffed when he first got the idea for the T-shirts: "Drepung Monastery / World Tour 1995," written below a striking red-and-gold silhouette of a monk in profile with ceremonial headdress. They suggested that he was reducing a proud, millennia-old mystical tradition to the level of a rock concert. Once you started in that direction, they maintained, there was no limit to the junk you could hawk. Key chains. Sun visors. Beer coolers. They imagined a long list for him, trying to shame him.

Meanwhile he was thinking, No, but what about incense? Tibetan incense would definitely sell, being as dimensionally superior to the variety found in American 7-Elevens as vichyssoise and peppercorn pheasant are to a cheap canned chili.

He explained to his doubting friends that the narrowness of their misguided idealism ignored the fact that for an entire generation of American youth any concept that can't be represented on a T-shirt is only marginally real. Turner avowed that, with this tour, he wasn't going to let people off that easy.

He would not be satisfied with bringing to their very doorsteps the cutting edge of human sentience within the known universe, the majestic crystalline music of the spheres with all its attendant terror and grace. No, he was by-God going to rub their noses in it. He would meet them on their own ground and so disenchant them with the pureed pap and propaganda of cultural determinism they are given in place of a life that they would forever become thorns in the heel of any system, any regime, whose existence is in thrall to less than the full and free functioning of their minds and wills.

So what about television? his friends wanted to know. Had he worked a deal with cable yet? After all, if you're going to kowtow to the American masses you may as well go all the way.

It's not the same thing, he said. Television's different.

Different how? they wanted to know.

Television is reductionistic, he maintained. It makes everything smaller than life.

Unlike T-shirts, they said.

The difference of opinion had remained unresolved, but for Turner it was made irrelevant every month when he sat down to do the books and was able to send the Drepung monastery a grand or two from the proceeds of T-shirts and incense alone.

Admittedly, it was a drop in the bucket where the restoration needs were concerned. Because when the soldiers of the Chinese revolution had hit Drepung they'd done a creditably thorough job. Three of the four main buildings had been gutted, and of more than a hundred thousand sacred texts in the Hall of Truth barely two thousand had escaped whole. The rest were either burned outright or ripped into loose pages which the soldiers had used to line the central courtyard, a fit carpet for the monks they herded out at bayonet point, sunrise and sunset, the holiest times of the day, and led in singing loud songs to the glory of The People.

Fully half the monks at the monastery now were too young to remember the purge years. They assumed that holiness was by its nature somewhat shabby, assumed that Drepung had always been poor.

Backstage the monks wandered in slow, aimless circles, wearing looks of contentment and patting one another on the shoulder when the arcs of their paths chanced to intersect. Turner hefted the packing case with the T-shirts and incense and trotted out to the foyer where the students of Kennesaw College were gravitating into a loud queue, their money already in hand. As he laid the merchandise out on the tables the monks began drifting up front one by one.

The last to come was Beh Vah, his face glistening wet beyond any exertion he had performed. Draped around his neck with a studied casualness was a white bath towel with the insignia of a hotel they'd stayed at in Reno the week before. The older monks pelted him with looks of disapproval. He took a detour to the nearby men's room from which he soon emerged, dried off and properly prayerful, the casino towel folded meekly under his arm.

The first student in line bought an extra-large T-shirt and two packs of incense and directed his enthusiasm straight at Se Hon, without waiting for Turner to interpret. "You guys are . . . are . . ." His bearded face strained mightily, searching for the word.

" . . . *cos*mic," he sputtered at last, in a flash of inspiration. "You guys are cosmic."

Se Hon smiled courteously and waited for the translation, which was not immediately forthcoming. Turner paused in making change and turned over in his mind the phrase's Tibetan equivalents, discovering in the process that none of them were true to both the letter and spirit of the idea. Se Hon, abetted by his expression of perpetual nearsightedness, was the most intellectual of the monks, but also the one who knew the least English. In frustration, aware of the importance of keeping the line moving, Turner fell back on the translator's ace in the hole, the absolutely literal.

"He says," Turner told Se Hon, "that you and your group are definitely a part of the universe."

Se Hon waited expectantly for Turner or the boy to elaborate further, but when he realized that the exchange was complete he stared straight ahead and blinked several times, pondering all the idea's implications.

"The universe," Se Hon repeated in Tibetan, making sure he'd understood. Turner nodded. Se Hon looked up at the boy who, eager to help, nodded also.

Se Hon asked Turner, "Had someone told them we were *not* part of the universe?" The idea appeared troubling to him, that someone would spread false information to young seekers of knowledge.

"No, no," Turner said in Tibetan. "It's more the sense that you . . . make him *think* about the universe."

"Make him?" Se Hon looked apprehensive. "We *force* him to? He is saying we interrupt his meditation?" The boy, sensing a question had been asked, nodded eagerly. "No, no," Turner said in Tibetan. "There's a cultural supposition here which I'm not communicating very well. In the sense that, say, a person . . ."

"Two mediums, please." The girl who was next in the T-shirt line elbowed the intense boy aside and flashed a perfect smile.

" . . . the sense that a person is not ordinarily *given* to contemplation, then anything that has the effect of, say, guiding . . ." Turner fumbled behind him in the box of medium T-shirts and came up with only one. The supply would have to be replenished from the van.

He glanced around for help. Beh Vah had loaded the van last. He'd know exactly where the new box was.

"Beaver? Can you help me a minute?"

Getting no response, he leaned around Se Hon to see Beh Vah engaged in a lively conversation with two blonde girls in cheerleader outfits. Beh Vah was trying valiantly to surmount the language barrier by the use of elaborate hand gestures, to which the cheerleaders responded with cascades of giggles and even more elaborate hand-charades of their own.

Turner decided to go for the T-shirts himself. He looked around for the program chairman and found her hovering nearby, waiting to be of use. "The *temporal* universe?" Se Hon was asking Turner, "or more in the sense of . . ." The boy nodded fervently. "Be right back," Turner said. "Right back." The girl in the sun dress agreed to make change while he was gone.

After the cool drone of the building's air conditioning, the blinding blue Kansas sky struck Turner's sight like a thunderclap. Small wavering funnels of heat swirled up from the sidewalks and the portico of the building. While he was at it, he'd pull the van into the shade and roll down the windows so it could cool off. He felt in his pocket for the keys.

That was the moment he first noticed the cloud.

If cloud was the word for it. Hovering directly above the van, some twenty feet in the air, was a continually shifting shape only slightly darker than the sky behind it. A shadow, Turner would have called it, had there been any object around to cast it or any surface to cast it on.

As it was, the haze of dark flickerings, a kind of sheet lightning in reverse, seemed less like a shadow than an indistinct aperture into a place of shadows—the innards of some ancient movie house with its roof suddenly ripped away, the images on its screen not quite extinguished by the harsh incursion of sunlight.

But the more Turner squinted and tried to focus on the shape the less visible it became, at one point disappearing altogether and making him think he'd imagined it, that the occurrence was some manifestation of the heat. Then he tried a trick of night vision he'd learned in the jungles: looking way to the right or left of the thing you wanted to see, putting it at the very periphery of your vision, which had the effect of intensifying its brightness at some expense of clarity.

It worked; the shadow images bloomed again—not just bloomed, but boiled. Inside the hazy opening, shapes tumbled over shapes, wrenched of all their colors and discrete edges.

It was a distillation of nightmare so thick and potent as to defy description: wide-shouldered *mafiosi* with the eyes of reptiles, axes flecked with black blood ricocheting down an infinity of carpeted stairwells, deformed fists the size of bulldozers crushing the world's great art with assembly-line efficiency, black-helmeted troopers with clubs and bayonets ransacking a hospital nursery, oxcarts of corpses raining down through trees trailing putrefaction and bile.

There were sounds too, not from the direction of the cloud itself but seemingly from within Turner's own mind: cries of pain, shouts of disbelief, the rhythm of marching boots in nighttime alleys, the pleading of women as their defilement began, the percussive *thack* of shrapnel striking flesh, the far-off surrealistic wail of two-tone ambulance sirens.

Turner glanced quickly around the square to see if anyone else was watching. There was no one in sight. Nothing moved, not even a grass blade. The wind had stopped and the heat was stifling. In the excruciating stillness he realized suddenly that the chaotic sounds had stopped, too. Sure enough, when he looked again toward the van there was nothing above it but seamless, broiling sky.

Nothing, that is, except for the crow.

Strutting in a lazy ellipse across the roof of the van, seemingly oblivious to the scorching metal and its waves of heat, was a huge ragged crow. Beyond its look of general ill health, there was something else not quite right about the bird—nothing so obvious as an outright deformity, but rather some subtle lack of symmetry in its wings and feet which was compounded by the stiff, machine-like way it moved its head and wings.

Abruptly the crow paused in its methodical walk and for the first time appeared to notice Turner. It tilted its head side to side, studying him with an almost theatrical exaggeration. Then the bird did something clearly impossible: it smiled. The dull-orange beak broadened and broadened, contorting upward at the edges into a revolting caricature of a smile that Turner had seen only once before on a human being: the first man he ever killed.

With the speed of a thought, Turner found his hand around one of the large white rocks that edged the sidewalk. Knowing full well the futility of what he was doing, he threw the rock at the bird's head with such force that his arm socket felt on fire. The bird's smile faded.

The throw looked absolutely true, but at the last possible instant the rock seemed pulled by some surge of unnatural gravity and dipped by a good foot-and-a-half, splintering the van's side window with a ringing crash. Just at that moment a diminutive coed in shorts and sandals came around the corner with a towering stack of books. Seeing the explosion of glass and Turner hefting another rock, she dropped the books with a shriek and ran back the way she'd come.

The second throw had so much added velocity it sailed a good arm's length above the crow's head, prompting the return of the grotesque smile. But by the third throw Turner got the range just right, and the crow had to do a frantic backward somersault as the rock sang through the exact air where it had stood.

As Turner reached for another rock the crow shakily took flight from the roof of the van. But rather than fleeing over the circle of low buildings it flapped straight toward him, one final taunt. As it passed above his head, almost close enough to touch, he threw his last rock so hard that he lost his balance and fell to the ground, knocking the wind out of him.

Even as he heaved to get his breath back there was no mistaking the faint inner sound he heard, or the words the crow's lips shaped as it passed over:

For now.

After several seconds or several minutes, he wasn't sure which, Turner slowly pushed himself upright. As he dusted the grass clippings from his clothes he felt the sudden return of a breeze. All natural sounds resumed, birdsongs and a distant factory whistle and a sprinkling of notes from the chapel carillon, as if the top of some gigantic bell jar had been lifted and life let back in. The moving air loosened the last few fragments of the van's window, which fell to the pavement with a faint noise like a wind chime.

At the van he found the box of T-shirts he'd come for, and with the back of his hand wiped it free of shattered glass. But when he put the box to his shoulder and turned to slide the door shut, all the reinforcement went out of his legs and he had to sit down.

Goddamn it, he'd gotten soft. He could feel it, a laxity like the beginnings of nausea in the fibers of his muscles. And not just that, but spiritually, too. His meditations were easily distracted, the universal song too easily drowned out by the chattering of his mind. A mistake. For a warrior, maybe a fatal one.

As a test of his centering he tried to visualize the classic golden sphere within a golden sphere within a golden sphere, each one rotating independently of the others, all floating at the height of a man's head through a peaceful forest and trying to follow, without looking down, the shining path along the dark footing of moss.

But after just half a minute, maybe less, he was picturing in his mind's eye the cloud again, hearing its voices. He had heard them before this, in the war years, had watched as the troubled aperture opened like a maw to consume the whole world. Worse, he'd been its unwilling handmaiden.

He had known it would be back. He hadn't thought it would be this soon.

With his eyes shut he felt a sudden shadow fall around him, then the force of a hand on his collar. A split second in advance of any logical thought he found himself on his feet, arms flexed to strike.

What he saw was only the placid face of Se Hon, inquiring about his health with a melodic grunt.

"I'm fine," Turner told him.

But, being a monk, Se Hon was too adept at reading messages from eyes instead of voices. He grunted the dreaded syllable, a question, and gestured with a precise tilt of his head toward the skyward realm. Turner nodded.

Se Hon sat beside him, speechless, an arm around his shoulder. Turner tried to gather his thoughts, his energies, but all he could feel was an overpowering weariness.

Damn, damn, damn.

He'd thought he would have more time.

2

ON THE ROAD south to their next show, some small private college in the wilds of Texas, the van was quiet as a tomb. Despair reigned. Chai Lo was so withdrawn he didn't even object when Turner forsook the peaceful two-lane for an interstate. Turner's one try at making light conversation with the monks fell flat, as did his halfhearted attempt at a pep talk.

"Guys, I know each one of us had a picture in our mind," he told them, "of how far along we wanted to be, spiritually and every other way, by the time this whole thing started coming down, right?"

Nobody spoke.

"All I'm saying is, if you feel like you're sucking wind at this point, then you're not the Lone Ranger, okay?"

Six uncomprehending faces. Hard as Turner tried to keep figures of speech to a minimum in dealing with the monks, an idiom or two always crept in when he was tired or preoccupied. He knew how frustrating it was for them, himself having mastered only a few dozen of the thousands of Tibetan figures of speech which came to them as naturally as breathing.

He didn't have the heart to translate, this time. "Just scratch that," he corrected. "What I'm saying is, if Won Se were here right now, I'm sure he'd tell us . . ." But his exhausted brain had suddenly beached itself. All that occurred to him were recycled Vince Lombardi bromides about winners never quitting and all of us being in this together. He realized with sad certainty that he hadn't the foggiest idea what Drepung's spiritual master would say to them at this point.

At that moment, though, he spotted a roadside rest stop with a row of phone booths out front and slowed the van to turn in. "Hell, why don't we call him?"

This brightened the mood of the monks considerably, so that by the time he picked a booth and began the arduous process of accessing the remote Tibetan village's single telephone, they were all horseplaying and jostling each other like grammar-schoolers, trying to be next in line to talk to Won Se.

All, that is, except Chai Lo, who wandered moodily to a nearby dog-walking area and with great concentration began studying the leaves of a parched water-oak.

Turner had never quite understood the relationship between Won Se and his second in command—whether his and Chai Lo's coolness to each other was the result of some past bad blood or just a mismatch of personalities.

During both Turner's stays at Drepung, he had not once seen Shy and Won Se actually have words. They obviously respected each other as eminent scholars of the Books of Chojung, the vast and complicated history of both the temporal and spiritual realms whose volumes filled an entire room of Drepung's library. But the precise formality with which they addressed each other in public, pleasant though it was, stuck out like a sore thumb in a setting where a touchingly childlike physical affection was commonplace, with no respect to seniority or scholarly ranking.

The telephone receiver crackled. "International operator," said a British voice made indistinct by static.

"Tibet, please," Turner told her. "Drepung." He spelled it for the operator, as he always had to, and then argued at some length that a telephone, if only one, did actually exist in the city. Finally he heard the familiar sigh that meant her computer screen was displaying for her the daunting maze of electronic connections such a call would require.

"Hold, please," the operator said grimly. A babel of foreign dialects filled the line.

At first Turner had theorized that Chai Lo might resent the fact he could never succeed Won Se as master of the monastery—the position being divinely appointed, not subject to human whim. It can only be held by a reincarnate monk such as Beh Vah, a young boy who turns up at the monastery's gate on the anniversary of the death of some great holy man and proves himself through days of intense questioning to be the new vessel of the great man's spirit, after which he's ordained to become the monastery's next leader when the current one dies.

But Chai Lo had never shown the least hint of jealousy toward Beh Vah. He loved the youngster as much as everyone else at Drepung did and was, like them, almost perpetually charmed by him, despite the boy's bouts of immaturity that kept the elders on the verge of pulling their hair out. Shy had, by his own admission, loved him like a son ever since the night Beh Vah knocked on the gate and recited for them the wisdom of Lim Rhya, a renowned Lama dead three hundred years. A reincarnate, for some reason, always came to the monastery at night.

Night. Shit. Turner was so preoccupied he'd forgotten to calculate the difference in time zones. In Tibet it would be a good two hours before daybreak.

The gruff voice of Nohr Bu, the village grocer, came on the line, slurred and thick from sleep.

"Unh?"

Turner greeted him in Tibetan and inquired, as was proper etiquette, about the health of his family, his thoughts on the pattern of recent weather, and the regularity of his bowels.

"Unh," Nohr Bu replied.

In his mind Turner could see the thickset man lighting the yak-butter candle on his bedside bench and pulling on a robe, readying for what he knew would be Turner's next request, trekking the half mile uphill to the monastery to awaken Won Se and fetch him to the phone.

"Unh," Nohr Bu agreed. There was a monstrous clangor as the receiver apparently bounced off the stone floor. When the noise reverberated away Turner could hear a plaintive yawn and Nohr Bu's receding footsteps.

A canny salesman from the comparative metropolis of Lhasa had convinced the grocer that the installation of telephones was about to boom in Drepung, and that he would have a tremendous competitive edge over other shops if his customers could phone their orders in for delivery.

But the communications boom had started and stopped with himself, and the unintended result was to confer on Nohr Bu, a reclusive sort of man for a merchant, the grave civic responsibility of being the village's sole conduit to the great world beyond the mountain rim. He was the *de facto* mayor of Drepung, and he took his duties seriously.

"Have you finished your call, sir?" the nasal British lady broke in.

"Ma'am, I'm holding," Turner said. "It'll be a while."

He pictured the monastery gardens luminous with fog under the waning moon and felt a sudden stab of homesickness for the place.

By now the two figures would be making their way down the white gravel path—frail Won Se taking the hill haltingly because of his arthritis, an old orange blanket around his shoulders against the chill; the dark bulk of Nohr Bu, muttering and wheezing, walking two paces behind the great scholar out of respect.

"Nu en! Tur-ner?" Even through the static Won Se's voice sounded strong and even, a fact which lifted Turner's heart disproportionately to the dark news he was about to relate. He made short work of the pleasantries, assured Won Se the monks were all healthy, and then immediately told him about the evil cloud.

The silence on the other end extended so long after Turner finished that he thought he'd been disconnected.

"This does not surprise me," Won Se replied at last. Turner could tell by the change in the timbre of his voice, though, that the news had shaken him. Won Se was a man of a thousand talents, but lying convincingly was not among them.

"What does it do to our timetable?" Turner asked him.

While Won Se pondered, the phone connection amplified unnaturally the background noises of the grocer's household: a maverick rooster crowing in the back yard, a musical dinging of silverware on crockery that meant the omnipresent urn of stout, bitter tea had gotten hot enough to drink. Nohr Bu would be adding the finishing touch, a spoon of fresh yak butter, to the cup he offered the great overseer. Turner heard Won Se offer his thanks, in Tibetan, and slurp a mouthful before answering.

"It will hurry it up, obviously," he said, managing to sound more assured. "We knew from the beginning that our times were, how to say . . . approximate."

"How *much*, though? By half? More? We were thinking we had a year or two." Turner felt a tug at his sleeve; Beh Vah, now at the front of the waiting line, was entreating him to hurry so he could talk to Won Se. Turner shushed him.

Won Se replied in Tibetan, a long and melodic proverb which, boiled down, said that if Buddha in his wisdom had meant for us to be concerned with how long something takes he would have replaced the cheeks of our rear ends with clock faces.

He knew Turner couldn't be pacified by aphorisms, though, so he followed it immediately with, "Three months? Four, perhaps. If I were fool to say." This confirmed what Turner feared. He felt his heart sink.

"Be heartful, Tur-ner," the distant voice chided him, as if by telepathy. "There is time to prepare. It is not like the realm has already taken form."

"What do you mean, 'taken form'?"

"When the outer realm is truly ready to enter our own, it must put on a body. Almost always an animal. So, if you haven't seen . . ."

"I have. I mean, it did."

Turner told him about the crow. The silence that followed was broken at last by a sigh that seemed to come from someone even older than Won Se, who was very old.

"Is it *that* bad?" Turner prompted.

"It was a crow that called out Rhi Gu Yan, the greatest warrior of all. The realm is, how to say . . . thinks high of you. That was in a Dragon Year too, like this one."

"How soon, then? If it's already taken form."

"You will do well," Won Se said.

"How *soon*?"

The lone rooster crowed again in Nohr Bu's yard.

"You will do well," Won Se replied. "We are praying. Know you have our love."

Suddenly the blazing sand-colored landscape outside the phone booth became liquid, decomposed itself into swirls of pure color that stung Turner's cheeks where it touched. As he wiped his eyes to clear them, he felt Beh Vah's hand tug anxiously at his sleeve.

In the snack bar, under the armadillo, was where the editor of Pickwick University's campus newspaper, *The Palindrome*, told Turner she'd meet him for an interview after the monks' show.

He got there a few minutes early and poured himself a cup of coffee at the counter. He took a seat against the far wall underneath the 18-foot-long wooden cutout of an armadillo, day-glo red, who grinned down lovably through buck teeth. The picture window across the way looked out on the low scrub hills of southwest Texas, where a lightning storm was approaching with ominous slowness. The snack bar was deserted. There was nobody at the register.

Turner felt confident he would recognize the girl when she appeared. Editors of student publications, he'd found out over the years, almost always stood out from the crowd by virtue of appearing to live in another span of time than what is generally recognized as the present. Prince Valiant haircuts, Galilean sandals, Confederate battle caps, Star Wars spandex jackets. Every campus editor who'd interviewed him would clearly look out of place at a Young Republicans' smoker.

At exactly the stroke of six o'clock, steps echoed in the hallway outside. The girl who materialized in the serving line wore Sixties' black from neck to toe: sweater, straight miniskirt, stockings and patent shoes. She scanned the room for Turner, waved at him, and deftly went about heaping two trays of food from the secret innards of the stainless steel ovens and warmers. With her long bangs, ironed-straight hair, and vivid eye shadow, she looked like a slightly more exotic version of Mary from Peter-Paul-and.

She brought the trays to the booth and slid one across to him. Enough steaming burgers, hot french fries, and ketchup packets for a family. Before he could protest the quantity she held out her small white hand for him to shake. It gave off the scent of expensive bath soap and something else more bitter, lemony, some rare flower or herb. Up close her face looked fragile and childlike in its armor of bright makeup, which didn't quite hide the faint crow's-feet at the corners of her eyes. From them Turner could guess her history: married in high school, divorced, back now to do the campus thing to the hilt. He pegged her at thirty-two or -three, maybe more.

"I'm already impressed," she said.

He snapped out of his reverie. "Beg pardon?"

"Your photographs don't do you justice."

Turner felt his face redden. "Well, you're mighty kind."

The editor took a notepad from her black shoulder bag. "I thought we could start with . . ." She broke off and looked at his tray in a panic. "Oh, no. I just realized. You're probably a vegetarian, right?"

"Actually, I'm not."

"Good, good."

Something about the woman's voice, her mannerisms, seemed damned familiar to him. But when he couldn't place why, he blamed the perception on encroaching middle-age; the older you get, the more everyone reminds you of someone else.

The editor thumbed to a clean notebook page, tossed back her hair, and took a deep breath before looking him in the eye. "First question. What's an international celebrity like you doing in a dump like this? Would you call it a fall from grace, or just slumming, or what?"

"Well, 'international celebrity' might be overstating just a . . ."

She pulled a sheaf of photocopies from a pocket of the notepad and read from them. "Let's see . . . 'Confidante To The Legends Of Music,' *Rolling Stone*, August '85. 'Turner To Topple Graham As Principal Promoter On Planet?' That's *Variety*, January '86." She smiled sweetly. "Shall I go on?"

"You've done your homework," Turner said.

"I'm conscientious at everything I take on," she said. She held his eye until he blinked.

"So, anyway," she continued, "it's clear from what I've read that you used to be really big."

"Nope," Turner said. "This is about the most I've ever weighed."

She fixed him with a smile that silently said, "Smartass," laid her pencil on the table and sighed.

"Okay, let's start over. If you play ball with me, I won't ask you about the, uh, *practices* over there. People get into some really wild stuff, from what I hear."

Turner looked blank. "Practices?"

"Sure. You know. The sex practices and stuff. Don't let your food get cold."

Turner grabbed a grateful mouthful of french fries and pondered his reply. The lightning storm over the low scraggly hills filled the whole horizon now, moving the world prematurely into dusk.

"To tell the truth, monks aren't much into sex," he said.

"But you're not a monk, are you?" She gave him a guileless, level stare until he had to glance away. At the beginning of the trip he'd promised himself, in the interest of concentration and endurance, that for the duration he'd be as celibate as . . . well, as a monk. Until now, the problem hadn't come up.

So to speak.

"True," Turner said, "but I'm afraid I'm not much of an expert on the, uh, social customs outside the monastery. I was hoping we could talk about . . ."

The *deja vu* that had been scratching at the back of Turner's mind ever since the woman arrived leaped suddenly to center stage of his consciousness, instantly transforming her face into Cassie McNamara, his first steady girlfriend back at Zion High.

Cassie, of the endearingly ratty beatnik wardrobe—the small town's sole revolutionary, who sang songs of justice and freedom on her battered Sears-Roebuck guitar. Cassie, of the nights parked in his paisley Volkswagen in storms like this one, him driven to delirium by hours of resuscitation from her tiny, miraculous mouth—only that, never more than that—while her impermeable bra cups made dents in his chest he could sometimes feel to this day, invisible stigmata recurring in late-night hotel rooms after sufficient quantities of gin and tonic. Cassie, of the first picture postcard he received at Tun Hoit base camp, a color scene of Haight-Ashbury at sunrise with a small ink-pen circle around an apartment window in the distance. *The guy I'm living with reminds me so much of you.*

Cassie. Here. Now.

His head swam. The perilous tilting of reality put him on guard for a malevolent spirit, but the wonder of seeing her real and whole after all these years so effectively sapped his will that he couldn't concentrate enough to perform even the first of the Five Tests.

"Cassie?" he heard himself say, a catch in his throat. Was he losing his mind? He'd had no realization of speaking until the word was in the air. Crazy air.

"Yes?" Cassie's face said. Longing in her eyes. It wasn't the first time he'd imagined seeing her, sure that he'd glimpsed her at the edge of his vision only to see her transformed into a stranger when he looked straight-on. But something felt off center here. Something not right.

With all his force of will he shut his eyes. "*No*," he shouted. When he looked again the woman's proper face had been restored, upturned and alert as if nothing odd had been said, no time had passed.

"'No,' what?" she asked.

"I need coffee," he said, getting unsteadily to his feet. "Can I bring you some?" She smiled and shook her head.

When he came back she said, "Let's talk about *in*side the monasteries, then. Is it true, the things we read about? Levitation, astral projection, stuff like that?"

"Look," Turner said, "I'm not trying to give you a hard time or anything, but that's a difficult subject."

"I'm a difficult woman," the editor shrugged. "And I've got plenty of time."

As always, when the conversation turned toward the mystical, Turner had dire presentiments of sensationalized newspaper headlines: *To Hell With Gravity, Says Bizarre Cult,* or *Move Over, Star Trek: Weird Monks Hop Through Universe At Will.*

Except that "monks," plural, would not be entirely accurate. Of the six who were traveling with him, only old Lu Weh had as yet mastered time and space—a source of great consternation for the other men, seeing as Lu Weh was such a maddeningly slow learner in the academic aspects of monkhood. He'd had to repeat some stages of enlightenment three and four times, the equivalent of flunking a grade in school.

This accounted for the fact that he was far older than any of them but was technically only now on a par of enlightenment with Beh Vah, the most novice of the bunch. Apparently, projection—or "transiting," as the monks called it—was not something you learned, but something you caught on to. In any event, Lu Weh had taken to it like a fish to water.

"Okay," Turner said finally, nursing his coffee. "If the question is, have I personally seen things happen that can't be explained through the physical sciences, the answer is yes. But there are two problems with that.

"Number one, people of a certain mindset start wanting you to prove it, whatever that means, so that the whole context of the original event is lost. It's like some cut-rate parlor trick. Number two, if you go to the other extreme and start accepting ideas with *no* proof, no testing, then what good is having a rational mind?"

She looked steadily at him, her pencil poised. "Is that a yes, or a no?" she said pleasantly.

"No," Turner said.

"No?"

"No, it's a yes *and* no."

With a deep sigh, she started scribbling in her pad. At that instant Turner heard in the air beside him, pitched just above temporal hearing, the familiar tweak of sound like two ping-pong balls colliding. *Please, Louie, not now*, he prayed silently. *Any time but now.* Suddenly Lu Weh appeared in the third seat of the booth, glancing around like a child at a carnival.

Any second, Turner knew, the editor would glance up and the shit would rapidly adhere to the fan blades.

When Lu Weh's gaze fell on Turner's french fries he scooped up a handful and gobbled them whole, with an expression of fearful delight. One troublesome drawback of projection was that it expended a supernatural quantity of calories, which is why Lu Weh always remained rail-thin despite three groaning spreads of food a day that made a halfback's training table look meager by comparison.

The other drawback was evidenced by the fact that he was totally naked. Because the process involved the body becoming a sort of oversized spiritual tuning fork, any inanimate encumbrances such as clothing refused on principle to go along for the ride. It was a perpetual annoyance that the most advanced masters solved by creating, in the minds of any people who happened to be in the vicinity, the illusion of a loincloth. That process, though, not only required the traveler to maintain a level of concentration above and beyond that already demanded by the travel itself, but as chance would have it the particular mental resonances involved in the two maneuvers were precisely at cross-waves with one another—making them the astral equivalent of patting your head and rubbing your stomach elevated to the twentieth power.

The occasions when Lu Weh had attempted to fake clothing, he had gotten the two energies just enough out of sync that the illusion he generated was not a loincloth but rather a vivid transformation of his genitalia into strange new life-forms: once a grotesquely elongated chicken head with Groucho Marx-like eyebrows, another time a great disembodied black hand which swung with the coarse grace of an elephant's trunk when he walked, its fingers conducting some unheard symphony.

The villagers in the area around Drepung, of course, took such failed experiments in stride. When people gathered at the tavern or in the market stalls they would comment at great length on the spiritual exploits of this monk or that, much as people elsewhere follow the fortunes of their favorite baseball hero.

Unfortunately, the good ladies of the East Canton Gardening and Benevolent Society had not displayed similar aplomb the month before when Lu Weh materialized by accident in the midst of their Spring Plant Fair. Turner understood later from newspaper reports that five police cruisers and two ambulances were required to quell the melee.

One of the braver of the women armed herself with a leaf rake and led the general assault on the intruder, which was repulsed only when Lu Weh, hemmed in and frightened, tried simultaneously to clothe himself and to transit away but in his confusion became locked in a sort of illusional overdrive which caused his pelvic persona to undergo dozens of transformations in seconds with the rapidity of fireworks, each version more splendid and terrible than the last until, trailing a giant red-eyed cobra between his legs, he leaped over the cotton candy machine and disappeared in mid-air.

The two women at first reported to have suffered strokes were taken to the hospital for observation, but were treated and released with prescriptions for Valium after it was determined that they'd only fainted. Experts from the Center for Disease Control in Atlanta who were dispatched to the site that afternoon placed the blame for the mass hallucination on a heretofore undiscovered bacteria found in the chicken salad sandwiches sold at the event.

By now Lu Weh had discovered the mound of ketchup packets on Turner's tray and was squirting their contents with a fearsome efficiency over the remaining fries. Turner made a violent facial pantomime toward Lu Weh, urging him to occupy a more discreet location in the room before the editor looked up. The monk paid no attention. He seized the boat-shaped cardboard container and catapulted the fries into his mouth. A blast of thunder vibrated the picture window.

"Spell that," the editor commanded, not looking up from her notepad.

Lu Weh wiped his mouth on his forearm and with a supernaturally-pitched *plink* vacated the booth, leaving the container to hover for an instant before settling to the table. Turner's pounding heart slowed to an almost normal rhythm.

"Spell what?" he asked.

"'Pallor trek'. Is that Tibetan?"

"Parlor trick," he corrected. "P-a-r-l-o-r. Didn't your grandmother have a parlor?"

When the woman looked up Turner thought he saw her composure slip for a second and a flicker of panic cross her face. But before he could be sure, the confident mask returned. "My grandmother died when she was very young." she said. "So, tell me . . ."—here she calmly turned to a fresh notebook page—"How did this whole thing get started, anyway? How does a capitalist, establishment, Western rock-and-roll impresario come to be traveling around the country, apparently on a shoestring, with a bunch of monks?"

Which was a question Turner asked himself frequently, but when confronted by a reporter he was always in a quandary whether to tell the short version or the long version. The short version, of course, began with Won Se's urgent letter showing up backstage at the Meadowlands during the climactic show of the Stones' tour. Just at the moment when his career was on some kind of ungodly smooth roll, the biggest acts in the business wanting him to manage their tours and the wanna-bes sending beautiful female messengers to wedge tapes through his mail slot at all hours of the day and night. Such a sweet, high plane of existence for a country boy to be on. So, so sweet.

And then the letter came.

But even as he was readying to say *I was backstage at the Meadowlands and I got this letter* he was aware of how diminished the accuracy of the story was—of any story, really—when you forced on it an arbitrary beginning and end, cutting off all the delicate tendrils of cause and effect that reach backward and forward and sideways in space and time.

"Well, I was backstage at the Meadowlands one night," Turner began telling her, "and I got . . ."

At that moment the granddaddy of all lightning slammed into the yard, sending a giant ball of sparks ricocheting like a pinball between the low buildings. Turner's latent Vietnam reflexes had him diving halfway under the table before he realized it, but the editor didn't appear perturbed. With a loud *whump* the electricity went off.

The woman merely sighed her impatience. "I suppose we'd better finish this up at my place," she said. "When the power goes off, it usually stays that way awhile." She got up peremptorily and put her notebook in her purse. "Come on. It's just a few blocks."

She was halfway to the exit before Turner caught up with her. "Whoa," he said. "As bad as that lightning was, I'd lay money your power's off, too."

By the residual flickers of lightning through the big window he could see her amused grin. "No doubt," she said. "That's why I keep candles." In the dimness all the black she wore had faded to nothing. She became an ivory-white head and hands, which moved a full step toward him until one of her hipbones brushed his.

"We could have a drink and talk," she said in a half-whisper. "I mean, *really* talk."

In the darkness her index finger went unerringly to his navel and traced a slow circle around it through his shirt. A tremor ran up him from his knees; he couldn't get a deep breath. Before his equilibrium could return he felt her other hand on the back of his hair, soft as a wing, urging his head forward to the place in the air where her mouth waited.

His brain going *Jesus Jesus Jesus Jesus* and when their lips finally connected in the paralyzed air some altogether new continuum was broached with a lurch like colliding boxcars and it was, it *was* Cassie McNamara's mouth, not a doubt in hell. It was elastical beyond measure, it was inexhaustible as loaves and fishes, bearing him up in a state of embryo-like grace. Nothing to fear, nothing. He could even taste in the archaeology of her teeth and tongue the licorice mints that had been Cassie's addictive passion.

Except it couldn't be. This woman, this hallucination, whatever the hell she was, stood upright on two feet—something Cassie had not done for twenty years and (the idea still struck him every few days out of the clear blue, like a knife-point wedged underneath his ribs) never would do again. And the low purr of pleasure in Cassie's, the woman's, throat was the slightest bit distorted, out of phase, like a voice passed through a window fan. Something not right here. Something damned strange.

Turner tried to raise his hands to stabilize himself but he was so weak it took three four five surges of effort before he gripped her with sufficient strength to separate her from him, his brain waging a laughably fragile *No* against the ten gravities that pulled him into her.

He held her at arm's length and looked at her—now in possession of her own face again, Cassie's having disappeared—while he regained his breath, as if from a long swim. Her lips hung slightly parted, her eyes damp, a look of subdued triumph.

"Listen," he said, in a voice he recognized as his own, "this is all real tempting, but I need to go check on the guys. If the power's off at the motel, they're probably pretty uneasy by now."

He was so disoriented he didn't realize that his stiff-armed resolve had weakened until he felt the fingertips of both her hands on the small of his back, kneading the tension away. She was on tiptoe now, breathing moistly into his ear. "Call them," she whispered. "From my place." Her small teeth took the barest nip of his earlobe, stopping just shy of pain.

Jesus.

Something not right.

He started inwardly reciting Lim Rhya's Twelve Tests of Right Action, but the rock-hammer pounding of his blood and the warm herbal scent that rose from the front of her sweater kept making his brain lose its place and start over at Test One: *Does it cause harm to any sentient being . . . does it cause . . . does it . . . does* . . . while the increasingly sentient being in his pants-front whom her hipbone caressed with such unhurried ardor shouted into his bloodstream that all the tests were satisfied, praise Buddha, clear to proceed, clear to proceed, three, two . . .

But some small voice of reason broke through the clamor and enabled him to hold the temptress at arm's length for the space of a breath, enough time for his brain to master language again.

"I've got to go," he said. "Got to go."

In the faint lightning tremors she appraised him with a look of scorn and disbelief. When she spoke it was not with her original voice. Not even with a woman's voice, but rather a guttural snarl, as if the gargoyle on an ancient building were given the power of speech:

"You . . . *dare* . . . deny . . . me?"

Her breath was the air from a tomb. Turner backed away and breathed into his shirt sleeve to evade the stench. His stomach churned.

"Who the hell *are* you?" he said.

The gargoyle voice growled low in her throat, a hideous parody of the sound she'd made when he kissed her. "Your . . . destiny," it said. "Accept it . . . now . . . and save . . . the pain."

Turner looked around desperately for another doorway than the one she stood in, but the glass and formica of the snack bar had been replaced by a shifting confusion of shadows. No way out.

"Baby?"

From no clear direction a young girl's voice, near tears. Turner whirled to see that the woman in the doorway had disappeared. In her place stood . . . oh, great God in heaven. No. No.

It was . . . *was* Cassie McNamara, center of his universe for four years and an aching vacancy in his heart ever since, the only woman he had loved with every recess of his being, holding back nothing. She wore the same leotard and floppy sweater as on the day he left for the Army, and with her sleeve she made an awkward swipe at her big wonderful sad Irish eyes, red from crying.

She was eighteen years old. Eighteen and beautiful and whole and standing, her body not yet broken, not yet a prisoner of the cold encumbrance of chrome rails and spokes he had never seen her in, but which rarely missed a day gliding just at the edges of his perception. It was worst on city streets, where every glimpse of a wheelchair, or even a half-seen bicycle wheel, drew a sharp involuntary snap of his neck, to see if the face was hers. But now here she was whole—the horrible deed undone, her hand outstretched toward him.

"Baby, they want me to talk to you," she said. A sob erupted from her with the violence of a hiccup, but she forced it back down. "Will you listen?"

"You're not real," Turner said. "You're some kind of witch. Cassie's forty years old, for Christ sake. Cassie's . . ." *Crippled* was what always came to mind first by habit, his grandparents' colloquialism, and by effort he replaced it. " . . . paralyzed," he said.

She shook her head vigorously. "That's all a dream," she said, wiping at her eyes again. "Just a bad dream. Or, it *can* be . . ."

Out. Out. He had to get out of here, clear his head. He tried to shove her aside gently as he could and make for the exit, but her hands went up to his cheeks and turned him to face her, and all the force went out of him. "Baby . . . ?" she said. The air became invisible molasses, trapping him in place.

"Imagine me and you," she sang in a whisper, with much feeling, "and you and me, no matter how you toss the dice, it had to be . . ."

A song from high school. *Their* song, played on the red transistor radio day and night by a wonderful group called The Turtles. Had life ever been so pure? This was not happening. Not fucking happening. This was a dream.

"Who else could know that?" the girl said, her face urgent against his, their foreheads touching. "Listen, baby. Please. They're scared of you. They know how strong you are, and what a good person . . ." Her voice broke again. She breathed deep to compose herself, exhaling a small warm wind of licorice scent.

"Who?" Turner said. "*Who* does?"

"Oh, God, I don't know. They say they're from the 'rim,' or something . . ."

"The realm?"

"Just hush and listen. They're willing to make a deal. If you'll send all the monks home, and start your life again from the day you got the . . . letter, some kind of letter, then the rim won't come to earth again for a hundred years. You won't have to fight them. They won't have to . . ." She swallowed hard. "To kill you all." The sobs rose up in her again.

Turner carefully pried her hands from his face and held them in his. "Look, Cassie . . . *if* you're Cassie, whoever the hell you are. Why should I trust the realm? They *invented* lies. They're the cause of all the suffering in the world. And they're saying I can shake hands with them and go home and everything's fine? That's bullshit, and you know it."

She clamped her eyes hard shut, sending a cascade of accumulated tears and mascara down the sides of her nose. But when she opened them again she was all business. Her even voice belied the desperation in her face.

"They knew you'd say that. They said to tell you the means . . . the means . . . oh, crap. I'm too shook up to think." She bit her lip and looked toward the ceiling, straining to remember. The gesture was so unguarded, so purely Cassie, that Turner had to fight an overwhelming urge to take her in his arms.

"The means . . . exist . . . to forge a contract . . . enforceable under universal law. At least hear them out." Her head collapsed to her chest with the effort she'd expended in getting the message right. When she raised up to look him in the eye again she only had one word to add:

"Please."

Turner's mind was a crowded rush of images, all of them imprinted over her impossibly large, imploring eyes: the monks at that moment in a dark motel room in a strange frightening land, hugging each other and saying prayers for his safety; the contorted face of the crow swooping down at him on the Kennesaw quad; Won Se in the Drepung garden on the day Turner and the monks departed for America, answering his question *But what if I screw up?* with a sad pantomime, the monk's small brown hands making the shape of a globe whose hopes disintegrated, poof, with the ease of a soap bubble. *Do well, Tur-ner.* What he wouldn't give to make it all a bad dream, to have his life back.

"I can't do it," he said, finally. "You know me better than that. I can't just walk away. It never works."

"But it *can*," she said, squeezing his hands. "Listen, we . . . you could start over."

"What do you mean?"

"I mean, from before it happened."

Her eyes welled over. The *it* was obvious. It, the accident that was in his store of permanent nightmares; not actually seen, only imagined, but replayed regularly, eternally, in slow motion—beyond changing but never beyond regret.

"It's part of the deal," she said, her face as hopeful as a child's on a holiday. "We get another chance." She tried to smile, but the quivering of her lower lip kept it barely incomplete.

At some level he knew the realm was playing with his mind, the way Won Se had warned it would. But the chance, even if illusory, of giving the old story a different ending tore at his heart like talons. All the careful stratagems Won Se had drilled him in, for catching specters and demons in their lies, turned insubstantial as smoke.

With all the strength he had, Turner shook his head. His voice was reduced to a whisper. "I'm sorry," he said. "I can't."

He would try for days to recollect exactly what happened at that next instant, what the sequence of events had been: whether the room exploded into light and flames before or after Cassie's body wrenched apart to reveal the gargoyle-being in all its rage at being spurned, its hideous face filling his vision floor-to-ceiling with the bulk and loudness of a speeding Mack truck, shouting curses whose force flung him backwards through a hurricane of broken glass.

But inexplicably, the vivid after-image on his shut eyes as he flew through space was not of the beast's face but of Cassie's, just before. Had the tiny amulet been around her neck the whole time, unnoticed by him, or had it appeared there only after her need for subterfuge was gone? Whichever, it would be engraved on his mind the next few weeks: a dainty silver chain, supporting the enameled silhouette of a ragged, misshapen black crow.

That much, the amulet, he was sure of, as he raised up groggily to sit on the dark grass. A soft rain was falling, one too soft to help extinguish the tall orange pyre the snack bar had become. He heard a far-off fire truck's bell and siren change pitch and grow louder as it topped a hill.

He was sure of the enameled crow. And of one thing more: the beast's last words after its curses were all spent, words that still reverberated in the darkness as Turner got uneasily to his feet:

No mercy, the thunder had said.

Twice.

No mercy.

3

TURNER WATCHED, out the window of the van, a pewter-colored sun rising over the marsh coast of southern Louisiana as delicate white gulls cut spirals in the mist. An occasional shrimp trawler on the horizon was the only sign of human habitation.

No matter how he angled his seat or the steering wheel, he couldn't find a position that gave any relief to the aching in his neck and shoulders. The lick he'd taken in last night's conflagration would have been a nothing, a gnat bite, back in his combat days. As it was, he came awake at 4 a.m. with the sensation of a hot poker being inserted between his shoulder blades. He was so stiff he had to roll himself out of bed.

When he went to find some aspirin he also found the electricity restored and the guys all awake, still too hyper from the events of the evening to sleep. They were eating leftover pizza and watching Oral Roberts on cable. When Turner suggested that they go ahead and hit the road everybody concurred. Five minutes down the highway in their familiar positions, though, and they were all dead to the world.

He remembered his naive plan, when they first arrived in L.A., of teaching all the monks to drive so they could share the road duties with him. No chance of that now, when every hour counted. He searched the glove compartment for more aspirin.

Chai Lo, reclining beside him in the passenger seat with his fingers laced on his chest, stirred and let out a vigorous yawn. Shy pressed the button on his armrest to return his seat upright, and the mechanism's spring propelled him forward with such force that his forehead bounced off the windshield with a resounding *konk.* He swore the mildest of Tibetan oaths, one often used by children because of its alliterative appeal.

A few seconds later the van coughed and sputtered, but with some careful coaxing of the gas pedal Turner was able to keep the engine from quitting. No aspirin in the glove compartment; he slammed it shut.

"What *is* it with us?" he said to Chai Lo. "We've been like the Three Stooges all week. Bumping into stuff, dropping stuff, tripping over stuff. And the van's quit, what? Three times? Four times? We're beating ourselves to death before the fight even starts."

Chai Lo stared ahead, thoughtfully silent. Finally he said, "Stew jizz?"

"Stooges. Slapstick . . . uh, comedians. Comedy." Turner heard movement in the seat behind him. Beh Vah stretched and let out a loud sigh.

"Wish Won Se here," Beh Vah mumbled. Chai Lo didn't reply, only stared grimly ahead.

"Me too, Beaver," Turner assured him. "Me too."

"Strength in numbers," Beh Vah added. The youngster was a veritable magnet for American proverbs. Since he'd been here he'd stitch-in-timed and sleeping-dogged them to distraction.

"Strength *here*," Chai Lo grunted, with more than a touch of pique.

Turner looked in the rear-view mirror. In the back seats Bah Tow and Se Hon snored loudly, but Wah So and Lu Weh had awakened and were playing patty-cake. Having lived in the monastery since they were toddlers, the pastime had escaped their notice until the day before yesterday when they wandered through a nursery school playground while waiting for Turner to check out of the motel. They were mesmerized by two small girls patty-caking near the swing set. Because the physics of the game were stunning in their simplicity but offered an absolute festival of permutations and refinements, the monks took to it with a wild joy; they had been slapping their hands raw ever since.

Strength here, Turner thought, watching them in the mirror. Oh, yeah. We're a goddamned powerhouse.

"We must trust in the plan," Chai Lo said.

"Oh, there's a plan? I thought we were just flying by the seat of our pants, at this point." He looked down at Chai Lo's robe, hiked to the knees. "*My* pants. Excuse me."

The van's motor started missing again. By gearing down and revving higher Turner was again able to keep the vehicle moving, though their speed slowed to about twenty. "Oh, great," he said. "This is great."

On the right of the road a ramshackle service station appeared where before there had been only swamp. Despite the early hour an attendant stood beside the two gas pumps waiting for trade, his hands in his pockets. Hand, rather. The old man had only one arm. Turner braked to pull into the driveway, and noticed that the man wore the first all-black work clothes he had ever seen, including a ragged black baseball cap. He looked like the cemetery caretaker in a horror movie.

But as soon as Turner left the highway he saw the rows of upturned roofing nails arranged on the concrete waiting for his tires. He saw, too, various tools of destruction propped against the gas pump at the old man's feet—a sledgehammer, a chisel, a pickax, a shovel.

A crowbar.

He stomped on the brake and swerved hard to miss the nails, which caused the sleeping Se Hon to roll from his seat and come to rest in the aisle. Before the van had stopped rocking on its shocks his piercing snore resumed, as did the game of patty-cake beside him.

It was then that Turner noticed the large handmade sign across the storefront: BLACKIE LeCROW'S GAS & BAIT. A round-bottomed signboard on the driveway appended the message, MECHANIC ON DUTY. The "I" was dotted with the stark outline of a crow in flight.

The realm's idea of humor, no doubt.

"I'm not believing this," Turner said. When he wracked the wheel hard left to pull back onto the highway the engine revved full and strong again and the back tires threw up a cloud of sand from the soft shoulder. As the gas station receded in the mirror he saw the man at the pumps raise his one good arm in a wistful salute.

"All right, Shy," Turner said after drawing a deep breath and letting it out. "Fact. The realm created that little drama especially for our benefit. They're toying with us, right? By making it so obvious, like a damned cartoon, when they're capable of much better. I mean, is that a fair assumption?"

Chai Lo scratched his chin and thought hard. After what seemed like minutes he said, "In the broad sense." It had come to be his favorite phrase in the English language. The distinction of *sense* did not exist in Tibetan, but because of its ability to instantly expand the number of levels of any argument he had taken it gladly to his heart and used it at every opportunity.

"Okay. So now the question becomes, are they *real*?"

Chai Lo let out a long sigh. "In what sense?"

The events of the last twenty-four hours had made raw meat of Turner's nerves. "In the *sense*," he said, "that if we'd gotten out, back there, could Boris have cold-cocked us with a fucking shovel? What other sense is there?"

"I do not know that type of shovel," Chai Lo said. His look of concern couldn't conceal the glint of mischief in his eye.

"What I *mean,*" Turner said, "is are they flesh and blood? Was the reporter? Was Cassie? Do they have lives and mothers and stomach aches and all that, or are they just fake protoplasm whipped up for the purpose?"

"Mmm," Chai Lo said. "In what . . ."

"In the *sense,*" Turner cut him off, "that if we turned around and went back to that service station right now would it still be there, or did they fold up their tent and steal away to nothingness when they saw we didn't bite?"

Chai Lo shrugged. "There is one way to find out."

"Thanks, Shy. That helps a lot. It really does."

Turner sifted through the contents of the cluttered dashboard trying to find his notebook, the one where he'd written the directions to their next stop. Some church with an odd name. The appearance hadn't been on the original schedule; it was a last-minute addition he'd only found out about the week before when he phoned the booking agency in Sausalito for his messages.

He found the notebook and leafed back several days. To get to the Heartily Overcoming New Deliverance Temple Unlimited, his scribbled information said, you were to stay on Highway 49 through Bogalusa and Stendhal and Shreveport and then about eleven miles past Shreveport turn left onto Route 116 which would seem to be taking you to the county seat of oblivion.

But persevere, his note said, and after seven or eight more turns which were painstakingly detailed across the next two pages you will find yourself in Bon Aerie, Louisiana, unincorporated, of which the H.O.N.D.T.U. is the chief landmark.

How in goodness, Turner wondered, did the place find out about the monks? Word of mouth from some college student home on spring break? Who could say.

The next road sign confirmed they were on Highway 49, and the sign after that told him it was seventy-five miles to Shreveport. He looked at his watch and did some calculation and decided that if the van held out they could make the church's eleven o'clock worship service with a good half-hour to spare.

"Okay, Shy," he said. "Second question . . ."

"Third," Chai Lo corrected.

"Third question. Is it the realm that's making us so damned clumsy, or is it something else?"

"Oh, no," Chai Lo said with assurance. "It's us."

"It's us," Turner repeated, looking confused. "*We're* making us clumsy? Why would we do that?"

"The heart's sad longing for certainty. You remember the teaching. Lesson Seventeen, Third Level? Won Se delivered it while you were with us."

"Refresh me if I'm wrong. 'The nature of man is that when faced with choosing among a number of outcomes, one of which is not *knowing* the outcome, he will choose almost any painful outcome just to avoid the not knowing.' Is that the one?"

"More and less," Chai Lo shrugged.

"I don't see the application."

"We cannot be sure we will win."

"Ah. But we *can* be sure we'll lose, if we screw up enough. So you're saying we're subconsciously beating ourselves up just because it's the path of greatest certainty?"

Chai Lo frowned. "Subcon . . . ?"

"In the heart."

The monk nodded. "More and less."

"But what does that have to do with the van messing up? It's just an object."

"So? You told us every object has subject."

"I was talking about grammar."

"Six of one, half of another."

"So you're saying that animate and inanimate are just different states of the same energy?"

"Did I? Sounds well."

"Sounds *good*."

"Me, too."

The sun was above the mists now, white and pulsing, already hot enough to make the black pavement dance. Turner pulled down his visor against the glare but after a minute raised it again, unwilling to give up that much of a sky so gorgeous. Especially since his days of seeing it might be severely foreshortened, if the realm had its way.

"In other words," Turner said, "until we get our act together we're our own worst enemy. Right?"

"No, no, no," Chai Lo said vigorously. "You . . . what is the words? You flatter yourself."

The thought of what might lie ahead sent a stab of cold into Turner's backbone, despite the heat and brightness of the perfect day. At moments like this, Won Se's puzzling words to him at the end of his recuperation twenty years ago, during the war, seemed in retrospect some sad joke: *You are the Hope*. Had other Hopes, in other times, felt this much like an impostor?

Nonetheless, that was what Won Se had said, the morning Turner left Drepung the first time. *The Hope*? This had made no sense to Turner. A big part of the time he'd spent at Drepung he was delirious from his injuries in the ambush at Tre Chinh and from the effects of exposure. Even afterward, when he'd mostly recovered, he remembered that he made himself about as welcome as a boil.

Lumbering along the silent hallways on his homemade crutches, interrupting classes and discussions left and right by his sudden oversized presence. And later, when he had picked up just enough fragments of the language to be dangerous, taking lecturers to task for their interpretations of the spirit life, playing devil's advocate for good old oversimplified Western rationalism. All in all, the intellectual equivalent of a bull in a china shop.

Miraculously, the monks at Drepung had rarely lost patience with him, and never over anything he would have expected. Their philosophy of life was surprisingly elastic; it seemed not only to tolerate him—a trained killer in their nonviolent midst—but in some unexplainable way to *contain* him before he ever came on the scene and, most likely, before he was even born. While *their* ways, meanwhile, meshed not at all with his blustery bravado, striking him on alternate days as being either enigmatically profound or maddeningly childish.

One example out of hundreds was the monks' consistent refusal to explain anything they said. To someone schooled in the give-and-take of Anglo-American debating tradition, with its point and counterpoint honing down disparate ideas to a single cutting edge of perfect reason, a discussion between Buddhist monks sounded for all the world like two people competing to see who could change the subject most often. Apparently this was a result of their belief that knowledge of spiritual matters comes not through gradual accumulation of detail but rather in great leaps and bursts, for which a teacher merely paves the way by painstakingly teasing the mind free of all preconception.

A process which even they conceded was pretty damned aggravating.

And so Turner had puzzled for half his life over the conversation he had with Won Se the day he left the monastery to rejoin his unit in Saigon for the trip home, the unit whose paperwork had listed him for those three months as missing in action and presumed dead.

Won Se was a dwarflike man who'd been about sixty-five then, with a permanently startled expression that belied his cavernous reserves of calm. Standing at the stone gate of the temple that last morning, he had squeezed Turner's wrist—because of Won Se's small stature and his arthritis, the highest point of the arm he could comfortably reach—and had said with peaceful assurance something so garbled that Turner at first chalked it up to his own ignorance of the language.

"Say again?"

Repeated, it sounded the same. "In the rightness of time, again you we will see."

Not being totally clear on the monks' view of an afterlife, Turner had to assume Won Se meant they would all meet up in paradise someday when their bodies had been transformed into spirit, when war was no more, away from this hellhole the world had become.

"The life after," Turner said, nodding.

Won Se shook his head adamantly. "The life before," he corrected.

"Before what?"

"Before . . . before . . ."

The old man slapped his own forehead with frustration and then, with his voice the nearest to emotion Turner had ever heard a monk's voice come, said what sounded like: "You, I hope."

The game was wearing thin. Ever since his first months in Vietnam, Turner had had no patience for obliqueness, for subtlety; he felt perpetually on the verge of some great existential violence he was too weary to perform. So he said, with more anger than he intended, "*Say again?*"

When Won Se looked up at him there were clearly tears in his eyes. "You . . . are . . . the Hope," he said, with a firmness that left no room for misinterpretation of the language.

Despite himself Turner laughed out loud. Looking down at his shabby form, the places where his old fatigues had been ripped with knives to accommodate the bundlesome homemade bandages and splints, and smelling on his skin the now-familiar convalescent mixture of adhesive and alcohol and faint excrement that was remarkably resistant to all forms of bathing, he told Won Se:

"Anything I'm the hope of is in piss-poor shape, buddy."

Won Se nodded heartily, smiling a sad smile. He put his arms around

Turner's waist, as high as he could hold, and they stayed that way until the car came.

The two prophecies would not become clear to Turner until almost twenty years later, just this past summer, when Won Se called him back to Drepung to show him the War Room. At least that was what Turner called the place; the monks had no name for it, as far as he could discern, but were amused by the irony of his choice of words and so the name had mostly stuck.

Their request for his presence had come at the worst possible time. That is, the best time of his whole life and then some, a week during which he pinched himself daily to ensure he wasn't dreaming. The landmark Stones' reunion tour was clicking up the Eastern Seaboard like clockwork, *clock*-work—D.C., Philly, Boston, with every stadium a sellout since spring. Seats were scalping a pair-for-a-grand in yuppie circles. The international press was in ecstatic tow. The wonderful weather was holding and every single aspect was going so ab, so, frigging, lutely, *perfect*. And now on the boys' very last encore of the very last night Turner was perched on a stratospheric scaffolding alongside the lighting crew while the overflow Meadowlands crowd spread out below screamed itself into nirvana, an upscale Woodstock revisited. The high-rigger roadies on the scaffolding were getting rowdy, hooting and tooting and popping their champagne corks to spray him down, and the Scandinavian cover girl who'd joined the entourage on a whim back in Denver, or was it Houston, was squeezing his hand and whispering in his ear that they'd better be heading down toward the stage so as to pose for high-fives with Mick and Company while fifty thou worth of fireworks pow-powed in the background. Then it would all be over, and he would wait for his cut of the tickets, the T-shirts, and the TV rights to accumulate in half a dozen banks in his country-boy, kiss-my-ass name.

At which point he nuzzled Greta's long blonde neck and reached to grab his walkie-talkie and his tote bag and . . .

And spotted the odd-sized, cream-colored envelope protruding from the bag's side pocket. The envelope bore no stamp, only his name—no address—in the spidery handwriting he'd not seen for two decades but whose source he knew in a heartbeat, as immediate and certain as his right hand finding his left in the dark.

He tore open the letter, while the grand pandemonium continued to erupt around him, and read:

All greetings, from your brothers at Drepung . . .

Despite Won Se's broken, rambling English, Turner clearly deduced that the old master was summoning him back to the thousand-year-old monastery on the sheer rock hillside, and that life and death hung on his response. Although *whose* life and death was a good bit less clear.

You are the Hope, Won Se's shaky handwriting reminded him.

And so the next morning Turner did the impossible: he slipped the knot of his so-sweet, pressure-cooker life and by a quarter to seven was staring blearily out the window of a ramshackle jetliner at the sun rising over the blue-gray Atlantic, alternately feeling excited and wondering if he had lost his mind.

4

ALL OF WHICH was how, that evening, he came to be sitting in the lower gardens with Won Se and the other elders after a joyous homecoming feast in his honor as they continued to discuss with great gravity and purposefulness his mission, as they had come to call it. In typical monk fashion, they had outlined for him in exhaustive detail everything that could possibly be known about the subject, with the small exceptions of (A) exactly what he was supposed to do, (B) when he was supposed to do it, and (C) why.

He gathered, in vague terms, that the monastery was under threat from some powerful entity, although his sporadic reading about the tiny nation's politics over the past several years led him to believe this was highly unlikely. The zealous Marxists and Leninists of the old revolution had long since been succeeded by cooler heads who were less concerned with glorious victories for The People than with getting just a small slice of the Western-dollar pie that Hong Kong and Japan were so greedily gulping. The new-day bureaucrats had the general mien of used car salesmen, not soldiers, and any of the region's resources not apt to turn a ready profit—Buddhist monasticism, say—were treated by the capital with benign neglect.

"Guys, you'll have to be patient with me," Turner said, at a pause in the talk. "I want to help you, but I'm catching on a little slow." The last of the sun was striking the old dilapidated stone building set into the mountainside above them, giving it a hundred orange eyes. A flock of swallows, dipping and swooping for insects at a great height, made a constantly changing Mobius strip against the fading sky.

"Now, if I understand you right," Turner said, "you're saying I'm the only person on the face of the earth who can do this . . . thing, this mission, whatever it is."

All faces turned toward Won Se, who was staring into the distance with the slightly pained expression he wore when trying to simplify some spiritual concept just enough for Turner to get his rational mind around it but not so much as to untie the perfect knot of contradiction he insisted was at the heart of all great truths.

"The only one . . . of many," Won Se said with difficulty, "who is now."

It was going to be a long evening, Turner saw. Damn it, he loved these guys, but why did they have to turn a simple conversation into a game of charades? He longed mightily for a good stiff cocktail, but in his haste he hadn't thought to bring liquor. And the monastery, he remembered, only uncorked its reserves of a sweet mead-like beverage twice a year, on festival days, both of which were months away.

Only one . . . of many . . . who is now.

"One of a long . . . *line* of people to do this, you're saying?" Turner offered. "It's happened before?"

Won Se looked puzzled. "Long line . . . ?" he asked. "Fishing line?"

"No, no. Long . . . *row.*"

"Long row . . ." Won Se pondered, "to fish in middle of lake?"

It wasn't the first time language had broken down just when he and the monks were near understanding on a crucial issue. At such times the only thing to do, he'd found, was drop back and punt. "Just scratch all that," he said, "and let's start again." While he sat for a moment with his face in his hands plotting a sneak attack on the language barrier, the evening quiet was broken by the sound of running feet on the courtyard gravel behind him.

A skinny teenaged boy with the severe haircut and saffron robe of the initiates sprinted into the midst of the seated group and stood before Turner with an expectant shudder. He was dripping wet, as if from a swim in one of the nearby mountain lakes, and he bowed deeply from the waist as he extended an awkward hand for Turner to shake.

"I am to meet you, please," he said, out of breath from running.

Won Se cleared his throat and whispered loudly like a stage prompter, "I am *please* to meet you . . ."

"Yes," said the youngster, nodding eagerly. "What he said. And I . . . am forward to be traveling you and your country."

"Beg pardon?" Turner said, but when he looked to the elders for explanation they were all as one glaring at the boy's back with such vigor that he finally glanced around and took the hint. He bowed again toward Turner. "I am excuse," he said, and ran up the path toward the main building.

Won Se gave a long, patient sigh and shook his head. "I apologize," he said to Turner. "Beh Vah is, how you say, full of hand."

"A . . . handful?"

"Most exactly."

Forward to be traveling you?

With tremendous sober effort, Turner directed all his brainpower toward a recapping of what he'd heard, or thought he'd heard, that the monks were wanting from him.

"You say the monastery is in danger. Danger from who, exactly?"

The elders looked at each other with what Turner took to be growing exasperation and shook their heads, then waited for Won Se to speak.

"Not the monastery," he told Turner. "The world."

"The *world* is in danger? From who?"

"The usual," Won Se said. "The dark. The warfare is, how to say, intenser by each day. It must soon break through."

Turner had the sudden eerie feeling of being trapped in a time warp. Whether it was a scarcity of oxygen to his brain from the thin mountain air or the dazzling dots of fire that pulsed hypnotically across the great building's facade, he couldn't say, but for a moment he almost convinced himself that he mustn't look down or he'd discover his 20-year-old self in torn fatigues bulging with bandages, all the intervening years erased like a dream.

Warfare? Of course, the monks didn't get newspapers or television here. Still, was it possible they were so far behind on current events they didn't know . . . ?

"But see," Turner said diplomatically as he could, "they're destroying more and more nuclear missiles every day now. Both sides. The armies are all being cut back. Sure, there are little pockets of trouble here and there, but a *big* war is less likely now than . . . well, probably any other time in our lives."

Won Se not only shook his head violently at this, he did what monks rarely ever do—he raised his voice. "*Flesh!*" he virtually shouted at Turner, before he reined his emotion in, and the tiny wattles of skin that quivered on his neck made it suddenly apparent how much he had aged since Turner was last here. "War of flesh, you are talking. I am saying warfare of spirit. The kind that never ends."

In frustration Won Se balled his frail, teakwood-colored fists and held them at arm's length in front of him, where he rotated them like planets in the last narrow shaft of brilliant sun that remained at the level of ground where the group was seated. One fist was high and centermost, basking in the light, until the crosswise orbit of the other fist began gradually to eclipse it with a swelling crescent of shadow that enlarged and enlarged until Turner believed, was sure, he saw the hands cease being hands and become contrary pulsing globes of distilled light and distilled darkness, the darkness clearly ascendant, the light being extinguished as slowly and surely as the windows of fire on the hilltop, winking out one by one as the shadow of the world rose to cover them.

Turner blinked hard, and the globes became just hands again, which settled onto Won Se's lap. The elders, sitting silently as a held breath, all looked at Turner.

"You're saying if I don't do . . . something, whatever, the world . . . goes dark? Eclipses? What?"

"Worse than darkness," Won Se said, sounding very tired. "*Spirit* darkness." Though his eyes were on the small gray gravel of the garden path, he seemed to be looking instead at some momentous brink of future time, too fearful to contemplate. The monks, with matter-of-fact expressions, all nodded their agreement.

"Evil is never far from our hearts," Won Se explained, now looking at Turner again. "In the best of times it is a, how say . . . lap-dog. It knows its place. In other times it roars, devours. Grows wolf teeth." He paused to read Turner's eyes. "Until," he finished, raising one slim finger, "there is hope."

The letter of last evening seemed a year and a world away, but Turner saw the cramped writing now in his mind's eye, packed away in his suitcase in one of the barren upstairs sleeping rooms. *You are the Hope.*

At the bottom of the hill, already in full darkness except for a faint wreathing of white fog, was the gate where Won Se had embraced him the day he left, twenty-odd years ago. *You are the Hope.*

"You knew all of this when I was here before," Turner said to Won Se. The elders nodded in his behalf.

"Then why," Turner asked, "are you just now . . ."

"The fullness of time," Won Se cut him off.

A sudden weariness overcame Turner—jet lag from the day-long flight, he reckoned—and he settled slowly backward until he was lying prone on the low stone bench. The twilight sky had shaded itself gradually west to east with color that ranged from a smoky rose to the rich purple-black of an eggplant skin, a particular combination he had seen no other place on earth but the small Alabama town of his childhood. Most likely there was a scientific reason—the mountainous terrain, the abundance of small lakes—but when he had healed here during the war he had taken the sky at dusk as a flat-out miracle, a balm for the heart. Lying here in this courtyard, back then, he could fantasize that he was back at home, waiting for his grandmother to call him in for supper.

A garland of brilliant stars appeared along the treetops to the east, and their immediate clarity somehow helped him see with new eyes how absurd the whole present situation was. Okay, the monks had saved his life, once. Agreed. But anybody who gets through a war in relatively one piece owes the same debt to dozens of people. Hundreds, maybe. Hell, take a number.

None of which changed the fact that what the monastery was proposing for him now—becoming some type of half-cocked traveling evangelist, reviling evildoers—just wouldn't wash. The only real question was how best to let them down easy and high-tail it home, maybe do them a fund-raiser somewhere down the road to salve his conscience.

He sat up and rubbed his eyes. "Guys, maybe my brain will be working better tomorrow. What say we knock off for now, and try this again in the morning?"

Won Se didn't respond immediately, but held a quick murmured discussion with his second-in-command, whose name Turner thought he remembered from the hurried introductions as Chai Lo. Though he couldn't hear much of what the two men were saying, it appeared from their expressions that Chai Lo was on the losing end. After the exchange was finished they both stood up, Chai Lo wearing a look of resignation.

"You will go to the room now," Won Se said. At first Turner thought he meant his sleeping room, upstairs, but when the procession reached the corridor leading to the monastery's steep basement stairs he realized Won Se had some other room in mind. At least he'd managed to change the subject, Turner thought.

The stone stairwell was illuminated by a row of torches. He had never ventured this far down during his first stay, mainly because of the difficulty for his crutches. The air smelled like woods-dirt and lichen. He could hear water dripping somewhere within the walls. The monks wore forlorn looks. None of them spoke.

Turner followed them down a long flight of stone steps. Then another flight, and another, and another. The surface of each step was slightly lower at the center than at the edges, a path of wear from centuries of bare feet. He lost count of how many flights they walked down. At each level the silence became thicker, more complete, until he could hear with amplified clarity every monk's individual breathing.

Then, beyond a certain point, the silence began almost imperceptibly to be replaced by the commodious hum of purposeful human activity, the click and clatter of small implements and machinery. The sound reminded Turner, for some odd reason, of the summer he'd worked as a copy boy at *The Birmingham News*.

When Won Se said "the room," Turner had pictured a small cell of the size the monks slept in, or perhaps the slightly larger communal rooms that were used for reading and discussions. So he was totally unprepared when at last the procession turned a corner and he found himself standing in the entranceway of a cavelike enclosure so vast he couldn't even see its farthest wall.

The layout looked like a gigantic laboratory from some past century, with monks manning dozens of experiment stations all subdivided by columns of stone and ringed with lit torches. At one station a young monk on a ladder crossed and recrossed the face of a twenty-foot-high map of the world, gluing and ungluing tiny beads of colored glass in accordance with instructions on a bundle of narrow fan-folded paper he kept referring to intently and then replacing under his arm.

Farther down the row, another monk on a ladder attended to a sort of three-dimensional abacus the size of a room, a forest of rods and counters that stretched from floor to ceiling. A number of the stations seemed to be only shelves of books, at which one monk sat on a stool reading while another sat nearby on the floor in an attitude of prayer.

But the installation that riveted Turner's eye was a long silver cage against the right-hand wall, extending backward horizontally until it was lost in depth and darkness, housing a single row of unblemished white doves. Just above the whole length of the cage ran an assembly of slowly revolving rods and tines like the innards of an oversized music box, from which emanated a low discordant chiming that the doves seemed to regard with fearful anticipation, blinking and looking around.

When Turner approached the cage more closely he noticed, here and there, gaps in the row of birds along the perch. Directly beneath each gap, in the cage bottom, lay a crumpled white form, some on their backs with curled feet raised in the rigor of death, others hunched quivering with their feathers fluffed out by illness. As he watched, one bird halfway down the line tottered and fell. It hit and lay with its neck stretched at an angle, one wing flopping monotonously like Morse code.

Out of the shadows came a sad-faced monk with a clipboard and a pencil; he noted the latest casualty in a column of figures and sketched alongside it what looked to be a diagram of the position of the section of revolving tines where the bird had been sitting.

From somewhere nearby, Turner heard kick into action what he could have sworn was the metallic chattering of the old Associated Press teletype machine at *The News*. A clear impossibility, since the monastery had no phone lines and no electricity.

Turner became aware of Won Se at his elbow.

"What *is* this place?" he asked him.

"It is how we know," Won Se said. "Or try to know."

"You mean, from here you can predict . . . things?"

Won Se didn't answer. He proceeded down the walkway and motioned for Turner to follow.

In a small alcove to their right sat, sure enough, a battered old Associated Press teletype, churning out dispatches on a length of yellow fanfold paper that accumulated in a wire basket beyond the platen. It could actually have been the same machine at *The News*, its olive drab casing darkened by years of inky fingerprints.

"Where did you get this?" Turner asked.

"A friend," Won Se said.

Turner walked around to the back of the machine and saw what he expected—its phone cable and electrical cord were both fastened into neat coils that hung down the rear plate into thin air.

He said, "But how does it work?"

Won Se shrugged. "Fairly well." He gestured for Turner to follow him to the left, toward the standing thicket of abacus rods. "It's of limited value in what we do, but it's good to have as a, how you say, backup."

The monk stationed at the room-sized abacus stood to one side in a seeming trance of concern, his head bent as if listening for something beyond the walls. Suddenly on impulse he climbed the ladder and moved two counting beads a rung higher on one of the rods.

"This is the Tally of Inner Blindness," Won Se said. Inner blindness, which he detailed for Turner at some length, was their term for people who, despite good minds and good eyesight, permanently shut out the parts of reality that don't mesh with their philosophy. In the manner of an elaborate seismograph, the abacus tenders kept a running count of the proportion of people in the world who were thus afflicted at any given time.

Turner walked the circumference of the rods, eyeballing how many beads were up and how many were down, but he'd forgotten how to read an abacus. "How are we doing?" he asked Won Se. "Is blindness up or down?"

Won Se looked around at the rods, perplexed, as if the answer were there for anyone to see. "Oh, up," he said. "Much up."

"And that's what increases the chances of this, uh . . . spirit war?"

Won Se grunted an unintelligible syllable.

"Pardon?"

In the silence the chattering teletype sounded ominously loud. Won Se grimaced and massaged his forehead with the heel of his hand. "Actually that is not true," he said.

Turner felt a flutter of hope. "What's not true?"

"The blindness is only one of things. One of hundred things."

"And you measure them all from here?"

Won Se began to walk on to the next station, but he stopped for a second to massage the tense shoulders of the monk who stood, head bowed, at the abacus. Then he gave him a slap of encouragement on the butt, like a coach consoling a team who's getting badly whipped in the final quarter.

"We measure all we can," he said to Turner as they walked. "The, how you say, technology is not all there yet."

Turner felt suddenly so closed-in and so unreal that for a few seconds he was afraid he would have to sit down. His mind was definitely overloading. The yawning torchlit cavern and the faces of the monks began to fall in and out of focus as if from the effects of anesthesia.

When the image snapped clear again he could suddenly see the vast absurdity of the whole undertaking. The realization pained his heart. He was in awe of the monks' wisdom, loved them like brothers, owed them his life—true, all true—but something looney-tunes was clearly operative here. Had Won Se gone senile, or was the whole monastery the victim of a group hallucination?

In that flash of insight Turner thought he understood the central secret of the process of brainwashing: don't begin with small lies, insignificant fictions, and work your way up; the brain will marshal all its forces of logic and order to resist from the very start. No, the secret was to hit your victim right off the bat with an illusion so ludicrous in its immensity that logic and order are left scrambling in the dust while the heart leaps up, streaming pure faith, to take the hook.

After all, wasn't it on faith that he'd gone to Vietnam when the draft took him, rather than packing off to Montreal as his ex-best friend had done? And wasn't it on faith that he'd just flown halfway around the world to end up in this nuthouse? Was he always doomed to be a sucker for a grand cause, an epic purpose? He wished, with the ferventness of prayer, that he was back at home.

Instinct told him to bolt and run, but judgment argued that he wait until morning and extricate himself with courtesy. He owed them that much. Tell them he had urgent business back in the States, but promise to give their proposal some hard thought.

At that moment Won Se, the gentle Won Se, fixed him with a look of cruel intensity approaching panic. Every cell in Turner's body prickled. Could monks read minds? No, ridiculous. More likely his doubt was written large on his face.

Won Se appeared to be making some grave decision. He breathed deep, and his placid expression returned. With perfect control he gestured toward the end of the row of columns. "Come this way," he said, "and you'll see the mandala itself."

Now it was the other monks who panicked. They looked at each other incredulously, then all protested at once in a babel of strained voices, Chai Lo's the loudest.

Won Se tried to quiet them with his outstretched hands and, failing, said to Turner, "Excuse us for a moment, please." With that, he herded the group some distance away where the animated conversation resumed, just out of Turner's clear hearing. Though he couldn't make out all of the discussion, it was obvious from the cadences and silences that Won Se's view of the situation was prevailing. Finally the exasperated elders turned and headed back up the stairs in what appeared to be the monastic equivalent of a huff.

"I apologize," Won Se said when he returned, "for our dissension. It is a troubled time for us. We have . . ."

He checked himself, apparently afraid he was talking too freely. He gave Turner one of the depth-searching looks he was capable of, looks greatly dreaded by Turner and the monks. Won Se's intensity seemed to burn away all layers of pretense and expose the vanity and self-delusion that lie at the heart's true core.

To Turner's surprise, Won Se seemed to find him worthy. He took Turner by the elbow and ushered him toward the passageway, continuing his thought as they walked: "We have reasons for to believe," he said, "that there is a traitor in our mist."

Despite himself Turner visualized some prowler in the fog of the gardens at night, even though Won Se clearly meant *midst.* Turner didn't like the direction things were taking. The hocus pocus aspect of all this was turning him off enough, without dragging a cloak-and-dagger act into it.

"A traitor?" he asked. "What makes you think that?"

Down the long passageway, the stanchions with torches grew less and less frequent until there was barely light to walk by. Turner looked over his shoulder, squinting into the peripheral shadows, and his apprehension began returning in a big way.

With an unnatural clarity his mind's eye showed him Greta at that moment, sunning her heartbreaking body by the hotel pool, her spun-gold hair cascading over the chaise lounge, waiters in safari shorts bringing piña coladas from the bar. But no, he had to make a side trip to this godforsaken place to incite a rebellion of monks.

"A week ago, maybe two weeks," Won Se was saying, "we found that the mandala had been sav . . . savage-taught?"

"Sabotaged?" Turner offered.

"Yes, exactly. Chai Lo discovered it. The damage was not great. It is repaired. But the hurtful idea . . ."

From no clear source, the illumination began to grow gradually brighter. Cool air washed over them. Ahead, the light outlined the edges of a long, curving wall. Turner thought he heard a sound come from behind it—like waves on a shore, except drier and more brittle. Some substance being poured between containers.

"You don't think it was somebody from outside?" Turner asked.

"No. He would have been seen. The only path to the lower rooms is through the prayer hall. You remember."

He did. The prayer hall, where a monk sat perpetually on the bare floor contemplating a single candle, praying for the peace and safety of his brothers. The men took turns at it, in four-hour shifts, so that the prayer never ceased. Turner remembered how comforting it had been, during his recuperation, to pass the soft glow of the central hall on one of his midnight rambles, when the pain and the nightmares kept him from sleep.

Won Se shook his head sadly. "The realm is powerful," he said.

"The what?"

"You will see. Not even holy men are a moon."

"Immune?"

"Yes. Exactly."

Turner trailed his hand across a section of the long wall. The material was too smooth, too grainless, to be stone. Clay, maybe. It had the satiny glaze of fine pottery. But what kind of kiln could have fired a piece the dimensions of a house? When he looked up, Won Se was gone.

Turner stopped and listened for footsteps, heard none. Suddenly Won Se's torso thrust out of the wall, waggling a finger at him to follow, and disappeared again. Turner felt along the surface like a blind man until he found a narrow opening in the clay, cut with such precision that it was invisible until you were directly on it.

He had to turn partly sideways to wedge through, and as he inched forward behind Won Se toward some great, diffuse light, his head swam as if from an excess of oxygen, though the air didn't smell any different. When the narrow squeezeway at last opened out, what he saw so shook his equilibrium that he had to steady a hand on the stone railing to keep from toppling over.

He was looking down, from a great height, at a flawless diorama of the surface of the world—continents and oceans and islands, all in the muted, unreal blues and greens and browns of satellite photographs but with a three-dimensional clarity.

A dozen or more monks busied themselves with its refinement, walking the circumference of the sculpture or clambering along a network of scaffoldings above it. They carried small buckets of what looked to be colored sand, which they applied to the surface with a variety of techniques—sometimes scattering it from up high in whole handfuls with a sowing motion, sometimes applying it almost grain by grain from down close, with tweezers or with a tiny funnel-like device such as would be used to decorate cakes for a doll house. The result was like being present at Creation; a continuously changing landscape, with the artisans who tended it serving as its weather, its tides.

Turner realized that Won Se was watching him, waiting for his reaction. "It's beautiful," Turner said. As beautiful as it is useless, he thought. Had men actually been laboring down here for hundreds of years in the dank, mushroom-scented dimness, knowing that nobody but themselves would ever get to see their handiwork?

"It does have a purpose," Won Se said, as if reading his mind again. "Beyond the ornamental." He went into a long explanation, where each color of sand came from and the lengths to which the monks had to go to get it.

The blue-green could only be found below a mineral deposit so high in the Himalayas, he said, that there was just one day a year, in the summer, when the rocklike shell of ice softened enough to let a pickaxe through. The ochre and black, likewise, could only be found one place in the world, a patch just a few yards square in the center of the bed of a half-mile-deep lake inhabited by stinging fish so transparent they can't be seen unless taken out of the water. Once a quantity of the sand is retrieved, at considerable cost of suffering, the mix has to be sorted grain by grain into its component colors before it can be used in the mandala.

And the sorting, Won Se said, has to be done by someone who is totally blind, who has the gift of reading colors with his skin. Because of the tediousness of the process and the quantities of sand the mandala requires, the sorting is a lifetime's task for whoever undertakes it. And by some marvelous cosmic clockwork, on the day that a blind-sorter dies, a blind youngster from the village comes and knocks on the gate of Drepung saying he's been sent there by he knows not who, and that he has the gift. And he always does.

Turner saw that the mandala lore could go on for hours. "That's very interesting," he said. "You were saying about the purpose of it?"

"Well, as the warning, of course," Won Se blinked, as if the point were obvious. "One of many ways, certainly, but by far the most manifest. Come. We have a nearer look."

Turner followed him down a spiral of stone stairs to the level of the floor. There, Won Se knelt alongside a low protective railing and squinted across the miniature landscape like someone preparing to forecast the weather.

Something at the far edge of the expanse seemed to catch his eye. He went over to the spot, and Turner followed. A tiny green-brown island in a sea of blue sand, apparently the Caribbean, was marked at one end by a barely noticeable webwork of red granules that none of the surrounding islands had.

As Turner watched, the sand grains that formed the asterisk-like red shape began multiplying at its extremities, spreading its reach across the land. He looked up, expecting to see a monk on the scaffolding, trailing the red grains from an applicator. But the section of scaffolding above them was empty.

Turner leaned forward over the blue-sand ocean to confirm what he'd seen, bracing with his arms on the railing until his eyes were focused. After several seconds a new red grain appeared, then another. Because of their minuscule size, he couldn't tell whether they were materializing into place or were the result of existing grains instantaneously metamorphosing their color.

"Where do they come from?" he asked Won Se.

The monk shrugged. "Lama Chi En once said that they come from the need to know."

"You said they were a 'warning.' A warning of what? War?"

"Better to say . . . distress. From much inner blindness."

"Distress that can *become* a war."

"Is only one war," Won Se said. "The darkness and the light."

From a corner, a young monk began chanting in a crisp tenor voice. All the mandala workers stopped in place and bowed their heads, the buckets and implements hanging by their sides. The prayer lasted about a minute, and then work resumed.

Turner asked, "How do you learn to do this?"

Won Se looked around. "To do what?"

"*This,*" Turner said, pointing. "The sand."

"Ah. You learn from elders."

"But how do *they* learn?"

"From *their* elders, I would suppose."

"How long has this been going on?"

"'Going on'?" Won Se repeated, looking around as if there were some facet of the mandala he'd missed. Turner kept forgetting that monks weren't accustomed to thinking in terms of linear time.

"How many years?" he amended. "Ten? A hundred? A thousand?"

"Oh, much thousands. At least. As long as men have lived."

This didn't sit quite right with Turner. He was no history major, but he was sure Drepung hadn't been around that long. Centuries, maybe, but . . .

"Not all from here, of course," Won Se added, sensing the question. "We became the keeper of the lineage only after Rhi Gu Yan fought the long darkness. It is him we number from."

"The Dark Ages, you mean?"

"Whatever," said Won Se, seeming to grow bored with such a clearly Western line of inquiry.

Turner stood up and walked slowly around the circumference of the cavern, dodging the monks who rushed urgently from spot to spot with the buckets. When he completed the circle back to where Won Se stood, he said, "Questions arise. Such as, 'Why me?'"

Won Se looked severely disappointed that Turner would pose a question whose answer was so obvious. "You . . . are . . . the Hope," he said firmly.

"I've got that, I've got that," Turner said. "I mean, who decided? Who appointed me?"

"Your name is in the book," said Won Se.

"What book?"

"The Book of Hopes."

Turner tried to keep a straight face. "You mean, you just opened up this book one day, and there was my name."

Won Se nodded.

This was too much. This was clearly too much. Turner couldn't keep from laughing out loud at that point. The nearest monks cast looks of solemn disapproval in his direction.

"I'm sorry," he told Won Se. "I'm extremely tired, and all of this is so very, uh . . . Could I *see* this book, by the way?"

"After," Won Se said. "Of course."

Turner felt the beginnings of a most singular headache, like pliers tightening on the soft spaces just behind his eyeballs.

"'After,'" Turner repeated. "You mean, after my . . . speaking tour, whatever? I didn't catch that."

Won Se looked at him harshly, as if his failure to grasp what was going on amounted to intentional non-listening.

"After the *battle*," he explained to Turner. He spoke with extra spaces between the words, the way you'd talk to a somewhat slow child. "After your calling-out."

"The battle," Turner repeated. "I have to *fight* somebody? Who?"

"Or what," Won Se put in.

Damn the word games. Turner bit his lip before steadying himself to ask, "Who . . . or what . . . are you saying I have to fight?"

"The same as all Hopes," Won Se answered. "You fight what you most fear. Made far worsened than in all your, how to say . . . nightmares."

"Oh. Well, that's different," Turner said, with a grin. "I thought it was going to be something *hard*."

Won Se stared back grimly, not choosing to catch the joke. "Say if you are with us or against us," he said. "There is much to do, and very little of this time you are so concerned about."

Some small pieces of the puzzle, at least, were starting to come clear in Turner's mind. He had never gotten a satisfactory answer, for instance, as to why during Vietnam he'd been brought all the way to Tibet to convalesce, while other wounded soldiers he knew who'd been found by monks were cared for in the local Thai monasteries.

And what of the letter that brought him here, the envelope which came to be in his tote bag on the Meadowlands scaffolding where he was sure no envelope had been five minutes before? Was it his imagination that made the paper feel as cold as the air in this mountain pass, and scented with the omnipresent yak-butter smoke of the temple? Or was it all some giant conspiracy? And what about . . .

His aching mind reeled. No, he was truly sorry, he would beg their pardon, but it was all just too much to swallow. Too damned much. Saint Turner, patron of epic purpose, patron of all suckers, had retired to live in the real world and would stay retired.

He saw that Won Se was waiting for an answer to his question, but seemed already to know what it would be.

"This is all very fascinating," Turner began. "I tell you what. I've got some really urgent business back at home, but I'll be giving this some heavy thought. I'll get back to you, and we can . . ."

"If you allow me," Won Se broke in, "I show you one more thing."

Turner forced a smile. "Sure," he said. What the hell.

"This way, please."

Won Se led him to where a set of ascending steps were cut into the face of the wall, their upper reach disappearing into darkness. Won Se went first, but when Turner put his foot on the bottom step two young monks who were nearby dropped what they were doing and dived toward him to put a restraining hand on his shoulder. Won Se turned around and rebuked them sharply in Tibetan. They had their mouths open to argue, but whatever Won Se said next, a phrase Turner had never heard, silenced them. They returned to their work, glancing back reproachfully at him and Turner.

As he climbed farther into the dark, Turner braced a hand against the wall for balance. Won Se, despite his age, walked with all haste, not needing any supports. Far above the softly-lit sand the steps leveled out onto a plateau where a narrow doorway showed more stairs. Now in almost pitch blackness, Turner followed the sound of Won Se's quick footsteps until they came out into an enclosure roughly resembling the projection booth of a theater. In the center of the small room a circular porthole looked directly down onto the activity below, the way someone orbiting in a space station might see the earth.

From here the broad gashes of red became more apparent. The Middle East showed as a veritable anthill of red, as did the countries in the upper half of South America. Another broad stripe painted the outlying western republics of the Soviet Union.

But because Turner had been conditioned by the nightly news to see strife as being elsewhere in the world, he failed to notice the deep red wounds across the continent of North America until Won Se pointed them out to him.

One of the worst, it appeared, was slightly below center in the grouping of southeastern states, somewhere in . . . it was hard to tell, without the familiar map lines. Alabama?

Impossible. He knew they were orchestrating this whole show-and-tell for the maximum tug at his heart strings, but forecasting big-league spiritual warfare to break out in Alabama was taking it to the absurd. He tried to keep a straight face.

"Hmm," he said. "That looks serious, doesn't it?"

"Your home, is it not?" Won Se commented.

Turner held his thumb at arm's length and sighted along it in an attempt to triangulate distances. Playing the game. "Nope," he said finally. "It looks too far north to be Birmingham."

Won Se looked puzzled. "*Birmingham* is your home?"

"Sure is. Maybe you're thinking of somebody else."

"I am speaking of your *heart* home," Won Se said. "The place your deepest heart lives."

Now, this was strange. This was totally strange. Turner had done more listening than talking, both times he'd been at Drepung. He'd volunteered very little about himself, and he was certain he hadn't mentioned the fact that his grandparents had raised him after his mother and father were killed in the wreck. Nor had he talked of the attachment he felt to their old farm, much less where it was located. The pit of his stomach suddenly felt hollow and unstable, the way it did on a fast elevator.

"Perhaps a nearer look," Won Se said, and reached into a recess of wall just above the porthole from which he withdrew what appeared to be a turret of antique lenses at the end of a counterweighted metal arm. He looked down into the eyepiece and rotated the turret until he found the one he wanted and clicked it into place. He stepped aside so Turner could take a look.

What he saw through the lens was impossible. Eerie. But undeniable.

An aerial view of Zion Hill, Alabama, authentic down to the broad, desolate gouges of clay and sandstone in the forests to the north and west of town, made by strip miners back when he was in grammar school. Except for a recently blackened strip of woods caused by this past summer's forest fires, the view was the same one he had seen from the window of the plane bringing him home from the war years ago, the same view that had made him weep uncontrollably on the morning of his return: hilly ground with a few broad pastures where cattle grazed, a scattering of fish ponds giving back the pale yellow wash of sunrise.

For a moment he'd even had a wild, errant inspiration to hijack the plane and make the pilot set it down on his grandfather's south forty, just for the gift of kneeling and kissing that ground two hours sooner than he would if he drove from the airport.

Heart home. An odd phrase. But an understatement where Zion Hill was concerned. He felt a twinge of serious guilt at how long it had been since he'd visited his grandparents. How in hell had Won Se gotten photographs of the place—and current ones, yet? As Turner raised up from the eyepiece he glanced around surreptitiously, looking for the projection device, but all he saw was stone and shadow.

"Let me get this straight," he said. "You're telling me that this . . . destruction and suffering you talk about is going to start in Zion Hill, Alabama? I mean, excuse me, but that's just a little hard to imagine."

"The Calling Out is always at the heart-home," Won Se said matter-of-factly.

"I see."

Turner leaned again over the eyepiece of the lens turret and looked at the woods and fields of Zion Hill. A movement in the upper left corner caught his eye—a band of brightness sweeping across the panorama of treetops, a slice of sunlight cast by the crevice between two fast-moving clouds. So what he was watching wasn't a still photograph at all, but a movie. At the bottom of the frame, more motion: a speck traveling the blacktop which he saw, by squinting, to be a log truck.

"This is amazing," Turner said. "How does it work?"

"Fairly well," Won Se said. "It has various . . . what do you call?

Magnifications?" He slid his hand into the crudely made banjo-works of wires and springs and levers along the bottom of the turret and adjusted something. Turner watched the image shift, the truck become large enough to see without squinting, become bright yellow.

Another click, another shift, and the lens zoomed close enough to show streaks of rust on the roof of the truck cab, the driver's thick tattooed arm trailing half a cigar out the window as the truck passed from sight. On the shoulder of the road lay a dead possum, blackened with streams of ants.

As Won Se continued his adjustments Turner saw the steeple of Zion Hill Baptist Church, the tin roof of Johnny Patterson's barn, the sun glaring white off old Mrs. Cicero's clothesline of fresh laundry. Another click, and suddenly he was looking at the roof of his grandparents' house. His grandmother, wearing her checkered sunbonnet, stood on the front walk watering the red and orange zinnias that bordered the yard. Homesickness, or some other vague regret, closed around Turner's throat like a hand.

The next click Won Se made sounded sprung and discordant, as if something in the machine had gone awry. It had the effect of kicking the scene's normal time rate into a frantic overdrive; the sun set and rose and set and rose, alternating day and dark with the rapidity of a strobe light, and various storms and mists and weathers blew in and out of the frame with blinding speed. Turner caught, or thought he did, a quick flicker of his grandfather's frightened face through the window of the house at an instant that would have been, will have been, dusk. Then, amazingly, he saw a figure of himself, he was sure of it, crouching in the shrubbery, running, crouching again, as a thick pall of smoke blew through the trees and dots of flame fell.

"What the hell is this?" he asked Won Se, whose face at that moment bore the full freight of realizing what had gone wrong. In the time that it took for Won Se to plunge his hand deep into the machinery again and wrestle with some stuck lever, a gnashing of gears, the violence Turner saw through the eyepiece came to include a scattering of running monks, aflicker and then gone, and a glimpse of what he thought was a wheelchair. There were other running figures in the smoke he couldn't make out.

Suddenly all was still again, except for the frenetic stroboscope of day and night. Seen from the air there was only a charred rectangle where the house had been, with pieces of clothing or of bodies, he couldn't tell which, protruding from under the edges of the collapsed foundation.

At that point, with a groaning sound, the progression of images came to a halt and proceeded to reverse itself at a rate several times faster than it had moved forward. Day and night merged into an optical-purple twilight, and in the space of a breath the scene was back where it had started. He was seeing his grandmother's sunbonnet again, her small shape placidly going about the flower garden with a watering hose.

"I said, what *was* that?" Turner demanded. Won Se was half squatting now, frowning and pretending to be engrossed in some assembly on the underside of the turret which he polished vigorously with his thumbs.

"I *said* . . ." Turner repeated, and when the monk continued to ignore him a rage boiled out in all directions from his heart and before he knew it he was jerking Won Se straight up by the collar of his robe to face him. "Don't pull this shit on me," Turner heard himself say through clenched teeth, but Won Se looked so truly mortified and repentant that he involuntarily relaxed his grip.

"You have seen the end stage," Won Se said in a barely audible voice. "I apologize. It was not intended."

"You didn't tell me my family was in this."

"I said 'the world'."

"That's different."

The room became so quiet Turner could hear the slow dripping of water, or of time itself, from no direction he could name.

"So according to this," he said, nodding toward the lenses, "you already know that I'd fail."

Won Se shook his head vigorously in denial. "This is almost beyond understanding," he said. "You must trust me to the uttermost."

"I'm listening."

"If you are asking whether the prediction is accurate, the answer is yes and no. Yes, in the sense that it truthfully reflects the outcome of the universal forces in the current state, being carried forward to their natural conclusion. But the, how you say, ointment on the fly is that the natural conclusion is never reached in totality because of interference by human beings and by others we cannot name."

"So you're saying the universe *assumes* we'd fail?"

"In the shell of a nut, yes."

Twenty years ago, such a challenge would have put fire in Turner's blood, set his adrenaline pumping. The young Turner, patron saint of the hundred-to-one shot. Now, though, all he felt was an all-encompassing tiredness; that, and the exact location of the steel plate in his troublesome hip that sprouted rheumatism all up his side when he was around this much dampness. He was only a bit past forty years old as yet, but the prospect of what Won Se was proposing made him feel easily eighty, a hundred, archaeological.

"But this is also what makes the victory so sweet, if it comes," Won Se said. "There is a legend that says the Hope . . ." He tottered slightly, as if the effort of the exchange had dizzied him. " . . . the Hope, at the instant of his overcoming, actually hears the uncoupling of the great engine that drives the spheres in their course. And in that small space of time, before the integuments of the core of all being realign to accommodate the change that he has wrought, he hears what no other human is privileged to hear. What leaks out into the stillness from the core of the core, the legend says, is a music so much purer than music that it can never have a name, and on hearing this, the Hope is forever changed. And then he receives his deepest heart's desire, whatever it may be at that moment."

Turner stood silently for several seconds, running his finger around the rim of the metal turret. Deep within the walls of the room, water dripped with eternal regularity. A far-off monk's chanted prayer rose and echoed away.

"Look, I'd like to help," he said. "You know I would. But whatever this, uh, book thing says, I'm not your man. I'm not . . . spiritual, like you guys are. I'm a damn promoter. If a spirit ever appeared to me, I'd start figuring how to make a buck off of it."

For the first time that evening Won Se smiled, as if the reply was just what he'd expected. "Lim Rhya said that the spirit speaks its secrets more sweetly to one who flees it than to one who pursues." When this didn't seem to cut any ice with Turner, Won Se added, "The Hope is a spirit warrior. You know you have a warrior's heart."

Turner gave a little snort and shook his head sadly. "Not the spirit kind, buddy. All I ever fought was flesh. And I never want to do that again."

Won Se said, "You are selling your, how to say . . . short self. What is required is . . ."

"*Listen,*" Turner erupted. With the palm of his hand he forced his own chin upward, exposing his throat. "This area right *here,*" he said, jabbing a finger into a spot near his jawline, "is the softest spot for a knife to go in. Jugular and carotid, right there for the taking. But if you go in *here* . . ." He jabbed lower, beneath his Adam's apple, and his voice broke. " . . . then there's a little more gristle, true, but you're below the voice-box so the poor bastard can't cry out and warn anybody. See? That's the kind of stuff *I* knew. Know. Spiritual enough for you?"

Won Se was apparently unshocked by the revelation; he kept looking searchingly into Turner's eyes.

"Oh, and here's the clincher," Turner said, trying hard to keep his voice even as the words tumbled out. "Why did this great Hope go the Special Forces route, be a hand-to-hand badass cut-throat instead of just your garden variety kind of killer with rifles and mortars? Any guess?"

Won Se didn't answer.

"Because he was a coward," Turner said. "He couldn't take the way they treated you in basic, the drill instructors. Screaming at you, dog-cussing you, shoving you around. The Hope'd cry at night, see, and wonder how he was going to stand one more day of it. And then he started seeing a few guys here and there, just recruits like him except they got treated like princes. They could wear regular clothes, and their heads didn't have to stay shaved, and nobody bullied them or cussed them out.

"And he asked somebody why, and they told him, 'Special Forces, man. They're in Airborne training.' So he signed up. Ain't that heroic? You like that?"

Won Se took hold of the metallic cases of the lenses and gently folded the assembly back into its receptacle on the wall. "The question," he began, "is . . ."

"I'm not through," Turner cut him off. "You need to know who you're dealing with, here. So anyway, when he got really good at murder I guess it rubbed off on his normal life. Because when he got to come home on leave, he almost let the only woman he ever loved get killed." He had to pause and take a deep breath to get his even tone back again. "But nope, not quite. No cigar. Not killed, just paralyzed. I guess he needed more training, huh? Get that old warrior heart pumping, and . . ."

Won Se turned from the wall receptacle and looked at him sternly. "You are telling me no news," he said. "The facts are all known, and I must say that you miss . . . miss representing them, but . . ."

"The hell I do," Turner said. "The story goes on, see. This woman he crippled? His grandparents knew where she was living, but they wouldn't tell him. Afraid he'd . . . what? Finish her off, I guess. So the Hope starts giving them misery about it, tells them he hates them, wishes they were dead, so on and so forth. Shuts them out for years. What a brave guy, right? So then . . ."

Without warning Won Se's hand shot out so fast Turner flinched, thought he was being hit, but only a finger was laid tightly across his lips, silencing him.

"Say if you are with us or against us," Won Se said urgently, through gritted teeth. The wrinkled finger under Turner's nose smelled like clay, oil smoke, centuries.

When the finger was removed, Turner said, "Look, if my grandparents are going to be in this, I need to go back and tell them. They'll have to prepare, too. My grandfather's not well, and . ."

Won Se shook his head summarily. "They are prepared," he said. "Come. Let us begin." He started to lead the way out of the chamber, but Turner didn't follow.

"*They're* prepared, but *I'm* not? Bullshit. They're eighty-four years old. They don't even . . ."

Won Se stopped where he was. The light from the aperture in the floor gave his face a Halloween intensity.

"From this point," he said quietly, "there is no time to explain. There is barely time to teach. You must say *now* if you are with us."

Turner looked down at the sand continents and oceans below. For fleeting seconds he measured the ache in his hip against the ache in his heart. He enumerated for himself all the perfectly good reasons he should spin on his heel and run back to whatever was left of his sweet, sweet life.

After which, his defiant damned heart, as he had known it would, leapt up, streaming pure faith, to take the hook.

Then, undergirded by the soft light of the cosmos, the two men shook hands.

At the intersection of two roads to nowhere, a four-way stop. Sea oats and brambles in all directions. Turner braked and looked for road signs to indicate he was still headed for Shreveport. The battered wooden crosspiece on the shoulder showed a bewildering array of road numbers inside outlines of Louisiana maps. But Highway 49 was not among them.

"That's impossible," Turner said, slapping the steering wheel so hard with the heels of his hands that the horn blew. "We haven't made any turns. How could we have lost 49?"

Lu Weh and Wah So got up from their patty-caking as if from a dream and came up to stand in the aisle. Chai Lo explained the predicament to them while Turner thumbed through his notebook. They surveyed the countryside in all directions with expressions of great consternation.

Suddenly Wah So said, "We look for Sleeveport?" and as Turner nodded absently the monk pointed through the rear window to a large green road sign saying SHREVEPORT: 39. The opposite direction.

"Crap," Turner said. He threw his notebook to the floor. "How did we do that? Now we're late for sure. Hang on . . ."

With that, he put the van in gear and stomped the gas, making a teetering U-turn that slung gravel and sand into the underbrush and roused a family of nesting white birds. The centrifugal force of the maneuver caused the forgotten Se Hon, still dead asleep, to roll from underneath one of the seats and come to rest inertly in the aisle, where he raised up with a confused look. "Sleeveport," Wah So explained to him, and Se Hon, apparently relieved, went back to sleep.

Turner watched the speedometer climb to sixty, seventy, eighty, and keep going. He had leveled off at eighty-eight, the arrest report said, when the Lolafalana Parish deputy's car clocked him on its radar and gave chase.

When the siren's wail pierced the blurred landscape and the spinning blue light filled his mirror, Turner's heart sank. He imagined the distant H.O.N.D.T.U. deacons' board pacing the foyer and looking at their watches. Great way to build international goodwill and affect the Tally of Inner Blindness.

"Shit, what else?" he said, as he looked for a part of the road shoulder where he wouldn't mire in sand when he pulled over. "Passports, guys," he shouted to the back of the van. "Get your IDs ready."

But his words were lost in the general merriment the monks were experiencing at the sight of the patrol car. "Mammy Vice! Mammy Vice!" Beh Vah whooped, bouncing up and down in his seat. The others took up the cry as well, adding refinements of their own. "Hi the stash!" growled Wah So, a gifted mimic of all things American. "They not take us a life!"

"Guys, really, this is not the time . . ." Turner began, but out the corner of his eye he saw a large immobile shape with mirror sunglasses, up close.

"How 'do," the deputy said. He stood slapping a thick ticket book into the palm of his hand while inspecting the van from top to bottom, end to end, as seriously as if he were about to make an offer for it at auction. "Whereabouts y'all from?"

"Alabama," Turner said, at the same instant that Chai Lo, ever helpful, said "Tibet," which was an instant before Turner remembered that the van had California plates and he was wearing a Texas Longhorns sweatshirt.

The deputy stroked his chin and took a step backward for another look at the van, as if some subtle clue in its design might explain the discrepancies. Then he leaned in the door again and glanced back toward the rear seats where the monks sat frozen with fascination—all but Lu Weh, who yawned and hiked his robe to scratch his bare stomach.

"Y'all some sorta performers?"

Chai Lo nodded eagerly in response. "Sing, play instrument, dance," he said.

The deputy made soft popping noises with his teeth. "And where'd you say y'all was headed?"

"Bon Aerie," Turner said, encouraged at the turn the conversation was taking. He bent down quickly to retrieve his notebook from the floorboard. As he came back up with it he heard the hammer of a pistol being cocked.

"I-I-I wish you wouldn't be doing no sudden motions, buddy," the deputy said. "Make a old boy nervous, out here by his lonesome."

"Yessir. Sorry about that." Turner leafed through the directions. "We're looking for the . . . Heartily Overcoming New Deliv—"

"Right. Right. I know it well." Though the deputy betrayed no shoulder motion above the line of the window, Turner heard the hammer unclick and the pistol drop back into the holster. "Let me make sure I got this real straight," the deputy said. He took off his cap and, frowning, rubbed his balding head to a high sheen as if to enhance his thinking. "Y'all are show people, so naturally this being a Sunday you're on your way to dance at a colored church." He looked to the group for affirmation.

Turner nodded hesitantly, but Wah So seemed intrigued by this revelation. "What color is the church?" he asked. The deputy shot him a sour look. When he spoke it was to Turner, in a confiding tone.

"Now, I know this is all true, what you're telling me, because y'all are obviously upstanding people. But if somebody was to . . . just say they *was* to call the, uh, reverend out there, he could . . . *confirm* all this, I reckon, could he not?"

"Oh, of course. See, the agency who books us . . ." Turner was interrupted by giggling from the back seats. When he glanced around he saw that Beh Vah had resurrected a packet of sugar from an old take-out sack and was emptying its contents into his palm. While Turner watched in horror he pulled out a plastic soda straw and, the moment the deputy looked toward him, pretended to sniff the white crystals through it into his nose, to the intense delight of Wah So and Se Hon, who pointed him out to the deputy as they dissolved in laughter. "Mammy Vice!" Wah So shouted. "Rest this man!"

The deputy, in slow motion, took off his mirrored sunglasses and turned his head so that his gaze rested fully on Turner. There was hurt and betrayal in his small, sleepy eyes.

"I need you boys to do something for me," he said, almost in a whisper. Bah Tow, eager to be of service, threw open the van's side door and hopped out to await instructions. "Don't, buddy!" Turner shouted. "Stay inside, please!"

At the sight of Bah Tow's towering figure the deputy did a quick backward shuffle and his right hand went to his holster again, but the monk's totally guileless posture apparently made him hesitate before drawing the gun. "Get back in," he said loudly, pointing a shaky finger at the van. "Right now." Bah Tow complied, looking mildly annoyed that the Mammy Vice couldn't make up his mind.

The deputy, his hand still on his holster, spoke quietly to Turner now. "Need you to turn around here and drive just in front of me, real slow, about thirty-five or so. About six miles up that way we'll come to a four-way stop, and . . ."

Turner laughed his friendliest, most unthreatening laugh. "Look, I know what you're thinking, but actually we . . ."

"Four . . . way . . . stop," the deputy repeated coldly, "and turn right. There'll be a railroad track and two red lights as you get into town, and then start looking for the station on your left. Jail's off to one side. Just park in between there and sit real still until I get out and come around. All right? And please don't get no ideas about throwing no evidence out no window."

As Turner made a slow U-turn to follow the deputy, the monks mumbled to each other in puzzlement. Se Hon turned around in his seat and said to them, "I think he helps us find the church."

This appeared to satisfy all except Wah So. "What color *is* the church?" he asked.

5

THE PHONE RANG and rang. When the church secretary finally answered it she was out of breath. "Good morning, praise God. Heartily Overcoming New Deliverance Temple Unlimited. Have a blessed day."

"Reverend Isaiah Pendleton, please, ma'am," the deputy said. He motioned for Turner to pick up the other extension on the jailer's desk and listen in.

"I'm sorry, but Brother Pendleton's in prayer and the service is about to begin." In the background Turner could hear a baby crying, the rattle of pots and pans, and a foot-stomping version of "The Unclouded Day" being played on an electric organ. "Might I take a message, and have him call you after service?"

Turner looked entreatingly at the deputy on the other phone.

"Ma'am, it's sort of urgent," the deputy said. "I won't take but a minute of his time. It's about some dancers that he, uh . . ." He apparently thought better of it, and let the sentence trail off.

But the secretary was sufficiently intrigued that she let down her defense. "I'll see if Brother Pendleton can come," she said, and the staccato retreat of her high heels could be heard through the phone.

The heavy gray door to the jail corridor opened and the sheriff ambled out, one of several reinforcements whose Sunday morning the deputy had interrupted to help him deal with the crisis. The sheriff was a stockily-built man of Italian heritage, and wore a white T-shirt and a yellow fishing cap dotted with metallic lures. He'd been at the lake with his seven-year-old son when they tracked him down, and to save time he'd brought the boy along.

The sheriff nodded amiably at Turner as he came to a stop beside the deputy, who looked up from the phone. "I'm on hold," the deputy said. "What you want?"

"They're singers, all right," the sheriff told him. "My boy says they're all over the TV. Bunch called 'Whiz and the Lizards,' or some such." The deputy's face sank. "Tony's back there getting their autograph," the sheriff added meekly.

The front door clattered and two officers in softball uniforms came in from the parking lot, grinning and carrying plastic trash bags. The deputy's expression showed renewed hope. "You know, if we played this thing right, there could be some good publicity in it for us." The sheriff looked at the officers, who grinned back.

"Who knows?" the deputy was saying. "TV cameras? A phone call from the President? I mean, this drug stuff is *hot* right now." He sensed a hesitation in the air and slowed down. The two softball officers were stifling giggles.

"Might can get us in a McDonald's commercial is about all," one of the men said. He held aloft a crumpled take-out sack he fished from the trash bag. "Got five counts of salt possession, three counts of sugar."

"Don't forget the lemon juice," the other officer said. "That stuff is *mean*, when you shoot it up." They collapsed into guffaws. The deputy clenched his jaw so hard the veins in his temple popped out like surgical tubing.

"This is Reverend Pendleton," a deep voice on the phone said. The sheriff had opened the big gray door and was shouting down the hall. "Tony? Let's go get them stripers, bud. Time's wasting."

"Hold one second," the deputy barked into the phone, and covered the mouthpiece with his hand. "If they's one square inch of that van ain't searched," he told the officers through gritted teeth, "I'll have your ass. *Both* of y'uns."

They appeared to undergo a slight change of heart. "Well," one of them said, "there's a box of incense."

The deputy slapped the desktop with glee. "Paraphernalia," he said. "Ain't that paraphernalia?"

The sheriff looked back, exasperated. "Jesus in a jacket, Randolph. *Tony* burns incense. It ain't crap. Use your head." He leaned back through the door. "To-o-*ny*? Come *on*, bud."

"Hello? Is anyone there?" the preacher's melodious voice demanded, over the phone.

"Reverend Pendleton? This is Randolph Stearns, sheriff's office? Listen, we got a crew of folks here that's sort of lost, says they're looking for you? They're singers, they say, and . . ."

The voice in the phone laughed a rich, exuberant laugh. "Yes, Lord, yes," the Reverend said.

"So you *are* expecting them, then?" The deputy's face sank. "Listen, I got the leader of them right here. I'm gonna let him talk to you."

"Good morning, Reverend," Turner said. The deputy, with a spiteful look, kept his ear glued to the other phone, alert for any misstep the conversation might take.

"Roscoe? That *better* be you, bro. We got enough chicken wings here to keep an airliner flying. When I announced the King's Four Eagles was gonna be at homecoming, Sister Myrtle hit the meat store that very *day*. You got a reputation to uphold, my man." The resounding laugh again. "We was starting to get worried about you. Where you at?"

"Well, apparently there's been some kind of misunderstanding. My name's Turner, and . . ."

"This ain't Roscoe?"

The deputy's face spread into a corrosive smile.

"No, sir," Turner said. "I'm traveling with a group from the Drepung monastery in eastern Tibet. The, uh, agency that books us has a new girl on the computer, Lucille told me, and I guess she just . . ."

"Lucille?"

"Right."

"Oh, a delightful child," the reverend said. "She's got every record the Four Eagles ever made."

The deputy's pleasure faded again.

"Listen, I'm sorry about the mix-up," Turner said. "We . . ."

"Whatchall do?"

"Pardon?"

"*Music*. What kind of music y'all do?"

"We perform sacred music and dance from the Buddhist monastic tradition. Some of it's thousands of years old."

"Do you do it in the name of the Lord?"

It was a question that Chai Lo, if he'd been present, could easily have spent months ferreting out all the senses of. But this was no time for theosophical contemplation. The clock was ticking and the deputy was holding his breath for Turner's answer, his last hope.

"Amen, brother," Turner said.

"Well, praise the Lord. We'd be glad to have you for homecoming. Let me speak with the good sheriff, please."

"Telephone, sheriff," the deputy mumbled, crestfallen.

"*To*ny?" the sheriff shouted. "Right *now*, bud. I'll go off and leave you."

KEEPING THE SPEEDOMETER between ninety and ninety-five with the deputy's flashing blue light as escort, they made it to the Heartily Overcoming New Deliverance Temple just as the noon meal was being spread on the sloping green lawn uphill from the building. The homecoming crowd, in their starched pastel shirts and dresses, looked from a distance like tropical flowers covering the hillside.

At the perimeter was a barricade made up of long folding tables draped with white cloths, which held enough crates and boxes of foil-wrapped food to serve as famine relief for a small kingdom. And more was being unloaded at that moment from the trunks of cars.

Turner parked the van and got out to say farewell to the deputy, but the patrol car didn't stop. It spun in a wide arc, slung a little gravel, and headed back toward the main highway, leaving Turner only a glimpse of the deputy's angry posture at the wheel, his uniform cap pushed partly down over his ears from the force he'd put it on with when the sheriff assigned him escort duty.

"Brother Turner?"

A massive man that more than fit his phone voice, Reverend Isaiah Pendleton came striding across the churchyard wiping his fingers on a napkin. He held out a hand for Turner to shake that seemed the width of a coal shovel.

"Praise the Lord," the preacher said. "We're glad you made it." He clamped his left hand over his right as they shook, enveloping Turner's completely. "You-all haven't had your noontime meal, I trust? We'd be proud for you to join us." He wore a flashy pink silk tie with a stickpin, but his small gold-rimmed glasses were in the style of a scholar.

"That sounds mighty good," Turner said. "We've come a lot of miles since breakfast." The monks were disembarking from the van and stretching their legs.

"Wonderful. Come help your plates and I'll introduce you around."

Beh Vah sidled up to Turner with a look of concern and spoke in a confidential tone. "The Mammy Vice told a fib," he said.

"Huh? What do you mean?"

"The church is not colored. It's white."

Reverend Pendleton threw back his head and emitted a laugh whose volume and abandon threatened the molecular structure of nearby objects.

"This youngster needs some fried chicken immediately," Pendleton announced to everyone nearby. He put his arm around Beh Vah's shoulder and walked him uphill toward the picnic tables.

"You're a breast man, am I right?" the preacher asked. Beh Vah acknowledged timidly that it was so.

AFTER LUNCH THE MEMBERS of the Heartily Overcoming New Deliverance Temple congregated again in the big sanctuary, with its stained glass windows depicting Bible scenes of the faithful throughout history. The building's air conditioners groaned out a valiant attempt at delivering the congregation from the sweltering heat of midday, and the deacons supplemented that effort by passing out stacks of cardboard fans imprinted with a message from the local funeral home: When You Go The Last Mile, We Will Ride You In Style.

The deacons had given up their seats of honor on the pulpit stage, decorated with blue carnations on the armrests, to Turner and the monks. While the pastor scribbled notes in preparation for introducing them, the soft metronomic sweep of the cardboard fans was punctuated by a baby's cry, but its mother made short work of its despair by unhitching the shoulder of her gown and freeing a splendid gallon-sized ebony breast which the baby's mouth seized audibly in midair and which she then modestly covered with a white lace handkerchief. Turner watched Beh Vah drink in the transaction with a reverence akin to a trance, his lips flexing involuntarily in empathy.

When Reverend Pendleton finally strode to the podium, the whole audience—with the exception of the mother and baby—leaped to their feet as one. "Let's glorify Him this afternoon!" Pendleton shouted into the microphone, and hundreds of arms went up in the air, cardboard fans and all, as the people shut their eyes and made a quick, fluid burst of utterance that was almost but not quite understandable speech, more like the tender cluckings and trillings that a resting flock of birds makes at nightfall. "Amen and amen," Pendleton said, and the crowd all sat back down with a scattering of handclaps.

"*God . . .*" the preacher began, letting the word hang in the air long enough to tantalize with its promise of revelation, "does not always send us what we expect."

Murmurings of acknowledgment. "Can I get a witness this afternoon?

I *said*, God does not always *send* us what we ex*pect*." Louder murmurings, a few amens.

"But aren't you *glad* . . . we serve a *God* . . . that's greater than Isaiah Pendleton's little old *half*-baked, *tid*dle-wink expec*ta*tions, amen?"

Enthusiastic amens.

"So . . . so . . . I know you all share with me a . . . a . . . *mo*mentary and . . . and tran*sition*al re*gret* that Brother Roscoe and the King's Four Eagles could not be with us today, but by the grace of God we have the privilege of . . ."

The back door of the church opened slowly with a loud squeal of hinges and a short, skinny black man came in and stood looking for a seat. In contrast to the finery of the other churchgoers he wore a gray T–shirt, Army fatigue pants, and a cartridge belt. As people throughout the crowd looked over their shoulders and spotted him, a nervous buzz of whispering made the rounds. From Turner's seat behind the pulpit he saw Reverend Pendleton's jaw muscles clamp in anger, and his sentence faltered before he regained control.

"We have the . . . the *pri*vilege of welcoming a group of brethren who have come from the very *farther*est, uttermost reaches of the *earth*, so to speak, in order to share with us today."

The only seat available was on the front row, so the small jerky figure, wearing a look of serious purpose, quickly made his way up the aisle.

"Brothers and sisters," Pendleton was saying, "I have the in*stinct*ive honor of pre*sent*ing to you . . . the monks of the Great Lung Monastery in Tie-bet. Let's hear it for them. Make them welcome."

As the applause began, the man in fatigues sat down in one of the spaces on the front pew. His seatmates on either side refused to acknowledge him and abruptly slid another space apart while looking into the distance, a clear snub. The object of their disapproval caught Turner's eye and gave him a snappy, military-style salute followed by a friendly wink.

Turner made the beginnings of a wave in response, but his line of sight was suddenly blocked by the looming shape of the preacher who gave him a quick bear-hug as he stood. Pendleton took advantage of the proximity to whisper a message in his ear.

"I truly apologize," he said to Turner, "but this man who just came in is a trouble-maker and a rabble-rouser. I only hope he'll have the common decency not to disrupt your presentation, you being a guest. He certainly has no respect for the rest of us, I can tell you that." Turner glanced past

Pendleton's shoulder as the embrace broke up. The man in fatigues sat with his hands interlaced in his lap like a choirboy, smiling the angelic smile of the wrongfully accused.

While the monks donned their headdresses and retrieved the horns and cymbals from behind their chairs, Turner stepped to the microphone and gave his standard brief speech about the role played by sacred music and dance in Eastern religious culture. The soft fluttering of the cardboard fans as he spoke gave him the sensation of talking to a garden being blown by the wind.

Meanwhile, in the front row, the skinny man in fatigues had produced from nowhere a small black binder into which he was frenetically scribbling notes on the proceedings. Except not notes, exactly, because Turner, from his elevated position at the podium, could see that the man was sketching elaborate spidery diagrams that looked like snowflakes turned inside out. Turner searched the man's expression for some clue to his purpose, but it was fruitless. As he drew in his book he scanned his surroundings with the intense, bemused objectivity of a naturalist. Or a cardsharp.

Finally Turner introduced the monks. The long trumpets sounded a low, warbling half-pitch note in unison, a signal the performance was beginning. The monks took the front of the stage and Turner sat down on the end beside Reverend Pendleton, who was studiously avoiding looking at the man with the notebook. Throughout the whole concert the man kept busy with his diagrams; his demeanor changed only once, when the low blatting of the horns began to be delicately stitched through by the not-quite-random tinklings of the cymbals.

At this juncture he shut his eyes, threw back his head with a look of sublime receptiveness, and clapped his small hands with such sudden explosive power that the two elderly women sitting on either side of him jumped several inches off the pew and simultaneously squealed their shock.

"Yes, *yes*," the man shouted out. "That's it. That's *it*, right there. That's perfection."

The rest of the congregation apparently mistook the isolated commotion for an outbreak of the spirit of revival, because by the time the changeable voice of Chai Lo's flute interjected itself in between the high-low pairing of pitches, the ground swell of excitement had spread all the way from the front row to the back. Two dozen people were on their feet, hands in the air, some shouting hallelujahs, others discoursing in a rapid flutter of unknown tongues.

The growing clamor of the response, in fact, threatened to drown out the music itself—a circumstance to which the monks, by and large, responded by methodically stepping up the volume of their playing without appreciably affecting its style; the one exception being Beh Vah, who was moved by the chaos to stamp his foot in time to the rhythm with the profane fluidity of a Mississippi Delta bluesman.

The other players were too preoccupied to cast Beh Vah any sobering glances, and as a result the disturbance continued to escalate, undampened, until everyone in the sanctuary had their arms up giving praise.

Even the steadfast nursing mother gave in to the shock waves of spirit and leapt up, passing off her startled charge like a pink football to her leftside neighbor in the pew. With one quick piercing hoot the mother became a blurring dervish of black lace and nylons from whose bosom the discreet white handkerchief fled like a leaf in a windstorm.

The centrifugal force of her rotations soon caused the fugitive breast to lift like a car in a carnival ride, until its growing momentum attracted the tentative notice of even the elderly man to her right who looked out at the befuzzed world through inch-thick eyeglasses. When he turned his head to inspect the event more closely, he chanced to intersect the growing arc of the breast itself, and the force of the blow, while not unyielding, had ample heft to propel him backward headfirst over the pew and in the process take out a number of worshipers like dominoes.

When he was shortly resurrected from the pile and helped to his feet, not only did he appear unhurt but he wore an expression of superseding radiance. A knot of deaconesses nearby, unaware of what had occurred, took his holy look as a new visitation of grace; the resurgent burst of hallelujahs spread through the whole congregation in the space of a breath, renewing their fervor at just the point where the music ordinarily would have been concluding.

But conclusion obviously would not do, under the circumstances. So the monks astonished themselves when, without benefit of signal or prearrangement, they not only began again at an identical point early in the composition but effected the loop so seamlessly that even Turner, who knew the piece so well that his brain sometimes sang it in sleep, didn't realize for several minutes that something about the structure was awry.

After several more repetitions of the song, when the activity of the crowd finally began to subside, a sweat-drenched Reverend Pendleton stepped weakly to the microphone.

"Praise God, praise God," he said. "Brother monks, we don't want to wear y'all out too soon. We're going to declare a short recess, here, let everyone take care of their personal needs, and we'll be back in about fifteen minutes, if that's acceptable to the congregation, amen? Amen."

The members were already pressing toward the stage in a gentle milling chaos, their arms outstretched to pat or hug each of the monks in turn. Turner caught a glimpse of panic in the eyes of Chai Lo, dedicated loner that he was, but as he moved forward to reassure him he was intercepted by a small nervous hand grabbing the crook of his arm and turning him aside, bringing him—with a little bending over—face to face with the man in fatigues.

"Cap'n Turner, sir? James Crowe, here. I was instructed to report to you, sir."

Turner was taken aback. He was sure the pastor hadn't introduced him by name, much less mentioned that he'd been in the military.

"Feel totally free to remark on my name, Cap'n," Crowe went on, "especially under your circumstances. I'm fairly well accustomed to all the jests. Only allow me to add, if I may, that it's 'James,' never 'Jim.' 'James,' sir. And that's 'Crowe' with an 'e', not the kind that's arrayed against you at present. Which, I would hope, should give you a bit of respite from your understandable suspicion."

He talked faster and with more animation than anybody Turner had ever seen, as if his syllables were being spit by a machine gun.

"I'm sorry," Turner said, "have we met before?"

"Most unredoubtably, sir. Tre Chinh, '68. Night recon. The week before Tet."

Though Turner was still seeing James Crowe's face, it dimmed in relation to the darkness that was flooding his mind's eye, like ink poured in water. The sucking sound of soldiers' boots in the marsh. Sky too cloudy for stars. The only light a sporadic incendiary rocket filtering through the low mists to the hellish chirp of Asia's version of the cicada, an ugly brown locust-like creature that only hushed its off-key cry long enough to crawl, dripping wet, into your collar and sleeves.

Turner's unit had been on reconnaissance for about three hours when the impossible happened—impossible, but not infrequent, this far in the boonies. In the darkness and mire they came head to head with another American patrol going the opposite direction, one group as unaware as the other that there was anyone else within miles.

After the first adrenaline panic subsided and the two commanders established that no one had been hurt in the brief bursts of fire that were exchanged, Turner sought out the other unit's radio man and got him to double-check their positions with somebody at base. When the reply came back garbled six times over the course of twenty minutes, Turner gave up.

"Maybe just as well, Cap'n," the radio man offered. "I think they get their maps at Texaco, anyways."

Turner held a short consultation with the other commanding officer and they decided just to go their separate ways, as per original orders, and pretend the screw-up hadn't happened, which was something everybody in the war did a lot of in those days.

But while Turner's men were hitching up and re-forming, the wiry black radio operator took him aside. "Beg pardon, sir, you say you're going northwest? Right now?"

"Yep," Turner said. "Why?"

"You ought not to do that, sir. If you could wait just ten minutes or so, it would change the . . . uh, circumstances an awful lot." The little man's eyes flicked side to side while he talked evermore rapidly, as if afraid of being overheard. "Ten minutes, that's all."

Turner shook his head. "We're a half hour behind, already, from *this* bullshit. I'll get my ass chewed four directions if we straggle in after daylight for no good reason."

"Ten minutes," the man whispered. He put a death grip on Turner's forearm. "Please, sir. *Please.*" His voice broke, near to crying.

Oh, great, Turner thought. *This is all I need.* He'd seen it happen before—too much reefer and imagination, and one's peaceable buzz could cross over into a wicked high paranoid roll. Wild beasts behind every tree trunk, catastrophe hovering in the air.

About the only thing you can do for the sufferer is to humor him, edge him away from the main crowd so his freaking will be less contagious. Sometimes eating a can of C-rations helped the dope metabolize faster, or a shot of whiskey. For God's sake no coffee, no speed. Calmative is the order of the day.

Except that at the moment Turner had no rations, no whiskey, and no patience. Besides, this was not his man, therefore not his problem. He eased out of the radio operator's grip as politely as he could, and headed over to discreetly alert the other CO to keep an eye on him.

He never got there.

He'd only gone three or four steps with his back to the man when the skinny black arm flashed scythe-like out of nowhere, catching his neck in its crook and doubling him over backwards, off balance, all while tenderly clamping his windpipe and carotid artery shut with the skill of an attending physician.

Turner grabbed and fought and struggled, no hope in hell of getting enough air to make a sound with, but his attacker agilely managed to stay just out of reach while tightening the vise a bit more. The giant purple amoeba of unconsciousness began blooming outward from the center of Turner's vision and he felt himself starting to go limp.

At the crest of blacking out, he heard the troops just beyond the wall of vines laughing at a joke someone had told. The sound came to him strangely amplified and reverberant as if the world was inside some huge tin trashcan, and he had a fleeting vision of the grand irony of it all—he had sidestepped sure death from the enemy's mortars and rifles so many times he'd lost count, and now here he was on a friendly outing getting his ticket punched by a good homegrown psycho from the U.S. of A.

But miraculously, as the final blackness was descending on him it hovered for a moment and then started to withdraw. His perception was drastically slowed, but it nonetheless told him he'd gotten a whiff of oxygen from somewhere. It was several seconds until he identified the source as the new blessed coldness at the back of his throat. The steel arm was lessening its pressure. Slightly, just slightly. But enough.

As his head cleared he could see the man's pained, upside-down face—above him, below him, he couldn't tell which—and without any conscious decision at all his lungs heaved with the scant air they'd stored up in an attempt at a scream. But before his mouth could open, the vise clamped down again. In the darkness the topsy-turvy face took on the compassionate chiding look of a grammar school teacher with a stubborn student, saying wordlessly *See? Now see?*

It went that way for the next several minutes, the restraining arm guiding Turner in and out of consciousness as precisely as a hand would tune a radio dial. His laboring heart was so all-consuming loud in his eardrums that when the first blinding blast of white light hit, turning the world into a photographic negative of itself, he thought for a second that it was a blood vessel bursting in his brain.

But then on the heels of that blast came a succession of bigger ones, kicking the whole earth, *wump-wumpwumpwump-wumpwump*, like popcorn from hell. The arm unclenched itself from his throat and was instantly replaced by a pair of concerned hands assessing the damage, massaging the blood flow through again. Figures leaped past them, strobed by the light, spread-eagled in confusion, and the first full breath of air Turner gulped had the unmistakable sulphur-and-crankcase oil tang of mortar shells in green vegetation.

In twenty seconds the whole valley to the west of them had been reduced to smoke and light. No, not west, Turner thought, as he sat up and got his bearings, still swilling the sweet air. *North*west. His planned route. And the very center of the inferno, he judged, was at the distance of the three- or four-minute walk he would just have completed by now if he hadn't been detained.

He looked around at his benefactor for some kind of answer, but the man was gone. In grand fuck-up style, yet a third unit of troops wandered up out of the dark, coasting on hash and lost as ghosts, and in the resulting confusion the group with the radio man somehow disappeared. Turner had never laid eyes on him again.

Until now.

"Jesus Christ," Turner said to James Crowe. "It *was* you. You saved my life."

Crowe nodded meekly.

"You said you were instructed to *report* to me?" Turner asked him. "Instructed by who?"

Crowe gave him a blank look. "I assumed *you* would know, sir."

"You don't know?"

"No, sir."

"I mean, was it a letter?" Turner asked. "Or a telegram, or a voice from the sky, or what?"

Crowe squinted and chewed his lip as if the question were a difficult one. "Nothing in writing, sir, no," he finally said.

"A voice, then?"

"I suppose it was," Crowe said. "Technically."

"You *suppose*? You don't know?"

Crowe shrugged. "You know how other dimensions can do you, Cap'n. They don't always translate precisely. I mean, look at *fractals*. Huh? Jesus."

On the invoking of the name of Jesus, the drenched shape of Reverend Pendleton materialized protectively at Turner's elbow, wearing a stern expression. James Crowe, taking the hint, rubbed his eyes wearily and said,

"I'll just plan to catch you later, sir, when things thin out a little bit." He turned to Pendleton and extended a hearty hand. "Reverend? It's been a pleasure, as always." The preacher refused to shake.

As Crowe left he snapped Turner a small, quick salute. "Later, then, Cap'n. It's going to be a pleasure traveling with you."

Pendleton stared after him with open disgust, shaking his head.

Only then did Crowe's last words register with Turner.

Traveling with you?

Turner made to follow him. "James?" He looked left and right throughout the crowd, but Crowe was nowhere to be seen.

OUT IN THE CHURCHYARD, the service long since concluded, the last family was boxing up its casserole dishes and folding its tablecloth to go. A young girl in a wheelchair, her white hair-ribbons brilliant in the sun, propelled herself across a level patch of grass in slow circles and figure-eights like an ice skater exiled into the wrong dimension.

As always, the sight of a paralyzed person chafed Turner's heart, resurrected the whole groaning cargo of regrets about Cassie and sent them cascading past his mind's eye with no order of rank or reason. Even his nightmares about her were confused; in them he often saw her as this girl's age—nine, ten?—riding in a wheelchair, though he knew full well the accident hadn't happened until she was twenty. It was as if the magnitude of the loss had retroactively taken her childhood, too.

Where was she now? When she thought of him, what did she think? At the time they were most in love he almost convinced himself they could read each other's minds, could have long conversations late at night without benefit of telephone across the mile of woods between their separate beds. But now when he tried to imagine himself in her skin the gulf was too great; it was as if he'd never known her.

Turner decided to make one more quick circle of the churchyard, to look for Crowe. No luck.

Strange, considering how intent Crowe had been on talking to him. Maybe Pendleton was right—maybe he *was* a little bit nutty. But how had he known Turner would be there in the first place? Ah, well. A moot point, now.

A caretaker was locking the building. The monks were getting into the van via their usual hierarchy, Chai Lo first by rank and on down to Bah Tow, patient at the rear of the line because of the contortion required to squeeze his ungainly frame into the cramped compartment.

Turner was about to slide into the driver's seat when he heard a tentative throat-clearing behind him. It was the girl in the wheelchair. "Sir?" she said, holding out her church bulletin, "Could I get your autograph, please? I already got the monkses."

"Sure," he said. He climbed down and squatted beside her chair, making his knee an easel to write on. He'd never seen the monks' signatures before. Wedged between the items in H.O.N.D.T.U.'s order of service, they looked almost like musical notation, or one of James Crowe's scrawled diagrams. Turner added his name in a space along the edge and handed the bulletin back to her.

"Y'all can sure enough play," she told him.

"Well, you're mighty sweet. Thank you for coming." He bent and hugged her neck. Her dress smelled of fresh starch.

At the edge of the parking lot, he looked in the mirror and saw the small figure waving. He rolled down his window and waved back.

Beh Vah, who occupied the front seat beside him, was already snoring softly. His big white casino towel was draped around his neck again, but this time nobody had the energy to chasten him.

6

BEFORE TURNER realized what a toll the day at H.O.N.D.T.U. had taken on the monks, he'd been in hopes of driving far into Mississippi before they stopped for the night. Or maybe even making Birmingham, where their next show was, if he could locate a thermos or two of trucker-strength coffee at critical points along the way.

If he drove straight through, he'd have time the next day to take a detour and check on his grandparents. Ever since the years of his long estrangement he had kept in touch with the diligence only a guilty prodigal could muster. They were never far from his thoughts anyway, but especially so after the night he'd seen them on Won Se's disaster-monitor, or whatever the hell it was. He phoned them every week and they purported themselves to be fine, but something in their voices left him unconvinced. He needed to see for himself.

The church road dead-ended into the main highway at a peaceful-looking bayou. Two boys on an old wooden rowboat were fishing with cane poles. The day's worst heat had passed, and the air smelled like salt water and asphalt that had been slow-baked together in some great oven.

Turner took a left, east, onto Highway 49 and the lowering sun made orange fireballs of all his rear-view mirrors. After a few miles he came to the entrance ramp for the interstate and, seeing as nobody was awake to protest, he took it.

He had just passed the first marker that told how far Meridian was when a rest stop presented itself on the right, and the row of phone booths out front reminded him that he needed to check in with their booking agency. The booths also reminded him that he missed the hell out of his cellular phone.

As if the prospect of confronting ultimate evil and battling for the future of the human race weren't enough, it turned out he had to do it on the cheap, besides—one of the many restrictions that filled a whole volume of the Books of Chojung. "Rules," it was called—a sort of Scout handbook on the care, feeding, and deportment of a Hope who was preparing to be called out by the realm. Under the section on Renouncements the book made it clear that once the final face-off is set in motion the hero has to lay aside all material things except the clothes on his back (or *her* back; the appendix of the book revealed that every once in a while the Hope was female) and use nothing but wits and grit to marshal his forces for the coming conflagration.

And so he had dutifully put his hard-won bank account in mothballs for the duration and hit the pavement as in days of old: finding investors, negotiating with agencies, printing up a zillion cheap brochures and mailing them to anybody with an auditorium—brochures touting the Drepung tour as the Most Important Event of the Age.

If only they knew what was really at stake. Another zinger that Won Se had dropped on him from the Rules book was the fact that Turner and the monks could tell nobody what they were up to on the large scale, i.e. saving the world from a plunge into spiritual darkness. ("As if anybody would believe us, right?" Turner had remarked to Won Se at the time. The old monk snorted. "Tell me about it," he said.)

Turner took the exit ramp to the rest stop and picked a phone booth. Lucille answered on the first ring. "StarShine Talent."

"Hi, lady. How's things on the coast?"

"The coast is clear, sweets. Ha. How's my boys? They getting climatized yet?"

"Pretty much. I thought we were going to have a mutiny when your peanut brittle ran out, though."

Lucille cackled at that. "You tell that little sweetheart of mine if he ever gets led astray, be sure to wait and let me be the one to do it, okay?"

She meant Beh Vah. "It's a struggle," Turner acknowledged. "Listen, about that last gig? We got our wires crossed somewhere. They were expecting a quartet called the King's . . ."

" . . . Four Eagles. Right, right," Lucille finished for him. "I apologize. We've got egg on our face, big time, hon. There's a new girl on the computer, and . . . anyway, that gig was on us. We'll credit your account, just like you had got paid."

"But that's what I'm saying. We *did* get paid. They liked us."

"Well! See? What'd I tell you? Listen, sweetie, are you up for an interview?"

His pulse did not race. After the events of this week, he didn't look forward to another session with a campus editor.

"Who with?"

"Try Paul Zotfeld, *USA Today*."

"Aw. Get real."

"I'm serious as a heart attack, darling. I met him at a party last week and told him the whole scoop on you. He wants to catch your show in Birmingham."

"How can we ever repay you?"

"Straight fifteen off the top, baby. Hit the big time for momma. Uh-oh. Other line. Gotta go. Hug everybody for me . . ."

Turner was several miles down the interstate, pondering the question of whether they should jazz up the show for the entertainment editor's benefit or go for the authenticity factor, when he realized that not everybody in the van was asleep. There was a hushed, urgent conversation going on in the back, whose subject he couldn't quite make out. He was sure he heard the words "periodicity" and "molybdenum," neither of which he would have thought the monks knew.

He took his eyes off the road long enough to switch on the dome light and glance toward the back of the van. Sure enough, there was James Crowe, his feet up and his duffel bag beside him, animatedly lecturing to a rapt Se Hon and Lu Weh while the other monks dozed.

Turner braked quickly and pulled off onto the shoulder of the interstate. The eighteen-wheeler that was on his rear barked at the van with its air horn and roared around him.

"So they thought they had this whole new periodicity worked out," Crowe was recapping for Se Hon as Turner walked the aisle to the back. "They're predicting the bifurcations . . . you know, the little branching-offs on the graph . . . right down to the *tee*, I mean pow-pow-pow-*pow*, just like that." Crowe kept in a constant state of motion, his long fingers making a frenetic ballet to accompany his talk, as if trying to help his ideas pole-vault above the limitations of language. "And then up jumps something stupid like molybdenum and it won't fit. Blows the whole thing. I mean, *molybdenum*. Shit . . ."

"Molybdenum," Se Hon echoed with disdain.

"Shit," Lu Weh said.

The sleeping monks were awakening from the van's stopped motion and rubbing their eyes. Turner stood above the confab with his arms crossed. "Excuse me," he said, at the first pause in the conversation.

"So I'm talking the dimension," Crowe went on, unfazed, in a tone of voice that befitted a dangerous secret, "that all the dimensions are just dimensions of. You dig?"

"Excuse me," Turner said.

Se Hon looked up. "He ride with us," he told Turner peremptorily, as if that made everything perfectly clear.

"So I see," said Turner. He squatted in the aisle. "How far are you going?" he asked Crowe.

"To the stone cold end, sir," Crowe said, sticking his small chest out proudly. "I'm with you the whole way."

Turner rubbed his eyes. It had been a long, long day. "Let's talk about that a minute, James," he said. "In private. Excuse us, guys?" The monks regarded him coolly.

As Crowe preceded him down the aisle, Turner reflected that the one drawback to having your life saved was that the savee forever after felt somewhat beholden to the saver. Even when said saver appeared, as in this case, to be a few bricks shy of a load. But no way, Turner thought, could he let a hyperactive war vet threaten everybody's concentration, what with things about to be coming to a head so soon.

As they stepped down to the grass of the roadside, he put his arm around James's shoulder. "Listen, James, I really appreciate your enthusiasm," he said, over the roar of traffic. He glanced behind him and saw Shy and Louie's faces pressed anxiously against the lighted windows of the van, eager for their lesson in theoretical physics to resume. "But right now I've got my hands full just keeping these guys out of trouble. So I really don't see taking on an extra, uh . . ."

Crowe stiffened slightly.

"And our finances are kind of tight, too," Turner went on, "with the van threatening to break down again, so . . ."

With that, Crowe pulled loose from Turner's grip and stood apart to face him. "Begging your pardon, Cap'n," he said, drawing himself up to his full five-four or so, "but I ain't a 'extra' anything. I was *sent*." There was righteous indignation in his eyes.

"You were sent," Turner repeated tiredly.

"You bet your ass," Crowe said. "With all due respect, sir."

"But you don't know *who* sent you. Right? And you don't know what you're supposed to *do* after you . . . 'report' to me."

"Sure, Cap'n. I'm to help y'all out." He beamed proudly.

"Help out? In what way?"

Crowe looked astonished that Turner wouldn't know. "Why, with the *math*, sir. I thought they told you."

The math. Lord, Lord, Turner thought. We have a card-carrying nut case, here.

A passing eighteen-wheeler blasted its air horn, making Turner jump. He looked around at the van and, sure enough, Beh Vah was hanging out the driver-side window doing the time-honored arm signal of children everywhere, pleading with truckers to sound off. The wake of the rig's passing sprayed Turner and Crowe with road grit and the stink of diesel.

Turner had an immediate pressing need to toss Crowe his duffel bag and watch his scrawny countenance receding in the rear-view mirror, but his conscience couldn't abide just leaving the man on the roadside. Kid gloves were called for, here.

"The *math*!" Turner said. "Of course! How could I forget?" He slapped his forehead, making a show of great chagrin. "Listen, the latest word is, you're supposed to work on the math at . . . at *home* for a while longer, and then we're to call you when it gets a little closer to the time. Tell you what . . ." He put his arm on Crowe's shoulder again and steered him toward the van. "We can get you a Greyhound in Meridian, have you home by bedtime, and then tomorrow . . ."

Crowe resisted the vanward path of movement. He mumbled something as he backed away. His eyes looked crazed.

"Say what?" Turner asked.

"I said don't bullshit me, Cap'n. All due respect. I hate to have to do this—" Crowe's hand flashed into the big pocket of his fatigues, where Turner belatedly noticed a bulge. Oh, Jesus, not a gun. Let it be a knife, not a gun.

In the slow-motion thought that precedes violence, Turner judged the distance to the van door and decided against making a run for it, particularly since Lu Weh and Se Hon's faces were still pressed to the glass, an easy target.

"Get down!" he shouted at them. "Get *down*!"

They complied, dropping from sight like rocks, but the commotion they made in doing so engaged the curiosity of the other four monks, all of whom pressed their faces to the glass to see what the clamor was about.

When Turner spun back around, Crowe's hand was coming out of his pocket. All thinking time had expired. Turner knew there was nothing to do but take him on. *Go.*

He crouched, pivoted, stiffened his left arm like a club in a roundhouse motion aimed at Crowe's forearm with, he hoped, enough momentum to break his grip on the weapon before it appeared. But a split second too late to change his trajectory he saw Crowe take a step backward with an almost supernatural nimbleness, so that the blow only connected with air. As did his second punch, which was to have been an uppercut but only served to throw himself further off balance, stumbling to keep from going down.

In desperation he made a diving tackle toward Crowe's feet, but it was likewise sidestepped with a swiftness that made Turner feel spastic by comparison. He hit the ground and rolled, and when he looked up it was too late. Crowe stood over him in full possession of . . .

A pocket calculator?

"This'll just take a minute, Cap'n," Crowe told him. "*Chill*, sir. Please." He began punching in numbers and functions with the speed of an office typist, while Turner got unsteadily to his feet. All six monks were at the van windows now, looking perplexed by the odd roadside drama.

Crowe mumbled to himself as he worked. "Reference . . . plane with . . . factor of . . . yeah, that'll work." He replaced the calculator in his pocket, took a deep breath, and clapped both his hands to his head, squeezing his cranium with such ardor that Turner could feel the pain.

In seconds the patch of gravel Crowe stood on began pulsating with a neon-like glow, which slowly spread until the whole roadside, and then the asphalt itself, was ablaze with phosphorescent color, red, green, blue, throbbing like a neon diner sign in overdrive. The atmospheric pressure did a rapid jitterbug from low to high, making Turner's ears pop.

There was a thunderclap of pure light. As it echoed away and the world returned to dusk again, a huge dark tower stood solidly astride the near lanes of the highway, blocking out the sky.

It was . . . he was . . . hallucinating. Had to be.

Because the towering shape was clearly a giant redwood tree. Gianter, in fact, than any he had seen in California. Taller than an office building.

A fact which did not escape the notice of the driver of the wide load eighteen-wheeler now hurtling toward the tree at a good eighty-five. The scream of his locked brakes rent the air. The big truck, trailing a plume of black rubber-smoke, started swapping lanes in a valiant attempt to stay upright.

A look of horror crossed Crowe's face. "Oh, shit." He jerked out his calculator and frantically punched some keys. At the last possible instant a U-shaped tunnel opened up through the tree's solid heart and the truck wailed safely through.

"Happens every time I get in a hurry," Crowe apologized.

The monks all poured from the van and with delighted cries ran over to inspect the tree. When they patted its bark and found it to be authentic temporal matter they turned toward Crowe and gave him a spontaneous round of applause, which he acknowledged by bowing meekly.

"Cap'n, sir . . ." Crowe began. He was interrupted by a screech of brakes, and then another and another, as motorists from both directions of the interstate stopped to gape at the new landmark. They began getting out of their cars.

"Cap'n, sir," Crowe said, "we need to talk."

Turner felt better when he had put several miles between them and the world's first giant Louisiana redwood and convinced himself that the witnesses to its creation would not think, in the confusion, to jot down the van's license number as it vacated the area with all due haste.

When he was able to quit checking his mirror for blue lights, he gathered enough presence of mind to hear Crowe out.

Or try to. Crowe ensconced himself on the floorboard alongside the driver's seat and began a frantic headlong treatise on the protocols of dimensionality.

"Whoa, whoa," Turner said. "From scratch, here, please. First, tell me how you did that."

"Did what?"

"The *tree*, damn it."

"Well, like I was saying, Cap'n."

"James?"

"Yes, Cap'n?"

"I'm not a captain any more, James. I'm radically civilian. Just 'Turner,' please."

Crowe snapped him a brisk salute. "Gotcha, Cap'n. I hear where you're coming from. I got no problem with that."

"You were saying about the tree."

"Right, Cap'n. Lemme just start at the beginning . . ."

Which was the story of how Crowe had survived, against any sane person's odds, in Vietnam. Time and time again he was delivered from sure destruction, he said, bobbing safely to the top of hell's cauldron of dead and dying. Four companies, to be exact, had been shot out from under him in as many months, himself the only survivor.

By the time he was assigned to the fourth one (317th Recon at Tre Chinh, the place where he'd saved Turner's life) his reputation preceded him. Owing to the perverse pragmatism-cum-superstition of that grim time and place, he was viewed not as one blessedly lucky black child, which he felt himself to be, nor as a lethally savvy jungle fighter they might learn from, but rather as a one-man contagion of the worst possible fortune.

There even came to be a saying derived from his experiences, which he heard one man of the 317th tell another when they thought he was nowhere around: Bad luck, worse luck, Crowe luck.

The crazy thing was, he didn't seem to be doing anything unusual in the field that would account for his personal good fortune—just following the conventional drab battle wisdom they teach you in Advanced Individual Training, some grizzled alcoholic veteran of Normandy droning on and on under the buzzing fluorescents restating the obvious from the training manuals with the dark-olive canvas covers.

Crowe followed the conventional wisdom, that is, except in situations when he was scared so shitless he did the first thing that occurred to him. It was a tendency which caused various young lieutenants no small measure of apoplexy, but no sooner than they would go pop-eyed and purple and dog-cuss his very name and tell him he was going to get himself killed, then the Red Sea of destruction would suddenly open out into a straight paved highway for Crowe. It turned out that whatever he had done was exactly the right thing to do, after all. Because when the smoke finally cleared, every time, his was the only protoplasm for miles around that was still capable of movement. An orphan again, just like in childhood.

And his initial elation at coming through alive came to be replaced by an acid-like dread, exhumed whole and dark and potent from the depths of memory, at the thought of meeting his next parents. Er, platoon. The cold-eyed evaluation underneath their pasted-on smiles which gradually fell away as word of his past circulated. *Crowe luck. Crowe luck.*

When the fourth and final go-round of all this took place, just weeks after his brief encounter with Turner on night recon, he was in the field riding the rough tail-end of a two-day high set in motion by some immaculate Thai cocaine that had clapped him firmly astride God's own motorcycle. He was then made to resonate into more fine-spun orbits by the leavening action of great quantities of prime Cambodian hashish; both of whose declines in effect he was doctoring as best he could with some truly vile local whiskey on that gorgeous fog-laced morning as they were breaking their encampment by the Lo Duc River and the ambush came.

Instant firefight, sky where the ground was, even the rocks exploding. Despite being filtered through the fog in his brain, the prospect of what had by now come to be the certain outcome—his miraculous survival merely so he could tuck the dying's guts back in and then later help bury the dead—seemed to him immensely grotesque and perverted. He'd had enough.

So rather than returning the enemy's fire or diving for cover, Crowe unhurriedly drained the last swig from the whiskey bottle, savoring its aftertaste of tapioca. He threw down the empty and smoothed back his hair, knocking from it a few stray embers from an exploding tree beside him. He looked around to see where the enemy contingent was most concentrated and, having determined, he waved his arms above his head to get their attention, all the while jumping up and down for maximum visibility.

In the relative silence that ensued he turned his back to the attacking forces, dropped his dark green trousers to his ankles, and bent over so as to better expose the richly gleaming ebony of his buttocks to the pinkening morning sky. He accentuated the gesture by animatedly pointing at the target with both hands and shouting a stream of bitter, pent-up invective of which *murdering cocksuckers* was by far the kindest and gentlest part.

The force of his words wilted a small circle of tender green undergrowth directly around his feet. Still he grew louder, belittling their marksmanship, their eyesight, the gram-weight of their genitalia, and their mothers' proclivity for entertaining pack-oxen in their boudoirs on Sundays. He dared them, double-, triple-dared them, if they had so much as a hope of a single hair on their sorry saffron hindquarters to prove it by blowing him so high and wide the maggots couldn't find a mouthful with a microscope, goddamn it, were they deaf, not next year, NOW.

Behind the silence the universe breathed. Once, twice. Then the volley began, jarring and slicing the earth, Beethoven riding the devil's shoulders conducting hell's artillery, and the magnificent pounding heat and flash of it made Crowe weep joyful tapioca tears at the nearness of his deliverance.

But when the storm of smoke and metal began to subside and he could again hear the river lapping fluidly against stones and could taste the tender tang of snot and tears that had collected in his upside-down head he surmised that he hadn't died and opened his eyes to discover why.

What he saw, on the small patch of green hillside immediately in front of him, was a remarkably precise silhouette of his bent-over self etched ballistically into the vines and undergrowth, every curve and notch and appendage in sharp relief—even his most-favored appendage, suspended in the middle like a carpenter's plumb-bob—with a skill a world-class sculptor would envy.

He felt of himself all over, in stunned disbelief—legs, head, shoulders, belly—and determined that except for a few rather nasty powder burns and a big shard of glass impaled just below his left ankle, presumably a ricochet from the whiskey bottle, he was unhurt.

In his jagged mental state this proved the very bottoming of his already lethal despair. Desperate with disappointment, he threw himself face-first to the dirt, fists and legs going like a baby in a tantrum, screaming denigrations of himself and the day of his birth and God Almighty with a violence and cunning of metaphor that made his previous barrage of insults toward his attackers sound like a letter of recommendation.

No sooner was he prostrate, though, than the screaming grandmammy of all mortar shells came low-skimming across the clearing and bisected the exact void of air where he had stood examining his wounds just a second before. When the round hit, it made flaming smithereens of the statue the first barrage had carved and then, its destructive gusto barely diminished, reduced the entire hillside immediately beyond to dust and smoke, with a concussion that scalded Crowe's exposed neck and shoulders and jarred loose three large Army-issued fillings from his jaw teeth and half covered him with silt and debris. But, none to his surprise, he was otherwise unhurt—his head much clearer now—and stoically resigned to the mixed blessing of continued existence.

He lay breathing gently, hopefully an indistinguishable part of the blackened scenery, as the cautious voices of the approaching enemy soldiers advanced toward and then beyond him. As they passed, one man gingerly prodded his side with the toe of a boot.

He lay there for minutes or eons, no idea which, until birdsongs echoed again with their full strength up and down the channel of the river. He could feel the tentative probings of root hairs from microscopic seeds seeking sustenance from the sweat in his clothes and hair. When he finally rolled over and sat up and shook off the ashes, a by now familiar prospect met his view.

He spat out his dislodged fillings and walked down the black, denuded stretch of hillside toward the river, stepping carefully to avoid the corpses and corpse parts scattered so liberally over the area they would have stretched arm to arm, if so arranged, to the very edge of the water, which was frantic now with small brown somersaulting birds and great white slow-motion cranes with beaks like sabers.

That was when the revelation hit him. At the riverside, amid streamers of low-lying fog made from steam expelled into the brisk air from the wounds of the dead as one organ or another shifted slightly in acclimation to its ceased function, while the cranes caught small silver minnows for their breakfast.

A-rith-me-tic. The word entered his brain in luxurious slow syllables sounding like some exotic foreign city, a thought so totally unprovoked and unpreceded that it seemed to come directly from God's mind to his own.

Arithmetic. His only talent in school, more curse than blessing because it drew attention and thereby ridicule to his ugly duckling self—*Go figger little nigger go figger little*—whose knees knocked together when he ran and whose words always came out in a wad rather than a neat row like they were supposed to.

The hell of it wasn't that he could do math, but that he couldn't *not* do math. Taunt him with a long division problem and he'd answer before he realized; he could square root and cube root like a scalded dog and not even know he was doing it till he'd done it.

Which had naturally made him the apple of the eye of old lady Farquhar, math teacher at Indigo City High for at least a hundred years, who would adjourn to the cloakroom every morning to take her toddy and then glide to the blackboard like a great brown steamship. She'd fix the class with her frog eyes and begin their daily catechism—*What is thuh universe Thuh universe is God doing math*—before infusing them with such quantities of it that the fainter-hearted would weep and tremble and sometimes pass out.

And here was radioman James Crowe halfway around the world in hell and the math still working crazy-alive inside his skin so silently he didn't know it was there, except what else could keep delivering him so regularly from the vast dark disorder of this place? What else, if not the math?

Which was the question he put to Turner now, his tale having ended.

But Turner had questions of his own. "Let me see if I'm following. You can use math to . . . manipulate reality."

"I guess you could say that."

"All right. So the reason you're here is that you sat down one day and did, say, calculus or whatever, and the figures you got told you some monks would be at Reverend Pendleton's church."

"No, sir. *They* told me."

"The people at the *church* told you?"

"No, sir. The people that's *running* this thing told me."

"Running what thing?"

"I was hoping you could tell *me*, sir."

A light rain began hitting the darkened windshield. Talking to Crowe was taking so much of his energy that Turner had serious doubts about driving straight through to Birmingham tonight.

"Okay. Different topic. Tre Chinh. When you kept me from walking into that ambush, you were using math to predict the future, right?"

Crowe looked blank. "I guess so, Cap'n."

"So show me how you do that. Tell me what's going to happen to us tonight. Or in the morning."

"Can't do that, sir."

"Why not?"

"Because that night at Tre Chinh was the first, last, and only time I've done that. Damn if I know how, sir."

The rain had increased so that Turner had to put the wiper on full power. He decided to look for a motel, then get an early start in the morning. But, as if on cue, the van's motor coughed, then coughed again. From the back seats came a credible imitation of the sound, followed by light applause. That would be Wah So, who was so fascinated by this country's preponderance of mechanical things after living his whole life lacking in them, that he was sometimes moved to imitate, in homage, their complex sounds.

The motor, as if goaded to top him, sputtered more violently still, a sound the monk mimicked with less success. Wah So tried the effect again, at increased volume.

"Warsaw?" Turner said toward the back. "I need to concentrate, here, buddy." Wah So's efforts lapsed into silence.

This time no amount of gas-pedal coaxing or positive thinking could help the van regain its former momentum. The engine quit altogether and Turner coasted to a stop on the gravel shoulder, to the accompaniment of loud sighs from the back seats.

Turner raised the hood and stood looking into the flashlit depths of the big motor, a cold rain raking his back. The greasy machinery looked inscrutably back at him. No obvious trouble, like a wire loose or a belt broken. He came to be aware of James Crowe's head under the hood, alongside his.

"Carburetor, you reckon?" Crowe guessed. "Maybe trash in the fuel filter. You got a ranch?"

"Do I have a *what*?"

"*Ranch*. Little hex ranch, monkey ranch?"

"No. We don't have any tools." As he stared into the motor again, Turner was struck by the ludicrousness of the situation. "James?"

"Yes, Cap'n."

"Let's use our heads, here, bud. If you can do a tree out of nothing, a carburetor ought to be child's play. Get your calculator."

Crowe creased his forehead. "I don't think that's a good idea, Cap'n."

A hard gust of wind swept rain up under the hood, sent some of it down Turner's shirt collar. He felt his frustration level rising. "You don't think it's a good idea," he repeated. "Might I ask why?"

"Well, sir, we don't want to waste another one this soon."

"Waste another what?"

"Supervention, sir. Them mothers are scarce."

"Supervention?"

"Messing with matter. Do it too much, the balance gets cockeyed. I mean, deep shit. That's why there's like, a, whatchamacallit on 'em. You know, that gizmo on an accelerator keeps it from going too fast."

"A governor?"

"Governor. Right. Right."

By the glow of the flashlight, Crowe's eyes were looking crazed again. Turner heard the familiar sounds of triple patty-cake coming from inside the van. He thought, Why me?

"Let me get this straight. The number of these . . . miracles you can do is limited?"

Crowe looked offended. "Super . . . *ventions*, Cap'n, not miracles," he said. "Superventions. I ain't Jesus. I just got his initials."

"So what's the limit?"

"One per person per year, sir. They're very strict about it."

"You mean to tell me you had one mir— er, 'supervention' that could have helped us in the final battle, and you blew it on making a damned *tree*?"

Crowe glared at him. "Begging Cap'n's pardon, but . . ."

"Turner!!!" Turner shouted.

"Begging pardon, sir, but you didn't leave me no choice. You was kicking me off the bus. Didn't take no math to see that."

"But what's the *point*, if you've used up the one . . ."

"Letting me finish, please, Cap'n," Crowe said coolly, "I was going to say I been saving 'em up."

"Saving up superventions."

"Three years' worth, sir. Up till . . ."

"The tree," Turner finished for him. "Meaning two left, now."

"Exactly, sir. I think we should use them wisely."

Turner clicked off his flashlight and looked in one direction of the highway, then the other, for some glow of light denoting civilization. The two horizons were equally black.

"And Cap'n . . . uh, *sir*, if I might add one more thing?"

Sure, Turner thought. How much wetter can I get, standing here? But he only gritted his teeth and said, "Yes, James?"

"I know Cap'n's . . . I mean, I know you're thinking you've hooked up with a one-trick hoss, here, what with this supervention thing. But I just want to say that, in all humility, I have a number of other talents that can be useful to you. I been through a hell of a war, like you have, and I learned a lot of stuff."

Turner sighed and switched the flashlight back on, took a benedictory look at the dead engine before slamming the hood. "In particular?" he prompted James.

"Conceptualization," James said, without having to think. "Long-term strategizing. The broader, if you will, logistical picture. Which is one of the things they said you were lack . . ." The speaker froze, his eyes in the faint glow of the flashlight stricken with embarrassment.

"Go on," Turner said. "'Lacking in'?"

Crowe stared down meekly at the roadside gravel.

"'One of the things *they* said'?" Turner quoted. "*Who* said?"

"Well, the people that's . . ."

"' . . . running . . . this . . . thing'," Turner harmonized. "What else did they say I was lacking in?"

Crowe shut his eyes tight and swallowed hard. "I'm not really at liberty, Cap'n . . . uh, sir. Sometimes I talk when I ought to be listening." He gave Turner a sheepish grin. "That's one of the things *I'm* lacking in."

Turner switched off the flashlight again, and looked up and down the highway. No illumination, no sign of life.

"Sir?" James said. "If I might add one more thing?"

"Oh, feel free," Turner said, raising his face to the rain.

"Just so you won't think you're stuck with some kind of prima donna," James said, "I want you to know I'm still an old infantry grunt at heart. I slog through shit, happily hump and tote. I ain't proud. I want you to put me to use. I'm glad to be in your command, sir."

When Turner looked down from the rain he saw Crowe's small hand extended toward him. He sighed and shook it.

Put me to use, Turner replayed in his mind. Hmmm. Like humping his grunt self down the pavement to find a tow-truck, perhaps?

But then he made a quick mental inventory of the van's passengers, trying to judge which of them would have the best luck thumbing a ride on a late-night western Mississippi highway. A crazed black man in combat fatigues and a cartridge belt? A saffron-robed Tibetan monk?

His choice was clear. He gave Crowe his flashlight, and instructed him to watch over the guys and keep the van doors locked until he got back. Then, taking a deep breath, he slicked back his wet hair and started walking east, his thumb out invitingly, wearing the same aw-shucks, country boy smile that had won him Willie and Waylon in one fell swoop to perform at the Vet Aid benefit, back in what now seemed prehistoric times.

Thumb, grin, thumb, grin. All to no benefit, as it turned out, for the first seventeen motorists who passed him.

Make that eighteen.

7

THE COUPLE WHO'D given Turner a lift in their aging Volkswagen van were proving to be ideal company in his search for a garage. Throwbacks to the Woodstock era, they seemed as weary and bummed-out as he was; after initial introductions the pair were content to listen in silence to the van's aging tape player, the first eight-track machine Turner had seen in more than a decade. The scratchy, apparently endless tape had all the classics of that summer. Hendrix. Joplin. Crosby, Stills and Nash.

He listened, daydreaming and half-dozing in the vehicle's faintly pot-scented air, until in the interstice of silence between songs on the tape he heard, embedded in the static, a low echo of the next song's beginning, and the hairs on his neck tickled in recognition. Please, no. Please let it be some other song.

This is the dawning of the
Age of Aquarius . . .

Shit.

Age of Aquarius
Aquarrrrr-ius . . .

His last defense against the dreaded memory crumpled then, and he knew that even if he made a spectacle of himself by turning the stereo off it was still too late, the song was already in his head and would play there till conclusion, dredging up what baggage it wanted.

He gave in to the flashback, let it run its course, remembering ruefully what his grandfather had once told him—that the chief sorrow of growing older is not the decline of the body, as most believe, but rather the swollen webwork of connections in the mind that makes everything in the present remind you of something in the past, so that no object or face or tune or odor can ever be merely itself but comes freighted for better or worse, generally worse, with your whole jagged history.

The postcard.

Was how it started.

The one object from that other life that he'd kept.

The postcard from Cassie, with her apartment window circled.

The guy I'm . . .

Ice-pick in the heart.

. . . living with reminds me so much of you.

Nights at base camp he would write long letters to her. But only in his mind, never mailed. And once a week, a color postcard to his grandparents—the touristy kind sold in the PX, happy peasants working rice paddies at golden sunrise, children playing jump-rope in front of moss-covered Buddhist shrines. *I'm fine and am staying out of danger*, he would write, a total lie. *Please don't worry.* And *Pray for me* he would add, only partially for politeness' sake, because when the adrenaline of being in the field subsided he felt even more alone than he had when his parents died, felt cut off from the woods and rivers of his childhood, a lost ball tossed off the edge of the world into high bamboo.

So that when his chance came that summer to go home, if only for a two-week furlough, he was beside himself with joy. Word came one Friday night, while a bunch of them were drinking beer at the PX, that their latest exploits—capturing a major hunk of territory at the northeast perimeter while suffering only four casualties, three guys who took rounds but were able to say, like in the movies, *It's only a flesh wound*, and a recon man who burned pure shit out of his hand when he triggered his own trip-flare—had so impressed General Somebody that he'd ordered two-week passes for the lot of them.

They were hot. They were the elite. Kick ass and take names, by God. Turner felt so compact and godlike, so sweetly immortal and omnipotent, waiting at the Saigon Airport that Sunday morning in his creased khakis with the ticket crisp in his hand, SAN FRAN USA, that the much-folded postcard in the inner sanctum of his billfold—Cassie's apartment building with the faint ink circle around her window—took on a bold new life. It became a clear plea for help, *Take me away from all this*; why else would she have written, why else so specific about the exact spot, and why hadn't he realized it before?

He studied the picture so intensely on the interminable flight over that he dreamed the building when he dozed; a kind of peripheral imagined vision set in, so that he saw plainly all the features of the park whose trees framed the hillside street, smelled the espresso and croissants from the coffee shops and bakeries that must surely be just out of camera range. More than three-dimensional, more than real, the scene became the stage-set for the movie of his triumphant return.

He would knock on her door and . . . no. He'd wait in the park, watch for the guy she was living with to leave, and . . . no, there'd be dozens of people in the building, he couldn't tell one guy from another. Even though when he pictured Cassie in San Francisco, the attendant hot pain like a straight razor slicing through his insides, he pictured her with a kinder, more polished, better-looking version of himself . . . hadn't she said *reminds me so much of you*? Except she probably didn't mean in looks; women almost never meant something the way you took it.

No, he'd wait for her to come out of the building and he'd call out her name and she'd be so surprised to see him she'd run into his arms. They'd go somewhere to talk, a coffee shop maybe, and by the time he finished his elaborately reasoned argument, she'd understand that he was a different person now, more sure of things; would understand how much he still loved her and would confess that she felt the same; would understand that the war was not like she'd thought, that it was necessary and right and he would come through it healthy and alive because he was smart and didn't take chances; would understand that the two of them could no more go through life without each other than a planet could suddenly pick another orbit, that their love was not just love but was physics and preordained no matter what misunderstandings and stray paths might make them momentarily feel otherwise.

He would watch the perfect architecture of this idea assemble itself gradually in her dark eyes while she listened and drank the sweet bitter coffee she'd mentioned in the postcard. And when the pieces of his reasoning came together in her heart like the girders of a building he would see her face change, see it hold and mirror him like it used to, which would be his cue to squeeze her hand and produce with a humble flourish the extra airline ticket in her name, from San Francisco to Birmingham the next morning.

A week was all he asked. One week driving the old roads and walking the old footpaths and eating his grandmother's cooking and talking about their future. And if being back in Zion Hill with him didn't feel right to her, infinitely more right than the crazy life the west coast offered, he'd buy her a ticket back and that was that. No theatrics, no regrets. Swear to God.

He knew it would work. The maneuver was unassailable in its rightness and logic, no loose ends or loopholes, as nailed-down righteous as the maneuvers in the field their platoon leader sketched on the big map for them by lamplight—skinny Puerto Rican named Ludlow, figure that, but Turner loved him like a brother. So that on the long cab ride from the airport to the park at Haight-Ashbury, the obstacles and objections to her leaving with him that raised themselves in his mind as the pink Sunday sun first emerged from the fog between the pillars of the Golden Gate Bridge were so quickly overruled that they eventually died out altogether and he could lose himself in the scenery: hillsides speckled with houses the color of seashells, cable cars with antennae like insects sparking up and down the steep streets.

When the windows of the cab suddenly darkened on all sides to show only rich green foliage Turner sat up out of his reverie as if dropping from a dream, rubbing his eyes and looking around.

"A spark," said the driver, an old Chinese man, but as the man thumped the fare meter to indicate the amount Turner realized he'd said *Is park.* When he held his hand out for the money, concern showed in his eyes as he glanced up and down the length of Turner's crisp starched uniform. "You sure, here?"

Turner got the cash from his wallet, and then took out the postcard too, read the fine-print caption on the back. "Golden Gate Park?" he asked.

The driver nodded, and Turner paid and got out. He stood for a minute with his duffel bag, squarely facing the front of the apartment building, before he took the magic postcard from his pocket again and unfolded it to the circled X. Matched against reality, the only visible change was that the uniformly white curtains on all the windows when the photo was made had been transformed by the Age of Aquarius into a checkerboard of bright colors, no two alike. Some were flags, some were peace symbols, some were stripes and checks and patterns.

Cassie's would be one, two . . . third floor, he counted, on the card. First, second, third, fourth . . . fifth door down. Simple enough. Three up, then five. The window was open. The curtain that belled out softly from it was a deep sky blue, Cassie's favorite color, and covered with a pattern of stars.

The sight gouged up a memory of himself with her, late at night in Zion Hill, in summer. They lay on their backs on the old wooden boat dock, heads touching, watching the pulsing constellations while a lake full of bullfrogs grunted a two-note song. *I want a bedroom like this*, she'd said, and he promised her their first house would have one, with day-glo stars on the walls and ceiling. And he promised her . . .

The memory threatened to open a floodgate of more, which he couldn't handle now. He pinched off the flow of it as cleanly as he'd been taught to stanch a cut artery, held it and felt the throb and cleared his mind for the task at hand.

The old building's stairwell smelled of pot smoke and cooking spices and patchouli incense. A phonograph played softly somewhere, muffled by the walls, and he recognized it as an album one of his buddies had—Oriental-sounding music, weird, like a guitar turned inside out. A man named Sitar playing something called a shankar, or vice versa. He could never keep it straight.

The planks of the steps groaned and squawked so violently in the near-silence as he climbed that he stopped once and tried proceeding on tiptoe, but if anything it only stretched out the groaning, made it worse, and he went back to regular walking.

The dark third-floor hallway had a runner of carpet worn so thin you couldn't tell what the pattern had been, roses or seashells, and the apartment doors were painted vivid, glaring colors—all different, like the curtains that showed from outside.

The fifth door on the right was jet black. In the exact center was a tiny crucifix, carved out of ivory or bone, and hanging upside-down. Something in Turner's heart sank, and he felt almost as far from home as he had in the jungles.

But he'd come too far to quit now, he told himself, and stood to his full height and knocked three sharp times on the door, with what he hoped was a proper mix of politeness and authority.

No sound came from inside. He waited a full minute and knocked again. This time there was a loud scraping of furniture and the thump of running feet. Something heavy slammed against the door from within, with so much force he thought the wood might splinter.

"Hello?" Turner said. "Cass?"

After a minute the knob rattled and the door opened a crack. Half the face of a dried-up old man looked out, wild white hair and a hollow eye. Turner glanced down and saw the skewed leg of the sofa that had been upended against the door.

"Morning," Turner said brightly. "Hope I didn't wake you up. I'm looking for a lady name of McNamara? Cassie." The inflamed-looking eye stared straight at him, vacant of any intent. "Reddish hair?" he added. "Kind of long?" As he said it he realized her hair could be any length now, any color, in the year since he'd seen her.

The door was suddenly jerked open a foot wider, the sofa leg scraping raw against the wood of the floor. The man's whole withered head showed now, with a growing smile. Turner saw beyond him that the curtain in the window was black, not blue. He knew he hadn't counted wrong. Did some of the rooms have two entrances, or two windows?

A shaky hand came up from behind the door, pointing straight at Turner's face. "What do you . . ." the old man said, wheezing with the effort. "What do you think . . . of your blue-eyed death *now*, mister boy?"

"Sir?" Turner said.

"Soul . . ." the man wheezed, his smile turning to a sneer. "Soul . . ."

"I'm sorry I bothered you," Turner said, starting to back away.

"Soldiers driving fr-fr-friggin' . . . ambulances, what the p-p-piss is the whirl comin' to, son of a . . ." The old face seemed to lose itself in reverie until the reddened eyes glanced up and noticed Turner's slow departure, which drew a new burst of resentment.

"Damn . . . *vulture* . . . done taken *one* p-pretty . . . girl, how many of 'em you . . . *need* for your filthy d-d-death . . . bed . . .?"

"Sorry," Turner kept saying, "sorry," and beat a slow retreat toward the stairs until he heard the black door slam shut on the incoherent mumblings. He waited a few seconds in the silence and then tiptoed back down the hall and knocked on the door to the right of the old man's. It was dark blue and had at its center, he noticed now, a tiny silver pasteboard star, the kind Sunday Schools used to give for good attendance.

After a minute he knocked again. He thought he heard a floor plank creak inside, but couldn't be sure it hadn't come from an adjoining apartment. "Cass?" he said softly. "It's me."

No answer.

He headed downstairs, meaning to go out on the street and match windows to the postcard circle again. But coming to the first-floor landing, he noticed a wall of ramshackle mailboxes that he'd overlooked before, off in a dark alcove of the foyer. A closer look showed that only a few of the numbered boxes were labeled with names, none of them Cassie's; the rest were either blank or had small colored drawings of zodiac signs and magic symbols. One drawing showed a fat smiling Buddha, the kind he'd seen in stone carvings at the entrance gates of small temples in Vietnam, way out in the bush.

When he stepped out onto the sidewalk to take stock of the third-floor curtains again, the sour-sweet scent of baking dough washed over him and his stomach started growling more vigorously than before. He traced the scent to a small shop across the street. Hell. Maybe he could think clearer if he had something to eat.

He made a quick circuit of the apartment building to be sure there weren't other entrances he could lose Cassie to, if she went out, and he thought with fleeting irony how it was the same thing he did to the enemy whenever his patrol ran across one of the million underground tunnels that honeycombed the ground, over there.

But there was just the one entrance, not counting the fire escapes down the back. He scanned all the adjacent streets for her old bottle-green Chrysler, the one she'd left for California in, but he didn't see it. Had he really helped her pack, watched the creaking boat-like sedan rock out of her driveway and recede toward the interstate? Had he really been that bad a sucker for the bullshit slogan on the butterfly poster in her bedroom that summer, *If you love something, set it free . . .* ?

He'd been so sure, so blithely conceitedly sure she'd never get there, would come to her senses and turn around in Mississippi or Louisiana, that he hadn't lost the least bit of sleep that night or even the next. But when the August days stretched like a desert toward the X on his calendar, his date with the draft, the slow tide of panic that rose in him was confirmed by the terrible jangling midnight phone call (in her excitement she'd forgotten the difference in time zones) from a booth beside the ocean.

"Hear it?"

She'd held the receiver out the door for him to listen. As she described the campfires on the beach and the dark figures surfing by moonlight—"So free, here," she kept saying, as a cricket called from the sill of his open kitchen window—the joy in her voice told him without words the chances of her coming home, and when he heard himself snap back without thinking, "Nothing's free; it's all got a price," he felt a dark noxious gulf open around his throat. He suspected he would not handle the rest of the call very well and he hadn't.

The man behind the bakery counter, a sorrowful-eyed Greek of about fifty, took his order and made change, all wordlessly, glancing disdainfully at the uniform. Turner carried his tray of sweet rolls and coffee to a table at the big windows facing the street, and sat watching the entrance of the apartments while he ate.

No sooner than he'd finished his first sweet roll, the door opened and Cassie came out. Her hair shorter, but he knew it was her.

Her. Real as life. He slid back from the table so fast he knocked his coffee over and, leaving his duffel bag, took off at a full run across the street.

"Cassie!"

She showed no sign she'd heard him, just continued to walk slowly, deep in thought, toward an old maroon Fiat convertible with its top back, parked halfway down the block. She had on faded jeans and a man's white shirt, the tails tied at the waist. She'd lost a little weight, was almost too thin, but she was more beautiful than he'd ever seen her. Stunning, even.

Turner opened his mouth to shout louder, but a buoyant swelling of sorrow or joy or both had plugged his throat and hampered speech. His heart raced, and a stinging numbness coursed down his arms. This was not in the plan. Suave was the plan. Calm and reasoned and self-secure, a new man. Accent on man. But the state of his heart told him that at the moment he was not above begging, that tears weren't too far away.

Not in the plan. He slowed to a walk, took deep breaths and let them out slowly through his mouth. When he finally caught up with her she was already in the car and reaching to shut the door, still not having seen him.

He tried to say her name, but his throat was still constricted. He laid his hand gently on her wrist as she shut the car door. Bad move. She gave a sharp little cry and jerked around to face him while her other hand fumbled frantically for the switch key and started the motor.

Seeing her up close was a shock. Her eyes were . . . ravaged, was the only word. Red and swollen nearly shut from crying, no recognition in them of his face at all—just the same steeled desperation in the eyes of the last remaining victim in a horror movie as she faces the monster alone, her friends lying slaughtered around her.

He found his voice. A whisper. "Cass? What's wrong?"

In her dazed expression he watched her mind name him, place him, all in slow motion. When her terrorized face finally kindled with the knowledge of him, it was as profound a transformation as when a flower bud blooms, or the door of a dank room is flung open to air and light.

Her arms went desperately around his neck, a move which required her to half stand in her car seat, unwilling to wait for the opening of the low door. Turner buried his face in the wildness of her hair, the world topsy-turvy and half dark and red-edged. He crushed her so hard in his arms he felt their bones scrape, saw dim stars of pain before he got control again and eased off, freed his hand to trace slowly the length of her spine through the thin white cloth of the shirt. Her whispering the whole time oh God oh God, heedless of the fact that one of her feet had slipped against the gas pedal and was revving the little engine to a frenzy of sound.

When he was finally able to disengage himself enough to shut off her ignition and hand her the key, she looked at it without comprehension, having begun to tell him in great gouts of breath some long confused story he could make no sense of—phrases without connection, actions with conflicting tense. *Told her and told her, knocking and she won't*, all of which circled helplessly back to the orphaned words *I* and *she*.

He opened the car door, put his arm around her shoulder and steered her toward the building. He thought fleetingly of his duffel bag still in the restaurant, decided to hell with it. Her torrent of talk didn't lessen the whole way up the stairs and down the hall to the door with the Sunday School star, though at times the invective seemed directed not so much at him as at some omniscient witness to whatever terrible event she sought absolution for.

The apartment was spartan, to say the least. Odds and ends of salvage served as furniture, the kind of shipping crates and wire racks and giant wooden spools that could be had at night with a minimum of stealth in a city of that size, though each piece was made festive beyond its origins with the addition of bright-colored spray paint, applied in kaleidoscopic puffs and topped with a sprig of artificial flowers or the glued settings from broken costume jewelry.

The only store-bought items in the place were a battered stereo, a stack of albums, and a low black couch with a back but no arms. He sat her down on the couch and knelt in front of her as the distressed talk continued. She was shivering, though the room wasn't cold, and he briskly rubbed her upper arms to warm her, looking around in vain for a jacket or a spread he could wrap her in.

Underneath the talk he became aware of the sound of water running, from a room off to the left. In her agitation she must have left the bathroom shower on.

"I'll get that," he interrupted her. "You sit still." But when she belatedly heard the sound and saw what he meant to do she sprang up in panic and took his arm.

"*No,*" she said, with a stricken look. "It's . . . it's not . . ." Turner felt his face flush then at his stupidity. She wasn't alone. Some guy was there, in the shower.

"I thought he . . ." she said, "I didn't, uh . . . let's go. We can talk in the park. Just let me get . . ."

As she pulled loose from him he noticed a dark album cover lying on an apple-crate end table beside the couch. It was swirled with white powder, like a child's finger painting, and a thin pipette of glass lay alongside. She was too distracted to see him see it, or else she didn't care.

After a minute he heard a commotion from the direction she had gone, the doors of cabinets jerking open and slamming shut. He followed her. The tiny curtainless kitchen, surprised by the new sunlight, was a ruined warren of empty cans and packages, stacked plates stained with food. Cassie, her back to him, held one hand aside in a careful fist while with the other she ransacked the shelves and drawers, her shoulders quaking. Still unaware of him, she produced a clear glass bottle off a high shelf and drank from it greedily. For a second she half-strangled and coughed, and from across the room Turner could smell the medicinal tang of vodka.

With a practiced move she threw back her head and raised the favored fist to her mouth, releasing a small rainbow of capsules which she followed with another draught from the dwindling bottle, shuddering as she swallowed.

"What the hell are you doing?" Turner shouted. She spun, startled, and the bottle shattered on the linoleum. The sharp reek spread quickly into the general decay of the room.

"Are you stoned?"

She backed away as he approached her, more a threat than he intended.

"Huh? What did you take, just then?"

Her reddened eyes overflowed again, though she made no sounds of crying.

"What the fuck are you trying to do, kill yourself?" He saw his hands go of their own volition to her shoulders and shake her so violently her head wobbled. "*Huh*?"

She jerked out of his grasp and caromed off the small cluttered stove before coming to rest with her back against the wall, her arms against it to steady herself. Her expression was half terror, half disbelief.

She said something to him, but it was lost in the noise of a passing car.

He moved toward her, cupping his ear. "Say what?"

In her alarm she pressed harder against the wall, her forearm making a swipe at the new wetness in her eyes. By some sleight of hand she suddenly held her car keys. When she spoke, the quick bloom of the liquor and pills had magically settled her speech from the frantic jagged high she'd been on.

"I said, this is not *you*. They've done something to you."

He shook his head slowly and forced a smile. "Same old me," he said. He patted his chest for emphasis. Feeling the stiff packet of airline tickets in the pocket of his shirt surprised him, like some remnant from a previous life, so foreign to this present scene it made him want to cry, or laugh.

"*You're* the one that's changed," he heard himself say. "You're the one that's fucking up your life."

Her eyes hardened. "I hate that word," she said. "You never used to talk like that."

Something ignited in Turner then, the accumulated night sweats in bamboo hell and the slantwise sneering looks of the airport crowds eyeing his uniform and the old man's gibberish about death and . . .

He laughed loudly. "Never used to *talk* like that?" He held his arms wide, as if asking invisible onlookers to acknowledge the absurdity of the remark. "*I* never used to *talk* like that? Well, *you* never used to get stoned, and, and . . . shit-faced . . . and fuck people off the *street*! Goddamn it, I'll talk any way I want to!"

He was embarrassed by his sudden tears, which was probably why he felt obliged to slam his fist onto the small kitchen table for emphasis, not reckoning that its rickety condition would catapult several plates to the hard floor. In the confusion of his anger he bent to retrieve them, but when he saw how many directions the pieces had gone he straightened and turned toward Cassie to apologize.

She wasn't there. He saw a glimpse of her white shirt through the doorway, looping fast around the couch. She lost her balance for a moment and steadied herself against it before running on.

"Cass? *Cass*! Don't . . ."

He caught up to her at the front door, grabbed her hand on the knob before she could shut him in. "Cass, don't . . ." He wrestled both her wrists into his grasp and pushed her backwards with force against the blue door to get her attention. Her face looked cornered, wild.

"*Listen* . . . I'm sorry, I . . ."

He only half knew he'd relented his grip on one of her wrists until the hand streaked up at him with surprising speed, the longest key thumbed like a weapon, straight at his cheek. He jerked away and deflected the jab with his arm, holding more tightly to the one wrist he still had. She kicked out at him but hit the door instead, slamming its knob hard into the plaster wall, all while the hellish hiss of the bathroom shower continued unabated.

Suddenly her face was inches from his, her eyes wider than he'd ever seen them.

"You're not Turner," she said, in an eerily measured voice. "I don't know you. You let go of me, or I'll scream. I swear to God, I'll scream and scream."

All sound stopped but the distant hiss of water. Turner stared her down, but she wouldn't blink.

He let go.

She continued watching him a full second before she meticulously straightened her collar, dusted at the skewed front of her shirt, and turned to walk away.

"Cass?" he said softly.

Where the hallway met the landing of the stairs she stumbled slightly, grabbing to the fat stairpost for support, glowering over her shoulder at him before going on.

As she went out of sight a bolt of impulse swept him, head to foot, to run after her and restrain her whichever way, damn the consequences; what made him hesitate was some far-off inner voice, partly himself and partly Ludlow, his platoon leader. *Gotta know when to let somethin' go, mon.*

He listened to the reports of her heels on the descending stairs, fading like the last chorus of a radio song. Only when the awful finality of the building's slamming front door registered with him did his mind rouse itself from the befuddling gauze of the moment and remember with piercing clarity the glint of her car keys.

Bullshit, his inner voice raged, overpowering Ludlow's, *she can't drive like this . . .*

The stairs were a blur as he rumbled down them. Just before he reached the entranceway he heard the small motor fire up outside. He flung open the door to a passing streak of maroon.

He ran up the hill after her, ran for his life, but as she dropped into second gear he began to fall farther and farther behind. Just when his chest was near bursting he noticed the traffic light at the end of the next block go yellow and then red and he praised what he remembered of God but she hesitated at the light for only a moment before downshifting and blaring her horn and going through. Then the car was over the lip of the trolley-cabled hill and gone as cleanly as if it had never existed, except for the sound of the buzzsawing engine and her continued frantic shifting, that hung for the longest time in the warming air before it died away.

At seven-thirty that evening he was still sitting on the front steps of the building, waiting for her. At eight, stars began showing through the red and purple dusk, sky the color of cockscombs in his grandmother's flower-yard, and the silent streets began gradually to come alive.

From the park, and from apartments above him, came the sound of unseen radios: Beatles and Hendrix and hard obscene jazz and "Age of Aquarius" no telling how many damned times *mystic crystal rev-e-la-tions . . .* Long-haired people strolled by in twos and threes with their arms around each other, laughing and drinking from dark bottles of wine and occasionally breaking loose into a free, languid dance. The air became layered with pot smoke and wood smoke and the smell of meat cooking on open coals.

At nine o'clock she still hadn't come, and the brightness of the porch lamp above him was making him such a target in the festive darkness—bums had approached him twice begging quarters, and three Hell's Angels walked by slowly, eyeing him, turned around at the corner and came by again—that he went into the foyer and, using the retrieved duffel bag to cushion his back, settled himself in the shadowy space underneath the stairwell where he had a view of the front door.

At nine-thirty there was such a commotion out on the steps, loud voices and glass breaking, that he thought someone was fighting until he heard laughter rising above it. The front doors opened and a wild-haired boy with a cigarette, no shirt, came through leading a skinny laughing girl with hiccups who brushed at a purplish wine stain on the front of her dress. They went into the apartment just opposite the stairwell.

The loud laughter out front quietened somewhat, but the celebrations up and down the street kept on. Turner made himself wait what he judged was a half hour before checking the time again, but when he held his watch out into the thin band of light from the streetlamps only ten minutes had passed.

Now he regretted not stopping the couple and asking them if they knew Cassie, if they'd seen her since she left. When he'd almost decided to go knock, though, a noise strangely like a cricket started deep in the wall where his head was laid, and it wasn't long until the quickening of the rhythm told him it was actually bedsprings.

Over the next hour the front doors didn't open again as the creaking note quickened and slowed, quickened and slowed, came to be punctuated with a high, otherworldly moan he tried to picture, then tried not to picture, coming from the sleek blonde throat of the girl with the wine stain, and with his knuckles deep in the sockets of his eyes he prayed to know what he was being punished for, where he'd gone wrong.

Next morning on the plane, the sun rose from a boiling lake of white clouds somewhere over northern Colorado. He drank his free coffee and sat alone in the center of a section of three airliner seats with Judy Collins singing through the headset of his tape player: *Amazing grace, how sweet the sound that saved a wretch like me . . .*

He was so lost in thought that he sang the bass part from habit without realizing he was doing it, the part his grandfather had sung at Zion Hill Baptist when Turner was a boy. *Come up and sit by me, buddy. Help me sing bass.* The thrill of being fifteen, when his voice finally changed and he really could. The old song sank like a kind of salve into all the wounds his insides had suffered these past months, and he pictured his grandparents meeting him at the airport in a few hours, pictured driving them home in the old white Pontiac they'd kept all these years, the Indian-head hood ornament—standard issue, that model year—that lit up at night, a pale orange star they navigated by, driving home from church.

He caught himself singing and stopped, hoped he hadn't been loud enough that someone had heard. Then the song ended and another one began.

Bows and floes of angel hair
And ice cream castles in the air
Feathered canyons everywhere
I've looked at clouds that way . . .

He hated that song, even more than the Aquarius bullshit, could never figure why it triggered such an overwhelming sense of sadness and loss in him, while her big bright voice and the happy little keyboard curlicues seemed to mock him for feeling that way.

Looking out at the calm sea of clouds, he realized the part about clouds was coming up, *but now they only block the sun*, and he clicked the tape off before it got to that.

A San Francisco newspaper lay folded on the empty seat beside him. He picked it up, opened it, and changed his life. Unalterably.

At least that was the way he would always picture it in the years to come;

would see with an unnatural clarity his hands unfolding the newsprint, as if that single act were the cause of everything afterward, as if he could have laid the paper down then without ever opening it and life would have gone on exactly the way it was.

He skipped over the front page stories with their blaring headlines, as he would do later ten thousand times in memory—charges of corruption in some obscure city office, a prison riot at San Quentin, a rally of Berkeley students protesting the war—and settled on a story at the top of Page 2, about the predicting of earthquakes.

He'd read the first column and was about to jump to the top of the second when a small headline at the bottom of the page caught his eye.

> **Double Tragedy At Haight Apartments**
>
> A young woman is dead, the story began, and another critically injured in two apparently unrelated incidents on Saturday, according to police.
>
> Laura Faye Conroy, 21, a native of Branson, Missouri, was found unconscious early Saturday morning by Cassandra Denise…

No.

> . . . McNamara, her neighbor and former roommate, at the Bay Cliff Apartments, 1750 Haight Street. She died shortly afterward at Cedars-Sinai Medical Center. Officials say the cause of death was an apparently accidental drug overdose.
>
> Acquaintances told police Miss Conroy, a fashion model, had been "tired and overworked" in recent weeks, but not particularly despondent.
>
> Miss McNamara remains in critical condition at Cedars-Sinai . . .

No, Turner's mind screamed. The sibilant pressurized air of the cabin became ice.

> . . . from injuries she received when her car left the road at a high rate of speed and overturned at about 10:15 a.m. near the beach community of Point Croux. The wreck was discovered, minutes after the crash, by two men who had arrived at the remote area to surf.

> A hospital spokesman said Miss McNamara, 20, underwent surgery to repair abdominal and spinal cord damage received in . . .

No.

> Details were not immediately available on the cause of . . .

The moments after the newspaper slid from his hands were a riot of pure color and motion, devoid of all sense, someone who looked like him going up and down the aisle, his mind so wired he didn't realize what the terrified face of the stewardess was saying to him until the pressure of restraining hands on his shoulders made him see for the first time his fists on the woman's lapels and though he willed them to let go they held heedlessly on until he felt himself dragged backward and the hands finally loosened of their own accord, the palms staring up at him like separate unrecognizing faces.

You, his mind raged at the empty hands, as he felt himself steered to a seat and held down. The palms looked back blankly, offered no defense.

8

LYING ACROSS HIS bed in a room of the Black Flamingo Motel, waiting for Lu Weh to get out of the bathroom, Turner took some solace in the news that a really good mechanic would be doctoring their ailing Chrysler the next morning.

With any luck, they would even have time to swing through Zion Hill and check on his grandparents before heading down for the show in Birmingham. He'd looked forward for months to the monks finally getting to meet them. And getting to sample his grandmother's cornbread, which visitors were duty-bound to do if they stayed for more than fifteen minutes.

As Turner dozed off he sank into the silvery kind of morning in summer that isn't too warm, yet, but still holds the threat of heat. Cicadas at the edge of his grandfather's field cried out the old news of yesterday's parching. A solitary chicken hawk circled so slowly on a high updraft of air that he looked to be hanging motionless, a small brown kite.

His grandfather was plowing. He pushed an old spraddle-handled wooden plow, the kind with a single iron wheel in the front. Turner, a boy in the dream, walked after him trying to keep up.

But the faster he walked, the farther he fell behind. The plowed-up dirt was soft as pillows, making him step wobbly. The field had become limitless, the curve of the earth on all four sides reaching off to nothingness.

When Turner stumbled in the dirt and fell, crying out, his grandfather left the plow and ran back toward him in the shuffling, stunted motion characteristic of nightmares. What the boy saw as he drew closer was even more terrible than the thought of abandonment had been. From the neck downward his grandfather's body was eaten by raw, oblong holes, through which the frantic workings of his insides could be seen, making a sound like a hissing calliope.

Despite his wounds the old man made good progress, approaching with his arms outstretched, the sluggish gravity of the dream having been somehow cut loose so that the speed of events kept increasing, an engine out of control.

The sun swung to noon, then three, then down. Twilight fell as abruptly as a lamp blown out. An evil, copper-colored moon swooped up out of the trees beyond the tool shed and careened over the field like a kamikaze pilot, so low it knocked his grandfather's hat off, trailing cold air.

To the boy's shame he found himself running in the other direction, away from the old man's looming terrible embrace. But the farther he ran the more the rows opened out and deepened until they were chasms, whole dark cities beneath the earth, with only narrow ribbons of land between them.

He kept on, a tightrope runner on the tiny strips of dirt, until his luck went bad and his foot hit a sandy spot that sent him tumbling into the gaping dark hole, end over end through the new night sky to sure death below.

Through the rushing wind in his ears he heard a wailing that he realized was himself, his adult self, but when he was within inches of hitting the rocky ground he hit instead a motel bed in Yazoo City, Mississippi and leaped up, full of electricity, the truncated scream still in his throat.

A dull ache, low in his belly, bent him over. He traced it to his bladder, and as the evening reality of Yazoo City sifted down into him he remembered he'd been waiting a long time for a shot at the bathroom.

The door was still shut, a stripe of light showing underneath. For some reason the monks found johns ideal for meditation.

Turner tapped the door with a knuckle. "Louie? You about done, bud?"

No answer.

Lu Weh didn't have the keenest ears in the world. His parents had both gone deaf at an early age, so the genes were against him. Still he wouldn't abide Turner's suggestions about a hearing aid, because the disability allowed him to get some good meditating done in noisy situations that got on the younger monks' nerves.

Turner banged the door hard with the flat of his hand. "Louie?" he shouted. "How about it?" The silence that met his call filled him with dread. Lu Weh seemed healthy as a horse, but his age plainly put him on the threshold of heart-attack country. Turner tried the doorknob—luckily monks had no use for locks—and pushed the door open.

Lu Weh wasn't there, only his robe and shoes where they'd fallen when he dematerialized.

Turner wasn't surprised. The whole time they were checking into the motel, Louie was rattling excitedly about Crowe's theories of dimensionality. Turner could tell he was itching to experiment with them the next time he transited.

Turner stepped around the clothing and treated himself to a long and pleasurable leak. But when he was done the ache was still not gone. It had moved to a spot just behind his heart. He was remembering the dream.

THIS TIME WHEN Lu Weh reached the edge—the point in the void at which the atoms and sub-atoms quit rushing past your ears as softly as fur and suddenly ignite, with a *kr-r-r-ack* like five billion pool balls colliding, into blue points of perfect light—he hesitated.

A thing which is much easier to do by accident than on purpose, as he was doing now. Because if you have more than a split second to think about what you're up against, so to speak, you lose your nerve and want to reincorporate without completing the transition phase. Which is possible but not advisable since the after-effect makes a hangover seem like a picnic by comparison.

Now, by virtue of his hesitation, the time-drift carried him slowly toward the edge of the edge of the edge, to the place where logic foreshortens and all things become possible and impossible at once. Lu Weh suppressed his fear as best he could by severe concentration on what he was looking for, the hunch he'd suddenly had that afternoon when the little dark man was talking about the edge.

The only way you could describe the point of transition to someone who's never done it is to say, picture all the cars on the Los Angeles freeway at rush hour as a single infinitely-thin plane. Now imagine that slice infinitely replicated and stacked on top of and beneath itself without limit. Picture a similar stack of planes intersecting with all of these at right angles but with such synchrony there are no collisions ever. Call this, say, the north-south stack, and jam into it a third, infinitely other, stack angled east-west.

Your own humming atoms and sub-atoms are waiting on the entrance ramps, so to speak, of all three coordinates, for just the gap in traffic where your whole self will fit without losing a piece. And meanwhile you're being jostled from behind by all the bodies in the universe who are making the same passage at any given time, spiritually rowdy as kids in line for the diving board.

Lu Weh had felt the breath of Buddha himself, from behind him in line, on more than one occasion. Once he'd even heard a playful shoving match between the Great One and Sri Onh Ta, a holy man from the 12th Century. Sri Onh Ta was so patient and steadfast in his spirit life, legend has it, that he taught plants to transit with him, a grand accomplishment by any standard but one which also had the practical benefit of solving the nakedness problem. An old etching shows Onh Ta strolling among some startled foreign villagers in his kilt of hydrangeas.

But now, as Lu Weh hovered at the precipice of substance, there were fortunately no other transiters in queue behind him and he could take his time and watch for a dimension of the dimensions that was sure to exist if the dark man's theory was right. Although Lu Weh's own eye atoms were in great shape despite his age, he had never noticed any sign of what the dark man had alluded to—which could only lead him to conclude that it had to be looked for in some different way.

His hunch was to pretend that, rather than watching a storm of light-specks rocketing forward through a black void, he was seeing instead its opposite—an infinite pock-marked black cloud rocketing *backwards* through the great light, a fugitive Swiss cheese of blackness with no beginning and no end.

But every time he succeeded for a moment in seeing it just that way, he was overcome with such vertigo that his brain revolted and switched back, against his will, to seeing it the old way. Finally he steeled himself and readied for the cockeyed feeling that would hit like a fist when he tried again. *Three* and *two* and on *one* he saw the backwards-fleeing dark, saw it whole and believed in it, and before his brain could shut the process down, his every particle made the leap of faith and was swept counterclockwise with such instant velocity he felt impaled on the prow of some fearsome locomotive in absolute cold dark, with a sound in his ears like a tornado blowing across the mouth of a gigantic jar.

When he was just at the point of panic, the awful roaring in his head began lessening and the inelastic blackness that gripped him began opening out into what could loosely be called a place. A dark place, like a desert at night, to judge from the configuration of its horizons. The night sky had glowing, red-edged clouds despite there being no source to illuminate them.

As he neared the ground the landscape became a stark succession of chimney-like towers of rock, vaulting up randomly with an ugliness that somehow reminded him of deformed limbs. He felt the familiar tingling as his atoms started to coalesce and take on weight. In seconds he was landing on his feet with a jarring *thump* alongside one of the gnarled towers of rock.

He braced against the tower with both hands, waiting for his head to clear from the jolt of his incorporation. The stone was warm to the touch, and moist—oily, almost—in spite of a cold desolate wind that gusted at him randomly, first from one side of the column and then the other. It carried a fetid smell, sulphurous and yeasty at once, like a den of newborn animals tainted by a rotting afterbirth.

When Lu Weh got his bearings sufficiently to walk around—a task made difficult not only by the effect of the cold air on his worsening rheumatism, but also by the multiple red shadows of himself cast from the strange clouds, which made him dizzy when he looked down—he noticed that the back side of each rock tower had a line of primitive foot-holds chiseled in it from base to summit.

For some reason the indentations were all child-sized. He put his foot into one, and only half of it would fit. The same with his hands—a precarious hold at best. Suddenly his stomach gnawed at him so fiercely it bent him double. What with the chill wind and his long hard transit, cross-grain to the fabric of natural existence, he was clearly running on empty. There had to be an answer to the food problem for transiters. Something on the order of Onh Ta's hydrangeas, except edible. A belt of broccoli, maybe, or a headdress of cauliflower. Maybe fruit was the answer. Either way, a lot of work to be done on the problem. For now, he would try to stay busy enough to forget his hunger.

He got a double handful of the dark dirt and rolled it between his palms to heighten his grip. But it stung him like nettles and he had to wait for the feeling to come back in his hands before he started up the tiny holds in the side of the rock.

About midway up the side, his teeth clacking in the chill, he got the eerie sensation that the random push and pull of the wind had been replaced by a pattern like steady breathing.

Undaunted, he kept at his slow progress until he reached the place where the top of the column began to flare out, a rough mushroom shape. The indentations had disappeared and he despaired of going farther until he noticed, in the shifting light, a row of iron spikes imbedded in the dark rock, extending up and over the lip of the summit.

He tried his weight on one and it held. As he climbed he felt a small tapered span at the center of each rough spike that was as polished as glass, rubbed smooth from long handling. This was not a new path he was traveling.

He began to hear, above him, a rustling and murmuring against the rock. Whether it was human or animal or altogether other he couldn't tell. But when he reached the top and peered over into the concave belly of the peak, he saw the source: a straw nest the size of a parking lot, teeming with hundreds of tiny black hatchlings.

Their suspirations and quiverings against one another combined with their dark oily sheen to give the surface the slow roiling look of some nightmarish stew simmering on a fire. Here and there a tarnished yellow beak or claw would show itself for a second before becoming subsumed again in the perpetual rearranging of bodies. But despite the grotesque aspect of the scene, the trillings and sighings the infant creatures made in their sleep seemed to express only safety and contentment.

As Lu Weh leaned across the rim of rock and braced himself to take some of the weight off his aching left knee, his curiosity momentarily overcame his revulsion. He reached down into the warm morass of hatchlings and, with two fingers, pulled one up by a wing to inspect it more closely.

As soon as the creature met the cold air it became a squawking blur of feathers and talons, drawing sudden stripes of blood from Lu Weh's forearm. The harder he tried to fling it back into the pile the tighter it held on, until he noticed its head and beak were swelling and wrenching themselves, with a sound like cartilage tearing, into the shape of a miniature human face.

The creature had the face of the first corpse Lu Weh, as a boy, had ever seen. It was real, down to the huge purple globe his forehead had become by the time Lu Weh led the crowd of stunned villagers through the fragrant night woods to the place beside the tracks where the train had thrown the body. The frail, haunted orphan who had been his best friend the summer he spent with his aunt in Xian Thu province.

Whether the boy was demon-possessed or just in outright despair when he leaped in front of the train, ragged as a scarecrow in the great knowing beam of light, Lu Weh would never know.

His escalating horror notwithstanding, Lu Weh was compelled, now as then, to look and keep looking and take in every detail of the head far past any point of revulsion or pain.

Except that this time the misshapen head did in reality what before it had done only in dreams: opened its swollen eyes and spoke, saying *Why did you go with me? Why did you let me? You knew what I was doing. You knew.*

Except that he *had* and he *hadn't*. (He had since puzzled all this out at great length in a plea for some peace.) Rather, he *hadn't* known and then he *had* but by the time that he *had* (oh, the rancid meat of regret) the transpiring reality was lockstepped precisely one thought ahead of his own. So that no matter how many times he replayed those seconds forward and backward in memory the outcome was in every particular the same, and beyond all fathoming.

The creature took advantage of the instant of Lu Weh's trance to rake blood from both his wrists. The new slashes caught with such nettle-fire that this time he managed to hurl the hatchling far into the midst of the heap, where it made only a momentary ripple before it sank back into the general population. He was assessing the damage to his arms when he heard a different pitch of noise come from the farthest edge of the pile.

Gradually he became aware of pale shapes at either edge of his vision, approaching him. He blinked, and blinked again, but they stayed what they seemed: the most incredibly beautiful human babies he had ever seen or imagined. Twins, toddling naked toward him on a sort of walkway that extended the length of the rock rim.

By instinct he began performing the sacred mental gymnastics that are traditionally used to test for the presence of hallucinations and other illusions. To the last, the tests drew a full blank; the twins, with their reality assured, picked up speed until the nearer one tripped and tumbled headfirst toward the rock wall Lu Weh was braced against.

He grabbed for the baby just in time and lifted it up by its armpits, tender as chamois, to face him. He was rewarded with a peal of giggles and an adoring smile. As he experimented with the various mouth sounds he had perfected when his nieces and nephews were small he lost sight for a moment of the other twin until a flash of motion drew his eye.

By then the twig-sized dart was already in midair, and though he ducked violently, the movement came too late to avoid the sharp tip lodging near his temple. Coronas of pain radiated from the point of penetration. Before he could set down the baby he held, it leaped or flew directly at his face, a dervish of tiny fingers clawing at his eyes, his mouth, his nostrils, with the strength of a mountain cat.

Then like lightning the one who'd shot him was on him too—now he could see the dart pipe on the thong at its neck—targeting its flurry of blows on the area of his shoulders and chest that was exposed above the rock rim.

His foothold on the sheer face of the wall suddenly seemed meager indeed. If he raised his arms to flail back at his attackers he lost his slight purchase on staying upright, so he found himself fighting with one arm and holding to the rock with the other. This gave his face some small relief from the hail of knocks and scratches but also let the overall progress of the struggle, he saw now, go against him.

Each time he regained his hold on the wall his grip was a little less substantial. Fraction by fraction his center of gravity was being forced back, back. The pain was receding enough to be bearable, but he was sensing some new menace in its effect that his mind couldn't immediately calculate—a lethargy, but more than that, a . . .

As a small contingent of neurons near the base of his brain stem followed their brothers into the encroaching white oblivion they offered up a message they hoped Lu Weh might find of use: a page of some sacred text he had read long ago, offering practical instruction on the confrontation of demons.

Unlike agents of good, the text said, evil spirits are bound and obliged to identify themselves if you demand it of them, face to face. Or, if the demon is not of sufficient heft or consequence to rate a name, it's then obliged to name for you its higher-up (or technically, lower-down), the being whose immediate will and purpose it is working upon the world at that moment.

But when Lu Weh opened his mouth to make the demand he found himself suddenly bereft of speech, and only then did he discern the true effect of the dart's quick poison: not paralysis or sedation, but loss of memory. He couldn't speak because he had forgotten what he was going to ask, then he forgot that he was even going to ask anything. But then he forgot that he'd forgot and so remembered.

As he opened his mouth and formed the first word, though, the being nearest his head had prescience enough to forestall what would come next by cramming its entire tiny fist inside his mouth. Lu Weh was able to free himself from choking only by pulling sharply away and striking at his adversaries with both hands. It was not until he felt himself released backwards into the pure startled air that he remembered he'd forgotten he needed one hand to hold on with.

Plummeting in free fall through the nettle-smelling red darkness, his ears whistling, he felt his cells of memory and cognition winking out one by one like extinguished stars until the galaxy of his former thoughts was whittled down to a bare Pleiades of ideas. Then even those began blinking away as if being shot out by a carnival marksman until only two remained and the most vocal of the two screamed its message *name name name name name* and at its imperative he shouted upward into the receding vortex of conscious light at whose apex two small faces, white as peeled onions against the overhang of stone, watched his descent.

When he shouted up at them *Who is your master?* the name they shouted back in unison was not one of the infernal deities he had learned about in the sacred texts but, to his surprise, an English-sounding name, one he thought he had heard before but couldn't place.

When he tried to file the answer in his brain, though, the cell that had been so intent on obtaining it had become inert. So as his ears juggled the fresh name with no destination for it, the name's faint neural existence was immediately drowned out by a far more urgent message from the last remaining cell, which ordered him to discorporate with all haste before he struck the ground and was killed.

Discorporate discorporate discorporate it roared. *Discorporate discorporate.* Then realizing with panic the luxury of syllables at such a point in the plummet it amended its command to a more efficient *go go go go.*

Lu Weh finally managed to marshal all his energy into discorporation, a bare gnat's-width before his right buttock—lowermost at that instant in his tumbling fall—would have led his splatterment into the ground, and in achieving transit left in his stead only the barest suggestion of pink mist through which the dislodged dart passed to impale itself in the sand as the final echo of the name vanished past all usability.

9

"TELL ME THIS," the daytime mechanic asked Turner, wiping his hands on a rag after his initial inspection of the van's dead engine, "when hit quit, did hit make like a *chit-chit-chit?* Or was hit more of a *chub-chub-chub?*" The boy was exceedingly earnest-faced, a teenage Charles Bronson in a Valvoline baseball cap.

All around them, Yazoo City was coming to Monday-morning life. At the Ford dealership next door a workman with one arm was busy hosing down trucks in the explosive sunshine.

Turner yielded the question to Wah So, who stood by with a purposeful look waiting to perform what had become his official function whenever the van quit. *"Uh . . . sklhk sklhk . . . uh . . . sklhk sklhk,"* Wah So said.

The mechanic stroked his mustache gravely. "That'd rule out the manifold. Hit'd make more of a *urmp-urmp-urmp*."

Wah So nodded, excited. "Two song," he said.

"Say what?"

Turner interpreted, explaining that the manifold had been the cause of their breakdown in Tucson, and then excused himself to go look for Lu Weh. He was beginning to get worried. Louie frequently went on all-night expeditions, but he'd never failed to show up for breakfast before. After a particularly grueling transit he sometimes required three omelets and a couple of stacks of pancakes just to knock the edge off his appetite.

But back at the room there was still no sign of Lu Weh, the clothes on the bathroom floor untouched. Turner felt a nagging fear he'd mixed up his coordinates again. When Lu Weh had his full concentration he could transit on a dime. But if he got the least bit rattled his accuracy went totally to hell.

The day he'd run afoul of the ladies' club in East Canton, for instance, he was in such a hurry to escape that he misfigured and touched down in a city park a mile and a half from the motel the monks were staying at. He crouched naked in some shrubbery for nearly an hour before he was able to talk a bag lady out of one of her grocery sacks, which he wore like an oversized brown diaper to get himself home.

As Turner was leaving the room to round up the monks for breakfast he noticed his telephone's red message light was blinking. The mechanic with some more questions, surely. Nobody else knew they were here. Or maybe the motel's front desk. He had a sinking feeling. Had his Visa card been refused? He knew he'd mailed the payment. A few days late, but still.

When he phoned the desk, though, the number the clerk gave him to call had a California area code. Urgent, the man said. Turner recognized it as Lucille's number, at home. Why would . . . ? His first thought was that something had happened to his grandparents. With a rising dread, he punched the digits.

"Yello?"

"Hi, Lucille. Turner. Is something wrong? It must be three in the morning, where you are."

"Nothing wrong, babe. Something *right.*"

"What do you mean? And how did you find us, anyhow?"

"Aw, that's the easy part. Call every flea-bag dump along your route. Just another friendly service of StarShine Talent. Listen, babe, you got a pencil? Here's how you can earn back momma's phone bill."

"Just a sec. Okay, pencil at the ready. Shoot."

"All right. You know that Birmingham gig?"

"Don't tell me they're canceling."

"*Au contraire,* punkin. How'd you like to play a bigger hall?"

"How much bigger?"

"Ever hear of a band called the Wizened Lizards?"

"Sure."

"Well, they're playing Birmingham tonight. Whatever the big stadium is there . . ."

"Legion Field? Listen, what has this got to do with . . ."

"Right, right. Now, the Lizards' warm-up band is called Poison. So Lucille hears through the grapevine that Poison is sidelined in Richmond for a few days and can't make the trip. They've got food poisoning. Ain't that a hoot?"

"Wait a minute. You're not saying . . ."

"It's okay. Don't thank me."

"Lucille, I appreciate the hell out of it, really. But the guys have . . ."

"' . . . never played a crowd this big before.'"

"And a heavy metal audience? They'd eat us for dinner. Besides, the van's broken down, and Louie's off God-knows-where in some bushes, and . . ."

"But babe, Zotfeld's having wet dreams about it. *USA Today* thinks it's a great idea. The guys' first big break, East meets West, all that crap."

"Zotfeld? Oh, shit. *He*'d be there?"

"Listen to momma, sweets. Go look in the mirror, okay? This is not some local yokel I'm talking to. This is the great Turner. The legend. Have you ever missed a show? Huh?"

"But . . ."

"Huh? Of course not. Go get 'em, tiger. Peckers-in-the-dirt, okay? Showtime's at eight. Make momma proud."

When Turner hung up he looked at his watch and did some calculating. Clearly the side trip to Zion Hill was out, but if the van got fixed within the next, say, two hours, and if Lu Weh showed up and if nothing else went wrong—hell of a lot of *ifs*—they could make it to Birmingham with an hour to spare. Which was the absolute minimum time he'd need to go over some rudimentary lighting cues with the Lizards' road crew, do a sound check, and . . .

No. This was insane. They weren't ready. Exposure's all well and good, but not if you end up looking like some damned oddity—especially with a national reporter to chronicle it for posterity. No, the sensible thing would be to call Lucille back and beg off. She'd be hacked, but she'd get over it.

But as he picked up the phone, a scene flashed onto his mind's eye so vividly that he wondered for a moment if old Won Se back at Drepung was using some sort of telepathy on him. What he saw was the floor-to-ceiling abacus in the War Room, the Tally of Inner Blindness.

When the confrontation with the realm comes, Won Se had explained, a terrible disparity occurs—while the personages of evil can fight freely and unfettered, the Hope is encumbered by a sort of invisible ball and chain around his heart, one whose weight is composed of all the inner blindness remaining in the world at that moment.

Won Se's eyes had looked immensely saddened as he told Turner this, while monks scurried around in the shadows of the abacus updating the tally. "So you see why you must spread the news of the path, until the Calling Out occurs," Won Se had concluded. "Even though you can only affect a, how you say, tidbit of the blindness. One person, inner blind, could be the . . . break that strews the back camel, if you will."

Turner had let the figure of speech go uncorrected. "How come the realm gets to make all the rules?" he asked.

"You will have a chance to ask them," Won Se had said.

The tour was making such slow progress at lessening the blindness tally that Turner had lately quit asking Won Se for a reading when they talked on the phone. "Blindness is down," Won Se would say when Turner asked. But when he asked "How *much* down?" Won Se only answered, "You do well."

Turner was halfway through punching Lucille's number when he stopped and slammed down the phone. By God, let's do it, he thought. If converting eighty thousand screaming adolescents isn't a sufficient chunk to register on the tally, Drepung ought to get a new abacus.

He got out his notebook and started writing reminders to himself about details of the monks' act that might need polishing in order to be ready for major public consumption. No pandering, though, he decided. No frills. Authentic to the bone, that was the way to go. Rub the kids' very noses in the wonder of it.

Turner's adrenaline was pumping as it had pumped in days of old. He stuck the notebook in his pocket and got up to go tell the guys the news. Now if the van will just get fixed, he thought, and Lu Weh shows up, and nothing else goes wrong . . .

But then the door of his room flew open—monks had no use for knocking—and a stern-faced Chai Lo stomped into the room with Beh Vah in tow, the youngster looking angry and confused, his eyes wet from crying, and Turner knew immediately that something else *had* gone wrong. Very wrong.

At that moment Lu Weh hit butt-first on the bathroom tile, the clumsy kind of landing he always made when he had to discorporate in a hurry. The impact shot a bolt of pain upward from his tailbone. He rested his head on the commode lid, out of breath, and gingerly felt all around his hindquarters until he'd satisfied himself nothing was broken.

At least he hadn't missed the target altogether, like he'd done the time the lady leaf-rake warriors were chasing him. He stood up to relieve himself but when he bent forward to raise the toilet seat he became so dizzy he almost fell over. He had to sit and pee like a woman while he waited for his head to clear.

As he did so, he slowly became aware of a terrible stinging in his arms and chest. By the dim light from under the door he could barely make out great black scratches crisscrossing from his navel to his breastbone and along both wrists, caked with what he determined was blood. What . . . ? When . . . ?

He was certain he had just returned from a transit because of the telltale tingling of his atoms, still abuzz like hornets in a jar. But for his life's sake he couldn't remember where he'd gone or what had happened there. Just red . . . shadows, and . . . what else? Nothing else. Nothing.

He flushed the toilet and got up, feeling for the light switch so he could assess the damage in the mirror. The switch wasn't where he remembered it. He patted higher, lower, along another wall, all with no success. He permitted himself a mild oath.

His hand was on the doorknob to the bedroom when he remembered his nakedness and it occurred to him that Turner might still be awake. Not wanting to alarm him with the blood, he thought better of opening the door and squatted down to feel for the robe he had vacated in his transit. But he found only cool bare tile the whole width of the floor, and permitted himself a more strenuous oath. Turner must have picked the robe up.

Lu Weh had no choice. He opened the door to the room, one arm protectively across his worst wounds. "Tur-ner?" he whispered. No reply.

When he opened the door wider he saw that some sorcerer had been here in his absence, redistributing the world. Where the sparse motel furniture had been, there was now a richly carpeted hallway the color of caramel cake with rooms opening off on either side.

Lu Weh tiptoed along the hall looking for anything familiar, but the doors to all the rooms were shut. All but the one at the end, cracked an inch or so. He pushed it gently.

"Tur-ner?" he whispered into the dark. Then louder, his fear rising. "*Tur-ner?*"

The only reply was a small questioning grunt, the half-word of someone roused from sleep. But uttered in a small, pure voice. Not Turner.

Lu Weh found the light switch and the black room blazed open into a carnival of light: bright-colored cartoon animals on all the walls, a ceiling of midnight blue dotted with silver constellations.

And a canopied bed with a tiny blonde-haired girl in it, sitting up rubbing her eyes as if she couldn't believe what she saw. "Whizzard!" she said, pointing at Lu Weh. "Teevee!"

With an excited squeal she threw back the covers and toddled unsteadily toward him, wearing only pink-frilled panties. Something of her sudden rushing movement made him draw back, made a chill of panic race over him, something dimly remembered . . . from the red . . . shadow place . . .

But when her insubstantial weight collided with his knee and gave his leg a bear-hug and her big sleep-caked blue eyes looked up at him, his heart melted and he knelt down to hold her.

"Play?" he asked. "Pat cake?"

She nodded enthusiastically and held out her small pink palms, challenging him to make the first slap. He patted tentatively at first, then their motions began picking up speed. Tiny as she was, she knew variations of rhythm and impact he had not explored yet with the other monks. He made mental notes of the most impressive ones, for showing to Beh Vah when he could figure out where the sorcerer had put him.

The girl squealed with laughter. "Pat cake whizzard!" she said. "Teevee!" Lu Weh laughed too, at her uncontained glee.

A *thud-thud-thud* intruded from somewhere outside their circus of warm light. Frightened running feet. Nearer. Then more feet, heavier THUD-THUD-THUD and a woman screaming to fill the whole world and a man's voice behind him *Bastard* the last thing he heard before a great ceramic weight exploded against the crown of his head, tumbling him forward into a blackness with no sound.

"OUR VEHICLE IS repaired," Chai Lo said, standing before Turner in the motel room with Beh Vah's skinny arm turning white in the grip of his left hand. Chai said it sarcastically, his face almost in a sneer. Beh Vah looked at the walls, the floor, everywhere but at Turner sitting on the bed, and every few seconds he was shaken by hiccups that threatened to turn back into sobbing again.

"Okay, guys, spill it," Turner said. "What's wrong?"

"Better to ask our young star, perhaps," Chai Lo replied, his voice dripping with irony. Turner noticed he had one hand behind his back, as if concealing a surprise. The other hand tightened its hold on Beh Vah's forearm, making him flinch. Beaver raised his head and stared defiantly at a point two feet above Turner's eyes.

"I don't have time to play games," Turner told Chai Lo. "Look, we have sit-down every Friday to work out our differences. Can't it wait?"

"You be judge," Chai Lo said. "I found . . ."

Beh Vah couldn't hold his rage any longer. "Det," he said, shaking his head violently. Again, louder, as his tears started: "*Det!*" In Tibetan it was the strongest possible denial of a thing. Most Tibetan words were notoriously lax on the idea of tense, but *det* combined all tenses in one quick explosion of teeth and tongue: *Did not have not will not could not no no no no no.*

In answer Chai Lo flung down the contents of his hidden hand onto the pink chenille bedspread: a wadded scrap of black cloth, no bigger than a playing card. Turner picked the scrap up and unfolded it. It looked like a piece of washcloth that had been used to clean engine parts. It smelled of oil and gasoline.

"Why are you showing me this?"

"From our carbohydrate," Chai said. "Ask him."

"From our *what*?"

"Carbon . . . ate?"

"Carburetor?" Turner offered.

Chai Lo nodded furiously.

"Chai, I don't have time for . . ."

"*Look* at it," Chai commanded, his voice rising toward hysteria.

With a sigh, Turner leaned over to hold the scrap under the bedside lamp. The pressure is getting to Shy, he thought. He needs a break. Hell, don't we all.

Turner smoothed out the scrap in his palm, trying not to get the oil on his fingers. The bright lamp showed glints of gold inside the greasy nap of the terrycloth. Metallic threads that made letters: *E* . . . *N* . . . part of an *O*.

"I don't get it," Turner said, and then it struck him. Reno. Home of Beh Vah's cherished bath towel.

"Det," Beh Vah said, a hateful whisper. He pulled himself out of Chai Lo's grasp and sank down on the edge of the bed like a scolded child, his head on Turner's shoulder.

"They would not listen before," Chai Lo said. "Perhaps now."

"*Who* wouldn't listen?"

"Won Se. The elders. Not their sweet boy. Surely not."

"Wait," Turner put in. "You're saying . . . ?"

"He was on prayer duty the night the mandala was torn apart. 'Happens dance,' Won Se said. Now this." He indicated the scrap of towel. "This happens dance, too?"

Beh Vah burrowed deeper into Turner's shoulder. Turner reached to pat his knee. "It'll be okay, buddy," he said. The youngster's breathing quietened somewhat.

"Okay," Turner said. "Devil's advocate, here. Say he did it." Beh Vah raised up indignantly, glaring at him. "Just say," Turner repeated, patting his knee again. "Hypothetical," he explained. Beh Vah turned his head away, unappeased.

"You can't have a crime without a motive," Turner said to Chai Lo. "Why would Beaver work against us? What could he gain?"

"It is clear you do not know the Chojung," Chai Lo said—a bit condescendingly, Turner thought. He pictured the roomful of worn volumes, each the size of an unabridged dictionary and written in a patois of obscure Tibetan dialects spanning several centuries.

"Not by heart, no," Turner said. "Which part? Specifically."

"The part of the Betrayer," said Chai Lo. "With a Hope, also a Betrayer. Most usually a friend. A least-expected. In your scripture, a . . . dude's chariot, if you will."

"Judas Iscariot?"

"Whatever. Won Se did not tell you of this?"

Turner looked around to see Beh Vah's big, guileless brown eyes staring back at him. Somehow he didn't quite look the part of a traitor.

"No, he didn't mention it."

"An oversight," Chai Lo said, his voice sweet with sarcasm. "You remember, in your own scripture. The one who laid his head on the master's breast." He smiled at Beh Vah, who stiffened and stared daggers back at him.

Turner said, "So you're saying there *has* to be a Betrayer. Always."

Chai Lo wouldn't quite meet Turner's eyes with his. "Almost always," he said. "Sometimes two."

"Sometimes two," Turner repeated. "But sometimes *none*, right?"

Chai Lo nodded grudgingly.

Turner wadded the blackened scrap of towel and threw it at the phone table, missing. "I asked about motive," he said.

"Heart's desire," Chai Lo answered. "Riches. Lust. Famousness. All held out on a platter, by the rim, for a Betrayer who succeeds." He didn't refer to Beh Vah's vulnerabilities in that regard. He didn't have to.

There was a knock at the door. That would be Lu Weh, Turner thought with relief, getting up quickly to open it. Of course he wouldn't have his key. At least with Louie back there was one less thing to worry about.

He opened the door. It was two men in police uniforms, their caps in their hands.

"Mornin'," the bigger man said, without expression. "We're lookin' for some friends of a Mister Louis . . ." He examined his clipboard. "Louis . . . Whey?"

Turner's heart knocked in his ribs. "What's wrong? Is he hurt?"

The man held out his hand to shake. "Sergeant Grimes," he said. "You'd be Mister Turner?" The shorter officer peered around the other one's arm, suspiciously eyeing the two monks.

"I *said*, is he okay?"

"Yessir, in a manner of speakin'. But we got a pretty big little problem, here. I think you need to come with us."

THE YAZOO CITY police chief's cramped office was a maze of paperwork and styrofoam coffee cups, all overlaid with a gray haze from the Winstons he chain-smoked while listening to Turner's story. Over his shoulder, an old black-and-white TV, its sound turned down, showed commercials for pancake syrup and used cars.

Turner gave his best shot at explaining how no real crime had been committed, just a cultural misunderstanding brought about by Lu Weh's poor sense of direction. He left out the part about the transiting and, of course, the part about the realm's accelerated attacks on their frail, besieged mission to save humanity from destruction, of which Louie's arrest was most likely part of the latest volley.

Instead he spun a compelling narrative which touched on the monks' impeccable moral fiber, how easy it is to get lost in a strange place, and how appearances can be deceiving, and then topped it all off with the honest country-boy smile that had long been his most powerful negotiating tool, a smile which he had partly modeled on the painting which hung in his boyhood Sunday School room, of Jesus sitting among the little children.

The chief responded with a long silence and a skeptical fish-eye. He was a balding, hang-jowled man with a drooping mustache, whose slick three-piece suit looked out of place in the massive shabbiness and disorder that surrounded him. He kept glancing around his office, nervous from the sudden incursion of visitors.

Wah So, Se Hon, and Bah Tow fingered his office's wall-hangings with the curiosity of schoolkids. Chai Lo stared darkly out the window. Beh Vah, in his shame, sat on the floor with his knees up and his head buried in his arms. The dark exclamation point that was James Crowe paced restlessly, cracking his knuckles and keeping an ear toward the conversation—the only black person, Turner realized, he'd seen since they got into town.

"Now, all of what you're saying may be true as gospel," the chief said to Turner, stubbing out his cigarette. It was clear from his tone of voice he didn't think so. "But what we got right here is the facts . . ." He tapped on the clipboard that held the arrest report. "And the facts is all a law enforcement officer's got to go on, am I making myself clear?"

As Turner was nodding his understanding, Se Hon knelt at the desk alongside his elbow, holding open a thick volume of the criminal code he'd found on a shelf. The monk's expression, even more nearsighted than usual, was the tip-off that he was primed for an intellectual discussion.

"Are you a criminal," he asked the chief, "or just us?"

"Criminal *justice*," Turner rushed to interpret, as the chief glowered. "He's asking if you're in criminal justice." Then, to Se Hon, "Buddy, this needs to wait. We're talking some important stuff, okay?"

"Do you kill people?" Se Hon pressed on, with great concern. "Do you punish them with big letters?"

"Punish . . . ?" Turner wracked his brain. "Uh, *capital* punishment is what he's asking about," he told the chief, forcing a smile. Then, patting Se Hon's arm, "Really, bud, this is not the time. We'll talk later." Se Hon wandered off dejectedly to the corner of the room and attempted to read the big book again, holding it close to his face.

The chief sighed and looked at Turner. "I'll read the charges in order," he said. "'Criminal trespass, breaking and entering . . .'"

Turner interrupted before he thought. "He *didn't* break and enter, he . . ."

The chief looked up from the list expectantly. "He what?"

Turner was trapped. The truth would only make matters worse. He held his peace.

But the chief wouldn't let it rest. "If he didn't break and enter, then he just . . . materialized in these good people's house. *Whoooom*. Like a ghost, you're saying." He covered his mouth with his hand to keep from breaking into a grin.

What the hell, Turner thought. How could things be worse? Give truth a chance.

"It's called 'transiting,'" he said.

The fish-eye again. "What is?"

"The process they use to travel great distances by pure force of mind," Turner said. "They train the atoms of their bodies to vibrate in a certain way that lets them bypass the time-space continuum. That way, their bodies can 'discorporate' in one place, and then 're-incorporate' in another."

A long silence ensued. Without taking his eyes off Turner, the chief shook two Winstons out of his pack and lit them both at once. The soundless television on the shelf was showing the morning news. A reporter with a microphone motioned toward the giant redwood tree in the highway behind him, surrounded by a growing traffic jam. *Last night,* read a graphic across the bottom of the screen. Flashbulbs popped throughout the milling crowd.

The chief took a powerful draw of double-barreled nicotine and stood up at his desk, a vantage point from which he could eye Turner head-to-toe. Judging from his expression, Turner thought, he appeared also to be gauging the distance to the door in case he needed to make a run for it.

But then he looked at Turner again and his face softened. He took the pair of cigarettes out in order to exhale, and erupted into an enthusiastic belly-laugh.

"You really had me going there for a minute, you know it?" He sauntered over to Turner and punched him fraternally on the shoulder, then shadow-boxed several steps backwards. "Sunva bitch," the chief said, still laughing and shaking his head. He walked across to his office door, looked both ways, shut it, and returned to his desk, giving Turner a conspiratorial wink.

"Seriously, though," the chief said. "Let's get down to the nut-cuttin', here." He turned the arrest report around so that it faced Turner, and took out his ink pen to draw a line through the first two charges.

"These here, we can take or leave," he said. "But *this* sucker . . ." He hammered the third line hard with his penpoint. Turner read *Sexual molestation of . . .* and had to look away, his stomach in his throat. "We got some serious shit, here, excuse my French. Because your complainant is not your everyday Dick or Harry off the street. He's the city council president. Man that signs my paycheck. Com-pren-day?"

He scanned Turner's face to see if the gravity of the situation had registered. Satisfied, he went on: "In other words, if I don't get a conviction, it's safe to say they'll hang my balls from the courthouse clock and spend two hours drawing a crowd to watch."

Turner thought of Lu Weh's defeated face in his cell, minutes before, the bandage around his head tied in a rough bow on top that made him look like an aging schoolgirl waiting for someone to ask her to dance.

"What if I could get the complaint dropped?" Turner asked. "Just let me talk directly to the girl's parents, and I think we could straighten all this out." He looked at his watch. He would have to talk beautifully, and very fast, if they had any hope of making the show in Birmingham tonight.

"Not very likely," the chief said, with what seemed like satisfaction. "They just left for a week on the coast, to recuperate from all this upset."

"What about bail?"

"The judge sets bail."

"Could you call him and see how much it is?" Turner thought ruefully of the profits from his cut of the Stones' tour, still piling up daily in neat certificates of deposit in his off-limits bank accounts. Damn the Book of Rules. He'd have to throw himself on the mercy of the local bail-bond shop, maybe get Lucille to co-sign, and . . .

"No need to call," the chief said cheerfully. "I can tell you right now how much bail is."

"Good. How much?"

"Five dollars more than you've got. The city signs the *judge's* paycheck, too, you see."

Turner drummed his fingers on the desk for several seconds, his mind firing blanks. With a good enough breakfast in him, Lu Weh could transit from his cell to the van in an eye-blink. And with luck, if the jailer didn't notice him gone until they had enough of a head start to . . .

But it was no use. Springing Louie would buy them a few hours, at best, and then the situation would be worse than ever. You couldn't exactly go underground with six performing monks in your charge.

"Excuse me a minute," he said, and stood up. "James? Conference, please."

When they had stepped just outside the door Turner said to Crowe, "I think we need a miracle, bad. Excuse me . . . a supervention."

Crowe looked sorely troubled by the suggestion. "But Cap'n, sir, we've only got . . ."

"Two left, and the final confrontation hasn't even started; I know, I know. *You* analyze the problem, then. Show me some of this stuff you're so hot at." Turner's face tingled with embarrassment after the words slipped out. Sure, Crowe's roadside character analysis the night before—"*They said you were lacking in long-term strategizing* . . ."—had stung him, but damned if he wanted it to show. "Scratch that," Turner said. "I apologize. What I'm saying is, I'm open for ideas."

Crowe's pout was of very short duration before he took him up on the request to analyze things, marked by his immediately going into a kind of analytical trance in which his eyes moved rapidly by microscopic increments as if examining and discarding a list of alternatives that was very long—at least ten to the fourth power, say.

Finally he looked at Turner and shrugged resignedly. "I see your point, Cap'n," he said. "What you got in mind?"

10

TURNER DROVE through the outskirts of town with the windows down, marveling for the second time in as many days at how inexpressibly sweet the everyday air smells just after you've escaped the bowels of confinement. But the slamming of cell doors still echoed at the fringes of his memory, and he couldn't resist glancing in the mirror every now and then to reassure himself that Lu Weh was in fact with them.

He was. Somewhat the worse for wear, true; he kept tenderly touching the huge knot on his head he'd gotten from the enraged homeowner and wincing. He even interrupted a spirited patty-cake session between Se Hon and Wah So, calling for silence by pointing to his cranium and pantomiming a person in the throes of death.

The Yazoo City police had apologized profusely for detaining Louie, and the chief handed out baleful tongue-lashings to his men who were involved in the arrest after they admitted, one by one, that they hadn't the foggiest idea why they'd brought the monk in or how he'd gotten his head-knot. A thorough search of their paperwork turned up no clues either; apparently the officers had forgotten to fill out an arrest report.

But Turner remained unconvinced at heart. He wished like hell they weren't so pressed for time, so they could avoid taking the interstate up ahead and go a less conspicuous back-road route to Birmingham, in case the police had second thoughts and radioed ahead for a roadblock. Just then a Mississippi Highway Patrol car pulled out from an intersection and fell in line directly behind them. Turner's knuckles turned white on the steering wheel, and he let out a gasp.

"*Chill*, Cap'n," James Crowe said. "We're fine. We're free as the breeze. Don't you trust me?"

"Oh, I trust *you*. I'm just afraid something might remind them, and . . . "

"Nothing to be reminded *of*. It never happened, see? Once I collapsed the wave function into this outcome, it's history. So to speak. It *stays* collapsed."

As if in demonstration, the patrol car on their back bumper slowed and turned off leisurely into the parking lot of a coffee shop. The blood flowed back into Turner's knuckles.

"But if it never happened," he argued, "how come *we* still know about it?"

Crowe sighed patiently. "Because we're the progenitors."

"Of . . . ?"

"Of the initiative that *predicated* the function collapse. So in that sense we're external to the causality loop."

"James? Translation, please. Simplify."

Crowe smiled broadly. "We cool."

Signs flashed past, alerting them of the imminent interstate. At a stoplight, Turner pulled into the turn lane for the entrance ramp. He glanced at his watch. Then shook it, thumped at the crystal.

"Damn," he said. "What time do you have, James? My watch must have stopped."

"Nine-fifteen, sir."

"*Nine*-fifteen? That's impossible. We were at the police station for at least two hours, and then breakfast, and then . . . " Directly across the street, the message board of a small savings-and-loan blinked out the time and temperature: *78°,* it said. *9:16.*

"The supervention, Cap'n," Crowe said. "When it negated the circumstance, it excised the length of time the circumstance had existed. See, in terms of particle states, just think of it as . . . "

"I'll take your word for it," Turner said, as the light changed. Instead of veering toward the on-ramp he made a sharp U-turn. "Now we've got time to go the back road."

He didn't realize how frequently he was still checking the rear-view mirror for blue lights until Crowe began clucking his tongue.

"O, ye of little faith," Crowe said.

By now it had dawned on the monks that the accursed interstate was to be avoided and a raucous cheer went up, which was cut short when Louie clamped his hands over his ears, wincing, and shushed them vigorously in the name of his headache.

"I'm just in the mood for a scenic route," Turner told James. "All right?"

As he turned onto tree-lined old Highway 11—a narrow two-lane with crumbling shoulders—the monks, in deference to Lu Weh, re-did their cheering in immaculate pantomime, clapping and shouting and raising their arms triumphantly, all in perfect silence.

WHEN THEY STOPPED for gas in Carrollton, Alabama, James Crowe pointed out a brochure in a rack at the service station advertising the town's sole tourist attraction, The Face in the Courthouse Window. Turner remembered seeing it once when he was a kid. Purported to be the ghostly visage of a black prisoner, supernaturally frozen onto the attic pane of glass by a massive lightning bolt as he looked out on the lynch mob which would in minutes storm the courthouse and haul him off, it dated from the 1950s Dark Ages before the concept of civil rights made its turbulent inroads into the region.

The face phenomenon seriously intrigued James Crowe, having as it did obvious overtones of physics beyond its historical value. He and the monks lobbied Turner for a side trip, and because they were making excellent time due to the gratis hours Crowe's equation had afforded them he relented. Minutes later, they found themselves standing on the almost-deserted courthouse square in the sleepy noontime heat feeding quarters into an ancient sightseeing telescope focused on the upstairs window.

The monks let James use the scope first, since the excursion was his idea, but even without magnification the smeared blotch of face was clearly visible in the low-left quadrant of pane—white on the darkness of the window, like a photographic negative. Through the telescope you could make out, with only minimal imagination, the nuances of the man's terrified expression and moreover distinguish something of the medium of his entrapment—a sort of frosty suspension, overlaid with the faint rainbow sheen of an oil slick on water, that appeared to be contained almost hologram-like within the glass.

A property which no doubt gave rise to the assertion in the brochure text that the manifestation had proven impervious to all manner of cleansers from Windex to high-test gasoline on down, and that once when the more conscience-ridden of the community conspired to remove the affected pane altogether and replace it with an untainted one, the heavens raged all night with an unseasonable electrical storm and by morning the face was back, precisely as before.

The monks one by one had a long look through the eyepiece without comment. Then Beh Vah, whose turn was last by deference of age, said "He must be proud."

The other monks had drifted off toward a narrow kiddie park at the next corner where some of them were already flying in lazy arcs on the swings, just visible above the bright-colored fencing.

"Proud? Why's that, Beaver?" Turner asked.

"To be so much loved," Beh Vah beamed innocently. "That they would make him a, how you say, monument. He must be a good worker for them."

Turner looked around to see if James had heard the exchange. Their eyes met and he knew he had.

"No, Beaver," Turner began. "See, what happened . . . "

But Crowe, just out of Beh Vah's vision, was signaling Turner with a solid head-shake, *No*. Don't spoil it for him, his expression seemed to say. Don't uncork the whole race nightmare for him now, when his energies need to be focused toward the show tonight.

Besides, it had been a major leap of faith that a youngster, whose religious training since infancy had been the wholesale effacement of the self, could spontaneously see the merits of singling out someone for personal recognition. He would make Drepung a good, tolerant master someday, Turner thought, Chai Lo's jealousy be damned.

But Beh Vah hung on Turner's interrupted sentence. "'No,' what?" he prompted.

"No, he, uh . . . " Turner stumbled. "He doesn't actually *work* at the courthouse. He works somewhere else."

Lu Weh appeared then, tugging at Turner's sleeve and pointing out the tall Dairy Queen sign at the end of the next block. His massive post-transiting breakfast must have been wearing thin.

"Round up the guys and we'll walk over there," Turner told him, looking at his watch. "We can get some sandwiches and eat while we drive."

He had an afterthought. "Louie?" he shouted. "Remind everybody no sugar or salt packets, okay? Use them there; don't take them with you. I mean it." Turner put his arm around Beh Vah as they walked. The youngster returned his embrace, but at the news of the sugar prohibition he sighed wearily and rolled his eyes.

Barely a mile out of town, just as the Dairy Queen bounty was being apportioned throughout the van, they passed a small white A-frame church that sat off the road in a grove of hardwoods on a slight incline of grass.

Turner had to blink to make sure he wasn't hallucinating this, because it was an exact double of the old church of his childhood, Zion Hill Baptist.

Though the sign out front said Mineral Springs Independent Fellowship, it looked to be the same building, down to the board and shingle—even down to the outdoor toilet, and the row of concrete picnic tables out back where such heavenly lunches used to be spread during cemetery Decoration Day and all-day gospel singings. "Dinner on the ground" was the formal term, "ground" having over the years been shortened from "grounds," which led to ongoing confusion among the youngsters. Every time an all-day singing announcement was made from the pulpit, kids would elbow their parents and ask why did they have to eat on the ground, when they had tables?

Zion Hill. Turner had slowed the van and began pulling onto the shoulder of the road before he realized it, for a longer look. Sure, there were only so many ways to *build* a church, but . . .

So exact.

About that time the monks spotted the shady oasis of picnic tables and a general buzz went up requesting they stop and eat there. Turner got his road map out, used his knuckle-length to measure the miles to Birmingham, and consulted his watch.

"Twenty minutes," he pronounced. "Then we have to be back on the road. Absolutely have to." Lu Weh covered his ears in anticipation of the celebratory outburst, but though animated it was blessedly soundless.

After he got everyone situated at the tables Turner took his burger and quietly walked the circumference of the church building, marveling again at the similarity. Even the cemetery, extending down the hillside to the east where a caretaker on a riding lawn mower slowly circled the graves in the baking sun, was so similar to the one back home he had the eerie feeling that if he walked to the outer edge of it he would find a gravestone with his parents' names.

He walked up the concrete front steps to get a look through the window, see if the resemblance prevailed inside as well. But the small diamond-shaped panes in the doors were just frosted enough to prevent him from seeing in. Ah, well.

Before he turned to go, he reached by reflex to rattle the doorknob, and to his surprise the door wasn't locked. While he looked toward the far-off caretaker again, deciding whether or not he should go in, the building's trapped heat of the day breathed out at him like a conscious act, carrying the familiar scent of hymnals and varnished wood, the chlorine residue of the baptistry, the infinitesimal traces of perfume and aftershave and talcum and mentholated ointment that accumulated and blended in any confined space inhabited mostly by the old.

He went in.

The pulpit. The pews. The black spidery fans in the ceiling. The framed Church Covenant on the back wall, alongside the painting of Jesus with the little children. The "Attendance" board that showed with moveable cardboard numbers how many people were at morning worship, at Sunday School, the amount of the offering.

And though he hadn't been inside Zion Hill Baptist in more than twenty years, he knew immediately beyond question that this place was the same. The same, by God. Every detail. The very same.

His throat tightened. Somebody was telling him something. The damned paisley van, and now this. Not coincidence. For years he'd enjoyed an uneasy peace with his history, and now twice in two days a blast from the past had slammed into his wretched memory bank like a wrecker ball into a dime store piñata, sending fragments of the dark yesterdays tumbling shrapnel-like through his insides.

Why? Just to rattle him, sap his strength for the coming confrontation?

And *who*? Not the realm, apparently, if the tests were to be believed.

Think, Turner. Think. What would James Crowe say, he of the hotshot analytical skills, if he were approaching the situation? Turner sifted through the reams of commentary Crowe had offered so profligately, maddeningly nonstop the past few days regarding the relationship of mathematics to everything under the dadblamed sun, and suddenly a tiny nugget from those thoughts showed itself as gleamingly as gold in a pan.

No, no, no, Cap'n. You're sorting by differences again. That's the fallacy of everybody from Newton on back. The trick is you sort first by commonalities.

Sort by commonalities?

All right, then. What do a paisley VW van and an eerily exact replica of Zion Hill Baptist Church have in common, on the memory continuum?

The answer was so near at hand that he said it out loud without knowing he was going to.

"Cassie."

No, this was clearly not going to be a productive line of reasoning. Not when he'd spent half his life trying to unlearn his mastery of self-flagellation, trying to impersonate a normal individual. Not the time now, to get out the whips again. Clearly not the time, with so much at stake.

Out of here, bud, he thought. *Now.* He walked fast down the hardwood aisle toward the door and his freedom, but as he reached the backmost bench some overpowering magnetism of the heart drained his will and made him stop, hold to the pew-rail for a second, and finally sit down. He stared at the half-eaten hamburger in his lap.

How many years? he asked himself. *How much regret is enough*? If some . . . *person* were forcing him to watch these humbling *deja vu* re-runs rather than merely, as he was coming to suspect, his own pathetic lack of resolve, he would at least have a focus for his anger.

The building's frosted windows all dimmed as if a light switch had been turned off. A cloud over the sun. The only sound in the world was the buzzing of the distant lawn mower.

Then a sudden violent resurgence of sunlight hit the windows like a silent bomb blast, titanium white, glancing and reverberating off all the small sanctuary's polished surfaces: the wood paneling, the picture frames, the implements for Communion. And in that instant the mute language of the light, in some way he didn't even vaguely understand, revealed to him a truth he had heretofore, amazingly enough, camouflaged to himself. Now it reared up, bright and real and unassailable: namely, the talons that raked his heart at times like this weren't in the service of regret, as he'd made himself believe; some part of him had made a kind of peace with the regret. Rudimentary and unadorned, but peace.

The fact.

The fact was, he still loved her. Actively. Devoutly. Loved her. Even though he hadn't seen her in twenty years.

This was sick. This was extremely sick.

This was . . .

The bench. The very bench, the exact spot the two of them had sat the night Cassie dropped her bombshell on the congregation, the night that was to become her last as a member of Zion Hill Baptist Church.

They were . . . what, fourteen? Almost fifteen. Drowning contentedly in the throes of first love. Her father and his grandfather were both deacons, which meant that on the first Sunday night of each month their families had to be there an hour before preaching started while the deacons conducted the business meeting of the church.

This particular August night as they sat on the back bench Turner was so absorbed in the wonder of her, the wonder of *them*, the sweet dampness of her hand, the way her hair barrette caught the light, that throughout his sporadic whispered conversation with her the deacons' sober voices from the front of the sanctuary were not words to him at all but a recurrent low drumbeat of sound, on a par with the buzzing *whock-whock* of the old black ceiling fans.

Until Cassie interrupted his whispering with a finger to her lips, *Shhhh*, and after attuning herself for several seconds to what was being said up front she looked at him with concern and disbelief.

As he surfaced gradually from the subset of her singular face to the doings of the real world he noticed belatedly that there were a lot more early arrivals than usual for the deacons' meeting. The sanctuary was better than half full, and instead of the usual scattered pairs of deacons' wives quietly talking dress-patterns or recipes the congregation was largely men, hushed and expectant whenever the pastor, Brother Worth, or one of the deacons stood to speak.

Worth had the floor now, an intense little red-faced man with receding hair saying, "All I know is, the scriptures tells us to 'Study, and show y'selves approved, workmens that needeth not to be shamed.' And if y'all have been studying this nigra business like I have, you know we need to have us a plan." There were general head-nods, around.

It had been barely two months now, the pastor reminded them, since Governor Wallace had stepped aside from the door of the state university and let the federal marshals escort the first nigras in, or blacks as some of them preferred to be called. And in that short period of time there had been, not six, not seven, not eight, but nine incidents the pastor knew of *personally* where delegations of nigras had been sent to white churches around Birmingham to integrate their Sunday morning services.

And it was usually the case, he noted, that when something started in Birmingham—anything of the devil, whether it was fornication and drugs among young people, or women wearing immodest clothes—mark his words, it was only a matter of time before such like worked its way out to Zion Hill. A matter of time. And it was the same for this integrating, demonstrating business.

He stopped and let the gravity of this sink in. A few people groaned softly; many shook their heads.

"What's surprising to *me*," Brother Worth went on, "is that it ain't been in the papers or anything. I mean, since they're clearly doing it for the publicity. I don't know how it's being kept out of the papers.

"And while I'm on that subject, just let me say a word here in fairness to our nigra brothers and sisters in Christ. If *we* was a third . . . I said a *third* . . . as faithful about visiting the sick and winning the lost to Jesus as they are about this civil riot business, we'd see such a revival break out in this community and in this poor troubled land that even the devil hisself couldn't contain it. Can I get an *amen*?"

A drumbeat of utter silence.

"Amen," a deep voice rang out. Turner recognized it as his grandfather, and felt an inrush of pride. He gently elbowed Cassie and leaned over to whisper to her not to worry, that her father and his grandfather would very shortly set the preacher straight. They were well known to be two of the more moderate people in Zion Hill on the question of the "nigra business"; the only oath Turner had ever heard his grandfather use was toward a black field hand he'd hired one summer who, on his first day at dinnertime, stood wringing his hat in his hand and declined from embarrassment to come inside and eat with the family—just pass him a plate outside, please sah, and he'd sit on the porch steps and eat.

Wrong. If he was too good to eat at Granddaddy's table, he was told, he could damn well find another job.

But when Turner started to whisper a reminder of this to Cassie, she shushed him again and he sat up straight, stung by the rebuff.

Brother Worth still had the floor.

"I've prayed and prayed on this," he was saying, "and I'm sure the rest of y'all have, too. And it's very plain to me there's only one thing *to* do, and stay within the scriptures, if some nigras was to show up next Sunday morning and try to integrate us."

Turner detected a slight lessening of tension in Cassia's intense profile. For once it seemed reason was going to win out, even if under the guise of the scriptures.

Then Worth said, "I think we have to deputize somebody to watch by the door, and if they see anyone approaching for that purpose they would let us know, so we can all quickly stand and have a very, very short prayer of dismissal and then go home."

Cassie looked stunned.

"Now, it would be *different*," Worth interjected, a red finger stabbing the air to draw the distinction, "if they was coming here to worship the Lord in their hearts. If that was the case, we'd be duty bound to welcome 'em in and worship with 'em. But it's very clear the Lord's not in this. They're only coming to stir up trouble and dissension, and that's of the devil, and we need to have no part in it. Amen?"

Scattered *amen*s.

"So. All in favor signify by saying 'Aye' . . . "

There was a large round of *aye*s.

"All opposed . . . "

Turner waited for his grandfather and Cassie's father to lead a chorus of *nay*s, but as the silence lengthened it became obvious that was not going to happen.

"So carried," Brother Worth said. "We'll get together after service and work out the details of how to divide up the watch."

Turner thinking there must be something he didn't understand about the situation, some crucial fact or facts that made it only *seem* . . .

"Our next order of business is . . . "

Before he knew it, Cassie was on her feet.

"Excuse me . . . ?" she said loudly.

The congregation looked around at them in surprise, and Turner felt his face go a dark shade of red. Cass usually wasn't quick to volunteer her opinion, but once she got going she was like a freight train on a straight rail. In desperation Turner tugged gently at the sash of her cotton print dress where it was tied in a bow at the back, urging her to sit down, but she glanced around and gave him a look that immediately quashed that initiative.

"Yes, hon?" Brother Worth said, flashing a beneficent smile and winking toward one of the deacons on the front bench. Her father, Turner supposed. "You have a question?"

"I was just wondering," Cassie said in a strong, level voice, "how it is you can see into people's hearts, and know what they're thinking? I thought the Bible said only God could do that."

In the ensuing silence some members of the congregation looked anxiously toward Brother Worth for his answer, while others pretended a sudden consuming interest in the mechanics of the ceiling fans, or the spiraling path of a sluggish red wasp buzzing in and out the open side door.

The smile left Worth's eyes; only his mouth stayed upturned, by sheer force of will.

"It *does* say that," he conceded. "It does. But the Bible's a very complicated book. It also says, 'By their fruits ye shall know them,' and if you look at some of these nigras' fruits, I'm talking mainly the younger ones now, they're not sowing a thing but upset and hard feelings. They're tearing down, not building up. I just can't see the Lord at work in that."

There were several hearty head-nods throughout the rows, and a couple of murmured *amens*. Turner intently studied his fingernails.

"Yes sir," Cassie followed up, "but isn't there something too about, 'Judge not, lest ye be judged'?"

Worth erupted in a booming, mirthless laugh, and held his arms up like someone mock-surrendering in a battle. He shook his head resignedly. "Our young people do know their scripture, don't they? Who deserves credit for that? Who's your Sunday School teacher, hon? Sister Myrtle, idn't it? Myrtle, is this your good work?" There were a few nervous chuckles throughout the crowd. Sister Myrtle, a heavy-set widow with pin-curled gray hair, dipped her head shyly and waved the preacher's joke away.

"Seriously, though," Worth said, "there *is* a lot more in the word of God than *my* poor little mind can ever get ahold of. I think we just have to go by faith and, and, pray a lot for each other, as we try to do our best at living for the Lord. But, uh, we need to move on to other things, now. Is there a point you wanted to make, sugar, or . . . ?"

Cassie's steady voice when she spoke next belied the white-knuckled grip she had on the back of the next pew.

"I guess," she said, "just that if some people here that I know really looked into their *own* hearts I think they might not want to do this." The eyes of the congregation stayed strictly forward; no one faced around.

After a long pause the preacher said, "I thank you for that contribution, hon. We'll keep you in our prayers. Let's see, our next order of business is . . . "

Cassie was still on her feet. "Sir?"

Brother Worth sighed audibly. "Yes?"

"Can you see mine?"

"Your . . . ? I don't understand, darlin'."

"My heart," Cassie said, her voice breaking the least bit. "Can you see into my heart right now, what I'm thinking?"

Worth sighed again, looked out the side door and rubbed his mouth roughly with his hand. "No, hon," he said finally. "I don't have that power."

"Thank you," she said, and gracefully sat down.

While the deacons' topic turned to the cost of waterproofing the Sunday School rooms in the basement, where Sister Weems's primary class had seen a good bit of water damage during the heavy rains of early summer, Turner hesitated to look fully around at Cassie because he could hear how she was struggling to bring her breathing under control, trying so hard not to cry, and he was afraid any contact might set her off.

. . . my understanding Sister Myrtle's son can get us a fifteen percent discount on the water-seal from the hardware store he works at, but they only carry the high price brand, so I think Brother Ronnie's looking into . . .

When Cassie's breathing finally eased, Turner reached for her hand. She pulled it away, full and exact payment, he knew his trying to make her sit down a minute ago. He waited a short space of time and reached for it again, and this time she let him take it. He brought the hand up and brushed it lightly with his lips, which caused her to lay her head against his neck and begin, in absolute silence, the great outpouring of tears she'd tried so hard to contain before.

Her anger dripped inside the loose neck of his shirt, and when it had pooled alongside his collarbone it spilled over and ran hot across the nipple of his left breast. "It's all right," he whispered into her hair. "It'll be all right." But still it came.

He thought fleetingly about the colored preacher they'd seen on the TV news, the one who started it all, thundering *And justice roll down like water*, but when Turner would remember the deacons' meeting in years to come it all resolved into a single image, and Cassie's last night at Zion Hill Baptist became the hot wetness down his chest and the bitter wildflower scent of her shampooed hair, nothing more.

WHAT BROTHER WORTH couldn't see in Cassie's heart was that the following Sunday morning she would be walking through the waist-high field of amber sedge-grass that was the shortcut from the main road to St. Joseph Baptist Church, Turner a reluctant half step behind her reminding her of the reasons this was probably not a good idea.

When they came up into the clearing that served as a parking lot, surrounding a massive gnarled oak whose lowest limbs grazed the building's old red-shingled roof, Turner was surprised that there weren't half a dozen cars there, even though service was about to start if it hadn't already. Then he looked beyond the clearing at the graveled streets of shotgun houses radiating out through the distant pine thickets like the awry spokes of half a wheel, and he remembered from driving through it with his grandfather how compacted the colored camp was, compared to the rest of Zion Hill;

most of St. Joseph's members would live within walking distance of the church.

As he and Cassie walked up onto the shade of the small cement porch they could hear the piano inside beginning a hymn: "Rock of Ages." The piano's soundboard seemed to have a broken place somewhere in its linkages; one specific note of each low rolling bass run interrupted the resonance with a dulled *thuk* as if a tiny hammer were missing.

Cassie put her hand on the doorknob and then took it away. She looked around at Turner and at the trunk of the giant oak, near enough to the porch railing to touch. She shut her eyes and took a deep breath and let it out slowly, the first time that morning she'd showed any apprehension about what she was doing. What *they* were doing.

It would have been an opportune time for Turner to recite his litany of doubts again, but something about being so near their objective had oddly calmed him, resigned him to the fact. He didn't speak. Cassie clamped one of her hands tightly around one of his and pushed open the door.

Let the water and the blood
From thy wounded side which flowed . . .

They didn't sing it like Zion Hill did, a quick metronomic pace, but stretched out words like *water* and *wounded* to the length of several notes, and scat-sang little rills of higher and lower flexings onto the ends of them like old blues singers would. The air held an end-of-summer mustiness, overlaid with the smells of pine floor cleaner and women's perfume, almost funereally sweet.

The piano's booming under-rhythm stammered momentarily when the broad-set woman at the keys looked up and saw Turner and Cassie, but she quickly recovered. The congregation, almost as one, glanced back over their shoulders at the cause of the tremor. The fifty or so black faces registered a mix of curiosity and, Turner realized with a sinking feeling, outright fear. He lowered his head and steered Cassie toward a seat on an empty back bench.

A tall man strode toward them from the front of the church, and because of his white shirt and tie and little wire-rimmed reading glasses it took Turner several seconds to recognize him as old J.C., who plowed for his grandfather. He shook Turner's and Cassie's hands.

"Miss'er Turner, glad to have you," he said. "You too, ma'ams." He took a dog-eared red hymnal from under his arm, opened it to the appropriate number and gave it to them. But when he turned to go back to his front seat, his face suddenly showed a troubled afterthought, as if he'd been remiss in something. He knelt beside the bench and whispered to Turner, "Yo' grand-poppa dudn't need me f'something, does he?"

"Oh, no sir," Turner said. "We just came for church."

J.C. nodded and smiled his uneasy smile again as he went. They sang several more songs before the preacher, a Brother Ravizee, got up and welcomed visitors. His hair was flecked with gray, but he had the wide-necked solidity of an athlete. And though he welcomed the visitors more than once, with a vigorous smile, the way he kept bringing out his big white handkerchief to blot sweat from his face despite the morning being cooler than normal for the time of year told Turner the unaccustomed presence of white teenagers was making him uneasy, scattering his thoughts and cramping his language.

The sermon was about Moses looking over into the promised land but not being able to go in, though Turner remembered very little of it afterward because he knew what was coming next, and he dreaded it.

Finally the message raveled down and the preacher ask for them to stand and sing the invitation hymn, "You Can Tell Jesus," and before the fourth and final verse (*Maybe they do the church-joining part different from us*, Turner was praying, *Maybe they don't do it in public*) the preacher said almost word for word what the white preachers did.

"As we sing the last verse, if there's anyone who would like to unite with the church family, either through baptism or on promise of letter . . . "

Turner's hope slowly eased out of reach, like a rowboat sliding away from a dock.

" . . . ask you to come forward at this time. The doors of the church are open."

Cassie stood stock-still, staring straight ahead, until they were almost to the chorus. Then she looked around at Turner, her eyes freighted with the entire week of contention between the two of them over the subject *Cass, I can't do that to my folks, I can't* and silently reproached him *Last chance* before stepping out into the aisle *Your family moved here, but Granddaddy founded the damned church. He founded it, Cassie* and with her heels clicking confidently on the worn bare floor walked to where the preacher was standing and shook his hand, just as the last words of the chorus echoed away in a flourish of piano notes.

Total, awesome silence. Even a whining infant near the center of the sanctuary hushed, sensing something in the air. No one seemed to breathe.

Brother Ravizee put his hand tentatively on Cassie's shoulder and huddled with her in murmured conversation, their heads almost touching, while with a finger of his other hand he nervously kept trying to gouge slack between his collar and tie, as if his supply of oxygen had been cut off.

Finally he eased Cassie around to face the congregation and, after taking the deepest of breaths, said, "There comes now, to unite with St. Joseph's, Mizz . . . Cassandra . . . Denise . . . MacLemore . . ."

Cassie whispered to him.

"McNamara," he corrected, and rushed through the next without lingering as if he didn't want to dwell on all the implications of it, "upon-promise-of-letter-from-Zion-Hill-what-is-the-pleasure-of-the-church."

The primeval silence returned. When a voice was finally heard, it was old J.C.'s.

"I move we ex-cept her into pre-visional mem'ship on till such date as receival of said letter," J.C. intoned in a kind of singsong chant as if, by age or office, the task traditionally fell to him, "and at t'at time extend to her priv'leges of full fellowship if be t'will of God, amen."

Cassie appeared remarkably unflustered, her pale-peach shift and matching headband the only bright objects in Turner's field of view, giving the illusion that she was singled out by an invisible spotlight. She stood looking, he realized, directly at him. The reproach was all drained from her; in its place was the triumphant weariness of a runner or climber at the end of an arduous course.

The silence again.

"Sec'n," a young man's tenor voice said from the bench just in front of Turner, and he recognized him as the quiet skinny boy who mopped floors at the Jitney Jungle market in town.

"Moved and seconded," Ravizee said. "All-favor-signify-by-th'-raisin'-y'right-hand." One by one hands began going up, tentative as the first raindrops of a summer shower. Normal sounds filled the room again; even the baby resumed its weary whine.

"Amen," said the preacher, with unhidden relief, as the seesawing rhythm of the piano started up again. "Come forward now and welcome her with me." The members thronged slowly into the aisle, hiding Cassie and the preacher from Turner's view.

It was done.

When school started back, there were amused mentions of the incident for a week or two, never quite to his or Cassie's face. But the novelty soon wore off and the junior high's winning football team edged out most other areas of popular concern.

The day Brother Ravizee would call on her was the fifteenth of September, an unusually cool Sunday afternoon with the smell of wood smoke in the violently clear air. Turner and Cassie were sitting in the swing on her front porch when the preacher's old black Plymouth lumbered up the redrock driveway and parked a deferential distance from her family's car.

As soon as he got out, still in his Sunday suit, Turner knew from his slow walk and the contained torment on his face that he had some death or disaster to relate, but when he sat across from them in the white wicker chair he remarked first on the weather and then on the symmetry of the trellis of climbing roses at the corner of the porch.

Turner was thinking he'd guessed wrong, that this was strictly a social call, when Ravizee's face caved in and he said, looking at the porch floor, "I guess you-all have heard." He nodded toward the transistor radio on the window sill, its volume turned so low that you could make out the tune of a Beatles song but not the words.

Turner and Cassie looked at each other. "Heard what?" she asked.

The preacher rested his forehead in his hands, as if he were praying. "Them blowing up the church," he said tonelessly. Turner could have sworn he said *blowing up the church*.

"*Your* church?" he blurted out. "Who did?"

Ravizee shook his head impatiently. "Not ours," he said. "Birmin'ham. The big Sixteenth Street." He raised up and looked straight at Cassie, as if the next were meant for her. "They kilt four chirrun," he said, his voice going high and insubstantial on the last word.

"God," Cassie whispered. She looked to the grove of trees beyond her father's tool shed, thirty miles beyond which lay Birmingham.

Turner said, "You mean . . . *white* people did . . . ?" As soon as it was out, he realized how stupid it sounded.

But the preacher treated it seriously. "Don't know," he shrugged. "You would assume . . . "

He took his big white handkerchief out of the pocket of his coat and blotted his face with it, and then looked up pleadingly toward the bug-filled light fixture in the porch ceiling, fixing in his mind what he would say next.

His expression reminded Turner of the painting on the church's cardboard fans, Jesus in prayer at Gethsemane: *If it be thy will let this cup pass from me.*

"The deacons," Ravizee began, "and myself have, ah . . . " He looked at the floor again. "Lord God, it's hard for me to say this." He laid his wide hand across Cassie's forearm where it rested on the swing, eclipsing that portion of her skin. "We've discussed the . . . situation, this, ah, sad way the world is going, and it's our feeling that it's not, ah, a propitious time for a church of our color to be attracting attention unduly by, ah . . . "

"Meaning me," Cassie said. Her eyes were still on the grove of trees.

Turner didn't know yet that the grove would become her church by default, that she would appropriate from her parents' garage an antique park bench, bought at a rummage sale, and set it against the grove's biggest oak, like a pew. Turner helped her build a shelter over it, with some scrap fiberglass from her father's boathouse, and Sundays when her mother and father would leave for church she would go, in all seasons and weathers, to sit there under the trees and read and think, and eventually they even gave up arguing with her about it.

"We have come to love you," the preacher said. "Y'all both, it's just . . . oh, sweet Jesus. Sweet, sweet Jesus." He dabbed his big handkerchief to the corners of both eyes. "Please, ma'am, understand our hearts."

"I understand."

"Just for a while," Ravizee went on. "Till things gets better. It can't go on like this. This way is death."

Cassie nodded.

"We'll pray for you," the preacher said. "This bad old world needs you."

He stood up. It was done.

11

"HANG Y' JOCK STRAPS 'ere, gennermen, and come with me."

The Wizened Lizards' road manager, one Harley Garbo, was referring to the fact that the dressing rooms at Legion Field were, in real life, football locker rooms and bore the unmistakable imprint of decades of fermented sweat. "Y' names, once more? Me brain's 'bout rotted, I apologize."

Garbo was a little fireplug of a man, with waist-length hair as black as an Indian's. He wore biker boots and an oversized T-shirt with his group's insignia, two lizards copulating against a full moon. His gait and mannerisms brought to mind a hobbit on steroids.

Turner introduced the monks all around again, while they continued finding lockers for their instruments and ceremonial dress. Bah Tow, Se Hon, and Wah So gave up on getting their long brass trumpets into a locker—even telescoped down, the horns were a good eight feet—and propped them in a corner instead. James Crowe passed through, wearing an extremely worried look, with some boxes of Drepung T-shirts and incense to add to the table of concessions at the gate. Lu Weh had taken off his head bandage but kept tenderly touching the knot. Chai Lo practiced his flute in a corner, pouting over Turner's refusal to banish Beh Vah immediately and giving a wide berth to the youngster, who was beside himself with anxious joy over the prospect of meeting the Lizards.

Outside, on the field, the band had taken to the stage to tune their guitars and do a sound check; the concrete walls of the locker room vibrated with each amplified note. One of the players did a quick riff that had the approximate pitch and volume of a chain saw cutting fiberglass. Beh Vah, recognizing the song from television, shook with anticipation, biting two of his knuckles at once.

Harley Garbo suddenly appeared deep in thought. He stood tapping the side of his head. "Turner. Turner. *Turner*?" he said. "You wouldn't be no kin to the famous bloke, would you? The one what books all the shows?"

"That's me," Turner said, grinning modestly.

Garbo glanced over at the monks, then back at him, with a look of fierce amusement. "Yah-hah-hah-hah!" he laughed, machine gun-like. "In yer friggun dreams, right? Me, too. That wanker's on easy street, wot?" He looked around the locker room. "Where's the rest of y'stuff? I'll have me grunts go tote it in."

"This is it," Turner said. "What you see is what you get."

Garbo's good cheer subsided somewhat. "For real?" he said. On one of the long benches Se Hon and Wah So and Bah Tow, apparently spurred on by one of Crowe's physics lectures, were experimenting with a three-way patty-cake.

"We travel light," said Turner. "Float like a butterfly, sting like a bee."

"Cap'n?" James Crowe said from behind him, "We need to talk."

Garbo looked soberly at his watch. "Meet me on stage in about five," he said, "and we'll go over y'numbers."

"*What*?" Turner asked Crowe when Garbo was gone. "What is it?" Crowe's face was as woeful as if he had a death to relate. He looked over at the monks, then put his arm around Turner's shoulder and ushered him into a shower stall.

"I may have screwed us, Cap'n," he said. "Bad."

"How? What do you mean?"

"I was thinking back over the numbers I ran, for the supervention? And I realized . . . you know the part of the function that negated their memories? Well, right along there, the function . . . it . . ." In his torment, his voice cracked. He had to take a deep breath before he went on.

"It *what*?" Turner asked. "What did it do?"

"Damn it, it bifurcated, sir." He hung his head, contrite. "The little mother bifurcated on me, and I didn't even notice. Anytime I get in a hurry, I . . ."

"James? Translation, please."

"Of what?"

"'Bifurcated.'"

"Well, see, Cap'n, if you're going by Boolean logic, and you assume that something like the Mandelbrot set is non-recursive . . ."

"James . . ."

" . . . and its *complement* is non-recursive too, then you can say it's enumerable and you can define its cardioid in the Argand plane by . . ."

"*James.*"

"Yes, Cap'n?"

"*Bi . . . fur . . . ca . . . ted.*"

"Branched off. Split in two."

"Okay. So?"

"So it could be construed as two equations."

"James. Translate, please. Boil it down. We need to be on stage right now."

"I'm saying it might be considered two separate superventions. We may have shot our whole wad and not known it, sir. I'm truly sorry."

When Turner looked at the ceiling to ponder this new information, a rusting shower nozzle stared blankly back at him. He had a fleeting vision of turning it on and lying down in the spray, clothes and all, to see if it would wake him from this massive bad dream.

"You say '*might* be,'" he told Crowe. "How can we know for sure? Is there like an 800 number you can call, or . . . ?"

"The only way is to try one and see."

"Try a supervention."

"Right."

"And waste it."

"Right."

"Shit."

"I'm sorry, Cap'n. I'm truly . . ."

"Okay, okay. If you had to give odds, what are the chances we've still got one left?"

"Well, if you consider the first branch as a string within the Godel, instead of . . ."

"*James*. Ballpark, please."

"About fifty-fifty, sir."

Beh Vah came in, his hands shaking so much that his tri-cornered cymbal almost played itself. "See lizards now," he said, his eyes full of hope.

"IT'S A BLOODY rip-off, is what it is," the Lizards' lead guitarist fumed, poking Turner's chest bone with his finger. "We can sue, y'know? That's a crock, right down there." He flung his arm out, barely missing Garbo, and pointed through the glass of the cramped sound booth to the monks on stage.

"Well, actually . . ." said Turner.

"Aw, I dunno," Garbo said diplomatically. "Imitation's the highest form of flat'ry, ain't that what Shakespeare said?"

"Now lemme hear those horn thingies on mike three," the sound man spoke into the channel of the monks' headsets. "No, the big ones."

"Bugger Shakespeare," the guitarist said. "Once in y'life, y' get a truly original eye-dear, and some knock-off artist tries to make a fast buck off yer." He bunched the gold fabric of his robe in his fist for illustration, which only served to show how shabby it appeared alongside the monks' authentic ones. He'd been interrupted at his makeup for the sound check, and as a result wore one high arched eyebrow and purple-sequined eyelid while the other half of his face looked like a 40-year-old factory worker out for an evening of bowling.

"Yowza, them there," the sound man said. "Hit me." The booth filled with the amplified blatting of the big horns. "Jaysis God," he whispered.

"Well," Turner began, "what you need to understand is . . ."

"It's just for one night, Sterlin'," Garbo said. "Be a sport, wot? Poison'll be back for the Memphis gig. I talked to the docs."

"Sport, me arse. I'll be a laughin' stock. The bloody robes go, or I do." He crossed his arms defiantly.

"Wunderbar," said the sound man. "Cymbals, now. Mikes one and four. Ring 'em out."

Garbo said quietly, "But what would they wear, Sterlin'?"

"The fookda *I* care? Their street clothes. Whatever."

"Those *are* their street clothes, sweetie," Garbo said. "They're monks."

"Cymbals?" said the sound man. "Earth to cymbals . . ."

The guitarist's high-arched eyebrow drooped a notch. "Monks? Yer mean, *real* monks?"

"Real monks," Turner nodded.

The speakers above the sound board suddenly exploded with guitar chords, which reverbed away to the accompaniment of riotous laughter from the stage mikes. The people in the booth craned their necks to see Beh Vah with a white Stratocaster strapped around his neck, doing a creditable duck walk atop the stage-set sarcophagus. The other Lizards, who'd clearly put him up to it, were collapsed around him like battle dead, laughing and holding their sides.

The real guitarist slapped the plate-glass window in fury. "Ay! Ay!" He snatched the sound man's headset off and shouted into its microphone. "Mitts off tha', yer li'l shit monkey! Damn it to hell . . ."

He flung the headset down in a squeal of feedback and shook his fist at Garbo. "I'll get yer back for this, Harley. So help me, I will." He bolted through the door of the booth, knocking over a small fellow in spectacles who was about to tap on the glass. "Beg pardon," he said over his shoulder, and kept going.

Turner and Garbo rushed to help the man up. They dusted him off.

"Turner?" He held out a hand. Turner saw that the frames of his glasses were bent at an angle. "Paul Zotfeld, *USA Today*? Howya doin', babe? Good, good. That's good. Well, let's get right to it, shall we?"

LIIIZZZ-ARDS! Liiizzz-ards! Liiizzz-ards!

The packed stadium chanted with one voice as the monks made ready to go on stage. Apparently word had gotten out about Poison's cancellation, but not about the monks filling in. Looking on the bright side, Turner thought, at least they'd have the element of surprise on their side.

But when Se Hon, at the head of their sparse phalanx as they ventured out into the careening colored spotlights, saw the size of the crowd and the thousands of glow-in-the-dark green lizards with oversized phalluses (a hot concession item) the audience were tossing back and forth, his knees buckled under him. He was forced to retreat to the safety of the wings to lead the monks in a minute of prayer before they tried their entrance again.

Paul Zotfeld was at Turner's elbow, as he'd been since his arrival, observing the scene with a manic intensity. "I suppose this is a very . . . oh, what's the word? *Exciting* . . . moment for you, isn't it? Your first major gig since your, uh, retirement, shall we say?"

"Well," Turner said, "actually . . ."

"Of course. Of course. It'd have to be exciting." He wrote feverishly on his notepad, silently mouthing the syllables: *Ex-ci-ting . . . mo-ment.* "Have to be. Have to be. You know it."

Se Hon stood with his back against one of the towering amplifiers, breathing hard as if he'd outrun a wild animal.

Liiizzz-ards! Liiizzz-ards! Liiizzz-ards!

The reporter turned his considerable attention to the monks. "How . . . do . . . you . . . guys . . . feel?" He shouted each word, proceeding slowly, which allowed him time to accompany each portion with broad and sweeping hand gestures, a bastardized form of sign language he seemed to take great pride in. Since his first introduction to the monks, he'd tried frantically to surmount what he perceived as a colossal language barrier by a combined tactic of volume, oversimplification, and visual aids. It proved such a fascinating spectacle that the guys were struck mute by it, which only reinforced Zotfeld's resolve and vigor.

"They speak English," Turner reminded him now. "Fairly well."

Zotfeld nodded feverishly, weighing this fact as grist for his notebook. *Eng-lish* . . . *fair-ly* . . . *well* . . . he mouthed as he wrote. He gave an exaggerated wink, an aside to Turner, as if announcing he intended to test this premise.

"Pab . . . lo . . . En . . . glaze?" he asked loudly. The monks looked at one another in confusion. "How . . . feelum . . . now?" he pressed. "Feelum . . . ex-ci-ted?" The monks shot glances at one another before cautiously nodding their consensus.

The crowd noise swelled in intensity: *Liiizzz-ards! Liiizzz-ards! Liiizzz-ards!*

"Oh, this is great stuff," Zotfeld mumbled as he turned to a fresh page of his notepad. "Great stuff." *Feel . . . ex-ci-ted,* he wrote. "Oh yeah, you know it. Have to be. Have to be."

Liiizzz-ards! Liiizzz-ards! Liiizzz-ards!

"'Ello? 'Ello?" Garbo's voice buzzed in Turner's headset. "We ain't got all night, mate. Need they arses out there, y'know?"

"Ten four," Turner spoke into the mike, and then slid the phones down around his neck. "Guys?" he said. "Time for a huddle, okay? Everybody together." He looked at Zotfeld. "Excuse us just a second?" The reporter stepped a polite distance backward as the monks and Turner formed a tight circle, arms around one another's shoulders. They stood that way for a moment, heads bowed, eyes shut, each member adjusting the rate of his breathing until they all inhaled and exhaled as one.

Liiizzz-ards! Liiizzz-ards! Liiizzz-ards!

"I hear the song," Turner began, in Tibetan. *I hear the song,* the monks repeated after him.

"Song within me, song without me," he said.

Song within me, song without me.

"Song before me, song after me."

Song before me, song after me.

LIIIZZZ-ards! LIIIZZZ-ards! LIIIZZZ-ards!

"Make me so lost I am only but song."

. . . *only but song.*

"A man," a voice said. Turner recognized Beh Vah.

LIIIZZZ-ARDS! LIIIZZZ-ARDS! LIIIZZZ-ARDS!

Turner broke from the circle and slapped the two nearest monks on the butt. "Do it, guys! Do it!"

Heads down, they walked toward the aperture of colored light with the somber purposefulness of the condemned. Turner's dislocated headset buzzed with imprecations from the booth. He looked around for Zotfeld and saw him against the back of an amplifier, turned half away. He had his glasses off and was wiping his small eyes, his notebook temporarily put aside.

By the time the monks were in position with their instruments at the microphones, the roar of the crowd had given way to a silence so total Turner could hear a small airplane passing overhead, not to mention the almost imperceptible wilting of ten thousand polyethylene lizard phalluses.

He sensed Zotfeld at his elbow and looked around. Eyes dried and glasses replaced, the newsman was back in reporter mode now, notebook at the ready. "I'm sorry," he said to Turner. "I get sort of . . ." His voice choked. "It's so beautiful. It's all I've ever wanted to do."

"Be a writer," Turner supplied tentatively.

Zotfeld sniffed his derision. "No. *That.*" He nodded toward the stage. "Walk out into the lights and fucking blow them away."

A subterranean rumble vibrated the thin platform they stood on, a sound below hearing that slowly fed on itself until it became the chaotic, throbbing *bla-a-a-t-t* of Se Hon, Bah Tow, and Wah So's horns, a note that blocked out all other reality, insinuated itself even into the fillings of your teeth.

"Jesus God," Zotfeld whispered.

As the first thrust of the note echoed away to silence, Turner heard the astonished giggling begin in the front row of seats. *Yes*, he thought, feeling his fists and shoulders release the tension they'd accumulated from the events of the day. *Yes. Do it.*

12

IT WAS ALMOST midnight when the van pulled into the gate at Turner's big three-story ante-bellum house on a hill overlooking Birmingham, darkened acre-size lawns separating the row of neighboring homes.

Providence (or else Leroy Milby, his part-time house-tender and maintenance man) had left the porch light on for them, and when Turner emptied the van's glove compartment and located his garage door opener he found to his delight that the batteries still worked. And when a re-search of the glove compartment failed to turn up his house key, he remembered a spare one he'd hidden under a garage shelf more than a year ago against just such an eventuality.

Maybe our luck's rounded the corner, he was thinking, in the sweet after-rush of the concert's success. "Somebody grab the champagne," he said, as the monks piled out excitedly into his garage.

The only one worse for wear was James Crowe, who got out of the van last, still a little wobbly on his feet after being trapped midstream of the near-riot that ensued at the stadium's concession tables when the supply of Drepung T-shirts ran dry. When they'd stopped for the champagne and a few groceries, James chose instead a pint bottle of Jack Daniels and, having put a good dent in it on the way home, seemed much improved in spirit.

Turner was unlocking the door to the house when he felt a tug at his sleeve. It was Wah So, who took him aside to whisper, "I sleep in van, okay?"

"What? Why would you do that?"

The monk looked at the garage floor in embarrassment. "Too little beds for all," he said.

"I've got plenty beds," Turner told him. "Really."

Wah So disputed this by pointing to the far corner, which was cluttered with camping gear that included three folding Army cots. Turner succeeded, with much effort, in keeping a straight face.

"More rooms than this," he explained, nodding toward the rest of the house. "Lots of beds. We'll be fine, Warsaw. Really. Thanks for offering, though."

"Shhh," Se Hon cautioned everybody as they opened the door and stepped into the darkened foyer. "Not wake others."

"No others," Turner corrected him. "I live alone."

The monks eyed each other over the preposterousness of this idea. Where they came from, a building this big would house several dozen.

The foyer had a musty, closed-in smell.

Strange. Leroy was always conscientious about keeping the place aired out and in tip-top shape during Turner's long road trips. But when they got to the living room and his hand went by habit to the light switch, there was a note taped to it.

Mr. Turner, it read,

I really hate to leave you in the lerch but my work release is not working too well right now and they are here to take me back. It's a long story, so I will just say best of luck to you and I would value the chance to work with you again when circumstances permit.

Sincerely,

Leroy

There was nothing to indicate whether the note had been left two days ago or two months, but the olfactory evidence suggested the latter. Nevertheless, the old house opened out in the light and took Turner in its arms, as it always did, and he despaired that this would be only an overnight pit stop. He couldn't imagine any richer heaven than luxuriating in the silence of the place again. Reading a book. Cooking a pot of soup. Sitting on the porch at night watching small rainstorms come and go over the valley to the north. The greatest sin he'd committed in this house, in hindsight, was not loving this sweet life enough. He wanted another chance. Someday, maybe, with luck, he'd get it. Not now, though. Definitely not now.

A low whistle interrupted his thoughts. "Nice digs," James Crowe said. The effect of the whiskey on James, Turner had noticed, was to slow his mind down from 78 rpm to about 45, making him reflective and more economical with words. If only there were some kind of intravenous arrangement for the van.

The monks, meanwhile, had scattered silently into the big room on cautious tiptoe, touching its furnishings as delicately as if they were scouting for geological samples on a strange planet. It saddened Turner to realize how narrow their experience of America had been thus far, being limited of necessity to truck stops and cut-rate motels. Not to mention police stations.

Beh Vah gravitated naturally to the stereo, where he stood passing his fingertips lovingly across the black chrome face of the CD player. "Plays music, Beaver," Turner told him. "You want me to turn it on?"

Beh Vah nodded enthusiastically. "Lizards?" he asked.

"Nope, sorry. How about some Gershwin?"

"Gershwin Lizards?"

Turner shook his head. "Rhapsody in Blue," he said, switching on the amp and loading the disc in the player.

Beh Vah looked adamant. "Raps is not blue," he insisted. "Raps is black."

"Just listen," Turner said, as the first sinuous clarinet began evoking a New York skyline at night. "Just try it."

A blinking red light near the doorway caught his eye. His answering machine. Shit. No telling when Leroy had checked it last. He knelt at the phone table and pushed the button to see how many messages he had, but the little red window only displayed a crazily alternating series of eights and zeroes. The phone chose that moment to ring, causing the window to flash a final time, very brightly, before expiring with a sound like a dying alien in a video game. Turner reached behind the table to unplug it as he picked up the phone.

"Yeah?"

"Proud, proud, proud, baby," Lucille said. "I don't know what y'all did in Birmingham, but you got *every*body talking."

By now Crowe and the monks had drifted off to explore the house—all except Beh Vah, who had his head laid back against a speaker and his eyes shut, aurally experiencing the Big Apple, and Wah So, who was lying on the big semi-circular couch leafing slowly through a copy of *Playboy* with an expression of fear and immense wonder.

"The guys did good," Turner told Lucille.

"Musta did better than good, honey. I got *USA Today* calling wanting color pictures so they can put the boys on the front page. I got . . ."

"Front of the entertainment section? Wow. That's not bad coverage."

"Not section, baby, front page of the *paper*. The whole shebang. I got TV crews wanting to follow you guys around for a week. I got . . . oh, I know there's something else. What was it? What *was* it?"

Turner had learned Lucille's tones of phone voice well enough to know she was playing with him now, making him wait for the grand finale.

"Somebody wants to give us a recording contract," he supplied facetiously.

The fun went out of her voice. "They already called you?"

"Just making a joke," he said. "What's the good news? You've got my curiosity up."

"That was it," Lucille said. "Somebody from Gamma's music division called me. I tried to leave you a message, but your machine sounds like it's on dope or something. You ought to check it, hon."

Turner could tell she wasn't playing, now. He said, "But . . . how . . . ?"

"They must have had a scout at the show, is all I can figure. Anyway, let me give you who to call. Got a pen?"

"Hold on."

At that moment Bah Tow strolled through, eating something from a soup bowl which Turner saw, to his horror, was furred with a poisonous-looking green mold. He made a dive for the spoon and caught it just millimeters shy of the monk's mouth.

"Bad stuff, Bartow. It's spoiled, see?" Turner took the bowl from him and made an elaborate pantomime of sniffing it and scrunching up his nose.

"Green mean fresh," Bah Tow said indignantly. "You tell us so."

"I meant vegetables, buddy. This is . . ." He looked into the soup bowl. "Something else. We'll cook dinner soon, okay?" He had a sudden vision of his refrigerator; as hastily as he'd left here, its innards must look by now like a high school science project run amok.

Back at the phone, he said, "Okay, ready. Who called from Gamma?"

"The lady didn't give her name. She was just calling for the person who wants to produce you. Here's the number . . ." He recognized a Nashville area code.

"Who's the producer?"

"Ready? C. . . . D. . . . Masterson."

The pencil froze in Turner's hand.

"Lucille, you're shitting me. Who is it, really?" For a dozen years or more, Masterson had sat astride the recording industry like God. Producer of the Year, repeat, repeat, Producer of the Decade, gold this, platinum that, Grammys enough to play chess with.

"Hope to die, sugar lamb. Wants you to call first thing in the a.m. I *told* you y'all done good."

"I've never . . . I mean, he . . ."

Turner, who by necessity had grown brass balls—albeit artificial ones—when his career took off, had tried possibly fifty times over the years to get through Masterson's cordon of assistants and protectors to talk directly to him on behalf of one act or another about a project, but all in vain. You don't call C.D., ran an old joke in the business. C.D. calls *you.*

Masterson's ironclad rule was no interviews, no photographs. Whenever there was an award to accept or a cause to support, he sent an assistant. As with most recluses, legends about Masterson abounded. The gossip tabloids regularly revealed him to be an albino, a midget, a giant, a computer program, a woman; their eyewitnesses disclosed that he was born without vocal cords, was horribly deformed, was an alien, was a Satan worshiper.

The only direct evidence Turner had ever gleaned was the revelation of a top session drummer, one night after too many drinks, that C.D. allowed no engineers in the booth while he was recording, ran all the equipment himself.

"Hello? You still there, baby?"

"I'm here. I just . . ."

"How's my boys liking Birmingham? They had any collard greens yet?"

"Not yet."

"Listen, Lucille's got to run. You be a good boy and call C.D., all right? Chow, sugar."

It was too much. Too much at once. Turner sat staring at the receiver until the dial tone reminded him to hang up. It was like old times again, when he finally broke through from troublemaking Vietnam vet to respectable promoter—such a long dry spell, and then one day, *boom,* you're standing under a rain of blessings with no umbrella.

But he had the nagging feeling he was forgetting something. What had he not done today? Something . . . something about . . .

Then the awful dream from the previous evening reassembled itself in his head—the haunted field, his grandfather's wounds, the falling into the earth. He hadn't even telephoned his grandparents in—what? A week, now? Ten days? Crazy days, true, but still. How could he have forgotten again?

He looked at his watch. Five after midnight. Over by the stereo, Beh Vah's head had gradually slid down the speaker cabinet and come to rest on the carpet, where he lay emitting a soft snore.

Turner started to get up and go to the kitchen, but the gnawing in his gut was more than hunger. The hell with the time. He'd wake his grandparents up. Make sure they were all right. Otherwise he wouldn't get any sleep tonight.

He punched the familiar number, listened to it ring. Peace swept over him, even though he pictured them waking up in a fright, finding their eyeglasses, feeling their way to the kitchen phone in the dark. Late night calls had always panicked them, because they'd lived long enough to know such calls are never good news. This time he'd prove them wrong.

The phone rang and rang. A dozen times. Fifteen. Twenty. Had he dialed wrong? He hung up and tried again. With the same result. The peace that had settled onto him vanished as quickly as it came.

He hung up and dialed the operator, got her to run whatever diagnostic they do to tell if a line's out of order. No, she said, their telephone was fine.

He got up and went out into the front yard to think for a minute. The lights of Birmingham ran from left to right like a river of sequins through the cleavage of the mountain. The moon was almost full. Turner stood looking at the valley farther to the north, where the interstate crossed the highway to Zion Hill. An hour's drive. Hour and a half, if you got behind a coal truck.

He was trying to decide whether to herd the tired and hungry monks back into the van and take them with him, or to go alone and trust James Crowe's new slow-motion self to get the guys all fed and bedded down, when a third option came to him. He could call his grandparents' nearest neighbor and get him to check on them.

Johnny Patterson answered on the third ring.

"Yo. Talk to me."

"Mister Johnny? This is Turner."

"Turner! Where t'hell you at, boy?"

"Back in Birmingham for the night. Listen, I apologize for waking you up, but . . ."

"Couldn't sleep. Watchin' a little TV."

"Anything good on?"

"Naw. Goddang ol' shoot-em-up. Ain't wuff a good halfa shit. Pauline had the cable took out. Too much nakedness. She was worried about Robert seein' it." Robert was thirty-seven.

"Ah. Listen, the reason I called . . . I can't get Granddaddy to answer his phone. You know any reason they'd be gone this late?"

Mister Johnny thought a minute. "Naw. Can't say's I do. I'd be glad to put on my ol' brogans and go see about 'em."

"I hate to ask you. I know it's a long walk."

"Bull dookey. I don't mind. Gimme your number, and I'll . . . uh, wait a minute. I just remembered. Your granny was telling Pauline a few days ago they'd been gettin' a lot of prank calls, middle of the night. Keeping 'em awake. They was thinkin' about unpluggin' the phone."

"Ah. That must be it, then."

"She said your grandpa fussed at her, said what if Turner tried to call. And she told him you wasn't no fool, if you ever couldn't get 'em at night you'd call us."

Turner drew a relieved breath so deep it seemed to have starlight in it. "Well, good, then. I appreciate you easing my mind."

"Be glad to go see about 'em, though."

"No, that's fine. No need upsetting them."

"When you gettin' out this way? I keep waitin' any time for that little jet of yours to light down in my pasture out here."

Turner laughed. "No sir, I'm on four wheels these days. I hope to get by Zion Hill real soon, though."

"Well, come see us."

"Sure will. Good night, now."

In the kitchen, James had spread the monks a champagne buffet from the grocery sack and then gone on to bed. Despite the guys' weariness, the champagne—obviously their first—was proving a ready source of entertainment, from the ballistic cork to the nose-tickling carbonation. The latter apparently caused Lu Weh's sudden sneezing fit, but the others took the discovery more sanguinely, following Se Hon's lead and holding the tiny glasses close to their eyes against the light to follow the manic upward progress of the bubbles. All but Wah So, who put his ear to the glass instead and was soon doing a laudable imitation of the hiss.

"Why the bibles all go up, not down?" Bah Tow asked. Se Hon volunteered to go rouse James for a technical explanation, but Chai Lo gruffly halted this. "*Bubbles*," he said, with irritation. "It is their way, is all."

"You can take a snack to bed if you like, guys," Turner said, motioning them upstairs toward the guest rooms. He made himself two liverwurst sandwiches and ate them with great relish while he showed everybody where they'd be sleeping.

When he was finally alone, the sight of his own bed, its covers pulled back in simple welcome as if none of the past year's events had ever happened, brought a lump to his throat. He lowered himself onto the sheets like a lover, saying midway a quick prayer of thanksgiving for the day's great blessings, and fell almost immediately into a soundless velvet sleep.

They got to the Birmingham airport an hour before C.D. Masterson's private plane was supposed to pick them up. Turner had tried to wangle an extra day at home to catch his breath, clean out the refrigerator, and take the monks to meet his grandparents just once before the official Calling Out came and all hell broke loose in Zion Hill.

But Masterson's assistant—Turner still hadn't gotten to speak to C.D. himself—was absolutely unyielding on the timing. "We're fighting the clock on this thing," she'd told him gravely. "You of all people should know that." For an uneasy moment he thought she was referring to the realm, the Calling Out, the whole ball of wax, and he was speechless. But that was nonsense. She obviously meant some window of marketing opportunity which he, as a promoter, could understand the urgency of.

So they'd agreed that Turner and the monks would fly to Nashville this afternoon on Gamma's company plane and get acquainted with the studio. Meanwhile James Crowe would drive the van up, with their instruments and other belongings, and they'd start recording this very evening. When he asked about making hotel reservations she informed him that was already taken care of. Nothing slow about C.D.

While they waited for the small jet to arrive, Turner bought James and the monks lunch in the snack bar and tried to read the local newspaper, but his brain was spinning so fast he couldn't get it to insert itself into the flow of words about bond issues and stabbings so he finally gave up.

Beh Vah was first to finish his lunch, and went off to sightsee the concourse. He returned almost immediately, excited with the news of a video arcade he'd found. Turner bought him a roll of quarters from the cashier and got an extra roll for himself.

At a coin telephone in a quiet corner near the snack bar's restrooms he dialed his grandparents. The distant ringing repeated itself a dozen times, then more. His nagging concern of last night began to re-establish its grip around his heart, but as he looked out the big plate glass at the blinding cloudless sunshine on the runways he realized what a perfect day it was for gardening. Of course they wouldn't be inside today.

The early squash would be bearing by now, and most likely the pole beans and okra. The corn would be head-high, with nubs along the stalks rounding out daily, almost hourly, into plump ears. His grandparents never looked so ageless and fit and hopeful as when they walked its straight dirt rows wiping sweat, plowing and hoeing in amounts that would completely tucker out someone forty years their junior. "My medicine," his grandfather would wink, pointing to the patch of ground. And it was. Enough good seed and enough rain, Turner sometimes fantasized, and the two of them might live forever.

"Paging a Mr. Turner," the PA system squawked. "Meet your Nashville party at Gate C-13. A Mr. Turner. C-13."

He looked at his watch. It was a good forty minutes before the plane was supposed to arrive. Maybe he'd understood wrong. He listened to the phone ring a few more times before hanging up. No need to worry, he assured himself again. His grandparents had Lucille's number, could get a message to him if anything was wrong.

The studio rep waiting for him at C-13 looked to have come straight from central casting: styled hair, mirror sunglasses, expensive dark suit with a slight Mafia sheen, pointed wingtips.

"You're with Gamma?" Turner inquired needlessly.

The man flashed a capped-tooth smile and held out his hand. "Kyle Hardeman," he said. "You'd be Turner?"

"That's me. You're a little early, aren't you?"

"We had a great tailwind," Hardeman explained. Perfect smile again. Out the window behind him Turner saw the sleek black Learjet refueling on the tarmac, quivering in the waves of heat. "Have your guys put their bags by the door and we'll be ready to take off in about five."

"No, our gear's going by car," Turner said. "I'll round everybody up quick as I can, but it might be a little while. I understood noon, from the lady in Mr. Masterson's office."

"She's new," the rep said quickly. "She doesn't know that when Masterson says 'punctual' he means 'early'." This time the smile seemed a little shopworn.

"I see. You've been with him a while, then?"

"Long while." Hardeman looked nervously at his watch, then out at the jet. The refueling truck was pulling away.

"I'll do the best I can. Don't leave without us, now," Turner winked, as he broke into a half-trot back toward the main concourse. Beh Vah was easy enough to find, being the only saffron robe in the dim, noisy cave of the game arcade. He had abandoned the high-tech intergalactic war games for an old-fashioned carnival amusement, a big glass cage that let its protagonist manipulate a pair of pincers on a chain to pluck dolls and other prizes off a bed of gravel. A small teddy bear and a pair of Mickey Mouse ears sat on the floor by Beh Vah's feet, and he begged to finish one more round while Turner was finding the other monks.

When he got to the snack bar, Chai Lo told him James had gone back to the van because he'd forgotten to put money in the meter. Turner knew they couldn't just hop on the plane and vanish without telling James they'd gone, so he sprinted out to the parking lot to find him.

By the time he found James and sprinted back to the snack bar, Se Hon was off tending to an emergency bowel movement brought on, most probably, by the foot-long chili dog he'd ordered for lunch. Turner took advantage of the delay to collapse in a chair and get his breath back. Would his ancient-feeling lungs ever again learn to take in enough air, as they had in old times, to do whatever was required of them? He prayed for at least one of the realm's first-string warriors to be arthritic or have a trick knee.

With Se Hon back from the john and the other monks in queue behind him, Turner loped off to retrieve Beh Vah and his plunder from the video den and then they all trotted the long concourse toward passenger screening.

This proved a slight bottleneck. Beh Vah's teddy bear set off the metal detector, and much gentle persuasion was required to convince him to surrender it to the security guard for X-ray; Beh Vah watched the guard with great apprehension as the offending bear was placed on the conveyor belt and carried into the maw of the ominous machine. When it passed inspection and emerged at the other end, he fell on it with cries of joyous reunion and stroked its small head.

By this time James had caught up with the entourage, and trotted along to the gate to see them off. When they got there Hardeman was pacing and looking at his watch, clearly in a foul mood. Without a word, he ushered the group out the portal to the runway.

Just to make conversation, Turner asked him as they walked, "Is Dave Fedders still with Gamma?"

The rep looked blank. "Dave . . . ?"

"He was an assistant vice president, last time we talked."

"Oh, right. Sure. Good old Dave." His smile flashed, but his composure seemed shaken. Something not quite on the level about this fellow.

At the end of the walkway the beautiful little jet gleamed in the sun. The pilot stood at the foot of the folding staircase to greet them.

Turner tried an experiment. "How about Stuart Isaacson? He still working on that antique DeSoto?"

"Oh, yeah," Hardeman said. "You know Stu. It's his pride and joy."

There was no such person as Isaacson. No car. Turner had a queasy feeling about all this. He slowed his walk.

"Mr. Turner?"

The pilot's firm voice roused him from his reverie. "Good to be flying with you again, sir." As Turner shook the outstretched hand he tried to fit the face to a memory: handsome, boyish, close-clipped military hair.

"You might not remember me. Vic Taylor? West Coast leg of the Phil Collins tour. Eighty-five, was it? Early eighty-six?"

"Right, right," Turner said. "Good to see you." Tours were always a blur to him afterward, a confetti of names and faces, but the pilot seemed vaguely familiar. His paranoia subsided. The nervous rep was probably just a low-level flunky who pretended to greater things; the industry was full of them. No wonder he wouldn't know all his company's officers by name.

As they walked up the stairs to the cabin, Beh Vah asked Turner, "Baby airplane?"

"Yeah, you might say that. It's called a Learjet. I used to travel in them when . . ."

Without warning, Turner's brain was sundered by the grandaddy of all headaches. The pain was so intense it blinded him for an instant; his head filled with a roar so loud it had texture and color, the static of an untuned radio cranked up to murderous volume. He stumbled and grabbed at the handrail to steady himself until he could get his bearings again.

"Tur-ner! All right?" he heard one of the monks ask faintly, miles away, through the static.

Then, as quickly as it had struck him, the roaring pain went away. He blinked and looked around. The long flat airport building wavered in the heat, exactly as before. He noticed a wicked-looking mess of antennas and microwave dishes on the traffic controllers' tower. Had some stray bolt of concentrated radio waves collided with his head? He didn't think such a thing was possible.

"I'm all right," he assured Chai Lo, behind him. "Lost my footing."

The air-conditioned cabin was frigid as a meat locker, but it was what Turner's head needed. He dropped into a plush seat and pushed the backrest as far as it would go, his brain still throbbing from whatever had slammed it. He hoped Gamma's jet had a stewardess; he would order a double whatever-was-closest and a washcloth full of crushed ice for his forehead.

Down on the tarmac, James Crowe was waving goodbye toward the plane's windows and glancing at his watch at the same time. He'd wanted to see the guys safely off, but now he was itching to get rolling. James couldn't stand in one place for long. Turner waved at him. The monks, still inspecting the plane's interior, didn't see Crowe to wave back.

Suddenly Hardeman, looking extremely rattled, came barreling along the aisle toward Turner. "You've got a phone call down at the desk," he panted. "They say it's urgent."

All the blood went out of Turner's heart. The call was about his grandfather. Had to be. His premonition had been right all along. He ran for the door of the cabin, gently pushing monks aside, and clattered down the roll-up staircase two steps at a time.

But just as he was sprinting past James Crowe on the runway the blinding pain slammed through his head again, even stronger this time, and he fell to the ground as cleanly as if he'd been shot. His hands went frantically to his temples, squeezing his skull, kneading his scalp, in a fruitless attempt to make the pain bearable. Through the static he was vaguely aware of James Crowe's slight arms underneath his shoulders, cradling him.

"Cap'n?" Crowe's distant voice was asking. "What's the matter, Cap'n?"

There was the slightest lessening of the pain as the deafening storm of static resolved itself into gruff slurred syllables, none of them intelligible, like a tape played at molasses-slow speed. Turner had the oddest sensation at that point, one he could only describe later as the feeling that he was not alone in his skin, and with it the distorted whirlwind of sound became a single clear voice. A woman's.

Don't be afraid, the voice said. *It's Cassie.*

"Cassie?" Turner heard himself say, and then flushed with shame at falling for the ruse again. What kind of monstrous bad joke was this? Didn't he have other gaping psychic wounds the realm could rub its salt into?

Crowe looked as excited as a kid at Christmas. "Where?" he asked, glancing around. "I thought she'd forgot about us."

The monks are in great danger, the woman's voice said. *Listen to me. Don't let them get on the plane. Repeat. Don't . . . let them . . . on the plane.*

Then the voice faded and Turner's skin invisibly emptied out until it contained only himself again, and the throbbing static came to be replaced by a high-pitched whine which he realized was the engine of the Learjet starting up. It was leaving without him.

He got up and shook his head clear as he could, pushing away from Crowe's questions, and took off at a run toward the steps. An arm came out the cabin door and began detaching the steps from the fuselage to make ready for take-off. "Shy!" Turner screamed, waving his arms over his head. "Get 'em off! Get everybody off!" But the rising volume of the engines drowned out his voice in his own ears, much less inside the cabin. As he ran he saw the confused faces of the monks at several windows.

Just as Turner reached the bottom step, Beh Vah bolted out of the cabin door onto the small platform that was now hanging precariously by one corner and came running down the stairs, looking agitated and shouting something that was lost in the noise.

"Ears! Forgot ears!" Turner heard as he passed by him on the steps. Beh Vah put his fists atop his head to illustrate his forgotten Mickey Mouse ears. Turner charged past him, three steps at a time on the wobbly staircase, and saw Hardeman's black-suited arm reaching through the door frame again to detach the remaining corner fastener as he neared the top.

He prayed he had the momentum to do what he did next, take a flying leap through the door and put his shoulder to Hardeman with enough force to knock him sprawling backwards into the entranceway before he could undo the last bolt and cast off the staircase. Chai Lo was the first one forward, apparently come to see what the hell was going on. Turner had his hands full trying to keep Hardeman wrestled down, but he managed to tell Shy, "Get off! Get everybody off!"

Chai Lo stood paralyzed with confusion and fear. The whine of the engines was increasing.

"Get *off*, goddamn it! Everybody! Now!"

This time Chai Lo got in gear and ran back to tell the others. But Turner paid greatly for his momentary lapse in concentration; Hardeman got sufficiently on his feet to throw a roundhouse punch that caught him on the side of the head, staggering him. Turner landed on his hands and knees, realized through the vortex of dizziness that he was blocking the monks' escape route, and with great difficulty raised to a crouch and made another lunge at Hardeman just in time to hear the blessed sound of the monks' running feet fill the entranceway and clatter down the steps.

Hardeman sidestepped him, but so barely that Turner knew he was weakening. Rebounding off the closed cockpit door, he put his head down and hurtled toward Hardeman's belly. When he rammed it he heard a combined groan and wheeze that signified he'd hit the best of the soft spot. The blow sent Hardeman's considerable bulk staggering backwards, bent into a standing fetal position to hug his middle. His elbow caught in the curtain that separated the aft compartment from the passenger cabin and pulled it down in a tangle around him, rod and all, and his back end hit the carpet and slid partway down the aisle.

That was all the respite Turner needed to get up and make a run for the door. But as he did so the plane gave a sickening jolt that told him it was taxiing for takeoff. When he reached the door he froze for an instant with his hands on the frame, watching the yellow dashed line on the asphalt blurring increasingly to a solid one as the plane picked up speed. The steel stairway still dangled by its one fastened corner, its low end striking sparks off the runway.

He didn't need James's calculator to tell him his chances for bailing out wouldn't get any better than this. He breathed in and out with the reverence of prayer and pushed himself through the door, grabbing the handrails of the staircase that was bucking now like a rodeo bronc.

Each impact with the ground sent a jarring of pain up his arms and into his tooth-fillings, but via some near-supernatural grace or luck he managed to put one foot in front of the other until he was some two-thirds of the way to the bottom of the steps.

At that point the taxiing plane banked slightly left and the low end of the staircase frame collided with one of the landing lights rooted at the edge of the asphalt. The unexpected impact deprived him of his footing and he took the last four stairs on his tailbone, *bangbangbangbang* like blows from a hammer, the friction of the hand-railings scorching his palms as he tried to slow his descent to the blurred ground.

No right angles! he heard his old infantry sergeant say, instructing them how to dismount from a moving vehicle. *No right angles! Rag-doll and roll! Rag-doll and roll!* But that first step had never gotten any easier and wasn't now, like stepping onto a giant grinding-wheel. He gritted his teeth and he *did* it, his right toe taking the first impact and the second impact sandpapering the soft right cheek of his ass and against all instinct he made of himself a loose-jointed ball and rolled blessedly free of the bucking stairway at just the instant the nose wheel of the jet went airborne.

When he finally rolled to a stop and found he was able to sit up without undue distress and figured out the only damage he'd sustained was a scalded buttock and one set of bloodied knuckles he thanked the name of Sergeant Scarlatti as silently as he'd cursed it all those months in training.

At the far edge of the airfield the small black jet banked right into a hard half-circle and screamed back the way it had come, low enough to the ground to deafen, still trailing the bucking staircase like some vestigial limb. From the direction of the airport Turner saw six dots of saffron and a smaller dot of camouflage fatigue running toward him across the wavering tarmac.

Then he saw that the plane's trajectory was taking it head-on into a small white jet approaching the same runway to land. The white jet's pilot, who must have had the reflexes of a cat, made an evasive right-and-up maneuver that was almost . . . *almost* not enough and then it *was* enough, the two planes' wingtips just a hand's-width from grazing as his wheels gained, though just by inches, the runway he'd aimed for.

As the jet fishtailed, struggling with friction to smooth out its bumpy touchdown, Turner noticed the emblem on its side: the familiar blue-and-white symbol of Gamma Records, the old Greek character stylized into a thin, modern wing-shape.

The black plane, meanwhile, pulled full-blast into a screaming straight vertical climb until it was just a speck against the sun. At the apex of the climb it slowed and with surprising grace did a swan-like back flip, then kicked on all its burners again for a high-speed dive toward the ground.

When the plummeting jet reached an altitude where it had clearly passed its last chance to pull up, its wings began twitching last-minute corrections and Turner realized to his horror what its target was: the monks and James Crowe, a terrifyingly easy mark running bunched as they were in the wide-open.

Turner got to his feet to signal them but discovered that his trick knee had taken a harder lick than he thought. It buckled when he put his weight on it, and sat him back down.

James Crowe was first to see what was happening and gave everybody the word to scatter. The white plane had barely braked to a safe stop at the far end of the runway and the monks were digging hard toward all points of the compass when the screeching black jet plowed into the ground at exactly the spot where the group had been bunched just seconds previous. With the blast of its impact everybody hit the dirt by instinct, their hands over the backs of their heads, as a blowtorch of flame shot upward from the wreckage.

It wasn't until several lifetimes later, after Turner saw with relief all the men one by one stand up whole, that the smoke began to dissipate enough for him to make out the impossible: where the impact should have blown a crater the size of a parking lot, the unbroken asphalt showed only a black syrup-like film on its surface, which served to fuel the inferno above it.

No wreckage, no plane parts, no corpses. Just darkness, burning. And the smoke, by now risen high against the noon sun, already congealing into the unmistakable form of a ragged crow.

13

THE ELEVATOR at Gamma's headquarters was a big bubble of glass that crawled twenty-five stories up the side of the glass tower to get to the studio's suites in the penthouse. As the compartment climbed, it gave its passengers a breathtaking view of downtown Nashville, spread along the red clay banks of the Tennessee River in the late afternoon sun.

Turner even pointed out to everyone the old, churchlike brick building looking forgotten amid parking decks and skyscrapers, and told them it was Ryman Auditorium, first home of the Grand Ole Opry before the show moved to a theme park in the suburbs. At any other time the monks would have been all eyes, consumed by wonder at being suspended in midair above a city. But even though they listened politely and expressed mild admiration of the view, it was clear their hearts weren't in it. Their eyes looked shell-shocked; they wore the dazed, patient faces of survivors.

And with good reason. The stink of the black plane's death smoke still hung in the fabric of their robes, a constant reminder of their close call. Even though Gamma's real pilot had insisted, along with Turner, that they make a detour to the airport restrooms to wash up and then to the sundries shop for mercurochrome and bandaids, in their duress nobody noticed the odor until after James Crowe had already hit the highway with the van that contained their one change of clothes.

As for Turner, he was making it fine on nervous energy, every promoter's favorite fuel, but he could tell he was pretty far into his reserve tank. The area around his pummeled tailbone throbbed in time to his pulse, and little rivers of soreness were awakening in muscles he hadn't thought about in years. He was not looking forward to walking in an hour and a half late for their first meeting with the great C.D. Masterson, their best shot yet at turning around the Tally of Inner Blindness in a major way and thereby giving himself at least half a leg to stand on at the final confrontation. C.D. was not famed for listening to excuses, even good ones.

As if all that weren't enough, he had this business of the voice to worry about, too. *Had* it been Cassie, really? God bless her, if it had. Turner had known several guys during the war who claimed they'd gotten a telepathic message from their mother or wife, even a dead uncle, warning them of some imminent danger, but he had always chalked it up as the scared-shitless brain talking to itself in the presence of loneliness and a good imagination.

This had been no still, small voice, though; more like a buzz-saw through the soft raw center of his brain. Could it happen again? He found himself flinching at certain frequencies of sound, panicky that they were the beginning of another pronouncement.

And what of James Crowe knowing her name? He'd been damned little help afterwards, stonewalling from the get-go.

You said 'Cassie!' like you recognized the name, James. Why?

Did I, Cap'n? I thought you did.

Hell, yes. You know you said it. 'I thought she'd forgotten about us.' What does that mean?

If I said that, then I, uh, spoke out of turn, Cap'n. I clearly meant nothing of the sort.

And so on. With Turner in his present frame of mind, it was probably a good thing Crowe had split off to drive the van up solo, thereby removing the temptation to strangle him.

James's continuing revelations and by-the-ways made Turner wonder if there was a huge instruction book for this whole endeavor awaiting him in a dead-letter office somewhere. At the outset he'd thought the final confrontation would be a good, fair fight; he knew fighting, at least. But if the weirdness quotient of this thing got any higher he'd need a program to keep all the players straight.

The elevator stopped and the doors opened out into a reception area the size of a hockey rink, an impression which was reinforced by the pale ice-blue of its carpet and walls. A strip of oak paneling ran the whole circumference of the room, and on it were mounted bronze heads of the mega-stars the label represented.

As Turner and the monks hiked across the vast carpet to the marble reception desk the size of a pool table he recognized Streisand and George Jones among the gallery, as were Tina Turner and Sinatra, Pavarotti and B.B. King. What a bizarre mix, all of them drawn like a magnet to Masterson's studio.

The receptionist, in a black leather miniskirt and a high-teased mane of red hair, was on the telephone. Several nervous-looking young men and women sat in the row of plush chairs nearby, clutching cassette tapes in their white-knuckled hands like life preservers, so deep in thought they paid no attention to the six monks who'd scattered to inspect the bronze heads. Songwriters, no doubt, trying to break in at the top of the top and obviously having second thoughts about it.

The receptionist motioned to Turner that she'd be with him in a minute, but the phone call went on and on and he noticed other buttons blinking, callers waiting in queue. A door behind the desk opened and a long-haired young man backed through it, his arms loaded down with thick reels of recording tape. He was having a hurried conversation with someone in the inner office; in the short time the door was open Turner glimpsed who—a woman in a wheelchair, wearing a T-shirt and jeans. A secretary, most likely. Dark blonde hair in a pixie cut, and eyes that . . .

Oh, shit. Hell's bells. Eyes and a face that were the very image of Cassie, or at least of the persistent doppelganger he'd carried in his mind's eye these twenty-odd years since he'd seen her, some automatic function of his subconscious updating the face while he slept—adding the slightest wrinkle here, a graying streak of hair a finger's width to the rightside crown of her head. Only the eyes were absolutely unchanged, with their greengold gift for burning away foolishness and pretense like a laser beam . . . no, not unchanged, *enhanced* if anything by the passage of time, until they looked precisely like this woman framed in the doorway who acknowledged his stricken stare by giving him a bittersweet smile just as the conversation ended and the door swung shut again.

Damn it, who *were* these dark-blonde wheelchair women *Cassie thy name is legion* he kept spotting in distant cities, all these years, ready to ambush him with sad accusatory smiles whenever his black-and-blue conscience showed the least sign of healing? He sent up a silent selfish prayer that at least this one would make herself scarce while he was here, now of all times when he needed his wits and concentration for dealing with Masterson. He had a sudden panicked vision of C.D. calling for a stenographer as their meeting got underway, of this woman wheeling in with her notepad to take up a position squarely in his own line of sight, twisting and twisting the invisible knife. Please, no, let her stay in the nether regions of this place until he could depart.

The receptionist's voice brought him back to reality. "You must be

Turner," she said. Her face and clothes were New York, but her voice was down-home Nashville.

While he was basking in being recognized, heartened that his former fame hadn't altogether fled during his long exile, Turner felt a tug at his sleeve. It was Beh Vah. Ah-hah. As the picture became clearer, his ego deflated commensurately. Traveling with six monks would be a pretty good tip-off as to his identity nowadays, wouldn't it?

"No Lizard," Beh Vah said disappointedly, indicating the bronze hall of fame on the room's walls.

"No, buddy," Turner said. "I don't think they record here." He turned to the secretary again. "I'm very sorry we're late," he said. "Is Mr. Masterson still available today?"

She gave him what he thought was a knowing smile. Knowing he'd get his ass chewed, most likely. "C.D.'s waiting for you," she said. "You can go on back." She indicated the door behind her. "To the right, then all the way to the end of the hall."

Turner rounded up the monks and led them past the big desk. He steeled himself as he opened the door where the woman in the wheelchair had been, but when he looked down the long carpeted hall in both directions there was no sign of her. Thank goodness for small favors. He felt his gripped chest loosen.

The office at the distant end of the hall had its door open. As he approached he could see a jungle of plants inside, illuminated by some soft and indistinct filtering of light. He stopped at the open doorway; the ceiling of the room was windswept clouds, seen through a full skylight of tinted glass.

He tapped on the door frame with a knuckle before delicately sticking his head inside. "Mr. Masterson? I'm . . ."

Sitting behind the desk was the woman in the wheelchair. His throat tightened. "Excuse me," he said. "I was looking for . . ."

At that moment pandemonium erupted behind him. The monks, with cries of great delight, stampeded past him through the doorway, spinning him aside. They flocked to encircle the woman behind the desk, squeezing her and patting her and bending down for hugs and pecks on the cheek, all while maintaining an excited babel of Tibetan greetings and small talk which, unless he was imagining it, she seemed to somewhat understand and reply to.

"Excuse me . . . ?" Turner said finally. No one paid him any attention.

He was dumbfounded and a little embarrassed. Was this some obscure native custom he'd never known about, a ceremony for honoring the handicapped?

"Guys? Please . . ."

Beh Vah had squeezed his way to the front of the ranks and knelt beside the wheelchair, where he bounced on his haunches and clapped his hands in nervous anticipation. He said something that sounded like "Spiders now!" and held his hands palm-outward toward the woman, waiting for her to respond.

She laughed and reached out to pat his cheek. "In a minute, Beaver," she said. "I need to talk to somebody first." With her other hand she blotted away the mascara-flecked pools that were welling, Turner noticed now, beneath each of her eyes.

She wheeled herself slightly backward and made an adroit half-turn, to come around the desk toward him. The monks stepped reverently aside to watch.

"I'm sorry if we overwhelmed you, there," Turner began apologizing as she neared him. "Tibetans are very, uh, affectionate by . . . nature, and sometimes they . . ."

Her fine, tiny chin was quaking, and her piercing green-and-gold eyes spilled over anew. She held her arms up toward him.

Everything that had been till now the world and his life and the destination of time canted liquidly and foundered broadside against the obstruction of this moment, like the instant before a streambed is forced by a dam to feel out new paths across dry ground.

"Cass," he said. Not a question.

In a kind of dream he bent down and took her in his arms. To his surprise his hands remembered the architecture of her shoulder blades as if he'd held them just this morning, the small fine horn of bone at the base of her neck that his hand surmounted on the way up to stroke her hair. As he watched the dark slow-motion clouds overhead peel vividly apart only to converge again at the perimeter of the tinted glass, he wanted desperately to bury her in his chest like this for entire weeks of time. He felt his eyes swell and flood with the changed, unencumbered stream, reducing the room around him to shapes and colors and choking off his ability of speech.

Across the room he saw the underwater shapes of the monks tiptoeing silently out the door to afford privacy. All but Beh Vah, who lingered hopefully in the doorway with his hands flexing like spiderlegs at his sides until a frowning Lu Weh leaned back inside and peremptorily yanked him through.

Turner basked in the new quietness, the urgent patterns that Cassie's small powerful hands were drawing on his back, and for a while gave up trying to find words until someone, a stocky black-haired secretary, stuck her head around the door and said, "C.D.? Ron needs you to listen to that re-mix in Four, when you get a . . ." She saw Turner and went silent. She put her hand to her mouth in embarrassment. "Sorry."

Cassie turned half away from Turner's chest and sniffed to clear her head. "In a minute, Annie," she said, and then amended, "I might be a while."

The secretary discreetly disappeared, easing the door shut behind her.

C.D., Turner's befogged brain heard, half a beat behind reality.

C.D. Masterson . . . is Cassandra . . . Denise . . . McNamara, who is known and loved by the monks, and whose warning voice lately slammed into his head unsurprisingly to James Crowe because . . . ?

Because . . .

Turner felt the reality of the moment bounding ahead of him like a crazed hare in the distance, his mind unable even to keep within sight of it.

As the silence lengthened and his hunger for holding her became the least bit quenched, his desire to prolong the moment was gradually overcome by his desire to take care of some long overdue business. He eased apart from her and knelt in front of her chair.

The sight of her face, whole and in real time, flooded his insides with a joyous taste like light itself. Whenever he looked away and then back he feared she was a mirage that would have disappeared or else another concoction of the realm that would peel off its skin to expose the beast beneath. No. Here, real. Now. Cass.

But when he reached to take both of her hands in his, his elbows brushed the lifeless insubstantial knees inside her jeans and the awful realization ricocheted through him as pungently wounding as on the morning he opened the fateful newspaper. He knew . . . *knew* that if taken to its natural limits there was madness waiting at the end of that succession of thoughts and so he tried to smother it down, see her in the now, use this miraculous chance he'd prayed for and so nearly given up hope of ever having.

He fixed on her eyes, calmed himself, squeezed her hands.

"Look," he said. "You can say this is bullshit, and you'd be right, because it doesn't change anything, but I need to say it. Please?"

She waited.

"If I could give up my life," he said, "just give it, an even swap, to go back and do that morning over again, I would." Cassie started to speak but he pressed on, disallowing it. "I don't blame you for hating me. You've got a perfect right. I was a . . . poison, back then. I was poisoning everything around me. I'm so sorry."

Cassie started to speak again. "Listen," he shushed her. "Sometimes I think if I could just . . ."

"*You* listen," she said, her eyes radiating green fire as of old. She laid her fingertips against his chest, keeping him the proper distance while she said what she had to say.

"I never hated you. But I know some things now I didn't know. You weren't poison. You were on a poisoned *path*, and I was on a *crazy* one, and until I got off, what happened would have happened. With you, or with somebody. If I hadn't gotten off when I did, I'd probably be dead. Who's to say? The point being . . ."

"Then why wouldn't you see me?" Turner heard himself say, feeling the seemingly inexhaustible sentiment of a moment before eroding to a crust around a molten core of anger he had so successfully hidden from himself that it blindsided him now. "Or at least let me know you were alive?" He heard his volume rise uncomfortably, but his mouth seemed a step ahead of his reasoning ability and he couldn't rein it in. "I mean, *Jesus*, Cass, *anything*. A *postcard* wouldn't have killed . . . you . . ."

Cassie's face registered the irony without comment.

Jesus, God, he thought. *This has to stop*. He shut his eyes and a silhouette of a dark mountain trail reared up on either side, teetering crazily, gnarled stunted plants on either side giving off a poisonous musk. *Good work, Hope. Go it, holy man. You're sure handling this well.*

"The *point* being . . ." Cassie said evenly. He opened his eyes. " . . . that we can talk about all this later. We don't have time now. How soon do we have to go home for the Calling Out? A couple of weeks? Maybe less. Trust me, here. Work now, talk later." She squeezed his hand as clouds cascaded overhead.

The words registered in Turner's mind with delayed speed, as if at great remove.

We.

Have to go home.

"How do you know about all this?" he asked. "Have you been to Drepung, or . . ."

Cassie sighed patiently and released his hands. "It's a long, long, long story. But right now we need to get started on the album." She wheeled back toward the desk to retrieve a notebook, and began quickly leafing through its pages. As Turner watched her small intense profile his mind whirled, kept filling with castoff bits and pieces of old conversations they had had, old songs. *Imagine me and you, I do . . .*

She said, "I was thinking, what we could do with the Mountain Fennel movement is to let it be a segue into the Starlight piece, and that way . . ."

"And James Crowe, too," Turner interrupted. "How did he know your name, when I . . ."

Cassie held her place in the notebook and wheeled sharply up to him, her eyebrows raised. "Read my lips?" she asked. "Work . . . *now.* Talk . . ." She made circular hand motions toward herself as if pulling the answer from an obtuse student. "*La* . . . ter," she pronounced for him, pointing to her small wristwatch.

Turner laughed in spite of himself. "I hear what you're saying," he said.

"I was thinking, what we could do with the Mountain Fennel is . . . "

"I like it already," Turner said.

WHEELING DOWN the hallway with Turner and the monks in tow, Cassie handed him a sheet of paper over her shoulder. "You can be looking over the song list," she said, "while I give you the nickel tour. James ought to be here with the instruments by then and we can get started."

Beh Vah, walking nearest her, cleared his throat nervously. He reached to tap her on the shoulder and then lost his courage, looking imploringly at Turner.

"We can work as late as you guys want," she said. "I've got you booked into the Union Station Hotel, just a couple of blocks from here. Old place, but it's very nice. You guys'll be eating dinner at my house, though. Is that okay?"

There were general murmurs of assent as Turner tried to focus his mind enough to read the song list. Finally Beh Vah could constrain his need no longer. He threw himself in front of her wheelchair as if challenging a speeding car.

"Spiders now?" he asked, his face desperately hopeful.

Cassie threw back her head and laughed. Not a demure princess-laugh, as you expected from her appearance, but the coarse booming laugh of an Irish milkmaid several times her size. One more thing Turner had loved about her, that laugh.

"I *did* promise, didn't I?" she said. "All right, but just one, and then we work. Deal?"

"Dill," Beh Vah nodded. She kissed her fingertip and touched it to his forehead.

Beh Vah raised both his palms to face her, as if for a round of patty-cake, but rather than slapping them Cassie met them gently with her own freckled, ivory hands, palm to palm, fingertips matching. She shut her eyes. Beh Vah did, too.

After several breaths she flexed her palms slowly, in unison, until just the fingertips were left touching his. With only milliseconds of delay Beh Vah did the same, fingers curving until only the tips touched. The arrangement looked like two spiders dancing on a mirror.

Eyes still shut, Cassie unflexed her palms in approximately the rhythm of breathing. When they reached the invisible plane of air where they'd begun, Beh Vah's were there instinctively to meet them. As their palms touched he made a sound that was between a laugh and a sigh. Perfect contentment.

Turner felt suddenly like an interloper in some private ritual. He glanced around at the monks with their big glasses of iced tea that Cassie's secretary, Annie, had brought them earlier. Chai Lo was inspecting a small intricate painting on the wall, but the rest of them had their heads back, eyes closed, as if they were somehow participating in the exercise.

Underneath the awkwardness of the moment, Turner also felt a little . . . no, he didn't.

Yes, he did. Jealous was the only word for it. Here he'd gone and spent a goodly chunk of his life trying to be accepted by the monks, answering Won Se's endless maddening Zen riddles that made him feel like a child with a learning disability, so slow was he to catch on, or rather, to *quit* catching on; eating the horribly spartan monastery food, enough rice cakes and yak butter tea to stock a supermarket; trying to master ambulatory meditation on crutches in the building's dank stone hallways only to keep falling square on his butt.

And now Cassie wheels up out of oblivion and they treat her like queen of the May. Hell, yes, it chafed. Why shouldn't it?

"That was nice," Cassie said to Beh Vah. She disengaged her fingers from spider mode and squeezed his hands goodbye. Then she clapped hers. "Okay, now. Onward. We've got a lot to do in a short time."

Beh Vah kept his hands up. He looked at her longingly. "Pat cake?" he asked.

"Pat cake later," she said. "Work now."

"I don't understand," Turner said. "Was that, like, some sort of . . ."

Her glare cut him off. "Later," she said.

As they proceeded down the hall, he gave his attention to the song list again. It was already in sequence, with an attached sheet giving liner notes for each piece. Damned efficient, she was.

They came to a large glass-doored control room and Cassie motioned them inside. The soft recessed lighting, a tint of pink, gleamed off a wall of tape decks and electronic components, fronted by a massive mixing board that ran the length of the room. A small window, opposite, looked down on the acoustically-sealed studio, likewise softly lit, with its arsenal of microphone stands. Beh Vah gave a shudder of pleasure at the panorama, and bounced up and down on his heels.

"I was thinking with the flutes and cymbals we can go direct to digital," Cassie explained. "Save a lot of time in the mix that way. See, I can preprogram the equalization to clip at different frequencies depending on the volume. It gives you a . . . *roundness*, sort of, that you don't get with the old analog compression, having to ball-park it. But now, the *trumpets* are a different . . ."

"I don't think all these are going to fit," Turner broke in. He held up the list and pointed to the songs at the top. "Mountain Fennel is, what, twelve or thirteen minutes by itself? And Swan Flight's at least fifteen. We might have to leave out the . . ."

"It's a medley," Cassie said, with an efficient smile. "The trumpets, like I was saying, we'll need to do analog, because the distortion, the blatting, is part of the experience. So why get it synthetically when you can have the real thing? Just a plain Sennheiser mike and an old Ampex two-track deck. We'll experiment with different loads, to see where the best bleed-over happens, and . . ."

"Medley," Turner repeated. "You mean, *pieces* of them?"

He looked around to see how this blasphemy was going over with the monks. Beh Vah was running his fingers lovingly over the black chrome of the equipment. Chai Lo, Wah So, Se Hon, and Bah Tow were holding their iced teas dreamily up to the source of pink light, comparing the patterns made by drops of moisture condensing on the sides of the glasses. Lu Weh was sprawled on a couch at the far side of the room, softly snoring. None of them appeared ready allies in an argument of any sort. He'd have to carry the banner for truth and beauty single-handed.

"With all due respect," Turner said to Cassie, "this music's taken thousands of years to get to its current state of refinement. To be butchering it up now would kind of defeat the purpose, don't you think?"

"Oh, absolutely," Cassie said. "'Butchering' the music would be unforgivable. Fortunately, that's not my line of work. I'm a producer." She gestured to the room around her, as if to note the total absence of butcher's tools.

Turner nodded. "A *gifted* producer, obviously."

"Thank you," she said. She turned the angle of her chair toward the door. "Follow me, guys, and we'll . . ."

"I just don't think the songs should be cut up," Turner said. "It takes the full duration of each piece for your mind to go to all the places it needs to go."

Cassie kept rolling toward the door. One of the monks shook Louie awake so he could accompany them. "That *would* be ideal, wouldn't it?" she replied as she went. "If we didn't have time limitations."

"So, we could just do fewer songs," Turner shrugged.

"It would diminish the range and the effect," Cassie said. "Besides, it's too late to change the liner notes. They're being printed tonight. We want this first pressing in the stores by Friday."

"Friday?" Turner was incredulous. "That's impossible."

"Thank you."

"Is it unusual for a group's manager not to have a say-so in any of this?"

"Highly unusual. Now, if we can get on with . . ."

"Listen, I appreciate what you're doing, and I'm not trying to be difficult, here. I just think these kinds of judgments are something we both need to . . ."

Cassie stopped her chair in the door and wheeled it one hundred eighty degrees in a heartbeat to face him, her eyes flashing.

"Look, I was *saved* . . . to do this," she said.

Turner wasn't sure he'd heard right. "Saved. As in, uh, religiously?" he stammered.

"As in, I was hooked up to a hundred fucking tubes and my newly crippled little ass didn't die. *Capiche*?"

The monks, arrayed on either side of her, looked at Turner as if he'd broken wind in public.

"Please," she said, her tone a little softened. "There's no time for this, now. We've got work to do. If it bothers you, you don't have to watch."

While Turner was deciding how to respond she spun her chair and headed toward the studio, her entourage in queue, leaving him alone in the room with his thoughts.

"BEAUTIFUL!" CASSIE said into the control room's microphone, when the last note of the song had faded to silence and the twenty-four dancing channel displays of digital red ebbed to a row of single dashes. "That was the best take yet, guys!" She turned to James Crowe for agreement and got a fervent nod, then looked across to Turner. He gave her a thumbs-up sign. The lady knew her shit, one hundred percent. The boys had never sounded so good.

In the small room on the other side of the glass, the monks' sweating faces brightened with the hope of release. Doing the same number ten and twelve times in a row with minor variations of rhythm and phrasing was a new and exhausting experience to them. Bah Tow and Se Hon and Wah So laid their huge horns aside and made fish-lips, which they blotted with their sleeves. Their mouths looked to be swollen from the friction of the low notes. They slapped their cheeks, trying to get some feeling back. It was serious nighttime by now. The office staff had left long ago.

"Let's do the same thing a couple more times for insurance," Cassie said through the monitor speakers. A look of ineffable sorrow fell upon all the monks' faces. Beh Vah, standing with his knees tight together, laid down his cymbal and meekly raised his hand.

"Mince rum?" he implored Cassie.

"Good idea, Beaver," she said. "Let's all take a bathroom break and come back in five. Coffee's in my office, if anybody needs it." She rolled back from the big mixing board and stretched her arms above her head. "James, my man," she said. "Got some good bourbon in there, too."

James seemed to find that notion appealing, which in turn seemed to please Cassie. The idea of James with a caffeine buzz was too fearsome to contemplate. He stalked off hyperactively to investigate the provisions, leaving Cassie and Turner in the control room alone.

"You're good," Turner said to her. "No, scratch that. You're *great.* You're the best I've ever seen."

She busied herself with adjustments to the knobs of the mixing board.

"That deaf, dumb, and blind kid sure plays a mean pinball," she said.

"Look, I'm sorry if I was out of line, earlier," Turner said.

The directionless pink light of the control room accentuated the bridge of freckles across Cassie's nose. She looked directly at him for several seconds. In the deep galaxies of her eyes, nighttime had come. Nothing revealed.

"It was a good sign," she said. "You're learning to stand up for yourself." She gave a small, fatigued smile. "You've come a long way."

He knew the rules, but the questions that fountained so insistently from his heart demanded release. In the mellowness of the moment,asking just one seemed worth a try.

"At the airport," he said, "when you were in my mind? How did you . . ."

Her hand went up, and with surprising tenderness the backs of her fingers followed the line of his jaw.

"Ears can't answer questions," she said. "You know that."

"Ears . . . ?"

"When I'm recording, I turn into one great big ear. At midnight I turn back into a person again. Then we can talk."

"No question too large or small?" he asked.

"You might say that."

He noticed the big digital clock on the wall behind her. "God, time flies in here," he said. "I need to use your phone."

"See the other big booth, straight across? Take the short flight of steps to the control room, and the phone's on the back wall." She looked around at the clock. "I need to check on something before the guys get back," she said, and wheeled down the hall toward her office.

As Turner passed through the big booth, the soundproofing made the silence seem unnaturally intense in his ears. But when he got to the high-up control room, natural sounds returned. The dimly-lit room was all tinted glass on two facing sides, one looking out on Nashville's night skyline and the other showing the maze of studios and supply rooms below. As Turner dialed his grandparents' number he could see Beh Vah, back from his bathroom break, reverently touching the walls of electronic gear in the room where Cassie was recording.

A busy signal. Well, that's progress, he thought. At least somebody's there. While he waited to try again, an image from the past came to him, out of the pure blue but fully rendered: old Won Se at breakfast one festival day, telling a convoluted story from his childhood about the tribulations of dealing with a stubborn yak. The big stone dining room filling up with rich sunshine the color of butter, the monks bursting out at each juncture of the tale with a laughter as unsullied as that of small children.

Turner had been superficially certain, then, that when his time came to die and he asked himself the requisite questions, *When were you really happy? When were you really loved?* the morning would play itself back for him, along with a dismayingly small handful of other perfect moments from over the years. Most of them at Zion Hill.

He wondered why pangs of homesickness for Drepung and Zion Hill never stabbed him through while he was looking at photographs of the places, or writing a letter to his grandparents or Won Se. Never when he was expecting it, was prepared. Always like this—before he realized, cutting his off-guard heart to the quick.

He dialed the number again and heard a blessed ringing.

"Hello?" His grandmother's voice, even and strong. Hallelujah.

"Hello! How are y'all doing, lady?"

"Well . . . pretty good. Where are you at?" Nothing wonderful or horrible ever happened in Zion Hill, only the *pretty good* and the *not so good.* Delicate variations in the stresses its residents placed on certain syllables were your only clues as to how good or bad a situation actually was. His grandmother had slightly accented the "pretty" over the "good." That was not good.

"I'm in Nashville," he said. "What's wrong? Have you been under the weather?"

"Jackson had a sort of . . . falling-out spell yesterday."

Turner's rise in spirit evaporated. Through the phone he heard a slight grunt and a sigh of cushions as she sat down on the couch. This time of night she'd have her blue chenille housecoat on, and her white hair would be up in rollers for tomorrow's prayer meeting at Zion Hill Baptist. The windows would be open to the lonely chitting of cicadas, and the big cast-iron window fan would be stirring the warm air.

"You mean he fainted?"

"On the toilet. I heard a racket, and there he was. On the floor." There was the least perceptible edge of fear in her tone of voice, one that a stranger would not have picked up on; she seemed to hear the variation, and pretended she had only needed to clear her throat. Her facade of normalness returned. "They kept him last night for what-you-call-it, observation, and then run a bunch of tests on him this morning."

"What did the tests say?"

"Won't hear back till tomorrow. They're hoping it's just blood pressure. But it's never bothered him before."

"How's he feeling?"

"Aw, sassy as a possum. Just his regular self." This was not a reliable guide, Turner knew. His grandfather was as good an actor as she was.

"Could I talk to him?"

"He's just dozed off, but I'll go and . . ."

"No, no, no. Let him rest, really. I'll call back tomorrow. Let me give you some phone numbers where we'll be, in case you need me." He found a directory in a desk drawer, gave her the number of the hotel and of Gamma. "We'll be down to see you in a few days, I hope. As soon as we wrap up some recording. I'm getting kind of homesick."

A silence at the other end of the line, then a weary exhalation of breath.

"It's time, you mean," she said.

Time? What . . .

"Oh, it's *past* time I got to eat some of your cooking," Turner said with a congenial laugh, just in case she hadn't meant what she plainly seemed to. "I've been missing y'all, real bad."

Silence again. She wasn't falling for that. In a flash of remembrance he saw again Won Se's somber face by torchlight in the Drepung basement, telling him *Your grandparents, they are prepared.*

"I thought it had to be pretty close," she said with resignation. "So many signs. And now this." *This*, the illness.

In the quiet he heard the spectral frequency of the cicadas and, farther off, a dog howling. One of Johnny Patterson's sleek coon hounds.

"Hon, we're praying for you," she said. "Just come ahead, whenever you need to."

He tried to think of something to say, in summary, that was both pertinent and comforting. But nothing came and, as was so often the case, she beat him to the punch.

"We love you, hon," she said.

THOUGH HE COULD see through the glass that the crew was reassembling in the studio below, Turner decided he had to call Won Se. He counted the time zones on his fingers and determined it would be early morning at Drepung.

As the phone rang, he noticed Cassie in earnest conversation with an attractive middle-aged man in a business suit. They were sharing a laugh about something. She patted the man's arm as he left the studio. Turner felt an instant pang of jealousy, which he tried to quash by reasoning with himself. *She's got a life, okay*? He turned his attention to the phone.

After the usual rigmarole of operators and connections, Nohr Bu the grocer came on the line. "Unh?" In the background were the sounds of livestock, and the voices of old men arguing spiritual politics around the store's oil-fired heater.

Turner started the litany of polite inquiries that amounted to a proper greeting, but Nohr Bu cut him off with a grunt that sounded like "Wait" in Tibetan.

"Tur-ner?"

Won Se's voice.

"Won Se? Nu-en!" Turner said. "Pretty good timing, huh?"

Won Se explained that he'd come into the village to call Lucille, in hopes of tracking Turner down. Some good news, he said. For a change. The Tally of Inner Blindness had taken its biggest one-day drop ever, so they must be doing something right.

"Biggest ever?" Turner asked. His pulse speeded up. "Really? So we're over the hump, you think?" He was thinking of how else to translate the figure of speech (maybe *out of the woods*?) when Won Se showed he understood by laughing sadly.

"Det, det," he said. Then a long Tibetan phrase that translated roughly as "still a ways to go." Turner knew better than to ask how far because the language purposefully kept the matter vague.

"You will do well," Won Se said.

Progress, though. At least they were making progress. They had to remember that, stay pumped up.

Won Se asked their whereabouts.

When Turner told him Nashville, he seemed—at least for Won Se—enthusiastic.

"Nashville! Cassie?"

Turner looked down at her again through the rooms of glass, still afraid that if he lost track of her, didn't keep verifying, it would all turn out to have been a dream.

"Cassie. Yes. Listen . . . why didn't somebody tell me about her?"

A loud, rollicking laugh came from Won Se, the kind of explosion that was apt to come from a monk who had just made, or watched someone else make, a leap of understanding about the nature of the universe. It was one way monks worshipped.

"She is wonderful, is not?" Won Se asked, when he'd got his breath. "A . . . how to say . . . firecracker."

"I said, why didn't somebody *tell* me about her?"

Won Se lapsed into a puzzled silence. "Tell what?"

"Well . . . everything. Anything."

"You would believe?" Won Se asked. "And if you had, what difference would you have done than what you do? Did."

Fractured verb tenses aside, he had a point, there.

Turner pressed on. "But look, I'm supposed to be in charge, right? And people keep popping up out of the bushes with orders to help us, and it's all news to me. First James, and now this. I just feel like I'm in the dark, most of the time."

"Good for eyesight," Won Se said.

When Turner, in exasperation, began to approach the argument from a slightly different angle, the old monk replied with a maxim concerning woods-rabbits, something to the effect that a watch pocket on one would be merely for decoration. Turner decided to drop the issue for now, get what scraps of information he could.

"So how does everybody else know her, then?" he asked. "When was she at Drepung?"

Above the long-distance hum he could hear Won Se gently clucking his tongue, a sign that he was deep in thought.

"Not easy to say," Won Se said, finally. "A story best to come from mouth of the hearse, when time is left."

"You mean, from the horse's mouth? When time is right?"

"Exactly. Not a fence."

"No . . . offense?"

"Good, then. Good. My love to all, Tur-ner."

A question flashed in Turner's mind. "Any news about the Calling Out? How soon it might be?"

Won Se took the slow, weary deep breath of an old man, a near silence which thousands of miles of static rushed in to fill. Turner was thinking he might have been cut off, when Won Se said sadly, "Understanding that we are, how you say . . ."

Turner had heard the caveat a thousand times; his patience gave out.

"Your methods are imprecise as the devil," he finished for Won Se. "Right. I've got all that."

"Devil not imprecise," Won Se said sternly. "Has better equipment. Do not denude yourself."

Turner started to correct him with "delude" but thought better of it. He got the message.

"How long, then?" he asked. "In your estimation."

"Weeks, at most. Two, three. Perhaps days."

Turner's response was a contradictory mix of emotions—excitement and dread, with the excitement slightly ascendant. It was impossible to explain to anyone who hadn't been in a war: the sense of exaltation, the bizarre joy, when you've waited days for the forces of destruction to show themselves, heard their breathings and mutterings in all the air around you, and finally the wall of bamboo opens and death comes at you like a horizontal rain. You'd rather be anywhere in the universe but where you are, but you feel the *there* with such rhapsodic sweetness, so much more acutely than any *there* before, Technicolor life to the tenth power, and all because you've just been set free. From the waiting. Insane, but true. How else could there be war? Except that during his training at Drepung, Won Se kept reminding him that the coming conflagration would not be quite like that. Somewhat, but not quite. *More a, how to say, spirit war.* When pushed to elaborate, he always demurred.

"Tur-ner. Are you there?"

"Just thinking. I have a hard time staying focused, these days. I feel so *old*. So scattered. I hope I can . . ."

"You will do well," Won Se cut in. "Most especially now, with your half another."

Other half, Turner translated silently, and Cassie's remark of a few hours ago came back to him. *We* have to go home . . .

No way, he thought. Though he hadn't told anyone yet, the first thing he planned to do when he hit Zion Hill was pack his grandparents off to safety for the duration—maybe with some friends who have a lake place a comfortable half-hour from where the hell would break loose. The last thing he needed was to put Cassie, wheelchair and all, in the way of danger too. She would clearly have to stay put, here. He didn't relish breaking the news to her, but it was a bridge he would cross when he came to it.

"Look," Turner said, "I really have some concerns about that. I think . . ."

"Tur-ner? Must go now. Nohr Bu requires the phone. A joy talking for you. Be heartful. You have our love."

Static. A dial tone.

Down in the booth, the monks were blowing and cymbaling with all their might. When Cassie wasn't turning knobs she was clapping along, swaying in her chair to a rhythm he couldn't hear.

"SEE WHAT YOU think," Cassie said to Turner as she cued up the tape for playback. It was clear from her expression, though, not to mention the looks of satisfaction on the exhausted monks who sprawled on the floor of the booth, that the stuff was good and she knew it.

The whirring tape reel braked itself and changed direction. A horizon of red LEDs glowed in the belly of the big deck, and with the first note of music the lights began their dance, the stack above each channel rising and falling to show the intensity of each instrument. James Crowe, back from his cocktail break and gliding easy, pulled up a chair alongside her and leaned contentedly toward the digital dancing colors as if toward a fire on a hearth.

"This is strictly a rough mix," Cassie apologized. "I'll do a cleaner one in the morning." But the sound quality was still gorgeous. Legend had it that C.D. Masterson's rough mixes were better than other producers' finished products. The monks, hearing themselves on tape for the first time, wore transcendent grins.

"It's perfect," Turner said. "Sounds just like being on-stage." Cassie smiled broadly.

Suddenly the music stopped. Cassie looked around for the cause, but everything seemed to be in order. The reels still turned. She flicked a monitor switch back and forth. No sound, no readout on the LEDs. "This is absolutely strange," she said. She leaned over and inspected a vertical column of tiny silver switches on the backplate of one of the machines, then began flipping them one by one with her fingernail.

Abruptly, the speakers blared with music—but a different song, and only a single instrument's part. There was distortion of some sort; the notes sounded muddy and far away.

Cassie reached for a panel of rocker-switches and hit STOP, then rewound and played the tape again, with the same result. "Well, shit," she said, hitting a switch to halt the machine. "Where's my brain? I'm not believing this."

"What's wrong?" Turner asked.

"Somehow I've managed to tape the second batch of songs on *top* of the first batch. Which ordinarily would mean the first batch is lost, but the second one's okay. *Except* that some of the track assignments have gotten switched, so I've only got partials on *them.*"

"Couldn't the guys play in sync to the partial tracks and fill them out?"

"Well, they could. But if you've never synced before, it takes forever. It'd just frustrate them. Plus, monks aren't playing to an external concept of rhythm in the first place. No two performances are ever exactly the same, and it's that little feather-edge of dissonance that contains their whole meaning. You couldn't create that artificially in a hundred years."

"Right," Turner said. "I wasn't thinking about that." What the hell was she talking about? How did she know all of this?

Cassie looked over at the mute tape reels and shook her head.

"So, the bottom line is . . . ?" Turner prompted, afraid that he knew.

Cassie clawed her hair angrily with both hands, making it look like she'd just gotten up. "The bottom line is, we're screwed," she said. "We have to do it over from scratch. I'm very sorry."

Se Hon leaned forward and tapped Turner's knee, looking embarrassed. "Which part did we scratch?" he asked.

"Oh, you guys did fine," Turner said. "That's just a figure of speech. We're having some technical problems, is all."

"Tech . . . nology . . . problem?" Wah So asked. Turner nodded. The monks all gave each other knowing looks, as if to say, what could you expect from technology?

All of them but Chai Lo, that is, who stood off to the side fuming over some problem of his own. He sidled up to Turner and said grimly, "We must talk. Alone."

"Un*less*," Cassie interrupted, oblivious to the monks and Turner as she completed some inventory of options in her mind. "Unless I did what I *think* I did, and stored the analog tracks in digital too, just as a backup." She wheeled to the opposite end of the wide console, and switched on a computer screen that was built into the wall. She ran her finger down a list of glowing orange commands, her smile slowly growing.

"Bingo," she said. "It's all on disk. Hah."

"Just a second, Shy," Turner said. "Is that as good?" he asked Cassie.

"It'll take an extra hour or two of monkeying with the EQ in the mix, but otherwise we're home free. Sure beats doing it over." Except for Chai

Lo, the monks' outlooks brightened considerably. Scattered about the floor in various attitudes of repose, they looked to have been ridden hard and put up wet.

"Let me just call up the file and double-check," Cassie said. She pulled a sliding keyboard from under the countertop and typed in a command.

"It is *important,*" Chai Lo whispered to Turner, through clenched teeth.

"This is too, buddy," Turner said, patting his arm. "Just a second, please."

The orange screen filled with a complicated menu; Cassie chose an option and hit ENTER. The screen went dark. Inside the wall, some giant disk drive made a grind and hum, then stopped. The screen filled with rows of nonsense characters and began flickering like a strobe light. Cassie tried to type in commands, but nothing fazed its rapid cycling of on-and-off.

"God . . . *damn* it," she said, slapping at the keyboard. "The program's gone haywire. I am absolutely not believing this." She sized up the glum mood of the gathering, and the fact that Lu Weh, whose head had slid gradually forward to his knees, was snoring softly.

"It might be a bug that's got into the code," James Crowe said matter-of-factly, stroking his chin.

"How can we find out?" Cassie asked.

James wheeled his chair toward the keyboard. "Get me back to its brain, please."

"Its what?"

"Assembly language. Its brain."

"How do I do that?"

"Just keep hitting *escape* till it won't escape no more," he said. Cassie began doing this, until eventually only a tiny glowing prompt showed at the top of the dark screen.

Turner knelt alongside them and put his hand on Crowe's shoulder. "James, I didn't know you were a computer expert."

"I'm not, Cap'n. But I *do* know hex."

"Hex? You mean, like voodoo?"

Crowe rolled his eyes. "The hexa*decimal* system," he said. "It's the way these little puppies think. And hex ain't nothing but numbers." He smiled mischievously, as if that shortcoming made the machine his oyster. "I just need a little time alone with it, is all."

"How much time?"

Crowe stood and professorially inspected the various components of the machine before shrugging his shoulders. "Two-three months," he said. Cassie put her hands over her eyes in despair.

"Just jokin'," Crowe said. "Maybe several hours, if I'm lucky."

Turner couldn't help being a touch skeptical. "But if you don't know how to *program* . . ."

Crowe looked to the ceiling again. "The program's just numbers, and the numbers are . . . a *pattern*," he said, opening his arms wide as if this explained everything. "You never read Heinrich's work on pattern recognition?"

Turner looked to Cassie, who shook her head. He looked to Crowe and did likewise.

"It's neat stuff," Crowe said, rubbing his hands, his former bourbon mellowness wearing off. "See, he thinks the missing link between the optic component and the cortex follows the Lorentz equation, with one big exception . . ."

Cassie laid a hand on his knee. "James? Would you try, please?"

"Sure."

"We could bring you some food and leave you alone." She looked around at the energy level of the troupe and said to Turner, "Why don't we just break for dinner, start again bright and early. And hope our luck's better."

The monks looked at one another hesitantly. Se Hon raised a timid hand and cleared his throat. "Not to be a, how say, Annie Social," he said, "but I would like sleep for dinner, my own self." This appeared to meet with general agreement, and Crowe turned expectantly toward the keyboard.

Chai Lo's face, with its grim imperative, suddenly dominated Turner's field of view.

"Excuse us, just a minute," Turner said to the group, and ushered Chai by the elbow out into the darkened hallway.

"What's wrong?"

"Can you miss it?" The monk sniffed bitterly. "Your sweet boy has savage taught us again. Beyond a shadow, this time. I see him with my eyes."

Turner groaned. He didn't have the energy for this. "Shy, this is ridiculous. There's nothing the realm would like better than to get us fighting among ourselves. We can't let that happen."

"With my *eyes*," Chai Lo repeated. "He sneaks back to musical room before us."

"The studio?" Turner said.

Chai Lo nodded. "I follow and see him touching machines."

Turner felt a twinge of unease. That much, he knew was true. He'd seen Beaver drift back to the studio alone.

No. Not credible. Beaver's tearful denial, the morning at the Black Flamingo Motel, played on Turner's mind's eye with full intensity.

Chai seemed to read his thoughts. "Oh, happens dance," he said, with an edge of sarcasm. "Of course."

"Shy, be reasonable. It takes *years* for somebody to master all that equipment. You think a kid can waltz in and figure out in thirty seconds how to throw a wrench in the works?"

"The rim gives knowledge. Powers," Chai said defensively.

"You're saying the holy reincarnation of Lim Rhya would take an . . . *electronics* course from the realm, just to be able to do us in? Who was it tested Beaver, as a reincarnate? You were in on that, weren't you?"

"With my eyes . . ." Chai Lo repeated.

"*Forget* your damned eyes for a minute, okay? Beaver was . . . what, six years old? Seven? And he could recite every *word* of the teachings of an eighty-year-old man he'd never heard of. Has a reincarnate holy man ever been a Betrayer?"

Chai Lo didn't answer right away. "Always a time for first," he said, finally.

Turner held his eye for several seconds until Chai looked off. "All right," Chai shrugged, turning slowly to go back to the room. "Happens dance."

But his conversion wasn't convincing. Turner waited, one, two, three, for Chai Lo to hesitate and face him again. Which he did.

"Lots of happens dance," he said, with a bitter smile. "Happens dance the Judas knew to flee the airplane before we did."

The lost mouse-ears.

Turner's shaken composure must have shown on his face, judging from Chai Lo's look of triumph. The monk paused just long enough for it to register and turned again to go. "Sweet boy," he said, as he retreated. "Much happens dance."

Turner looked up and saw Beh Vah's face against the glass of the studio door, watching the exchange of words with an expression that could have been exhaustion, or fear; from the shadow on it, he couldn't tell.

Circumstantial or not, the evidence hurt Turner's heart. The monks' lives were in his hands. He was the man in charge. The Hope. Could he afford to ignore even the least kernel of truth in what Chai claimed?

With my eyes . . .

Hurt heart or not, Turner knew, from here on out his own eyes would be on Beh Vah.

14

THE OLD FREIGHT elevator rattled and squeaked and groaned the whole way down, the dangling light bulb in its ceiling doing pendulum swings that made Turner's and Cassie's shadows yaw and tilt like a fun house ride. "Warsaw could have a field day imitating this thing," Turner told her.

"We have a piano tuner come out and work on it about once a year," Cassie said.

"Seriously?"

"No. We've done some taping in here, though."

"You mean, a record?"

"The opening of George Jones's 'Down, Down, Down.' Remember the sound effects?"

"Sure."

The big cage shuddered and whomped to a halt. Turner reached to throw the iron lever that opened the door, but Cassie beat him to it and wheeled out into the dark basement. A red sports car sat against the far wall. Several men in cowboy hats and sequin jackets stood around the car in an attitude suggesting threat, their faces in shadow.

"Are these people, uh . . ." Turner asked, reaching for Cassie's shoulder to hold her back, but she outpaced him and he had to trot. Only when he got closer did he see the figures were mannequins. He recognized Ernest Tubb, Bill Monroe, Hank Williams.

"My bodyguards," Cassie explained. "I've got a friend who's a stylist at the Opry museum. He leaves people here while they're waiting to be cleaned." She wheeled to the driver's side of the two-seater car, and before Turner could get near enough to offer help she'd already opened the door, vaulted herself inside, and was folding the chair to stash behind her seat.

When he opened the passenger-side door the green arms of a big fern sprang out at him, its pot fastened in place with the seat belt.

"Uh-oh," Cassie said. "I forgot about that."

"No problem. I can hold it."

"Could you? I don't live far."

Turner disengaged the belt and sat by the fern, then worked at wrestling the big pot over into his lap. A wave of exhilaration and disbelief washed over him from out of nowhere, as it had been doing ever since their reunion. Of the hundred lives he had imagined for Cassie in her absence, over the years—lawyer for the downtrodden, Peace Corps worker in some small peasant country, a teacher of children—none of them was remotely like this one. And in none of the imaginary lives was she alone and unattached, as she was appearing more and more to be; in his masochistic prescience he had always outfitted her with a strapping white knight at her side, a guy much wiser and steadier and handsomer, far less rumpled and wrinkled than himself, a doctor maybe, good solid pacifist during the war, who had helped her pick up the pieces of her life after the accident and was ever after reaping the benefits, a hell of a happy life, and who, during her occasional bouts of depression, listened to and abetted in her impassioned excoriation of the devil Turner and afterward, when her crying jag was spent, would make patient and redemptive love to her into the morning hours.

But by some inexplicable working of grace, Turner not only sat beside her now but felt, or thought he did, the old easeful connections of mind and heart re-establishing themselves—or, more amazing, as if they'd never been severed, but had existed in some continuum beyond conscious thought. There was special comfort in the silences between them because he felt, as in old days, that he could almost, *almost*, read her mind.

And so when he asked, "So, do you take your plants out to, like, movies and the zoo, or do they just ride around with you?" he anticipated the droll sidewise glance of her response.

"Smartass. No, this one's not mine." She started up the car and pressed a button under the dash that made the convertible top retract with a slight whine of gears. "It belongs to Ann. You met her. My assistant? It's ailing, and she wanted me to give it therapy."

She revved the motor a couple of times with the hand-controlled accelerator on the steering column and then shifted into gear, sending the car flying across the basement and straight toward a brick wall. Turner had his panicked hand on the door handle, ready to unburden himself of the big fern and bail out, when at some invisible signal a section of the wall sprang upwards and let the car sail through.

The narrow concrete ramp outside quickly surfaced to a deserted alley between skyscrapers; Turner looked back and saw the receding panel of brick lowering itself into place, its edges indistinguishable from the rest of the wall. He laid his hand on his heart to feel the pounding. So much for mind-reading, he thought.

Cassie glanced around and saw the aftermath of his shock. "I'm sorry," she said. "I keep forgetting you don't know all this stuff yet."

"A secret entrance?"

She smiled. "Every recluse should have one."

The dark alleyway opened out into a street of lights. Even at this late hour the row of record stores and souvenir shops was milling with tourists eating corndogs and taking snapshots of each other in front of Ernest's place and Roy's place and Loretta's place and Dolly's place. Cassie took a left, downhill, away from the lights and the city center. The warm night air tousled Turner's hair, made the fern in his arms dance.

Several blocks later they were into a forbidding-looking section of warehouses and vacant lots. The street lights got farther and farther apart.

"Hang on," Cassie said. She twirled the wheel and swerved left across oncoming traffic, twirled right again and goosed the hand-control brake to bring them to a perfect stop beside a newspaper machine at the curb. She got some quarters from a change purse on the dash and bought a paper.

"For your scrapbook," she said, tossing it in Turner's lap before accelerating back into traffic with sufficient verve to set his head backwards on his neck by several inches. Through the whipping fronds of the fern he could see that the front page of *USA Today* had a big color picture of the monks on-stage just below the fold. Scattered words of Zotfeld's accompanying story jumped out at him, though he was too tired and rattled to read it through coherently. Mystical. Cosmic. Life-changing. Breakthrough.

He felt the beginnings of the old excitement, the momentum of adrenaline, from the days when getting an inch of press was like pulling a tooth. Back when being the underdog was fun.

Cassie yelled above the turbulence of wind, "Sound like some eager record-buyers to you?"

AT AN OPENING in the trees they turned onto a narrow gravel road that carried them toward what Turner first thought was a spotlight but which, as the trees thinned, became the rising full moon. The road kept leading downhill. At a certain bend in it, the woods ceased altogether and the broad

Tennessee River opened out below them in the moonlight like diamonds on black velvet. No sign of a house anywhere, or of any light other than the moon.

"Not exactly on the beaten path," Turner commented.

"Nope," Cassie said, gearing down for a sharp left turn in the gravel that looked to lead them down into the river itself.

The gravel became a small concrete ramp, and as she pulled under a narrow car shed and shut off the engine Turner's eyes adjusted enough to the nighttime to see the huge dark bulk of a houseboat docked at the river's edge. The void of sound in the wake of the silenced engine quickly came to be filled with crickets and cicadas, and with the soft mutter and slap of waves against the houseboat's bow.

The effect on Turner was so hypnotic he didn't realize Cassie had gotten out of the car until she suddenly wheeled into his field of vision and opened his door. "I'll take that," she said, and before he could protest she swung the heavy pot of fern onto her lap and rolled, at a brisk pace, down toward the boat.

By the time Turner could follow, she had hoisted the fern into the jungle of greenery along a wide rail that ran the circumference of the boat's surrounding patio, and was digging for her door key in the pocket of her jeans.

"Come here," Cassie said, when she heard Turner clomp onto the planks of the entrance. He stopped alongside her chair. She was squinting across the water, though not in the direction of the moon, which was hidden at this low vantage. "No, here," she said. "Bend down."

With her hand she guided his head into place alongside hers.

"See that?"

At first he thought the speck of light in the woods was a firefly, but it blinked with such exact regularity he decided it had to be manmade—the kind of beacon that warns airplanes away from tall buildings.

"What is it?" Turner asked.

"My office. Straight down from the beacon, about the width of your thumb. You could see the light in my window, if it were on. And I can see my house from my office, when I leave a porch light on."

"Really?"

"Yeah. That's why I bought this place. It seemed like such a nice . . . symmetry, I guess. So near and yet so far." She unlocked the door and rolled confidently into the dark, turning on soft lamps as she went. The glow illuminated low couches, walls of books, voluminous green plants. The layout seemed oddly familiar to Turner; had he been on a houseboat before, sometime in his life? He guessed there were only so many variations on the space.

But this one was clearly her: much practicality, very little decoration for decoration's sake. He liked it.

"Drink?" she called to him from the kitchen.

"Anything," he said. As he bent to sit down, an icicle of pain shot from his hip to his bad knee. "And some aspirin would be nice."

"You're gin and tonic, right?"

"How did you know?" As teenagers, liquor had never darkened the doors of their teetotalling households—their only venture in that regard being an occasional furtive six-pack of beer at the notorious county line. "I said, how did you know?"

No answer from Cassie, only the clinking of glasses and ice. Just as she'd declined to answer how she knew the monks, and how she knew about the death-plane, and . . .

Something familiar had been tapping at the edge of his memory, and he realized now what it was. The lingering smell of incense. The good, full-spectrum Tibetan kind. Strange.

When she brought out the tray with their drinks there were two small citron-colored capsules alongside his glass.

"Aspirin?" he asked.

"Better. It's an herbal blend. I make it myself."

"What's it called?" He palmed the capsules and raised them to his mouth.

"Acid for beginners," Cassie said.

The hand with the medicine hesitated. He took a polite sip of his drink.

"A joke," she said. "Really, it's harmless. All natural. It doesn't just anesthetize your brain, it heals it. Go ahead. You've had a hell of a day."

He looked at the capsules skeptically. "I need to be clear-headed in the morning," he said.

"Don't we all."

How could he refuse those eyes anything?

"No after-effects. You're sure."

"Positive."

He downed the capsules with a swallow of the citrusy gin.

A wind chime tolled from the deck outside, sounding eerily like the one at Drepung. A tugboat, far downriver, blew its rough horn. In his throat, the capsules trailed rainbows of warmth all the way down.

"I was thinking maybe you'd serve tea and oranges," Turner said. "The kind that come all the way from China."

"What? Oh. The old Cohen song. No, I think I'm out of oranges. There's tea, though."

"*Suzanne takes you down to a place by the river*," Turner sang, *"She feeds you tea and oranges that come all the way from China . . ."* One of their favorite songs, that last summer. What did the next verse say?

"Rest," Cassie said. "Put your feet up. Dinner won't be long."

"Can I help?"

"By putting . . ."

" . . . my feet up. Yes, ma'am."

When he stretched out on the couch she put her hand to his forehead for a second, as if checking a child for fever. Her fingers felt cool on his skin, and smelled of thyme, or whatever she was cooking with. Turner shut his eyes for a second and felt the worries and fears of the day slowly shedding from him like an outgrown skin. The wind chimes carried him back to his small room at Drepung, waking late at night to see the moon rising through the coarse, rippled glass, changing shape as it climbed. "You know, I was just thinking . . ." he said, but when he tried to put words to his thoughts they eluded him. So peaceful, here, he thought . . .

A HAND TOUCHING his shoulder. He sat up. Woke up.

"What? What is it?"

"Dinner time," Cassie said. "We can eat outside. The rain's not blowing yet."

A flute played softly somewhere. Spice-scent blew through the room on the damp wind.

Rain?

"How long did I sleep?"

"Exactly long enough. How's your aches and pains?"

"Better. No. Gone, as a matter of fact."

"Good. Bless your heart. You had a rough day. Come on . . ." A small freckled hand out for him, to pull up from the couch.

Back beyond the kitchen, a small table outside on the canopied deck. A candle in glass, smelling of citronella. The tiniest crescent moons at Cassie's earlobes, catching the light. New, or had he just not noticed them before?

She poured them both white wine from a carafe. Their plates were steaming brown rice on beds of greenery, paper-thin slices of some delicate fish on top. The first bite, pungent and mildly sweet, settled onto his palate like a dream. A soft rain fell, gently percussive in the cloth of the canopy. The gauze of cloud across the risen moon made its reflection in the dark river indistinct and enormous.

"You're amazing," Turner said. "Is there anything you *don't* know how to do?"

Cassie looked at him, into him. "Lie to the Hope," she said. "What do you want to know?"

The omnipresent flute sailed an octave and a half upward, breaking new sonic ground. His head felt crystal clear, big enough to walk around in. Where to start. Deep, deep breath.

"What did you mean, when you said you were 'saved' to do our record? And how come all the guys already knew you? This 'spiders' thing, and . . ."

Cassie threw back her head and laughed a big, ego-less, child laugh that echoed across the water.

"The Hope is jealous," she said, with absolute delight. The tiny crescent moons flashed.

"I didn't say . . . I mean, I'm not . . ." Turner took a big swallow of wine. "Okay, maybe a little," he said. "But about the 'saved' part . . ."

He felt her mood shift, become instantly somber. She sipped her wine and looked out at the pattern the rain made on the water and for a few seconds Turner would not have been surprised if she'd started to cry. But then she stretched and sighed to herself and, when she looked at him again, seemed mostly restored.

"Not just to do the record," she said. "I mean for the whole thing. All of this. I . . . where do you want me to start?"

Turner hesitated. "The beginning, I guess."

"You mean, the day I left?"

Turner drained his wine glass in one gulp and refilled it from the carafe. "Yeah," he said, looking out at the water. "That day."

She sighed. A long silence. Then she said, "I was bluffing, for one thing."

Turner saw, as real as if it were in front of him, her departure for California in the white '62 Fairlane, her nineteen and seeing the world open up for her after waiting so long at its door; her parents tearful at the curb, reminding her that the place she was going was bereft of spiritual values and so she needed to keep Jesus always in her heart.

"Bluffing?" he said. "You mean you didn't want to go?"

"Sure I did. But not by myself. I kept waiting for you to make a scene, or something. Cry and beg, I guess. Well, no matter. Water under the bridge. I shouldn't have brought it up."

"Beg?" Turner said, struggling to force down his anger. "What about that 'If you love something, set it free,' crap? The damned *poster*, Cassie . . ."

"Poster speak with forked tongue. Look, I'm sorry I brought it up. It's not fair."

He collected himself enough to prompt her for more of the story. He'd wondered so long about it all, but suddenly he wasn't sure he wanted to know.

"So you studied history at the university," he said.

She shook her head sadly. "Tried to. But I auditioned for a little part in a play, and got it, and I was hooked. I switched to drama. And that's when everything started to go kind of crazy . . ."

Her first month in acting class, she told him, was mostly taken up with classmates asking her to repeat things she'd said, so fascinated were they by the novelty of her accent. For her professors, though, the voice was anathema, fingernails on a chalkboard. Fortunately she was good at other aspects of the craft, and so they doubled-teamed her with dialogue coaches until her voice held not a trace of the Heart of Dixie; she was so accentless that she began to have dreams about growing up in the Midwest, a whole new childhood installed by sheer persistence into her larynx.

When she appeared in her first major production, a piece by Brecht (whom she'd thought until that time to be a shampoo) the reviews were very positive. After the second night's show, a Bob Dylan look-alike in a Navy peacoat was waiting backstage to see her.

He was an advertising photographer, he said, and was about to start shooting a national campaign for a new mascara. They were looking for a fresh-faced girl-next-door, and would she be interested in testing as a model? She at least had enough savvy by then to ask for a business card and some references. Shifty as the guy looked, he turned out to be legitimate. After a hundred or so Polaroids in different clothing under various lights, he called her one morning and told her the agency approved. She had the job.

From there, it was pretty much your average Hollywood fantasy, the domino effect in ever-brightening Technicolor. The magazine ads led to a couple of TV commercials which led to more modeling and even to a bit part in a series, as a generic hysterical woman in a cops-and-robbers motif. She wondered if Turner had seen her in any of these, and then realized that he'd be overseas by then, in the war.

The money was good. Greater things were always just on the horizon. The parties were unavoidable, and very late at night after substantial drinks she would speak in Alabama-ese to everyone's uproarious delight. Afterward she would feel twinges of self-loathing but she learned to mix her drinks with two jiggers instead of one and the problem mostly disappeared. And there were men, men, abundant men. So lonely, her first few months there had been, and now in a cocktail crowd they lapped at her like waves at a shore and she luxuriated in it.

When being in the right places at night and being fresh-faced the next morning began to tax her stamina beyond endurance, the other kids at the agency explained to her that modern pharmaceuticals had conquered that age-old concern. The girl who was her neighbor and best friend after abandoning the dorm kept her pills organized by means of a small carrying case, a box with fold-out trays like a fisherman's tackle-box with the substances arranged by purpose and strength of dosage: chemicals for work in the top tray, chemicals for play in the bottom one.

Laura, the neighbor, conveyed to Cassie her cardinal rule, that you never work on coke. Coke is for after.

Except that when shooting schedules shifted, the "after" bled more and more into the "during" and vice versa, and it got harder to remember what she'd taken when and with whom, and so she settled back for the fast ride, just for a little while, fascinated as a child with the joy of watching her body perform on its own, as if by remote control.

Cassie stopped and poured them both more wine. She was saddened, subdued, from when they'd first sat down. Beyond the canopy, the clouds had gradually thickened until there was no sign of the moon. "If I'm telling you more than you want to know, just say so," she said. "I can cut to the chase at any moment."

"I guess I'm just wondering what your social conscience was doing, all this time," he said. "Did you lock it in a drawer, or . . ." As soon as he heard his tone of voice he shrank inwardly, thinking *Self-righteous prick. Cut the high-minded act, you're just jealous. But it's spilled milk, man. Shut up, don't blow this chance.*

Cassie's tired eyes regarded him evenly for long seconds until he glanced away. "I suppose I funneled it all into *self*-destruction," she said, delicately accenting *self.* "If I'd been more noble, I would have turned it on strangers. Right?"

He looked at her, his chest roiling. She didn't back down. "Truce?" she said finally, sadly, holding out her hand.

He squeezed it. "No death talk," he said. "I'm very sorry I said that. Where were we?"

She sighed. "The express lane to hell," she said softly.

At that point in time, she related, the happy fast lane accelerated and kept accelerating, and by the time it seemed the luaus and the aqua swimming pools and the pretty boys and the Kleig lights and the bleary morning mirrors were zipping toward the prow of her face like pavement beneath the hood ornament of a Rolls doing a hundred twenty it was way too dangerous then to hop off.

That was when she started hearing the voices, she said.

A rumble of thunder came from far up the river.

"What kind of voices?" Turner asked.

"Different people. Warning me that I was screwing up."

"Voices, like . . . the way I'm talking to you, right now, or voices in your mind, or . . . ?"

"Mmmm. That's a tough one. See, it wasn't the first time . . ."

From the time she learned to talk until almost the end of elementary school, she said, she regularly heard the voices of people she couldn't see. She assumed everyone had such internal conversations and therefore didn't think them strange until she found herself at age seven in some department of a big medical university, in a room with brand-new toys and a small dark pane of glass at the end and a series of soft-spoken men with notebooks asking her questions about the voices.

"You never told me that," Turner interrupted.

Cassie shrugged. "It was embarrassing," she said. "I was afraid people would think I was crazy. Anyway, it was a moot point by the time I knew you. The voices had stopped."

The men with the notebooks eventually concluded that her give-and-take with invisible personalities was merely an unusually vigorous outcropping of the imaginary-playmate syndrome—not uncommon at that age, especially in girls—and that her parents should humor her and wait for the phase to pass.

This despite the fact that several of the voices spoke in languages she didn't know. She reported the words phonetically and the men wrote them in their notebooks and had to admit that a lot of them bore striking resemblances to actual foreign languages. But seeing as that was clearly impossible they chalked it up as some latent form of racial memory, a term much in vogue in psychological circles then for anything that couldn't otherwise be explained. She cringed when her parents asked if racial memory would be affected by the new civil rights movement.

The voices continued as always until Christmas vacation of the sixth grade. The evening of the day she got her first period they ceased as suddenly as switching off a radio, and that was that.

Until the apex of her west coast fast-lane life, an August morning almost ten years later when she woke from some indistinct nightmare into a tangle of sweaty sheets and sat up in an oppressively hot room that she'd never seen before. The angle of sun on the curtains told her it must be past ten o'clock. She got up and looked in vain for a thermostat to switch on the air conditioning. The tissues of her nose felt swollen, and a pile driver slammed the top of her head with each step she took. No matter how hard she thought back on the night before, she realized with a rising panic it was blank, *nada*, nil. She fought back the urge to cry.

The view from the window was not much help. In the indifferent sunshine of southern California, a row of tourist bungalows in mustard stucco descended toward a remote-looking highway. The only landmark she recognized was her car at the curb. But rather than heartening her, the sight of it sitting between two runty palm trees with its fender inexplicably crunched and needing a wash so badly its paint was the color of silt, was catalyst for the crying jag she had till then kept pent up.

So it was in the bungalow's steaming bathroom, as she stood at the mirror taking methodical hits off a Vicks inhaler and trying with tap-water compresses (no ice in the refrigerator's ice trays) to repair the damage that sleep or the lack of it had done to her face, that the unexpected foreign voice with its halting English stepped to center stage of her brain with such authority she screamed and spun and dropped the washcloth, thinking the person was an intruder in the room with her.

Greetings and all love from your brothers at Drepung . . .

"Won Se!" Turner said.

"Except I didn't know that. Or what Drepung was. I thought I was going crazy. It was like . . . well, with the other voices, before, I had to sort of *want* to hear them. Had to ask them in. But *this* guy . . ."

"What did you do?"

"Freaked out. Big time."

Amazing, Turner thought, gaining a new respect for Won Se's spiritual gifts. Not to mention his thoroughness. Drepung could pooh-pooh its predicting ability all it wanted, but here they'd had the foresight, all those years ago, to intervene in Cassie's life for no other reason than that she was, despite his and her estrangement, near and dear to the future Hope and he would someday need her to fill just the crucial role she was performing now, recording the album to pierce the moral carapace of the masses.

Amazing.

But questions quickly clouded his piercing insight; why, then, the accident? Why hadn't Won Se . . .

The summer storm that had been threatening all evening came now in earnest, rain and nearby purplish lightning and gusts of ozone-smelling wind.

But Cassie had continued the narrative, and Turner's brain leap-frogged to catch up:

From a friend, she had gotten the name of a heavy-duty shrink who assured her such internal chit-chat was common as nails, and who almost had her convinced that what she was hearing was merely her brain's self-rescue function kicking in, warning her to hop off the fast lane before she crashed.

She told this to Won Se the next time he communicated, and with typical monklike grace he allowed that she could call it anything she wanted to, but the universe had business with her and would not be silenced until it was completed.

More specifically, he said, the world was nearing the end of a cycle in which goodness and tolerance and moral conscience and right living were becoming so atrophied that the godhead of evil was only biding its time until it could put on its party clothes and, with a *kr-r-a-a-ck* like the snapping of ten billion bones, fall flailing and flaming onto an unsuspecting planet and proceed to, in the parlance of Cassie's place and time, kick ass, a spectacle that would make the numbingly excrescent horrors of Vietnam seem by comparison like a children's tea party. No battlefields next time, he told her. The war will be in the streets. *Red-on-yellow, black-on-white* was the way he put it, making her think of the old church song, "Jesus Loves the Little Children," *Red and yellow, black and white, they are precious in his sight* which Won Se obviously had no way of knowing.

Cassie paused in the story, fingering her wine glass and looking out at the lightning. When she faced Turner again, she said, "At that point, naturally, I asked him why he was telling *me* all of this."

Turner nodded.

Cassie took a deep breath and let it out. "So that's when Won Se first told me that I was the Hope."

"The Hope," Turner repeated numbly.

It took the words a minute to sink in. When they did, he felt the universe tilt a full ninety degrees. *Sometimes a woman,* Won Se had once said. The boards of the patio decking under his feet felt insubstantial as sand. As the numbness receded, his brain warred with itself; half of it thinking *Of course, she* should *be a Hope; why hadn't he known?* and the other half growing mightily, exponentially pissed *No wonder he had felt like an interloper most of the time, waiting for clues; Drepung had lied to him;* she *was the real Hope calling the shots, he was just the backup version; evil's on the run, bring in the B-team. Multiple Hopes? Well, hell.*

His hurt ego stood and stiffened throughout his whole height, fierily tumescent, and he tried to vanquish it by the classic visualization exercises, picturing himself plunging to the center depths of a icy mountain lake and then ascending like a missile of pure spirit into the thin twilight air above Drepung, but his concentration was so rattled he couldn't make the whole circuit of thought, kept fixating on Cassie's pensive face awaiting his reaction, the minuscule stars of light on either ear.

His own face must have looked shell-shocked, because Cassie extended her hand across the tablecloth in concern. He took it, gave a light squeeze. "They chose well," he said. And meant it.

Fine, stinging drops of rain were whipping under the canopy now. The gusts rippled the skirt of the tablecloth like a flag.

"Let's go sit in the den," Cassie said, picking up the carafe. Turner carried their wine glasses. The soft flute followed them room to room, though he didn't see speakers or a stereo anywhere. In her wheelchair she led them to a low white couch; on the far wall, an old kerosene lantern burned on the mantel like the one from his childhood that his grandparents lit during storms in case the power went out.

She set the wine on the coffee table and slid herself effortlessly onto the couch, leaving the chair silhouetted against the sporadic bluish lightning of the picture window like a third person in the room.

"Won Se told you that you were the Hope, and . . ." Turner prompted, when they were situated on the couch, and braced himself against his apprehension at what else the story might hold.

The day Won Se dropped that bombshell, she told him, her therapist agreed to squeeze her in at five o'clock.

"Amazing!" Dr. Meigel had said. "Yes, yes. It's so obvious, I should have thought of it before. The repressed religious fundamentalism of your childhood is merely rechanneling itself into other avenues . . . your blind side, as it were . . . in an attempt to regain control of your thinking." He'd seemed pleased with himself for achieving this insight.

Cassie wanted to know what she could do about it. "Take the offensive!" Meigel answered with joyful assurance. "Challenge the voice to prove itself by performing some miraculous act in the real world. Then, when the voice of course *fails*, its hold over you will be permanently broken and you will return to health."

What kind of miraculous act, she wanted to know. The therapist, being a former Jew, referred her to the God-proving stories of the Old Testament—Elijah calling down fire onto the altar, that type of thing. But then why not just simplify, he said. Forego the flash and bravado and breast-beating. Seeing as those Eastern religions purported themselves as doing all manner of mystical things, such as rambling about hobo-like in time and space, she should ask this so-called monk to materialize in the midst of their next therapy session, at five o'clock tomorrow, and properly introduce himself.

She put this to Won Se the next time he spoke to her, that night while she was brushing her teeth for bed. He seemed a bit miffed, in a monkly way, and explained that he was old and wasn't physically able to get around in that manner as he used to. When she kept insisting, he said he would send a representative instead.

But the next day, to her therapist's evident glee, no one showed up. He used the fifty-minute hour to lecture her on the evils of drugs, and said he thought they could move their meetings to every-other-week for a while.

"What happened to Louie?" Turner wanted to know.

"Wrong building."

That next morning when Won Se rang up Cassie's head through the ether, she unloaded on him, calling him everything from a charlatan on down, even though if Dr. Meigel was right she was merely talking to herself.

But talking to Won Se didn't seem the least bit like talking to herself. He told her the history of the Hope, how much was riding on her eventual stand against the forces of the realm. But why *her*, she wanted to know.

Why . . . the hell . . . *her*? It sounded like a job for John Wayne. Or the Army. Anybody, actually, but a skinny, running-scared, semi-cokehead . . . there, she'd said it . . . who barely topped the scales at one-oh-eight on a full stomach. Why her?

"And what did he say to that?" asked Turner.

"He said brute force wasn't always a prerequisite, and that I must have some really strong inner qualities or else the book wouldn't have picked me. And I said . . . you know, just humoring him . . . 'A *book* picked me? Does that sound fishy to you?'

"He admitted it was strange, but he said it had been done that way since the beginning and the book almost always, in retrospect, chose the world's best Hope at that moment. I said '*almost* always?' but he kept changing the subject to how I'd be trained, and all that. So I finally gave up."

Outside, the wind was escalating into fiercer gusts; for the first time Turner felt the houseboat shift slightly in its docking, like a giant animal accommodating its body to a new sleeping position.

"Don't worry," Cassie put in. "It's sturdy. I've ridden out lots worse than this."

But Turner's mind was back in California, two decades ago, listening to Won Se. "So that morning was when you finally bought the idea, then?" he asked. "You believed what he was saying?"

"Oh, God, no."

Won Se hung in there, though, pitching like a trouper. He said that although it was nowhere near time for her to start preparing for the Calling Out, he was approaching her now because to be a Hope you have to be alive, and if her lifestyle kept going the same direction as currently, that seemed less and less likely.

She lost it, at that point, told him to get the hell out of her mind and leave her alone, and when he didn't she screamed loud enough to drown him out. By the time he finally went silent she had screamed so much she was hyperventilating and had to take two of the Valium from the survival kit Laura had packed for her and, despite the early hour, chase it with a good strong tumbler of straight whiskey.

"I was scraping bottom," she told Turner. "I figured if anybody could help me make sense of it all, Laura could. So I dialed her number to see if she was there. It kept ringing and ringing, and when I was about to give up, she answered. But she didn't say anything.

"I kept saying 'Hello? Hello?' and finally she made a sound that was kind of . . . between a groan and a whimper, and I realized . . ." Cassie's voice broke, and she stopped for a second to compose herself. "I realized she was trying to say my name. Then I heard her phone hit the floor."

Cassie had grabbed the spare key she kept and raced to the far end of the old building's long hallway, thinking fleetingly there might be a break-in, some intruder there. But her panic overcame her fear and when she burst through into the bedroom Laura was alone, crumpled beside the bed-table in an old nightgown. A thin stream of whitish blood spooled from the corner of her mouth, and there was a stain underneath her on the carpet where her bowels had failed.

When she took Laura's head in her hands it felt cold. The eyes were shut, but she tried to talk. *Just . . . wanted . . . to sleep*, she said. Cassie found the phone where it had fallen and called for an ambulance. By the time she got back from the bathroom with a warm washcloth the hemorrhaging was worse and she couldn't find a sign of breathing.

Not until the ambulance men were putting their electrode paddles back in the case and time slowed down like a bad, bad trip, did the obvious become so obvious to Cassie it forced all the breath out of her. Even though a babble of words hummed in her, like *responsibility* and *notifying*, she knew that if she rode in the back of the ambulance with what used to be Laura she would suffocate, and there'd be two for the morgue.

She went back to her own room and raised the window and leaned out to watch as the ambulance left—no flashing lights this time, no siren. When it was gone from sight she stared at the blank sky for what seemed an interminable length of time, feeling like a sleepwalker who'd been awakened in some unfamiliar place and was struggling to get her bearings.

It was only a matter of time until the police would come, she knew, with questions, questions, questions. She pictured herself sitting mutely through the interview, shrugging and nodding and shaking her head, responding in mime because no words would come. Would they believe her, or would they be suspicious and try to take her in, have her committed, or . . .

"I couldn't stand the thought of talking to anybody," she told Turner. "The room felt like it didn't have any air in it, and the wallpaper pattern kept zig-zagging, like I might pass out. I knew I had to get away. Had to run."

She paused and looked uneasily at Turner.

"So what happened *next*," she went on, "was . . ."

But Turner's gradual increasing dread over the past few minutes had already told him what would happen next.

He happened. His dumb-ass, lovesick Rambo act, paying no more attention to her demeanor or her feelings than if he were walking on the moon in the eerie monochrome silence he would watch on TV, the following week, in the barrenness of his grandparents' living room.

If only . . .

He must have mouthed the phrase half-aloud without realizing it, because Cassie glared at him and shook her head in refusal as she kept on with the story.

When she roared off in the car she drove all the way to the coast highway and kept going, and once when Won Se's voice started up in her head again she turned the radio loud enough to drown him out. Even though it was a flawless bright morning along the coast, azure sky and white foaming waves, she had the sensation of driving in a rainstorm because her eyes kept brimming and spilling until she wondered that she had any fluids left in her at all. *Fluids.* Some man would be draining Laura's fluids soon. That's how he'd put it, fluids. Bastard.

"Then I remembered," Cassie said, "the week before, when I drove a photographer's assistant to the airport. He left me a token of his esteem in the glove compartment, and now I thought, how could I have forgotten about it? If I ever needed something for my head, I need it now." So she pulled onto the graveled shoulder, she said, and let the engine idle as she located the beautiful powder of life wrapped in the tiny waxed-paper rectangle that looked ironically the same as the headache powders her grandmother used to buy.

She found the tiny wrapper and a plastic drinking straw, and as she looked down onto the rugged rocks with their phalanxes of glistening sea lions *orrr*ing and *arrr*ing in the rainswept brilliant daylight she inhaled some acidic crystalline grace *This do in remembrance of me* and the forces of the world began to right themselves. Within a minute she had quit crying and could see to drive on.

Except that after a while she could see *too* much, could see Laura again. Time was a tunnel or was it a funnel leading both ways at once, big end to small and back again actually both the same, she could see now. Why hadn't she seen before? She wasn't running away from the death but was racing to prevent it, the second death, the bastard with his tubes.

The car accelerated with a mind of its own, but not without conferring on her the special powers to handle it at this warp speed. Faster, effortless, faster, amazing control, the other automobiles she met not dots of color but streaks, and then out of nowhere a reflectorized red-white barricade filling the windshield with arrows pointing left, right, the straight ahead way not a possibility but her hyperspace momentum made it one and with a scream of tires she was airborne and floating and the bright sky blotted out or disguising itself as rocks and then a loud noise and then nothing at all.

Either that evening or the next, she woke from this bad dream in a quiet bed with a rectangle of midnight blue sky to her left, so near the size and shape of the window in her apartment that she reached over to turn her glow-in-the-dark clock around and see what time it was.

But her hand hit only a cold chromium railing, and the incongruity startled her enough awake to see the plastic tubes growing from her wrist through a bracelet of adhesive tape. The obvious first blast of thought from her brain stem was that the bastard had *her* now, too, some plot to . . . but never mind; now it was time to get the hell out of there. She undid the tape and pulled out the tubes and grabbed the rail with both hands and swung her legs up to vault over it. Nothing happened.

Legs tied bastard tied her legs . . .

Her best inner self counseled her not to panic, to think this predicament through, but her outer self began screaming like a banshee. And even before the doorway filled with running white uniforms and the devastated faces of her mother and father and the exploding fluorescent ceiling zapped her eyes, the voice began again. The same voice, but somehow older, sadder.

Greetings and all love . . .

This time, though, she had no desire to drown him out, felt as open to his message as screen wire is to the wind. Listened, now, not only to what he was saying but to what he meant.

Interim time has blurred exactly the moment when she realized what her brief life in hyperspace had done to her lower body—whether it was during her dreamlike conferences with somber doctors that next morning, or earlier, intuiting it from Won Se's muted tone of voice in the rich blue night.

Whenever, the realization of her new life as half herself fueled in her such a volcano of multicolored rage that it, the rage, without her conscious knowledge, mentally rang up Won Se in his sleep—which was how she discovered she could transmit as well as receive—and demanded of him why he and Drepung had intervened in her near death and prevented her from going the full route.

Because that's what his message—one of them—had been, that first night, telling her that as her consciousness had reacted to the car's first impact (the shock of so many synapses shunting away to silence) by plummeting down through layers of knowing toward the layer that is no knowing at all but a being known, a great alarm chime went off in the depths of the room of instruments and sent messengers racing up to rouse every monk from sleep into prayer.

So that as her mind in its descent of the branches of itself, know/not, know/not, reached the point of the final branching, the no-return one, her pain-besieged consciousness studied the choice of paths with the prejudice of a child forced to choose between ribboned candy or a coat against the cold. A thousand fervent and expert prayers leapt half the world to dim by faintest degree the gloss of the death-candy's stripes and make the coat's wool become scented with the barest tincture of the perfume her mother had favored when she nursed her, borne upward on the waves of warmth from between her breasts.

With this microscopic resurrection done the monks watched in their hearts as Cassie delivered herself by will back into the world we know, not realizing that in a day's time she would be cursing every prayer and pray-er, by name if she'd known them, for consigning her to this malevolent new limbo-life. More than dead, less than (that barbaric word) whole. Halved?

But as humanness would have it, as the weeks passed and the notion of continued living became to her more and more unavoidable, the byzantine tale of the Hope—which she had screeched and railed and medicated against in her relative health—was now transformed, in her incapacity and remorse, into a model of logic; a reason to live; a shining shining path. She wanted to learn, wanted to prepare.

This change of heart cheered Won Se immensely. He began coming into her mind for a minute or two at odd hours when there was nothing of import to relate or to warn against, sometimes even singing her mind an ancient Tibetan lullaby when she was on the brink of sleep.

So it must have been especially hard for him to tell her everything was off. Won Se hated it for her sake, thought it cosmically unfair, but the matter was out of his hands. He could foresee her in a wonderful support role, though, one crucial to the success of . . .

Why *not* her? she wanted to know. Just one good goddamn reason. What was the bullshit he'd fed her about inner qualities being strength enough, no need for brute force? Huh?

His only guess, and it was strictly a guess, was the line deep into the Book of Rules which said that at the Calling Out, the Hope must stand alone under the skies. A literal interpretation, of course, would mean . . .

I can stand, all right? I can fucking stand. I do it all the time. I just need to brace on something.

Won Se was very sorry.

And, under the circumstances, he was exceedingly loath to press this next request at all, except that it was of utmost importance and the clock was, how to say, ticking, and . . .

I can stand.

Admittedly a very unusual circumstance, he apologized, which according to Drepung's archives had never happened before, but which the authors of the Book of Rules, in their wisdom, had foreseen and provided for. Namely, a Hope who for any reason becomes incapacitated before performing his/her duties has the obligation, some would say privilege, of naming a successor.

Turner's scalp prickled. The impact of what Cassie was relating stole upon him gradually, too big to get his mind around all at once. "You mean, *you* . . ." he said, and found that no more words would come.

Cassie shrugged.

"He could give me a day and a night to pray about it, he said. I told him I'd forgotten how. So he said to just picture . . . my heart, and picture my hands touching all its insides, especially the deepest parts . . ."

Turner stared, not at her, but at a point in the air between them where the inescapable fact hovered. His throat tightened, and he felt a stinging at the corners of his eyes.

" . . . and that before I finished feeling, one of the hands would be the Everlasting's, and by then it'd be clear what I needed to do."

Turner rested his head in his hands, thinking *You.*

"And I asked him," she said, "if he meant Buddha, or God, or . . . who, and he said 'How many Everlastings do you think there are, in all of time?' and I said I didn't know for sure, and he said in that case I would choose well."

Turner tried to say *After what I'd done*? but it came out a stifled sound and he gave it up. He felt the wetness of his eyes run into his hands, the release.

"It wasn't hard to decide at all," she said softly. "You were the best person I ever knew."

The rush of events swarmed his mind's eye: the night alive with tracer fire on the crest of the Quang Tri hill where he got his wounds; waking from a dark forest of beasts and delirium at Drepung *You are the Hope* and the sweet homecoming half a life later—Won Se's face that first evening in the garden as he explained about the Calling Out, his frail fists eclipsing a planet in the late shaft of mountain sun. All proceeding from the source that sat before him now, in the flickering lamplight. Cassie.

"I just don't see how . . ." he began, but she cut him off:

"There's a *lot* we'll never understand. We just have to accept and go on."

" . . . but to trust me enough to . . ."

"It was more than trust," she said. "I could read your heart."

"Is that like . . . reading my mind?"

She swirled the wine in her glass and looked at the lamp flame through it, shaking her head. "No. Much more reliable. See, when the voices . . . the power, or whatever, came back, I found out I could do that."

He must have looked as skeptical as he felt. Cassie smiled at him. "Like now you're wanting proof I can read your heart, and you're also wanting to know what the hell the spiders were, with Beaver, but you're hesitating to bring it up in the whole scheme of things because you don't want me to think you're fixated on it, or jealous."

All of which were correct. His mind felt naked, exposed.

"Now that you ask," she said, "Beaver's the one who calls it 'spiders'. I don't think it really had a name, before that. It's . . . well, it's hard to describe. It's a little like a hug. It's a little like dancing with just your mind."

"So you *have* been to Drepung," he said. "When?"

She shook her head somberly. "Only in mind. It's not a bad way. But someday I'd like to go for real." Her mood brightened a little. "They kind of made me their mascot."

She seemed lost in thought for a moment, then suddenly said, "I want some pie. Come with me?" She spun one wheel of her chair to angle herself toward the kitchen.

He got up and followed her through the hall.

At the refrigerator she moved containers around on the shelves looking for the pie. The glow from inside it made the darkened room look oddly different, like the beam of a burglar's flashlight. Thunder blustered outside.

Turner was getting plates and forks from the cabinet when her voice said from inside the fridge, "I'm not believing this." When she withdrew she held up two small oranges in the brilliant bluish light, her face like a child who had won a prize. At that moment the forlorn tugboat, nearer now, blatted its horn again.

"I think they used to be stamped 'China,' but it got rubbed off," she said, keeping a straight face with effort.

Turner had to laugh. "*Suzanne takes you down*," he sang, *"to a place by the river, you can hear the boats go by, you can . . ."* He stopped abruptly, not remembering till then the concluding line of the verse, *. . . spend the night beside her.*

She shut the refrigerator door with her elbow and held an orange out to him in the dark.

She said, "You can, you know."

15

THE AIR OF THE bedroom was charged with currents of fascination and regret and miracle, when at breath-held last he began to unfasten the points of pearl light down the roseate silk of her shirtfront. The whole denim length of her unmoving legs became conspicuous outside the field of his vision and he hesitated, saying into her eyes, a whisper, *You'll have to show me what to do.*

He meant do differently, because of her legs, and immediately wondered if he shouldn't have asked it, because her expression grew somber and distant.

No, I'm making you guess, she said. *So I can hate you forever if you mess up.*

While he stared at her she broke into her freeing, musical laugh, and hooked an elbow around his neck so she could muss his hair violently with her other hand, the way the whole thing started. When they were twelve and she was new in town and the first step of courtship after outright enmity was public horseplay, he soon gave this up because despite her being half his weight she forsook the standard shrieking feminine retreat method and gave back twice as good as she got, that amazing strength. So rather than be a spectacle for the schoolyard he negotiated a truce, the first of increasingly long consults he held with her about the abuse of power and the meaning of life and the way Cincinnati kept shooting itself in the foot during the Series.

And besides, she said, as he watched her blue lightning-lit hands effortlessly whisking his own shirt buttons free, *I hear from ladies on both coasts that you know exactly what to do.*

He felt his face redden. *That's . . . I don't . . .* But her laugh again, in perfect key with the invisible music of the walls, told him he didn't have to pursue it. *All I need is a little special handling. You'll figure it out.*

When they both were finally free of clothes and encased in the cool sheets he raised himself on elbows above her and was smoothing the hair back from her ingeniously sculpted face when he felt the gentle imprint of a hand against his chestbone, restraining his descent into her encupping warmth. *Turner*, she said. His heart turned over with joy and a question: why had no one else in all these years bothered to learn the language of his name? Then:

There's something I should have told you.

A cold wind swept through his chest; his mind invented terrible revelations in the silence; he shifted his weight off to lie beside her. She must have sensed from the sudden disengagement how thoroughly the disclosure had wilted his ardor, because when her other hand brushed perfunctorily there to verify *No, no, no*, she said. *It's good. It's something good.*

He had caught then a pinwheel flash of light at the corner of his eye, and glanced down to see the silver spokes of Cassie's chair spin a scant distance away from the bedpost as an inrush of wave shifted the house slightly on its axis; when the floor righted, the wheel spun back to its place and the room was still.

Tell me, he said.

She drew his hand up to her lips, kissed it, and kept it at her cheek. *When we were young*, she said, *you were so patient with me, about . . . you know. You never tried to hurry me, or force me. I loved that, about you. But I took it so much for granted I never realized how special it was, until I got . . . out in the world. And I never thanked you for it. Thank you.* She took a deep breath and let it out. *End of speech.*

He lay in silence, and felt the drop of wetness on her cheek work its way along his wrist. *Any time*, he said.

And it *was* the end of speech, for what seemed hours or years of slow-motion time in the incense-smelling dark, until at a pause for breath and rest he realized the storm had blown away to reveal a constancy of stillness and high moon against the sheer curtains. He lay feeling his sweat cooling in the breeze from a distant window, his lips tasting across her shoulder and breast the intriguing new third substance it made when mixed with her own.

That was the point at which his thirst to know overcame for the moment his hesitancy to stir offense or pain, and while he was still weighing the appropriate words he heard himself ask:

What do you feel?

She studied the ceiling, as if the question had never occurred to her.

Most of what I used to, she said after a little thought. *Even more, in some ways.*

More? Turner said.

I never realized how nice hands could be, for one thing. So if you feel my hands going everywhere, that's why.

I love your hands, he said. *It's just . . . it's all so good for me, I want you to enjoy it too . . .*

She laughed and hugged him. *Think a minute, Hope. When I'm in your mind, I feel all of yours and all of mine too.*

He thought about that.

What's it like?

Even better than you imagine.

No, really. What?

It's like . . . oh, God. Surfing on fireworks, I guess. She laughed softly. *It's like a lot of different things all at once.*

He thought very hard about that.

After a minute she said, *I don't know. It could probably work, but . . .*

What could work?

What you were wondering about.

I wasn't . . . he began, but he knew he really had been.

Namely, if she could probe his poor worn brain sufficiently to feel his pleasure and hers too, then wouldn't it be possible for her to transmit that combined brimming of the two straight into *his* brain, the way she'd done with the warning message, which would mean in turn that she'd not only feel the pleasure she got from him and the pleasure he got from her, but also his pleasure at feeling *her* feel his pleasure, which *she*'d then feel, and . . . Holy Jesus. The prospect yawed enticingly in the scented darkness, mirrors within mirrors within mirrors. It boggled the mind.

Boggle alert, Cassie whispered, and stroked his head. *It would probably work, but it might be dangerous. I don't know, like starting a nuclear reactor or something. We'd have to go very slow, and not let it get out of hand.* She smiled in the dark. *And it would need to be when we don't have an eight a.m. studio session.*

Or a civilization to save, he said.

When she spoke again, sleep was contending for control of her voice. *Turner's a very good waiter, though. I think it'll be worth your while.*

I've never been a waiter, he said.

You know what I mean.

Her breathing slowed and lengthened and he tried to match it, to ease himself toward sleep, but his mind was too alive with possibility to shut down.

So you can come and go, he said, *in anybody's mind, any time?*

She shook her head drowsily. *No, just a chosen few. And only when they don't put up walls.*

How does somebody put up a wall?

Shhh, she explained. *You need to sleep.* She kept up her tender, monotonous stroking of his hair. *Besides,* she mumbled, *you'll be doing it yourself, in a year or two.* She added, *You're a latent, you know.*

A latent what?

You just need a good trainer, she said.

You mean . . .

Shhh. Sleep.

But the fireworks of possibility kept widening and widening in his mind's eye like rings rippling out from a thrown rock, until they became a lake of incendiary light, and it was not until some moment of the following day that he would remember the other, darker, part of the vision that had intruded at just the moment he began his slow fall into sleep.

What first emerged as the faintest of shadows across the center of the lake's brilliant surface, as if cast by a high gauzy oblong of cloud against the sun, was a shadow shape rising out of the depths with an aspect of pure threat, as slowly and inexorably as if it had started an eon ago and had not once changed its pace, could not be hurried. Or hindered.

IN THE DEEPEST recesses of a dream, he wakes up on the big feather mattress in his old room at his grandparents' house in Zion Hill. A rooster, he thinks, woke him. He gets up and goes to the window with the hulking iron window fan in it, motor shut off in the night by his grandmother so he wouldn't chill, and sees that the sky has turned from pure black to the deep regal purple of an eggplant in the garden; not long till dawn. The sky above the south forty still holds a few of its stars. And great, soft mare-tails of glowing magenta, remnants of the vapor trail from a jet, hang suspended above the rim of the world, dissolving like cotton candy in the fresh new light.

The room was his room when he was growing up, his now whenever he visited. At thirteen he'd lie under these covers with a flashlight long after bedtime and read Ray Bradbury's tales about life on Mars and Venus. At eighteen he'd come awake here with a start, late summer mornings and the room like an oven, to the *plink . . . plink…* of small pebbles hitting the window. Cassie, with a handful of wildflowers she'd picked in the woods, calling him out into the brilliant sunshine.

He put a fingertip to the blade of the big iron fan and spun it, pulling the scent of jasmine and cool black soil into the room. A rooster crowed again. The whole morning seemed poised on the verge of something momentous, the answer to some prayer. As he felt around in the dark for his clothes he could smell bacon frying, coffee brewing in the kitchen down the hall.

When he put his hand on the doorknob to go out and see what wonderful event awaited him, the softest hand from nowhere touched his face, caressed the line of his jaw.

His eyes sprang open. Cassie, sitting alongside the bed in her wheelchair, leaned over him looking into his face, her cool fingers on his cheek. Out the houseboat's big window, in the purple half-light, shreds of fog blew in slow-motion up the channel of the river, remnants of last night's storm. The smell of breakfast remained.

The slightest corner of Cassie's lip quivered, as if she were fighting back tears. "You flatter a girl, you know that? That room's your favorite place in the world, isn't it? Where you feel most loved."

He came awake enough to realize the import of what she was saying. For weeks now his dreams had been all dragons and death and disaster, black smoke and many-headed Book-of-Revelation beasts. But this dream left a sweet aftertaste, even as it sank to oblivion beneath the literal light.

"You were in my mind," Turner said, half asking.

Cassie nodded. "Still am."

"Then this won't come as a surprise to you," he said. He grabbed her small ribcage just under her arms and lifted her clear from her chair through the bacon-smelling air to fall on top of him. Her mouth found his, after the night's plentiful practice, and his hands went to the small sunken oasis just above the base of her spine which he kneaded through the white chenille of her robe like fine dough, making the warmth of her settle lower and lower onto the front of him as her back gave up its tension.

When she finally pulled her mouth away she was gasping like a swimmer in difficulty. "The eggs . . . will get cold," she said between breaths.

"You should have thought of that before you got those eyes," Turner said, borrowing one of his hands to urge her face back against his.

Unhurriedly devouring the lobe of her ear, and then beginning the slow pilgrimage toward its opposite, his mouth gliding along the path of her hairline and stopping at its splendid tender stations of temple and cheek and eyelid and widow's peak, skin fresh and renewed from last night's long use by a trace of some mint-smelling soap, he felt the last vestige of resistance leave her shoulders and her center of gravity shifting her to roll slow-motion sideways onto her back, pulling him after with hands and arms that possessed surprising strength. As he rolled with her, his grogginess and delight gave the circular motion the illusion of repeat and repeating, undoing time to begin again at the sweet first cusp of the night.

ALL OF WHICH lingered in his mind as the long white bridge they rode into town became the color of honey when the first of the sun struck it. Cassie had the top down again; the air was crisp almost as fall, the sky washed to a singular pure blue by last night's storms.

The wind buffeting Turner's face, supercharging every breath, seemed the embodiment of what his heart felt. He kept having twinges of outright joy from different directions; something as simple as the shape of a sparrowhawk against the sky could set him off. But whenever the joy struck he felt immediately a soft retaliation of guilt. It wasn't right to feel this good, with the confrontation maybe days away. Not right.

But what you feel, a voice said, *only adds itself back to the world. Why the hell would you deprive the world of joy?*

"What?" Turner shouted to Cassie.

"I didn't say anything," she said. But the faintest smile played for an instant on her face.

When they topped a hill and the copper dome of the capitol glinted against a forest of clean-washed skyscrapers, Cassie asked, "Trust me on something?" Her voice had a businesslike edge.

"Don't see why not," Turner said.

"I had somebody spying on us in the studio, yesterday. I didn't want to mention it to you until I knew if it was going to pan out. He's a producer. For my money, the best there is."

"Thin guy, with curly hair? Kind of professor-looking?"

Cassie nodded.

"I saw you talking to him," Turner said. "I thought maybe he worked with you."

"No. His name's Leland Hatcher. He's on the Opry's payroll. But he's got clients from all over the world. Sort of a strange bird. Very, very gifted, though."

"You said you didn't want to tell me until you knew . . . if *what* was going to pan out?"

"He's crazy about the guys' music. He wants to do something with them."

Turner reached to squeeze her shoulder. "We've got the best producer in the world, already. What do we need *him* for?"

"No, you don't understand. He's a *television* producer."

Silence. They were into downtown now. The shops of Music Row were still locked and shuttered; transients squatted on the damp sidewalk, their backs against the storefronts, taking in the brilliant free sunshine.

"I know, I know," Cassie said. "You hate television. But at this point, I think we have to consider . . ."

"It's got nothing to do with 'hating' it," Turner said. He heard himself take on the argumentative tone he so disliked in others, and he tried to soften it. "I've just seen it drain the life out of so many things."

"Drain the life? How do you mean?"

"Well, it's like . . . I don't know. You can't *measure* it, or anything. But when television was new, the perception was that it could take . . . ordinary events, and make them special by virtue of . . . looking at them up close, I guess. Or in the privacy of your living room, or whatever. But in reality it's done just the opposite. TV's gotten so pervasive, so damned . . . *ordinary*, that whatever you *see* on it becomes ordinary, too. Does that make sense?"

"I hear what you're saying," Cassie said thoughtfully. After the droning of wind in Turner's ears on the throughway, the interior of the car seemed filled with a great silence when they stopped for traffic lights. "So, does the war not count?"

"What war?"

"Vietnam," Cassie said.

"What about it?"

"Television stopped it," she said. "Single-handed, as far as I can tell. The politicians sure weren't going to. We'd be fighting over there today, if it hadn't gotten to where good, patriotic Americans couldn't eat their Swanson TV dinners without having to watch their kids get blown up on the evening news."

Turner pondered this for the duration of a red light. "That's an isolated case," he said, when they were moving again.

"My point, exactly," Cassie said.

Turner laughed out loud, incredulous.

"*Your* point? I thought it was *my* point."

"When you argue with a woman, you don't *get* points."

"I always *thought* that was how it worked. But I could never get a woman to admit it."

At the stasis of the next light she turned and looked at him, deep in thought. The wind had her hair tousled like somebody's tomboyish cousin, and the clashing of this image with the gold-specked galaxies behind her grown-woman eyes made Turner have to kiss her or die. He couldn't stop until a city bus behind them beeped that the light had changed.

"My *point*," she said, when they were rolling again, "is that ninety-nine percent of television is schlock. You get what you pay for. But because people don't *expect* much from it, when they *do* see something real and alive it takes their souls by such surprise it absolutely blows them away. Changes them, forever. And this guy Hatcher can *do* that. I've seen his stuff. He doesn't do schlock. He's got Emmys he hasn't even unpacked yet. He's an artist."

Turner thought hard about this but held his peace. He watched his index fingers of their own accord make like drumsticks and tap a solo on the edge of the dashboard, as they were wont to do when he found himself between a rock and a hard place.

"We need this, Hope," Cassie said, urgency unsteadying her voice. "My gut tells me we need this, bad."

He stopped drumming and contemplatively cracked his knuckles while looking up at the sky.

In the silence he could hear her mind working. "What if you get final refusal?" she said. "When it's finished, if you're not totally satisfied, it goes in the trash."

Turner sighed long and hard. "It's not that I don't trust you," he said. "It's just . . ."

Cassie took her eyes off the street and flashed them on him. Her eyebrows were arched hysterically, like something from the wild. "What if I told you," she screamed at him, "that if you don't say yes, I'll kill us both?" Without looking away she wrenched the wheel hard right with both hands, plunging them straight toward the side of a building.

Turner's arms jerked up by instinct to protect his face. "Jeeesus!" he said, and at the last instant before impact he dived for the steering wheel to swerve them away. Cassie's small hands were like steel, would not be moved. Her face stayed on him, resigned and calm.

Suddenly a section of the brick wall whirred quietly upward out of sight, letting the car pass through. In the darkness of the basement she handbraked to a stop alongside the far wall, beside the figure of Hank Williams.

Both of Turner's hands were on his heart. When the pounding subsided enough that he could hear himself, he said, "I keep forgetting you used to be an actress."

Her smile lit up the dimness. "I coulda been a contender, huh?"

"You're crazy," he said, feeling himself smile back, unbidden. "I'm in love with a goddamned crazy person."

She took one of his hands from over his heart and lightly kissed it. "You ain't seen nothing yet, sport," she said. "So is it a deal, or what?"

WHEN THEY OPENED the door to the main studio, Turner's heart sank. The slender shape of James Crowe was draped motionless across the keyboard, as if sleep had struck him a blow from behind. Turner touched his shoulder carefully.

"*Incoming!*" Crowe shouted, and jerked upright in his chair before diving to the floor. Turner, recognizing the standard Vietnam nightmare, knelt beside him and stroked his head. "James? You're okay, buddy. We're in Nashville, remember? Everything's all right. Everything's fine."

If only that were true.

Crowe's eyes gradually showed recognition and he got to his feet, a bit sheepishly. "Morning, Cap'n. Cassie. Musta dozed off, there."

"How did it go?" Cassie asked, her voice neutral of hope.

"Check it out," Crowe said, and leaned down to type a short command on the keyboard. The screen brightened to life, and he stepped aside so Cassie could access all the controls. She adjusted a knob here and there, then called up the file of the night before. The big monitor speakers filled the room with the monks' music. Beautiful music.

Cassie let out a rebel yell that vibrated the glass walls, then spun her chair around and embraced Crowe's midsection so fervently he almost lost his balance. "You did it! You saved us a day's work. Bless your heart, James."

"Good work, buddy," Turner said. "Go get some sleep, okay?"

"TELL A FISSION?" Beh Vah repeated, disbelieving, when Turner told them. Beh Vah looked around at the other monks for confirmation, as if to ensure some fluke of the language wasn't getting his hopes up needlessly when all Turner really meant was to tell them about some specialized recording technique or a new bath soap.

Cassie was next door hard at work fine-tuning the rescued tapes, and the guys all seemed greatly revived by their solid night's sleep.

"Tell a fission," Chai Lo said back to him, nodding. "Vid-yo."

Beh Vah, apparently still skeptical of such amazing good fortune, meekly raised his two index fingers to draw a round-cornered TV screen in the air and looked to Turner with the question.

"Right," Turner said. "TV." The other monks looked mildly pleased at the prospect, game to give it a try, but Beh Vah was overcome with equal parts of elation and fear. He bit his knuckle so hard Turner expected to see blood.

At that point Chai Lo felt obligated to begin his standard lecture on the subjugation of the ego, citing its particular necessity when facing exposure through a medium so allied in the popular consciousness with temporality and alienation and greed and the lusts of the flesh and blah blah. The other monks, seeming to know by heart the territory Chai's speech would cover, made a show for Beh Vah's sake of listening reverently although Turner noticed their pupils dilating ever so slightly, a telltale sign that they were far off in more productive realms of thought or prayer.

Beh Vah, meanwhile, nodded at exactly the right places in the monologue to indicate fervent comprehension, though his hand kept going of its own volition to smooth his short hair or straighten a fold of his robe, and Turner realized the youngster was not looking at Chai Lo but at his own reflection in the smoked glass behind him, beyond which Cassie sat cueing up a wide reel of tape.

When Chai reached a stopping place, Beh Vah glanced at Turner and asked shrewdly, "Lizard vid-yo?"

"Not the same producer, no," Turner said. Beaver seemed to take this with only mild disappointment, as if Lizard-quality had been too much to hope for. "But we'd be shown on the same *networks* that they are," Turner assured him. "If everything works out, that is. It's like . . . an experiment, say."

"Same net worth?" Bah Tow asked, snapping back from his prayer-realm with a look of concern. Bah Tow's curiosity about monetary matters had been considerably magnified ever since a financial adviser occupying the adjoining cell of the Lolafalana Parish Jail during their sugar-packet arrest analyzed the monks' solvency and prescribed a complex package of deferred compensation and no-load mutuals.

"No, buddy, net*works*. Uh, television . . . outlet. Station. Group of stations."

Chai and a couple of the older monks shot one another skeptical looks.

"Actually, I wouldn't even be *considering* this route," Turner explained, "if I didn't have firm assurances that the people doing the filming are sensitive to our . . . concerns, to the message we're trying to present. Are on the same . . . wavelength, let's say." Six blank faces. "Same mode of, uh . . . same *thinking*. Okay?"

"*There* you fellas are!" a high-pitched man's voice echoed from behind Turner. An oversized figure came lumbering down the corridor at a half trot, making the floor vibrate from the impacts. A round-faced man of about fifty, wearing a gold lamé jumpsuit and white tuxedo-shirt, he wheezed to a halt beside the group and ardently pinched Se Hon's cheek. "You *cahhhnt* escape me!" he growled, apparently in imitation of Tallulah Bankhead. "It's useless to even try!"

He spun around to Turner, clicked his heels and bowed from the waist, then took Turner's hand with an aristocratic flourish and chastely kissed the middle knuckle. "Aloha, sweetie. Charmed, I'm absolutely sure. Maurice Plum, here. Now, all of you just do what I say and I won't have to break any legs, all right?" He unleashed a buzzsaw of shrill laughter, then slapped himself on the cheeks with both hands to quell it. "Oooh, stop it, stop it! I *love* it when you talk rough like that, big guy."

Turner was speechless. He felt the monks' accusing looks, from six directions, become tangible as pin-pricks.

He extended his hand for the big man to shake, and prompted "You're with . . . ?"

"With Lee," Maurice said impatiently. "Lee Hatcher. I create the little storybook worlds for him to transmit, as he does so very ably, to the masses. Didn't they tell you I'd be working with you?"

"No. No, they didn't. You're his, uh . . . ?"

"Ar-*tiste* con-sul-*tant* extraordi*naire*," Maurice said, and added, a little defensively, "That's choreographer, to the uninformed. What did you think, I'm a longshoreman? In this getup? I'm here to help you be all you can be." He shut his eyes rapturously. "God, don't you love Army talk?"

Down the hall, James Crowe emerged from the break room refreshed by his nap but, sizing up the tableau, silently rotated on his heel and went back inside until things settled down.

Turner felt the collective weight of the monks' eyes still on himself.

"And Mr. Hatcher is . . . where?" he asked, diplomatically as he could.

"Supervising a shoot in London. He'll be swooping in tomorrow morning, on the red-eye? We start shooting at seven a.m. But *today* . . ." he raised a stubby finger in the air, imperiously, "today we *prepare*!" He gave the monks a smile of transcending benevolence. "Eh, my lambs?"

At that moment Maurice's eye first fell on the lamb Beh Vah, and an instant and visible lovesickness smoothed out the choreographer's features.

"Today," he announced to the monks, like a general in front of his troops, "I'll be getting to know you better. Each . . . and *every* . . . one of you will get my full attention." (This last was directed with a fatherly smile toward Beh Vah.)

Turner caught Cassie's eye through the smoked studio glass and pointed at Maurice in pantomime, with a what-the-hell-is-this look. She started to grin, but covered her mouth with her hand and swiveled to pretend one of the dials on the console required her immediate attention.

Meanwhile Maurice stepped tenderly toward Beh Vah, put a beefy hand square on each of his shoulders, and looked him up and down as if fondly admiring a new suit on a hanger. "What a fine, *fine* youngster," he said. "What's your name? Hah?"

Beh Vah told him, but he mumbled so low that the big man said, "Beela? Beelva?" He looked to the other monks for confirmation.

"Beh . . . Vah," Chai Lo repeated for him.

"Beaver!" Maurice said, his feet doing a small dance of joy. "Oh, I love it!" he said to Chai Lo. "Are you his pa-*pah*?"

The look Chai gave him was the closest a monk has to daggers of hate. "I am not," he said.

Maurice, who apparently had not flashed to the notion of celibacy yet, looked at the others. "Anyone? Is he here?" Lu Weh, toward the back, scratched his belly and gave a vigorous head-shake.

"Well, pa-*pah* is to be commended for a *fine* bit of work, is all *I* can say," Maurice finished enthusiastically. "And ma-*mah* too, of course. Can't leave *her* out, eh?" He gave the tip of Beh Vah's nose a tender tweaking, which the youth bore stoically though his eyes remained on Turner.

Maurice shouted, "Well! Let us begin!" and popped his hands so hard that Wah So, who looked to have been daydreaming, flinched as if at an incoming artillery shell.

Sitting at the desk in Cassie's office, Turner dialed his grandparents' number and heard the distant phone ring six, seven, eight times. He held a pencil, which he turned over and over to keep his free hand busy although he had no idea what he planned to write down.

The part of the wall that was a window faced south, and as he stared through its dark gray tint at the metallic tips of older skyscrapers shimmering in the afternoon heat he realized he was looking straight toward Zion Hill. He wished he had sufficient vision to penetrate the lake of haze over the faraway blue mountains encircling Nashville and get some glimpse of what was going on there that would cause his grandparents to abandon the telephone at lunch time, their favorite meal of the day.

But on the tenth ring, as he was just about to hang up, his grandmother answered.

"Yes?" She sounded out of breath.

He asked her what the tests had said.

"Well, pretty good," she said. He could tell she was lying. The reason she'd run to the phone, she explained, was that they were out loading the car to go into town. The hospital. There was one more test they needed to do, or do again, to make sure of something-or-other. On the word "sure" her voice broke, the least discernible bit, and Turner knew she was holding something back.

"You get a bad report?"

She hem-hawed something about it being too soon to tell, before she changed the subject by telling him the news about Mister Johnny. He'd been missing since yesterday afternoon, she said, when he didn't come home from the mines. The volunteer fire department from Bagley Springs was searching the woods west of town where he liked to turkey-hunt. That was what they were hoping, that he'd tried to squeeze in a little hunting after work and had maybe broken a leg in one of those steep ravines. The prospects for this looked good, since his shotgun was gone from home.

"You've hunted with him, haven't you?" she asked Turner. "I wish you was here to show 'em his stomping grounds."

Half the people in the county who owned firearms had hunted with Johnny. He never met a stranger in his life, never let a visitor leave empty-handed. A jar of Pauline's fig preserves. A pack of venison from the freezer. He was a hard man to out-give.

"Henry Justice is the man they need," Turner told her. "He could track a raindrop in a thunderstorm. Mister Johnny loved to hunt with Henry better than anybody." Did he say "loved"? Loves, he means. Present tense.

Why was he always thinking the worst, lately?

Because it was all beginning, now. It was all coming down.

"Henry's already with 'em," his grandmother said distantly. "I s'pose they'll do all right."

"Listen, when you hear something from the doctor, would you call me? No matter what time it is. You've got the studio's number, and the hotel."

"All right, hon."

"We've got some filming to do in the morning, but if everything goes right we'll be down to see you in a day or two. If you need me any sooner, just call. I can come tonight."

"Well, I need to go," she said. "Jackson's waiting in the car."

As he hung up he had the nagging feeling some unfinished business remained from what was said, and he replayed the conversation in memory to see what it might be.

I wish you was here to show 'em his stomping grounds. Even though she knew Henry Justice was already on the case.

What she'd meant, then, was just a way to avoid saying *I am scared for Jackson and I am scared for me and I need you here, would you come?*

God love them both, but the downside of having iron backbones is that you only know how to *give* consolation, not take it. Some congenital device in both their mouths eternally prevented them from forming the words *I want . . . I need . . .*

So how was it the goddamned universe could call on him for help, and yet the two people in the world he'd worshipped from the time he was in diapers *couldn't*? Damn them.

What had Won Se said? *They are prepared. There is no time to explain.* Well hell, so be it.

He got up, but after a pause of conscience sat back down and dialed the number in Zion Hill again. It rang and rang.

16

HENRY JUSTICE stood puffing and huffing on the high spine of Bentley Ridge, waiting for the searchers from the squad fanned out behind him to catch up and thinking Jesus, how much he needed to lose some of this lard. Last winter he said he'd walk it off, come spring and better weather, not much use trying till then, when he could have fresh green stuff to eat and not the pot pie garbage and Chef Bull-Yardy his old lady crammed the cupboards and the freezer with at first frost each year like she was stocking up a atom bum shelter. Wasn't like they got snowed in more than once twice a year and then for not long, that and the Russians too broke now to buy bum fuel, he asked her what was she scared of?

To which she'd say she didn't see him turning none of it down, when she tried fixing vegetables he wouldn't eat them. Her knowing good and well that froze and canned vegetables wasn't shit, might as well get you a good bowl of pond scum and try to swallow it. But now here was summer two-thirds gone and after all his big talk he hadn't even picked the first mess of poke salad, his sorry self. And that exercise bicycle his daughter got him for Christmas rusting in the basement because he felt silly on it and besides the hard seat hurt his prostate. Damn this belly.

"Which a-way now, Henry?" It was Dwayne Cicero beside him, one of the leaders of the squad.

Henry made a visor with his hands and squinted into the low slant of sun, the blueness rising in the valleys like a fog creeping up.

"Johnny hunts west of that canebreak, there, a good bit," he told Dwayne. "But I think we'd get more good out of what daylight's left if we walked the creek first. Just this side of where it forks."

"You the boss man," Dwayne said, and motioned with his arm which way for the boys to go.

They had to step sideways down the steep grade, holding to little runty scrub pines to keep from sliding. Henry thinking how it was a wonder

Johnny hadn't broke his neck before now, sumbitch with them long legs see a turkey or a squirrel and get so excited he wouldn't watch where he was going, cliff or ditch or anywhere, just like a little kindergarten young'un. Wasn't nobody loved hunting like Johnny.

Could eat you out of house and home too, and still stay like a beanpole. Henry guying him about it, how could he eat twice much as him and be so skinny and Johnny with a straight face saying he reckoned it all went into his peter development. Sumbitch keep you laughing the whole day and not crack a grin. Never met a stranger, either. Boy's a sight.

The big maple at the creekside where they'd sit to eat their sandwiches when they hunted was sunk in the blue shade three-fourths up its trunk, the sun making just a tad of green fire at the top of it like a candle wick, when Henry got near enough to see the elbow of the shirtsleeve around the other side of it, the long old bluejeaned leg spraddled out, Johnny sitting up against the tree like he owned the place.

Joy was like a little hand on Henry's windpipe for a second, shutting his breath off at the relief of seeing him alive and whole, so that by the time he could holler, "What t'hell you doing, boy?" he was near enough to see Johnny's best shotgun in his lap at an angle like he never held it and the fact that the shape didn't try to move or answer froze him in place and made the buzzing of the big flies sound supernaturally loud against the soft burble of the creek and he realized what he would see when he walked the last few steps, and he was right.

Oh, godamighty was all he could say when Dwayne and the others caught up with him. *Lord in heaven, no*.

On the way back from the hospital Jackson stopped the car and got Cordelia to drive so he could lie down in the back seat. The pain medicine they gave him at the hospital had made him a little light-headed. That, or the news he'd gotten just an hour ago.

Old, old news; he'd been bracing for it every daylight these past twenty years as the clock of his life wound slowly down like everyone's does, thinking it couldn't be so bad if everyone's does, but *step in my office please* then why did the words hitting him feel like pellets from a gun *some bad news sir* and the plummeting sensation afterwards *mostly keep you comfortable is all* freeze all the breath in place in his lungs like falling on the playground when he was little and getting his wind knocked out, the panic of having no breath to tell anybody you're suffocating.

He rode lying down until his dizziness went partly away, but as it did the fidgetiness in his arms and shoulders got worse. The Nissan's small back seat closed in on him like the sides of a casket, and he had to sit up or scream.

"What's the matter, sugar?" Cordelia said.

"Just needed to move."

She reached a hand back and patted the thinning top of his hair. "Bless him's heart," she said.

Dusk had come. When they topped the part of Bessie Mines Road where the trees recede and sky surrounds you on all four sides, the sky was the gray of charred wood. Their house was a good three miles yet, but for sixty years whenever he'd come back from a vacation or a trip to Birmingham for supplies he considered this next rise the boundary of home because you could see home from there, nestled dollhouse-size in the valley of pines and pastureland—his house, and the scattering of other houses that made up the community of Zion Hill. The small grocery, whose owner was so old now he only opened when he felt like it, one of its two gas pumps still catercornered from where a drunk Bobby Daltry backed his pickup into it twenty years ago. The Baptist church. The cemetery with his name and Cordelia's side by side on a granite marker the color, he realized, of this sky.

Some of his dizziness was coming back. He made a note in his mind to be looking toward the grocery rather than the graveyard when they passed it, and then cussed himself for the childishness of that. As a kid on his way to go courting, he would walk a little faster and sing some song to himself when he saw the gravestones in the moonlight, not a suspicion in hell he'd ever be among them, but here it was. His stomach felt sick, and he shifted position to lie back down.

But as soon as he did he felt Cordelia hit the brake. "Oh, dear Jesus," she said.

He sat up again. "What? What is it?"

The instant he sat up, he saw. Tall towers of black cloud, a dozen or more, filled the entire sky above the valley where their house was. The clouds roiled and percolated and churned inside themselves, black water boiling, out of keeping with any normal motion of wind. On the ground, one last beam of blood-red sunlight burst from a gap between hills and played itself crazily over the houses and land and church steeple like spotlights in old newsreels.

"Lord, help," Cordelia whispered, as she steered off onto the shoulder of the road.

After the first hot rush of fear subsided, something Jackson couldn't name lifted his heart, not just lifted it but swept it up like strong arms wrestling a drowning swimmer up to air. It was not until several seconds later, him wiping tears with the heels of his hands, that he was able to put a name to the source of his joy. *Let it be the rapture,* he thought, hoping against hope, knowing it was most likely the other. *Oh, let it be the rapture.*

But the only thing that happened next was that the beam of bloody light slowly played out on the ground and left behind a reddish tinge in the sky that the monstrous clouds kept boiling against.

Not the rapture. If it had been Jesus coming, he'd already have come and gone. Didn't the scriptures say *In a moment, in the twinkling of an eye*?

No, this was the beginning of an ordeal, not the end—the one the voice had spoken of to his heart, how many years ago, forty-odd, now? Him arguing it blue-faced, claiming it wasn't in the Bible, until Cordelia had confessed to him she thought she was going crazy, hearing someone's voice in her head, and when they compared what they'd been told it was the same in every particular and they were forced to believe.

At last, it was coming to pass. Remembering part of the voice's long catechism he leaned across the seat back and cupped his hand around the rear-view mirror, turning it slowly half a hemisphere. The reflection revealed what he expected: the familiar valley peaceful and unclouded, the sun setting peach-colored in a swirling haze of pollen, the way the rest of the world was seeing it.

Cordelia's eyes were on the bright alternate reality trapped in the panel of mirror, idyllic against the dimness of the car as the little snow scenes you could buy, encased in a ball of glass. When she looked around at Jackson he knew she knew.

"Lord, of all times for it, now," she said.

As the world beyond the windshield went dark a new, smaller display of colors became visible in the direction of the church—the whirling reds and blues of an ambulance and a patrol car.

Cordelia gasped and put her hand to her mouth, whispering, Jackson heard, a prayer for the safety of whoever was in the wreck. He tried to extend *his* heart out into the dark world and make it hurt for them, like Cordelia was doing, but his mind couldn't get past the arrow of fire in his midsection: how big the tumor was, what it looked like. The failure shamed him.

The thing about women, he thought, is that in spite of all their shortcomings and the little foolishness they stay upset about, their God gift is that they can hold a dozen different feelings at once, lighting on one and then another like a butterfly. Where a man's mind is made like a pair of pliers, get ahold of one idea and steady do the hell out of it before you move on to something else. No wonder men can't figure women out.

"Go," Jackson said to her. His own mind's pliers were fastened on his ache, which was rallying again, and his numbness at Jesus's failed coming was overtaking his re-tightened skin, making it feel older than ever. "Go see."

His hand closed around the pill bottle in his pants pocket. It would be an hour before he could take another dose. *Even so come*, he felt himself telling the medicine. From here out the clock would be his mocker and his savior.

When they got closer to the site of the wreck he saw the tangled mess the two cars were in, one of them's headlights at skewed angles aiming up into the woods. No coming out of this one alive.

Cordelia stopped and they rolled down their windows. The crackle of the police car's two-way came to them, a voice confirming another ambulance was on the way. In the strobing colored light, two bundles of official-looking blue-green blanket lay on the edge of the roadway. Child-sized, both of them. A policeman was going at the crushed door of the nearer car with a pry bar, but there didn't seem to be any urgency about him.

Jackson recognized one of the ambulance men, Merle Quinn's boy Jamie, at the same time Jamie recognized him and started walking over. The boy had put on a little weight since they'd seen him. He touched the brim of his white baseball cap as he leaned up against the car. "Miss Cordelia," he said. He put his hand through the back window to shake hands with Jackson.

There was a strong smell of antiseptic about him, like the hospital they'd just come from. Even in the crazy spinning lights, Jackson could tell that the stains darkening the front of the white coveralls were flecks and spatters of dried blood, and his mind flashed back to the summer job he had in high school—sixty years now, sixty-five?—helping the butcher in the mine commissary's meat market. We come into the world doing hurt to things, he thought, and then some people have the gall to say we don't need Jesus.

"How's your daddy and them?" Jackson asked him. First things first, even if the world's burning down.

"Pretty good," Jamie said. "You knowed he had open heart."

"I heard that. Is he overin' it all right?"

"Fairly well. Momma has to stay on him about walking. He likes that ol' easy chair too much." One of Jamie's big stubby hands went up to dab at his eyes, and for the first time Jackson noticed his cheeks were wet.

"Looks pretty bad," Jackson said, nodding toward the wreckage.

"It's been . . ." Jamie began, but the pitch of the word went womanish and he had to clear his throat and start again. "It's been happening like this since one o'clock," he said. "This is my fifth call." He turned his head aside, and there began in him a high, keening wail like Jackson had heard once in a film on the educational television, an African tribe at a funeral.

But as the treetops beyond the boy filled with a frenzy of new colored lights Jackson realized the sound was not Jamie at all, but only the second ambulance arriving. Before Jamie trotted off to meet it, he braced both hands on the car's roof and leaned his head in Jackson's window as if to impart something in confidence, though Cordelia in the front seat could easily enough hear.

"I think . . ." Jamie said, with his glittering eyes and bitter coffee breath, before his voice got away from him and he had to start over. "I think there's some kind of hell loose, around here."

17

TURNER WAS BRUSHING his teeth for bed when he heard a door click shut from the end of the hotel hall where the monks' rooms were. Out of curiosity, knowing them to be at their individual evening prayers, he held the brush in his molars and went to his front door's peephole to see who it was.

The fish-eyed hole showed only an empty mauve hallway at first, but then a dot of yellow came in fast from the left and enlarged to fill the circumference of the view before receding toward the right, the direction of the elevators. Even in the flat distorted light Turner could tell it was Beh Vah, walking so soundlessly no footsteps could have given him away.

"Shit," he whispered, around the brush handle, as a vortex of old dread and disavowals opened underneath him where his sweetly anticipated sleep had been only seconds before.

He'd planned on spending the night at the houseboat again, until Cassie rightly suggested that the monks could use a good dose of handholding and reassurances from him, considering what they'd been through in the past couple of days, and what was ahead. Or else (was this strictly paranoia?) it was her polite way of saying they needed someone to keep an eye on them.

Now, unbidden, scenes from recent weeks paraded through his brain—Shy's accusations and Beaver's protests of innocence—with only the backgrounds changing, like bad snapshots you skim from a pack and then forget to throw away.

He ran to rinse his mouth and put his shirt back on, then stood at his door listening for the bonging and departure of the elevator before he stepped out in the hall to follow Beaver. He felt guilt as he did so, having maintained a gut feeling that the boy's heart was right, though he was hard put to explain the black strokes of circumstance accumulating against him. The realm's doing, maybe. Hocus pocus. Divide and conquer. Who the hell could know? And now Cassie's veiled suggestion . . .

He thought it would be easy to track a monk through the lobby of a hotel, but he was mistaken. Nashville's night crowd had invaded; cowboys in kerchiefs, street hookers in yellow suede and silver spandex, bar queens with their inch-long eyelashes and high-piled nests of bleached hair, and what Turner guessed to be a dragster or two, the whole bunch intermingling loudly with here and there some sheepish-looking older businessmen as escort, coming and going in pairs from the adjoining lounge. A Tibetan monk in a saffron robe was a sort of visual anticlimax by comparison, not rating a second look from anyone, and Turner made it all the way to the street before he caught a glimpse of Beh Vah, waiting at a corner for the light to change.

He was headed in the direction of Gamma's building.

No. Please, no.

Turner kept half a block behind him, the whole way. Beh Vah strode along purposefully with his head down. He didn't stop once to look in a store window, ordinarily one of his favorite things to do. Even when the route took him past an appliance store with the wall of television sets along its front all tuned to MTV, he gave them just a glance and kept moving.

When they got to the building, Turner hung back and watched through the glass of the revolving door as Beh Vah approached the guard desk. The white-haired security guard, his head propped in both hands, sat dozing peacefully. But Beh Vah stopped and dutifully signed his name to the clipboard anyway.

Pretty damned brazen, Turner thought.

Once Beh Vah was on the elevator, Turner tiptoed past the sleeping guard and watched as the glowing numbers in the call panel tracked the car's progress upward. At Twelve it stopped.

Leland Hatcher's offices were on Twelve.

Well, it stood to reason. With Cassie apt to be in and out of the recording studio at odd hours of the night, Beh Vah could hardly stroll in and twiddle whatever he'd twiddled to dump the good tracks. Might as well move on to grander things, try to fuck up their video.

The anger burned in Turner's throat as he got on the next elevator and punched Twelve. Little son of a bitch. Lie to me with a straight face. What was the last straw that made him go over to the realm's payroll? What did they offer him? Was his defection recent, or had he been a Trojan horse for the dark side all along, bred in the womb for the purpose?

The elevator door opened on blackness. As Turner's eyes adjusted, he saw a faint glow toward the left end of the hall and followed it. When he turned the first corner he saw, far down the corridor, the skinny silhouette of Beh Vah's back, heading for a lighted double doorway.

The soundstage. Sure, why not? Lots of little wires and connectors and gadgets to monkey with there. Anybody as cute as Beh Vah, Turner realized, was a crackerjack choice for a saboteur. He could ask people questions till doomsday about how their equipment works, his big innocent eyes shining, and nobody ever be the wiser. Now he was back to do the deed.

But no sooner than Beh Vah disappeared inside the square of light, it extinguished itself as quickly as a blown-out candle. Turner froze in the hallway, dark now as a cave, and his back sought out a wall for balance. His pulse quickened until it throbbed in his ears, the way it used to do on a moonless night in the delta when he'd hear a crackling in the wall of jungle blackness ahead of him and begin the nerve-wracking wait to see if the noise would be followed by another, and if their pattern was the skittering of an animal or something bigger, two-legged, with maybe a night scope drawing a bead on the bridge of his nose.

Sudden jet blackness was one of the triggers he'd brought home with him from the war. Every vet he knew had several, carried within his brain's circuit boards until his dying day: a simple sight or sound or smell that brought the whole hell of it back in a finger-snap, a perverse kind of miracle; the nightmare you thought was over and done these twenty years suddenly resurrected so real you can smell Satan's very ass again, and no amount of logic or positive self-talk can break you free until the flashback runs its course.

Then an even worse thought came, intruding from the present: *What if it's a trap*? He felt sweat pop out like dew on his palms and forehead. *What if he knows I'm on to him*? Beaver could be tiptoeing toward him even now, his bare feet soundless on the thick plush carpeting, and Turner would have no inkling of it until the first blow struck.

But at that moment an unearthly blue glow began to rise in the hallway, as graceful and blessed as dawn coming over the delta, and Turner saw that it came from the direction of the stage's big double doors.

He edged toward them, keeping his back to the wall, until he reached the door frame. He peered around it with one eye and saw Beh Vah hop down from the raised platform at the back where the control panel was, after having turned on the soft blue-gelled backlights.

Now Beh Vah walked reverently toward the center of the stage, shaking the tension out of his arms and neck, and knelt in the big open space with his head in his hands, looking tiny and vulnerable underneath the studio's indifferent catwalk sky of girders and wiring and darkened Kleig lights.

Because of the huge room's terrific acoustics, the words that Beh Vah murmured, then, came to Turner as clearly as if he'd been kneeling beside him.

"I hear the song . . ."

I hear the song, Turner's heart involuntarily supplied, as he felt the landslide of guilt begin from a point just behind it.

"Song within me, song without me . . ."

So that by the time Beh Vah concluded and stood to begin practicing again the dance he would do the next morning with video watching, Turner had seen enough and turned to go, grateful that his spying hadn't been detected.

As he got on the elevator he was more in a quandary than ever about whether they actually had a traitor aboard—hadn't Shy said *Sometimes two*?—or were just having a rotten run of luck. But when he started to push the button for the lobby, a phrase of the monks' music came to him from far down the hallway.

The sound was so faint at first he thought he'd imagined it, and as it grew in volume he realized that it wasn't coming from the direction of the soundstage, where Beh Vah could have picked up an instrument, but from the pitch-black corridor to the right. And it wasn't one instrument but all of them, going at full tilt. A tape? No, Cassie's studio was ten floors above this one.

Something not right here. He gritted his teeth and headed into the dark, dragging the fingertips of one hand along the wall and extending the other one in front of him, probing side to side like a blind man's cane.

He had felt the indentations of a dozen or more dark office doors when he came upon one with a dim wash of moving color inside it, a frosted glass door standing slightly ajar. The music was coming from inside.

Suddenly the sound grumbled to a halt, like a phonograph whose electricity is cut off. Then the music reversed itself and ran backwards, a mishmash of high-pitched notes, as frantic colors danced on the glass.

"Here, you think?" a voice inside the room asked. A brief burst of flutes played at speeded-up pitch. "Or here?" A mumbled answer came from a second voice, but Turner couldn't make it out. Maurice Plum, maybe? No, too deep for that.

Crouching so as not to show his shape against the glass, he stepped to the opposite side of the doorway so he could peek through the crack. He saw a dark-haired man's back, sitting at an editing control board in front of a wall of video monitors. The screens showed a freeze frame of the monks playing their instruments against the rich blue background of the studio set.

As Turner watched, the man punched a button and made the biggest TV screen go dark, then spun a wide knob which filled the screen with artwork of a hideous gargoyle-like face, one he seemed to remember from some Drepung textbook on devils and demons. "Or," the man said, and spun the knob again, this time bringing up the image of a woman's face wide-eyed with fear as the tip of a switchblade knife brings blood from her cheek.

The second voice mumbled a recommendation, and the man at the console threw back his head and laughed. From the laugh and the quick glimpse of his profile Turner recognized him now. Leland Hatcher, producer extraordinaire.

"Annie *did* do well with these," Hatcher acknowledged to the other person in the room, whom Turner couldn't see no matter how he maneuvered his eye at the door-crack. "Slice and dice. I think she's found her true calling. But you're right, we need to work up gradually to the gorier stuff, here. Big finish, huh?"

He typed in commands on a small computer keyboard and the big videotape machines in the wall hummed into action and made the edit he'd programmed. When he played the scene again to check it, the monks' pleasant golden faces and sweet flute music were the same as before, except . . . for one brief instant, a flicker of confusion too fast for the eye to comprehend, the place where the demon's head had been inserted.

The effect seemed to bypass the eye but land straight in the heart, Turner reckoned. Subliminal revulsion. The passage of music that had before been so pristine and so freeing now filled him with a sourceless dread, an anticipation of violence he couldn't put a name to.

"I love it," Hatcher said to his companion. "The audience'll never know what hit 'em, until they start getting the urge to slice somebody up." He leaned back in his chair, yawned and rubbed his eyes. "Wish that bitch would hurry up with the coffee," he said. "I need to finish this and get back to the coven project." He spun his chair around suddenly and peered intently toward the door. Turner jerked his head back from the door frame so quickly he was sure he hadn't been seen.

He was trying to decide what to do next when he caught the strong scent of fresh coffee. An arm went around his throat and a blade tip pierced barely skin-deep just above his collarbone. "Don't move on me, bastard," a woman's voice whispered, "or you'll be breathing through your collar, you read me?" The pain that spread like an ink blot from the point of insertion advised him not to call her bluff.

"Lee?" she said in a louder voice that sounded somehow familiar, "We've got company out here."

Hatcher sprang to the door and threw it open, a small black pistol ready in his hand. But when he saw Turner's face and predicament, his look of alarm dissolved into a broad smile.

"Oh my," he said. "To what do we owe *this* honor? You may release him, Annie." Hatcher looked vaguely like some game-show host Turner couldn't place.

There was a silence. The woman said, "But I don't know if . . ."

"Oh, go ahead. The good guys are never armed. Are they, Turner?"

Turner kept his stare on the "O" made by the tiny pistol's barrel-end, and guessed it to be roughly aimed at his heart. He'd shot a gun like that before. The .22 shell carried a relatively puny punch and its accuracy was miserable. But at a range of three feet, like this, both those shortcomings became moot.

His captor reluctantly let go of him and went across the hall to retrieve the tray she'd set on the floor, a big stainless steel pot and several cups. When Turner saw her full-face he realized where he knew her from. One of Cassie's assistants. The one with the sick plant, if he remembered right.

"Come in, come in," Hatcher told Turner, stepping back out of the doorway and gesturing a welcome with the pistol barrel. "We were just finishing up. You can be our premiere."

When the swing of the barrel reached the apogee of its arc Turner had a fleeting thought of diving for it, roll the old dice, but the coffee-smelling presence of the big woman at his back made him think better of it. He stepped into the editing room, keeping his eyes on Hatcher's pistol hand, his mind continually recalculating the odds.

The only light in the room, other than the color image of the monks on the frozen TV screens, was two small spotlights on a track rail in the ceiling, each one aimed at a portion of the big console board. Turner sensed, before he saw, a shape sitting in the well of darkness at the board's perimeter.

"I assume you two have met," Hatcher said, with what seemed an edge of amusement. After a moment of hesitation the shape stood up and let the harsh cylinder of light rake its face.

Chai Lo.

For an instant Turner thought he saw, perhaps because he wanted to so badly, a flicker of embarrassment in the slowness of Shy's eyes to meet his own. But if he did it was quickly remedied. Chai Lo's gaze became as timeless and steady as the void awaiting a mountain climber's misstep.

"Tur-ner," he acknowledged, with a suggestion of a nod. "I wish you had not come." This spoken with what seemed a sincere sadness.

"Sit down, sit down," Hatcher said brightly, the perfect host. "Let's see, do we have enough cups? Good, good. Annie's on the ball, eh? Hospitable Annie. Who *says* one can't service . . . er, serve two masters?" He gave her a lewd wink and she grinned inscrutably as she poured his coffee.

Hatcher laid the pistol close at hand on the countertop. His eyes connected with Turner's as he did so, a wordless warning not to try anything foolish. Chai Lo got up from his chair and leaned down to mumble something in Hatcher's ear. Its cadences had the timbre of a plea.

"Oh, I disagree," Hatcher said, with elaborate courtesy. "He definitely needs to see it. Who could do a better critique of all our hard work?" His hands were already flipping switches and punching keys on the console, shuttling the tape into high-speed rewind and adjusting the coloration of the monitors. Chai Lo sat back down resignedly and took a sip of his coffee, his eyes on the floor.

The portion of Turner's brain that kept recalculating his chances of getting Hatcher's gun came up repeatedly with the same two answers: slim and none. Hatcher glanced around at him and smiled, as if he'd read that conclusion in his mind. "Drink up, now," he said, motioning toward Turner's untouched coffee. "Please. I understand you have a long drive ahead of you this evening."

Turner didn't respond but the puzzlement must have shown in his face, because Hatcher continued, "Oh, yes. I forget that your communication system is a bit more, shall we say, primitive than ours. Fortunately, Mizz Masterson keeps us well updated. In addition to providing us with some excellent audio tracks, of course."

"You're lying," Turner said, all the while thinking: The guy's messing with your mind. Don't get suckered. Don't let your doubt kick in. It's just what they want. Do mental gymnastics, whistle Yankee Doodle backward, anything.

But then he found his mind something more productive to do, scanning the ceiling-high bank of equipment for the machine in which the master tape resided, just in case he got a chance to put a monkey wrench through it at some point.

Seconds before the shuttling tape clicked to a stop he spotted the changing digital counter and watched the green numbers soundlessly approach zero. A muffled *clink-clunk* deep inside the machine, and all the monitors bloomed to life with a test pattern of colored stripes that quickly faded to blackness.

Hatcher leaned back in his swivel chair and laced his fingers with satisfaction. The move put him crucial fractions of a second farther from the gun. But unfortunately not enough. Not quite enough.

"This version was Annie's idea," Hatcher said. He blew her a theatrical kiss across the room, where she sat in the darkness with her tennis shoes off and her feet pulled up under her in the chair. "It's the one we'll be supplying to the more . . . *adult-minded*, so to speak, of the cable outlets. We've got a different version for the kiddies, of course."

The deep rumble of artillery fire came from the big wall speakers, a percussive *room . . . roomroomroom* that still jarred his jawbone in nightmares. The black screen brightened to a picture of himself in grainy black-and-white, wearing a helmet and combat fatigues, his rifle braced on his hip. His first week in-country. That naive sparkle still in his eyes, belief in a sane world, a light that would go out in mere weeks and never return.

The picture slowly dissolved to a snapshot of scattered corpses, babies and young children caked with bullet-wound blood. My Lai? The bass notes of the artillery became overlaid with a rapid peppering of small-arms fire, which gave way to a wind chime and the opening phrase of the monks' music. And the sounds of a man and woman making love.

The sounds, he slowly realized, of himself. And Cassie.

"A nice touch, what?" Hatcher said cheerfully.

Betrayal is as colorless and odorless as a poison gas, but it has a kind of taste to it. A scalding, vinegar-like taste that slowly paralyzes the will. Turner's heart still cringed from the sight of Chai Lo's remorseless face just now, good workman busy at the tasks of the realm. But it was nothing beside the fact that Cassie could be in on this as well, which began opening like a physical gulf in the floor beneath him, a mire of hopelessness sucking him in.

If he learned anything in Vietnam, it was that the time to act is the very instant you feel the paralysis of doubt beginning. Seconds later, and you might not have the will.

Which is how he summoned the nerve to unhurriedly reach for his cup of coffee and hold it contemplatively in both hands while blowing on it to cool it, the sounds of his and Cassie's shared confidences grating from the console speakers like raw flesh peeled back.

Then suddenly, with no tics or hesitations to telegraph his plan, he flung the steaming contents of the cup straight across Hatcher's smug face and made a lunge for the gun, fumbled it once, and . . . *had* it.

Despite Hatcher screaming curses and the woman at the corner of Turner's vision in full flight toward him, he still managed to swing around and grab the big metal pot and slam it like a battering ram into the soft front innards of the appropriate VCR, and then again, and once more, until acrylic shattered and sparks flew and the machine in surrender ejected its mangled spaghetti of brown-oxide tape.

Hatcher had wiped his eyes clear now and was heading for Turner with seeming difficulty, one eye squinting, and Annie was coming at him from nine o'clock high preceded by the glint of a blade.

He spun and dug hard for the blank space between them, Saturday touch football revisited, that promised the precious door at the end of the room. But Hatcher in his rage covered ground faster than Turner had calculated and so he had to sidestep again and lose crucial balance—some of which he righted by throwing the heavy pot hard at Hatcher's head.

It barely clipped an ear, no damage, but made a direct hit on the speaker amp above the console. A blue arc illuminated its knobs and switches, and the short circuit set off a screech of feedback, ten times as loud as the siren for an air raid, that Turner feared would pop an eardrum. But the overload of power finally exited through the two big speakers, blowing out their cones like firecrackers and dispersing a thin yellowish smoke.

Three more steps and Turner would be home free, seeing as Chai Lo, sole constant in the room's confusion, hadn't moved to block his way but, whether from fear or some latent respect, stood rooted in place.

But then Turner's foot hit the puddled coffee on the tile floor and he watched his two shoes take to the air in front of him like some slapstick comedian. He tried to at least pick which side of himself he landed on, but he failed and as the elbow of his gun hand cracked the floor first and took his main weight he heard the sickening clatter of the pistol sliding away from him in Hatcher's direction.

Even before Turner had stopped tumbling, the hard bulk of Annie was on top of him, pinning his shoulder, her blade hand a warning in front of his eyes. In the aftermath the room filled with an unnatural quiet, which was relieved only by Hatcher's mannered voice, speaking as casually as if remarking on a polo play.

"Annie? Annie!" he said, holding the "O" of the pistol remarkably steady as his left hand dabbed at his face with a folded handkerchief. "Down, girl. Please. I have things quite well in hand, thank you."

As Annie grudgingly unpinned him and went over to inspect the damage to the equipment, Hatcher stepped slowly backwards toward the open doorway, glancing as he did so toward the immobile Chai Lo who refused to meet his gaze.

"I must say," Hatcher said to Turner, when he had positioned his back comfortably against the door jamb, "you certainly make hospitality more difficult than it has to be. Annie, Sweet? What's the verdict?"

"We've got a spare for the deck," she said, "but the edit master's ruined."

"I see. And the raw footage?"

"It's okay. We can re-cut everything from the time-code list."

"Wonderful. I was afraid our adventurer, here, had dealt us a real blow." He touched his face gently, where the scalded patches were starting to show, and winced. "Speaking of which, darling," he said, "a cloth and some ice water would be wonderfully soothing, if I could trouble you?"

Annie stepped wide of Turner to get to the door, careful to avoid the pistol's line of sight. "*Merci*," Hatcher said over his shoulder as she retreated down the hallway.

Turner sank heavily into one of the console's padded swivel chairs and rubbed the elbow that had broken his fall.

"Please, move away from the equipment," Hatcher said curtly. "I have no qualms about using this, by the way." He held the pistol's aim steady on Turner. "My friend here is emasculated . . . er, prevented from causing you direct harm by some stupid ancient rule or other. But I assure you no such restrictions apply to me."

Chai Lo looked at Turner and nodded sadly. "He is true," he said.

"So what will you do with me?" Turner asked Hatcher.

"Keep you out of mischief until our work is done," he shrugged. "After that, you're free as a bird."

Turner looked from Hatcher to Shy and back again. He'd been raised to believe that villainy made some permanent mark on a face, was recognizable in the jut of a jaw or the cast of an eye. But both these men looked good and upstanding, at peace with themselves.

"So, does the realm pay that well?" he asked them. "Or do you just enjoy seeing suffering, or what? I've wondered, what they offer you to go over."

Chai Lo looked toward Hatcher, whose face slowly lit up like a game show host about to award the grand prize. "So, you're wanting to do some moonlighting, then? I hate to burst your bubble, but it's all quite *pro bono*, Mr. Hope. For the love of it. Just like yours."

"I don't believe you," Turner said.

In the darkness behind Hatcher's head, a glimmer of brass, hidden from Chai Lo's view by the half-open door. Warrior's instinct made Turner resist looking toward it, not give the movement away by his eyes which were locked with Hatcher's.

The glimmer became the bowl of one of the monks' big sacred horns. It raised slowly toward the ceiling and paused, getting its range on the back of Hatcher's curly head, before descending hard with a metallic *thunk*.

For a second his face showed no reaction but a mild puzzlement and irritation, but then his eyes migrated backward in his head till only the whites showed and he sank loose-limbed to the floor. The pistol was still trapped in his limp hand. Turner scrambled to retrieve it, not waiting to see who his benefactor with the horn was.

Beh Vah leaped into the room astride Hatcher's crumpled form. He had the long brass instrument raised like a war club, his face alive with outrage and fury, scanning the room for a challenge.

When his eyes found Chai Lo, the look that passed between them was freighted with so many conflicting passions that it became a kind of perverse embrace, a contest to see who would first look away. Chai Lo was loser.

"They try hurt you?" Beaver asked Turner. "I hear sound and come." He advanced a half step on Chai Lo, his brass club in high readiness.

"It's all right," Turner told him. "He can't bother us. Come on."

Beaver looked dubious, was hesitant to give ground. Turner gently took hold of his arm to steer him toward the wall of tape machines. "Really, buddy," he said. "We need to get out of here. Now."

His hands shaking, he experimented to find an eject button on one of the decks, and then pressed it on every machine. When a tape came out, he added it to the growing stack he held under his arm.

But even after Beaver lowered his horn he couldn't take his eyes off Chai

Lo; he seemed to regard the fallen leader with the kind of trance-like compulsion people display at a terrible automobile accident or the site of a building collapse.

When the machines were all emptied, Turner had to physically pull Beh Vah away in order to break the spell. "*Now*, bud. Go. *Go*."

There was a slight delay at the elevator while Beaver wrestled to partially collapse his horn so it would fit through the door. Turner kept an ear out for Annie, and when the elevator door finally slid shut on them he leaned against the wall with his armload of tapes and got his first deep breath since the whole night's ordeal started. He'd worry about disposing of them later.

"Thanks for what you did back there, buddy," he said to Beaver. "I know it goes against everything you're taught."

Above a shy smile, the youngster blushed with embarrassment. "I learn from mad-gun," Turner thought he said.

"From . . . ?"

"TV," Beaver said. "You know . . ." He made his hand into a pistol shape and scowled across it.

"From . . . *Mag*num?"

Beaver nodded enthusiastically. But as the elevator bell chimed their approach to the ground floor he looked suddenly remiss in something. He began to feel in the folds of his robe, from which he pulled out an odd-sized, cream-colored envelope and handed it to Turner. "Is for you," he said.

It was *deja vu*, big time, as Turner read his handwritten name—no stamp or address—on the front of the coarse paper, still as crisp and cool as the air of Drepung. The fateful evening at the Meadowlands came back to him again, when he first read Won Se's "Greetings . . ." by the cascade of colored light pelting down from the Stones' finale fireworks.

But when he unfolded the letter inside, there were no greetings, no wishes for his health. Just four words, written in such haste the pen tip had here and there scratched through the paper:

It is now, Won Se wrote. *Go*.

TURNER SPRINTED across the hotel lobby just a half step ahead of Beh Vah. In dodging the thickening number of late-night patrons, he barely missed colliding with a small statue of a cupid and ended up taking a couple of long ropes of ivy with him from a hanging basket. He punched the elevator for their floor, and was disentangling himself from the greenery when he heard someone calling his name.

"Mr. Turner?" The young desk clerk came across the carpet at a gallop, holding aloft a pink phone message. "This call just came for you," he said, when he caught up with them. "It's very urgent."

Turner's first thought was that Won Se was hedging his bets to make sure he got word to him of the Calling Out. But the number on the message had an Alabama area code. His grandparents' number.

He knew what it must mean, and the knowledge must have shown immediately in his face. Beh Vah squeezed his shoulder. "Is bad," he said. Not a question. Turner nodded.

"Listen," he told Beaver as the elevator arrived, "you go get everybody up and moving. Tell James to bring the van around. I'll be there as soon as I make this call, okay? Five minutes, tell them, and we'll be on the road." When the chrome doors were sliding shut on Beh Vah's troubled face, Turner added, "Tell them not to take a lot of time packing, we've got to just go."

He turned and ran to the row of pay phones across from the concierge desk, thinking how stupid his injunction against packing had been. A toothbrush, straight razor, and a prayer book were about the maximum baggage a monk ever accumulated. And Crowe traveled nearly as light, himself.

Turner dialed long distance and punched in his credit card number, but in his haste he must have gotten it wrong because a recording came on and told him it wasn't valid. The woman's voice on the recording sounded so eerily like a mechanized version of Cassie that it cut him to the quick, started the gall-taste rising in his throat again, though his heart and logic both told him she wasn't capable of betraying anyone. Another trick of the realm. Whatever happened to all the nasal, spinster-sounding women the phone company used to hire to tell you you'd done something wrong?

He had to try twice more before he got all the digits right and Cassie's alter ego thanked him for using AT&T. When he finally heard the familiar ringing it was cut through by short bursts of static, as if there were terrible lightning somewhere in the intervening miles.

"Hello." His grandmother, as he'd rarely in his life heard her, all the starch washed out of her voice. His parents' death revisited.

"What's wrong?" he asked her. "What did the doctor say?"

"It's . . . not too good," she said. "It's . . ." He imagined he heard her frame her throat for the hard, explosive "C" of the word he knew she meant, but it was too terrible for her to say just yet. "It's a tumor," she said instead.

And then with no pause or transition, "When do you think you can come?"

"We're leaving right now," he said. "Right this minute. We should be there by daylight, easy. Okay?"

For a moment he wondered if she'd heard him; her mind seemed to be elsewhere. He pictured her staring out at the darkened yard, listening through the bedroom wall for any change in Jackson's breathing. In the silence he heard a brisk sibilant conversation just above the threshold of static and realized it was the subconscious prayer her lips performed on their own when she was worried, so barely audible you had to be very near her to hear it. *Jesus Jesus dear Jesus oh Lord Jesus . . .*

Then she said, with wearied resignation, "It's got to be near time for the other, too, there's just so much . . ."

"The 'other'?"

" . . . *ugliness* happening. It's like they've let demons loose. Mister Johnny . . ."

Jesus dear Jesus

"What? What about him?"

"We can talk when you get here. I'm sorry, I'm . . .

"What do you mean, the 'other'?"

She ignored him again, but the meaning was clear. Hadn't Won Se said *They are prepared*?

" . . . Just saying if you don't *have* to come tonight, for it, why don't you get some sleep and start fresh in the morning. There's so many wrecks now, you'd be better off driving in the daylight."

Sleep, he thought. Right. So much adrenalin was churning in him that it threatened to eat through his skin if he didn't expend it. He doubted a double syringe of morphine could make him sleep.

His hand went to Won Se's letter, crumpled in his pocket. "We need to come tonight," he said. "We'll be careful, I promise."

"Well."

"Try not to worry."

"Listen, hon . . ." Her voice sounded suddenly stronger, more business-like. "Can your preachers eat a regular breakfast, like we do, or do I need to fix them something else?"

Breakfast. Hell breaking loose, and she's thinking about breakfast.

"What I'm getting at, is," she explained now, into his phone silence, "they're not libertarians, or anything."

"What? Oh. No, ma'am. They eat meat, like we do. Listen, don't go to the trouble of cooking, with all you've got on you . . ."

"It's no trouble. I've got to cook anyway. Just be careful, hon. Please. If I had to lose you, too, I'd . . ."

"We will be. Promise."

When he passed by the door of the hotel's lounge on the way to his room, the crowd inside was in high gear, drinking with a heightened urgency as the evening waned and laughing loud enough to almost drown out the aging country singer on the TV screen above the bar, her spangled cowboy outfit flashing blue and red as the stage lights changed with the beat.

Turner thinking, as he'd thought so often during the war years, how can people's little one-person dramas keep going on like nothing's happening, the silliness and time-killing banalities, with the world on the brink?

He pictured the faithful acolytes around the miniature world in Drepung's vast basement at that moment, watching the continents' slight gouges and trickles of red sand becoming, minute by minute, great consuming rivers and gorges and geysers of crimson. The withheld evil of decades aligning its cosmic chess pieces, making up for lost time. Now. Real. And the largest of those red sand rivers, he knew, ran straight through the middle of Zion Hill, where he'd be by daylight.

The monks would be redoubling their prayers for him now, prayer without ceasing from dozens of good and holy men, their fervent outcries causing flurries in the cages of doves before rising up through the ancient building's catacombs into the sparse crystalline air like an almost visible mist.

So why, he thought, as the elevator closed itself around him, did he feel such an outcast, so alone? The polished chrome panels showed him four of himself, each violently alone and greatly aged since that splendid morning when he'd awakened to Cassie's face and the lapping of the water. No. Got to snap out of this. No time for self-pity. A clear head is everything. It's all coming down. All finally coming down.

You will do well. Be heartful. Know you have our love. He repeated Won Se's parting words over and over, like a mantra, as he sprinted down the long carpeted hall to his room. Suddenly James Crowe came around the corner, carrying a bucket of ice and yawning, and Turner had to make a mid-course correction to keep from running him down. "Evening, Cap'n," Crowe said, saluting tiredly.

Turner grabbed his shoulder. "It's time, James. We're leaving for Zion Hill, right now."

Crowe froze. "You mean . . . it's the big one?" Turner nodded.

"Holy shit," Crowe said. He threw down the bucket of ice and took off at warp speed toward his room.

When Turner reached his own door there was a moment of panic while he patted his pockets for the room key, before he remembered putting it in the pocket of his shirt. As he found it and started to open the door he noticed a dim light coming from around its edges, though he knew for a fact he'd turned them all off. His hand froze on the knob. Had some of Hatcher's henchmen made it here this fast?

He backed away a half step, breathed deep, then kicked the door open. As it slammed the inside wall he crouched and sought the safety of the door frame, peering around it for a sign of movement.

A dark figure sat in the entrance hall, silhouetted against the yellow glow from the far bedside lamp. A woman in a wheelchair.

"I'm sorry about your grandfather," Cassie said.

Turner said nothing. He'd been avoiding thinking of her as best he could, putting off the moment he'd have to confront her, for his own peace of mind, about Hatcher's tapes.

"Your grandmother called the studio first, trying to find you," she said. "I'm really sorry. I know how much he meant to you. Means to you."

Nothing he framed in his mind to say to her seemed equal to what he felt, to what he'd just seen.

He stepped wide around her chair, got his suitcase out of the closet. When he opened it on the bed and started throwing things in, she wheeled around and laid a hand on his arm.

"What's wrong?"

"It's happening," he said. "It's time to go home."

"I *know* that," Cassie snapped back. "I *mean*, why are you acting this way?"

She *knows*? Did Won Se send her a carbon of the letter, or . . . ?

"You're the mind reader," he said, hating the sound of his voice. "You tell me."

Her face, upturned in the light, didn't waver. Her eyes stayed fully on him. "I can't," she said. "You've put up a wall. Something's happened. What is it?"

He zipped the suitcase closed and looked around for anything major he'd forgotten.

She took hold of both his arms and turned him to face her. The same love and trust looked back at him from her gold green eyes. His deepest heart could never doubt her for long, but his mind kept playing back at triple volume the sweet breathlessness of their lovemaking profaned by the thunder of artillery and the faces of beasts. The tug of war between heart and head immobilized him, which clearly wouldn't do at this moment, and he found himself reading her eyes for some clue to break the impasse. Didn't eyes always tell the truth?

Chai Lo's hadn't, damn it. Or had Turner just been such a trusting sucker that he never thought to look for that, in him?

"Your friends Hatcher and Annie are working for the realm," he said. "Chai Lo, too. There's no time to talk about it now."

Cassie looked stricken. "We can talk on the way," she said.

Her guileless, trusting eyes.

A betrayer, almost always. Sometimes two.

No. This was insane.

At that moment a roil of vivid images plowed to the forefront of his mind, the ones he'd seen by accident that night in the War Room's future-machine: Zion Hill in smoking ruins, and the glint of light showing beneath the collapsed foundation of his grandparents' house—how could he have forgotten, till now?—had clearly been the remains of a wheelchair.

"What are you seeing?" Cassie whispered urgently. "Let me in."

What he was seeing, in agonizing slow motion, was another memory superimposed onto this one—his guilty hands flinging open her apartment building's door that ancient nightmare morning, too late to stop the blur of her car into hyperspace.

"Turner."

You are the Hope. Hadn't he said he'd give his life for the chance to do it over? He'd never have that chance. But he had this one.

"*Turner*?"

He picked up the suitcase. "You're going to hate me for this," he said, "but I can't let you go along. I couldn't live with myself if I put you in danger again."

She looked at him in disbelief for a second before her nostrils flared. "That's not your decision to make," she said.

He moved toward the door. "It has to be," he said.

"That's bullshit, Turner."

He was in the hallway, her wheeling behind him.

"Turner! Goddamn you, don't do this to me . . ."

He punched the elevator call button.

"Turner!"

The doors bonged open and he got on. "Trust me," he said. "Pray for us. I'll try to take my wall down."

The chrome doors slid shut across the last image of her he would have, her head shaking with the silent rage that pumped tears from her, and replaced it with multiples of his own expressionless face which stayed that way even as he heard her scream his name again and start ramming the now-receding shut doors above him with the frail metal of her chair's footrests.

Goddamn you . . .

His heart a confusion of images and feelings, all of them as dark as Chai Lo's shadowed face in the corner of the video room, until he became so overwhelmed he felt nothing, just kept tasting the taste.

18

THEIR GROUND assault on Bau Trai was to have begun at daylight, which was some four or five hours away when the thing happened. Turner's unit was encamped in a rough line around the contoured crest of a hill that reminded him for all the world of the hill above his old grammar school. Boys would lie on their stomachs in the walked-out bare clay, crawling cautiously up to the edge to peer over the low barricade of redrock and slag that someone had constructed as fortification.

Then, their prize in view, they would whoop like banshees and rain down volleys of imaginary warheads or flaming arrows or rifle balls—depending on their mode of war that day—onto the forces of oppression and humiliation and etiquette contained inside the low, flat-roofed building of yellow brick.

Except that this time the hail of fire, aimed at softening up the NVA's fortifications on the next hilltop in preparation for attack, was delivered by invisible bombers that thrummed like baritones in the black sky from which a fine mist of rain sifted. And Turner himself did the calling down, sleepily telling the voice on the radio whether the blooms of white flame the planes delivered were hitting the spots his men had drawn fire from, just before dusk. *Getting warm, warmer . . . now you're hot . . . nope, colder now . . . try about a fourth of a kilo east.*

When suddenly he heard, in the ear that was not against the radio's earpiece, a voice in the dark not three feet away whisper in flawless Vietnamese.

The lightning that shot up the length of his spine paralyzed him for one anguished heartbeat before he could react, but then he flung down the radio like a hot coal and hit the dirt, rolling by instinct in the direction his carbine lay.

When he reached for the rifle his hand hit, instead, a hand in the dark. His synapses going off like cherry bombs by now, his other hand scrabbling for the knife in his belt, but by some stroke of grace just as he hoisted the blade the *boompboomp* lightning firefall of red tracers and a blossoming bomb outlined the face of the intruder: a boy who could not have been more than three, even allowing for the stunting effect of malnutrition. He wore only muddy white underpants a size too big for him, the slack in the waist fastened with a safety pin.

How in holy hell he'd made it past the sentries was impossible to say, one more mystery in millions that the process of war, this war in particular, seemed by some quirk of its nature to spawn. Turner's rudimentary grasp of the language fixed on two or three words the boy kept repeating, and he determined the child was asking for some food.

Silent alarm bells went off in the back of his mind. He knew, too well, that the Cong had no scruples about using children for decoys or distractions. Or worse. A friend of his, furloughing in Quang Tri, had bought the farm when the enemy sent a toddler wandering into a crowded strip joint, enough explosives on him they never found a shred after he blew.

But Turner looked to the left of him, to the right, bald ground where anyone would show against the sky, and saw only silhouettes of helmet-tops of the men in holes on either side. He found his radio and started back calling the strikes, shouldering it to have his hands free. The far white bursts shed light enough he could find the can of crackers among his C-rations, and some packs of grape jelly he'd swiped at the PX snack bar.

The rain was coming heavier by then, so he settled the boy up into his lap to eat, underneath the folds of the big poncho, and talked to the invisible airplanes while healthy smacking sounds, such as a cat might make, came from inside the wet fabric. Him thinking how nobody back home would believe this in a million million years.

And then thinking something else, too, as the moment grew a halo around it, became a sort of place-marker for his life, thinking that this was quite possibly the first time ever he had known perfect peace. The first time, and he could keep it like a touchstone for whenever in the future he needed peace. Sheltering a warm other life in the dark and the rain, thinking about home, watching the red tracers and the white blooms of fire diffusing in the jungle mist like headlights and taillights on a highway.

"How far, Cap'n?" James Crowe asked, from the seat beside him.

More to make conversation against the lonely click of the wiper blades, Turner thought, than from any real need to know. The monks weren't talking, still had not fully absorbed the news about Chai Lo, and moreover were righteously pissed at Turner for not bringing Cassie. James, after hearing him out on that topic, had seemed to reserve judgment.

"Oh, a good two-and-a-half hours," Turner said. "Maybe more." The speedometer was brushing ninety, had been since they'd left the city limits. He figured he'd take a speeding ticket if he had to, would've gone even faster if the road hadn't been wet.

The traffic, mostly trailer rigs, had been heavier than he guessed it would be at this hour of the night. A couple of times he got safely in a fast truck's wake and high-tailed with it until the interstate forked, thinking most of them had radar alarms and made good escorts.

Right now the flow had thinned substantially and he was going it alone. There was a flicker in his mirror, and he glanced up to see a set of headlights topping the big hill a half mile or so behind him. The speed with which they enlarged told him a bad mother of a trucker was about to slice past him, and he eased off the gas a little in anticipation of catching the truck's side-wind.

But as he did, he noticed from the shape of the lights that they weren't a truck, but a car. And a small one, at that.

They grew and grew until they were nearly tagging his rear bumper, and instead of passing they flashed on bright, blinding him before he could look away. "Son of a bitch," Turner mumbled. "Go *around.*" The lights went bright to dim, then bright and dim again.

When he slowed even further, hoping the fool would pass, the car suddenly careened left around him, a slash of red with a black cloth top, then swerved back into his lane so quick its rear end grazed his left fender.

He braked hard as he could without throwing them into a spin, and wrenched the wheel to steer the van off onto the shoulder.

Turner said, "*This* guy is . . ." and was about to add *nuts* when the driver of the red car spun to a stop in front of him and flung open its passenger door.

This guy is . . .

Cassie. And fighting mad.

She jerked her collapsed chair from behind the car seat and slung it to the pavement in the arc of a bullfighter's cape, where it hit with such force that it assembled itself forthwith. She hoisted herself up by the door frame to swing over into its seat, then got a good grip on the wheel-rails and propelled the chair toward the van at top speed, her eyes in the headlights glowing like an animal cornered at night.

Turner was out of the van by now, stomping toward her, with James following. "Oh, that was smart," Turner shouted at her. "That was really smart."

"Well, how does one *get* your goddamned attention, then?" she yelled back. "Talking like a normal human being doesn't do it."

Behind him, Turner heard the van's side door open, then the monks' running feet.

He and Cassie were faced off on the shoulder pavement in the falling mist of rain, lit by the blue glare of both vehicles' headlights, so close their knees almost touched.

"You . . . listen . . . to me," she said through her teeth, in such a sudden utter calm that he had to. Her eyes were wet, looking up at him, and her chin shook with the containment of her rage. "I was *saved* . . . for this. And nobody can tell me otherwise.

"Now, if you've got something against me I need to know what it is. I keep trying to get in your head and see, but you've shut me out. So much anger. It blocks all the light."

He had no awareness of having done this, but it sounded true.

"The *clock* . . . is *ticking*, Hope," she said. "We can talk while we ride."

Turner hunched down to put his face more on a level with hers, hoping that by the time he did, some words would have come. But none did.

The look in her eyes was a vast, commingled rage and love that looked to have the power to vaporize solid matter, or to jump-start an earthquake.

Turner had to look away from that intensity if he was to gather his resolve again. But what he saw were the monks and Crowe arrayed at the roadside like someone waiting for a sporting event to begin. Only Beh Vah stood back from the line a little, looking sidewise at Turner with his chin down.

Cassie laid a hand on Turner's temple, turned him to face her. "Don't make me follow you," she whispered, too low for the onlookers to hear. "You can't stop me from following you. Unless you kill me."

"Oh, for Christ sake, Cassie," Turner said. He pulled away from her and threw his head back as if asking relief from the heavens. At the zenith of the sky, an incongruous ragged hole in the rain clouds showed twinkling stars.

The clock is ticking, Hope.

Turner heard an interrogatory cough beside him. It was a meekly smiling Se Hon, who looked at him and then at Cassie and said, "I suppose this would be not a good time for spiders." He shook his head as he asked it, ready to acquiesce but hopeful all the same.

Cassie held out her hand to Se Hon and he took it. "Not really, sweetie," she said. "Tomorrow, maybe." She kissed his knuckle and he nodded, satisfied, and went back to the group.

Tick, tick. All eyes on Turner. Soft rain falling, almost like smoke. Cassie regarding him with an expression that was no expression at all, the feeling wrung out of her like a cloth.

"Give me your car keys," Turner said.

Her eyes narrowed reflexively, the least bit, suspicious of his intent. "Why?"

"I'll pull it farther on the shoulder and lock it," he said. "It's a hazard, to leave it where it is."

Silence. Her small shoulders rose and fell with the effort of her deliberation. Turner had a sense of some faint probing force at the edge of his consciousness he couldn't have put a name to.

Cassie's eyes had filled up again. He didn't think it was the rain. "Let me in," she whispered. "Let me see."

Turner clamped his eyes shut against the soft intrusion.

"No," he said, with dead calm. "You have to trust me first."

The soft pressure subsided. When he opened his eyes she was looking at him with what seemed resignation.

Tick, tick.

She sighed, looked at the ground, and then reached in the pocket of her jeans. She held the key out to him wordlessly, still looking down.

"Guys?" Turner shouted, as he started trotting toward her car, "You want to give Cass a hand, here? The van doors might be a little high for her to negotiate."

When he'd started the car he looked back and saw that Wah So and Se Hon had linked their arms to make a kind of seat for boosting Cassie up into the van. James was folding her chair to stow in the back, and Lu Weh and Bah Tow were rearranging the luggage to make her a space. There seemed to be an air of festival around her in the lighted interior.

As Turner was putting the car in gear to move it off the roadside, some invisible obstruction in his consciousness seemed to roll away at the urging of invisible hands.

What poured in through the opening was such a balm to his hurt spirit—he imagined it as the consistency of honey, and thought for an instant he could taste some sweet herb—that he had to put his head down on the wheel for the space of a breath and focus his mind on the task at hand.

When he looked up again, Beh Vah was inserting himself into line ahead of Se Hon, wanting the first spiders.

"It was in the *plant*," Cassie said suddenly to Turner as he drove through the mountains of north Alabama in a moonlit fog.

They had already talked at great length about the treachery that had come to light, Hatcher and Annie and Chai Lo and Lord knows who else turning up in the dark side's batting order, any more of them and you'd need a printed program to tell who was who.

When Turner realized they'd spent nearly an hour rehashing it, stoking the hurt, kicking themselves for having missed what in hindsight were tiny warning signs, they put a moratorium on the subject and agreed to talk only about good things, things that would build their spirit for the ordeal that was just ahead. But in the midst of reciting one of the Buddha's teachings about inner peace in times of danger and trial, the idea of the plants hit Cassie like a thunderbolt and she blurted it out.

"*What* was?" Turner said. "What was in the plants?"

"The bug. The microphone." She hit the dashboard with both fists. "It was in the goddamned *plant*. Just about when the battery in one would have time to run down, she'd give me another plant to nurse. They knew every move I made." She shuddered and beat the dash again. "*Oooh*, goddamn her. After all I did for her? It's crazy. Why didn't I have a clue?"

"Hey," Turner said. "What's done is done. We've got to cut the death talk and stay focused. Sound familiar?"

Cassie sighed.

"It's been a long night," he said. "Do you think you could sleep a little, if I stopped and let you stretch out back there?"

She gave him a look.

"Okay, okay. So where were we, in the teaching? 'If the spirit is within the flesh, and the flesh within a larger spirit, then it follows that . . .'"

"I think," Cassie said, her mind off somewhere not listening, "that I could let it drop if I just had the least little foggy idea of why I didn't even suspect . . ."

"Who the hell knows?" Turner shrugged. "So to speak."

Lu Weh and another monk or two were snoring peacefully in the back. The others, he saw in the mirror, were reading their prayer books by the glow of penlights. James wore the same prayerful look as he played the mathematical equivalent of solitaire on his pocket calculator, its numerals glowing in the dark.

"Okay," she said. "I'll stop. Water over the dam, right? Who the hell knows. Like you said."

Turner took his eyes off the road long enough to touch her face and kiss her. "It's good to have you back," he told her.

"I wouldn't miss it for the world," she said. She cleared her throat. "' . . . And the flesh within a larger spirit, then it follows that the resources of that spirit are a bounty of hope no demon of the realm can pierce . . .'"

Turner took her hand.

By the time they reached the Robbins exit on Interstate 65, the night sky had gradually, imperceptibly, brightened from black to a dark, bruised-looking rose color. Sunrise was still twenty or thirty minutes away, Turner guessed, about the time they'd get to Zion Hill.

All the stars but one had disappeared, and the big moon was already growing pale in anticipation of the imminent wash of light; it looked almost transparent, like a thumbprint in damp watercolor. The exit ramp dropped the van into the thick of farming country, with here and there hastily cobbled fruit stands hugging the side of the road. Uphill behind them, simple frame houses with wide porches were dwarfed by the bounty of their fields and orchards: sweet corn and stick-beans and squash and kale, apples and peaches and pears and pecans.

His passengers were all asleep by this point, if not totally at rest. Now and then one of the monks, dreaming, would cry out a word or syllable Turner couldn't understand, a fragment of some exhortation to one's comrades in the face of danger.

Cassie slept too, but if she fought battles in her dreams it didn't show. Her head was canted backwards across the headrest, mouth the least bit open, in a kind of blissful surrender to unconsciousness, as if she didn't know or care how alarmingly vulnerable her small face and neck looked at that angle, a surface of eggshell rocketing heedlessly through the world.

It required a great deal of effort on Turner's part not to watch her constantly, to keep his eyes on the road. Her sleeping self seemed to him a sort of natural wonder, an exotic night-blossoming plant that only the faithful are privileged to see, and the control it took to tend to his driving made him feel like the helmsman of a boat fighting a steady sideways wind.

What kept coming to his mind in the silence, though, was a sense of some vague absence or imbalance in the familiar compartment, some error in judgment he had made. He finally realized the absence was Chai Lo's.

As he pictured the times he'd driven all night with Shy in the seat beside him, a frequent insomniac, and had poured out his deepest heart to the soft-spoken monk on an endless number of subjects both sacred and temporal, it dawned on him for the first time how massive, in military terms, a breach of security it all would become now upon Chai Lo's defection.

Because if Won Se were right, the evil realm's most dreaded weapons aren't its guns and clubs and bogeymen—though it can array those too, upon occasion—but rather all the ways it has of finding the most minuscule soft spot in your soul's defenses, its hellish persistence at homing in on weaknesses and fears you thought were well-concealed.

No disrespect intended, Won Se had said, but the realm's assaying gear makes God's look, by comparison, like a high school chemistry set. And now here was Shy gone over to the bad side; if the man had even half a memory, he'd extracted enough weaknesses and fears in those late-night confessionals to give some demon brigade a hell of a guided tour of Turner's heart's soft underside.

At the intersection of Morgan's Chapel Road, the old stop sign still leaned a good ten degrees to the right and bore the same perforations of rifle-shot that it had for the last twenty years. There was no car to be seen down any of the four directions of damp blacktop, but some deep genetic memory nevertheless made Turner brake to a stop before going on across.

The sky was brightening almost by the second. From here there was only one more turn, a right, just beyond Thornton Lake where he had caught his first catfish and first eel, when he was four. After that it was all a straight shot on Bessie Mines Road—six miles, maybe seven—to Zion Hill.

Turner already knew what he would do, just before they approached the last big rise. He'd wake up Cassie, so her first glimpse of their old hometown, his heart's home, would be the best possible view of it: a delicate tapestry of green pine and red dirt and neat rows of vegetable gardens, as miniature from that hilltop as if seen from an airplane, with the first gold strokes of sunlight fingering it as lovingly as a hand finding its way into a beloved, worn baseball glove.

For twenty years now it had been the place he escaped to whenever the world got to be too much for him. But this time the world had found the place too, and there was no escape. No, not the world. The realm. A difference.

A mist was rising off the lake when he turned at it. The van's passing scared up a flock of young partridges from the roadside weeds of the intersection, and they ran in a half-dozen directions, brown blurs of cooing and wings.

Not far, now. Turner saw that Cassie, as if sensing in sleep what awaited them, had gradually curled forward into herself, head down, and was bracing one arm in the niche between the seat and the door. Her blue-jeaned legs were splayed in the floorboard at an odd angle, like a child's.

Turner squeezed her shoulder one quick time and she instantly unfolded, eyes alert. "What?" she said, as casually as if there were an ongoing conversation.

"'What?' yourself," he said. She smiled at him and gently knuckled the corners of her amazing eyes.

"How far?" she asked.

"About five minutes. I wanted you to see something."

As they topped the final rise toward growing sunlight he slowed the van almost to a crawl, so they would have time to drink the vista in slowly when it showed itself.

"This is the prettiest . . ." Turner began, but as the valley came into sight it made a lie of that, and he hushed. His foot hit the brake, made the tires lock and scrape the pavement. The van came to a stop in the middle of the road.

Below them, sky to sky, the entire panorama was blanketed by a churning ocean of ink-black cloud, the edges of it crackling with tendrils of blue lightning, as if a bad storm front a hundred miles wide had somehow been condensed into four or five. No sunlight penetrated. The valley was an island of nighttime against the clean golds and blues of the dawn. It was like looking from the bright outdoors into a darkened room; the only objects that showed themselves were ones briefly outlined by a surge of the ghostly blue lightning, as liquid as flame. The steeple of the church. The iron fence around the cemetery. An angled tin roof that would be Mose Hartley's store.

"Good God," Turner whispered. Cassie raised herself in the seat and laid her hand on his arm that still clenched the steering wheel.

There were stirrings in the back of the van. When Turner glanced around, the monks and James Crowe were crouched in a clump between the seat-backs, their faces jockeying for a view. When they got it, all sound ceased.

Lu Weh was the first to speak. "Is right place," he said with grim acceptance. Nobody could add anything to that.

Except Cassie.

"Turn around," she said.

Turner looked at her as if she'd lost her mind.

"No, turn around in the *road*, I mean. Stay here, just point the van the other way."

Puzzled, he complied.

"Now look in the mirror," she said.

To Turner's amazement—but apparently not to the monks' or James's—the reflection of Zion Hill in the front and side mirrors was as bright and placid as on any fine summer morning; verdant, locked in dew, its ponds and waterholes giving back perfect blue replicas of a sky unsullied by the terrible black cloud.

"That's how it looks to the unknowing," Cassie explained. "That's the way we need to carry it in our hearts, till this is over. Be kind of two-hearted, so it all doesn't overwhelm us. The bad way's the way it *is*, but this is how it *can* be, again."

It was a long time before a tentative voice spoke, in the back. Bah Tow.

"Have some pray?" he said.

Everyone seemed agreeable to that. Beh Vah took Cassie's other hand, Turner took Lu Weh's, and the chain continued through the bunch standing in the aisle until James Crowe wordlessly took Bah Tow's left and Se Hon's right and completed the circuit of hands.

Turner glanced at each person's face before he began to lead the prayer, and out of nowhere an old song came to him, one he hadn't thought of in a dozen years: "Will the Circle Be Unbroken?" They used to sing it on decoration day at Zion Hill Baptist Church. He remembered sitting between his grandmother's high clean tenor and his grandfather's rumbling bass, the two disparate frequencies mixing in him like electricity on the chorus. *By and by, Lord, by and by . . .*

He couldn't have said whether it was the freshened Baptist memory or some other, more primal, need of his heart at that moment that caused him to eschew the genderless beginning of a Buddhist prayer and go instead with the way the men of Zion Hill Baptist used to pray; whichever, once he'd begun he couldn't call it back, had to let it pour out until its conclusion:

"Dear heavenly father," he said, his eyes squinching shut from old habit, "We ask now that you'd guide and direct us in what we are about to undertake, and that thy will would be done through it. We know, Lord, you've told us in your word that perfect love casteth out all fear.

"But we know, too, father, that our love for one another, and our love for thee, has never been perfect, and that we're very often afraid. We are right now, Lord." He felt the grip of Beh Vah's and Cassie's hands on his tighten the least bit. "So we ask that you'd just grant us enough of your own love, enough of your grace, to see us through what's required of us in this time of testing. Not because of anything we've done that makes us worthy of it, but just as a gift, Lord. Because you're the way you are, we know we can ask it.

"And just watch over us all, as we go forth from this minute, and we'll praise you for it. We ask in Jesus's name. Amen."

A man, Beh Vah's voice echoed with assurance, and a split second later the others. *Amen.*

When Turner opened his eyes he did so with both hesitation and boundless hope, with the faint unspoken expectation he'd had since childhood, and wondered if the men of Zion Hill Baptist did, too—the hope that this time you'd gotten the wording just right and God had immediately rolled out heaven's big guns, transforming whatever bleak circumstance had set you to praying in the first place.

So it was with a twinge of shame that he finally turned his head from the bright mirror and looked downhill to see the roiling ocean of cloud, absolutely unchanged.

19

AS THEY LEFT the hilltop and drove down into the valley, they immediately needed headlights to see. But Turner could have driven this last one-mile leg with his eyes shut, nearly, its topography being so cleanly engraved in his mind.

Against his expectation, there was virtually no wind at ground level underneath the churning covering of cloud. Though both of the van's windows were rolled down, the interior had filled up with a stifling, midday-feeling heat. Over at Hartley's store a single bare light bulb illuminated the crooked gas pumps from above, just as it did through the nights of his childhood, when he rode home from church in the dark after prayer meeting.

Across the road, the liquid blue lightning still fretted the low steeple of Zion Hill Baptist. When his headlights first raked the front of the building he thought they showed a dark square where the front doors were, the entry of some intruder, but when he blinked and looked again the weathered wooden doors were restored to their rightful places. No lights were on in the church.

A particularly large burst of lightning brought a low crackle of static from the dashboard, and Turner realized he'd left the radio on. He started to click it off, but instead began tuning around for a voice to tell him what was happening, out in the world.

A soft trill of flute filled the van, and Turner glanced in the mirror to see who was playing it. He'd thought all the instruments were packed away in the back. When he saw six elated faces looking back at him, he knew the music wasn't coming from a monk but from a speaker, and he turned the volume of the radio up. A syncopation of cymbals took the melody then, the flutes filled in the gaps, and the faintest hint of the big horns' low notes laid down a bass flooring in preparation for the piece's climax.

Turner looked over at Cassie, who had her eyes shut, nodding to the beat. Her left hand unconsciously assumed the position it had at the mixing console, turning an imaginary dial to keep the levels right. When the crescendo of the finish came, the monks and Crowe burst into sustained applause.

Turner reached for Cassie's magic mixing hand and kissed it. "When you said you'd get those tapes out in a hurry, you weren't kidding," he said. "That's amazing."

She grinned. "A lot of people owe me favors."

The announcer's voice on the radio began telling about the group, but he got no farther than " . . . sure you've been reading about them . . ." when the sound shut off. As the noise of the backseat celebration died away, it became clear in the ghostly total silence that the motor had died, too. And the headlights. Their small new success must have gotten the realm's goat, big time.

Turner knew that bringing the monks' sacred music to the masses was a quantum leap toward lifting people's inner blindness—the ball and chain that most fetters the Hope's heart in the final battle, as Won Se had told him. But now he began to wonder how much good it would actually do, if the realm only got aggravated and redoubled its efforts.

Turner coasted down the slight incline until he reached a solid-enough shoulder to pull off on, a gravelled access road at the lower edge of the cemetery. Before the van completely stopped rolling, James Crowe was already out the door with his flashlight, raising the hood.

Turner leaned out the window. "James? Let it go, buddy. It's only about a mile farther. We can walk it." When he turned to put the emergency brake on, Cassie was looking at him with one eyebrow partly raised.

"I'm sorry," he said. "I forgot."

"Keep forgetting. I take it as a compliment."

"It's mostly downhill from here, if that helps. Or you could ride on my back."

She shook her head. "Nah, better not. I've got a spur fetish. The chair's fine."

When he got out to unload it for her, his eye fell on the cornermost tombstone inside the fence and he saw by the dim blue light that it was engraved with his grandparents' names. The fact went through his heart like an electric shock before he remembered that this was nothing sinister, no trick of the realm; his grandmother had told him a year or more ago they were having the grave marker made, but the idea hadn't registered because he'd never seen it in the flesh. In the stone. Whatever.

As Cassie put her arm around his shoulder to help her swing out into the chair, Turner saw the monks lined up at the black iron fence, staring with curiosity out into the cemetery. It would be the first one they'd ever seen, except in photographs, and Turner thought how primitive the custom must seem to them, considering the way their own culture handles mortality.

He had been at Drepung several weeks, and had rambled increasing distances out into the countryside, before it dawned on him one day that he'd never seen a single cemetery or mausoleum anywhere. When he asked Won Se at dinner that night where Tibetans buried their dead, Turner blamed his own faulty command of the language when Won Se obviously misunderstood and answered, "In the sky."

"The spirit part," Turner responded. "Right. I know where the spirit goes. I mean the body. The remains."

But Won Se repeated his answer.

Because the land in Tibet was in most places solid stone, he explained, their forefathers had long ago abandoned the notion of graves in favor of sky burials.

"I don't understand," Turner had said.

And when he finally did, he had wished he didn't.

A funeral service is held, Won Se told him, on the night of someone's death, and the following morning at dawn the friends and family carry the body to some remote high hill. There, they anoint it with oils and herbs and then, using implements brought for the purpose, painstakingly carve the body into pieces small enough for vultures and wolves to carry away.

The grotesqueness of the proposition stunned him. He expected better of a people who had polished the spiritual part of their natures to such a fine, high gloss over the millennia.

But when Turner at last witnessed a sky burial he was surprised at how rational, how natural, the process seemed from close up. And partway through, when Won Se had looked up at him across the gradually diminishing corpse of the 97-year-old monk, and had wordlessly taken in Turner's distance and the unused knife at his feet, it was as if Won Se's expression said, "*You* loved him, too." Chastened, Turner knelt and took up the knife. And began.

After that day, his attitude toward dying underwent a sea change. Now it was embalming and caskets and gravestones—not sky burials—that seemed grotesque and primitive to him. Why make someone's preserved remains a touchstone of misery for the living, planted where they have to pass it every day and be reminded, all fresh again, of the pain of loss?

"Down this way, guys," Turner called to the monks, as he pushed Cassie's chair over the soft hump of soil and grass to get to the pavement. "I don't think there'll be many cars passing this early, but stay to the left anyway and keep an eye out, okay?"

James Crowe led the way with the flashlight, but once they got out from underneath the two big oaks whose branches overhung the road they found there was light enough without it to walk by. At the horizon to the east, the shape of the sun showed through the black clouds with a filmy, kerosene look to it, giving the same amount of light as a half-moon might in normal times.

The big fenced pasture to the left of the road, a part of Johnny Patterson's land that adjoined his grandparents', was empty except for two cowed-looking horses at the far edge of it, solacing themselves against each other's neck. Could they see this strange weather, too? Turner thought briefly of asking James for a mathematical perspective on who could see which of the realm's illusions, and why, but on second thought he hesitated to set off the frantic verbal cascade Crowe was capable of when he wrapped his mind around an idea. This mellow silence was more soothing to the nerves; he decided to let well enough alone.

When the fenced land ended, the road was again walled in by tall, coarse pines on either side, their trunks so impenetrably knitted together by kudzu and brambles that it was impossible to wander leisurely from the road down into the woods, as it had been so easy to do during his childhood—between the road and the distant Warrior River, hillocks and shallow ridges of clay and shale divided the forest gracefully into ballroom-sized enclosures of dappled sunlight, with a level floor of accumulated pinestraw that begged you to cast off your shoes and go barefoot. But those days were gone. Now, Turner calculated, your best companion on a hike to the river would be a good machete. If not a couple of canisters of napalm.

Cassie must have been thinking the same thing. "God, it's grown up," she said sadly. He realized she'd have had no reason for a homecoming, for years and years; her father had been prematurely taken by a heart attack barely a year after the accident, and her mother had moved off to Montgomery to be nearer her two sisters.

At the top of the next hill, the thick growth ended and the land to the left cleaved off into a vista of scrub pines and redrock that framed the familiar shape of his grandparents' pond. All light and life seemed gone from its surface. The only thing that distinguished it from its surroundings was the dim movement of angry black it reflected from the atmosphere; at its far side, the ruined prow of an old wooden rowboat protruded from a tributary of mud. The boat dock he and Cassie had watched so many sunsets from was a casualty of time, as well. None of the walkway remained, only stumps of the two outermost pillars tilted as unevenly as teeth in a jack-o-lantern.

Cassie stopped rolling and turned sideways to the slope of the road to keep from applying the wheelbrake while she paused to take a long look at the pond. Turner watched her face, expecting the forlorn view to deepen her already dark mood, but as Crowe and the monks caught up to them and halted, she shook her head and smiled.

"The senior party," she said. Turner hadn't thought about it in years; it was one of countless mental snapshots he'd expended monumental effort to keep locked in an off-limits bottom drawer of his mind, for sanity's sake.

She saw his blank look and prompted, "Your folks cooked barbecue, and we all went swimming in the pond."

He nodded, but the memory was all a blur to him until she added, "Remember Gayle?"

That would be Gayle Crosby, who set up her gypsy fortune-teller act in the front parlor, predicting amid clouds of dime-store patchouli incense all their futures for them. Gayle, of the vivid romantic imagination and astounding cleavage, who squinted at her crystal ball until it showed her plainly his and Cassie's lives. No, *life*. Singular. Marriage, of course, followed by Cassie's quick rise to popularity as a coffeehouse singer. Turner being her road manager, of course, until they got rich enough to retire and raise children and horses on a ranch in Montana.

Good old Gayle.

What if, Turner thought. What if, that day, she'd taken their lovesick selves aside in the dark parlor, sworn them to secrecy, and told them what the future *really* held? Would it have changed anything, to know?

Turner's contemplation was broken by a shout from Wah So, "Up! Look up!" simultaneous with an eerie, warbling whistle from overhead. Something was hurtling at them from out of the smoky sky. The whistling noise became edged, then replaced by, a harsh hissing sound like meat searing on a fire.

As the plummeting shape materialized in the smoke they froze for a fraction of a second, unable to believe the suddenly blatant threat was real. It was Wah So who first broke free of the inertia, his hyper-keen ears having given him a slight advantage of timing—he lunged toward the back of Cassie's chair, propelling her forward off the high lip of the blacktop paving into a shallow trough of nettles and vines, himself a saffron flurry of arms and legs in the air around her trying to cushion the worst of her headlong fall.

They had barely tumbled to rest when the huge globe struck the highway at almost the spot where Cassie had sat. Its destruction on impact was so deafening and immediate, an explosion composed totally of flinty shattering, that only by reconstituting a single freeze-frame of memory was Turner able to know what the object had been before the crash: a crystal ball of elephantine dimensions, at its center a splash of vivid red and orange that the containing glass distorted like a cat's-eye marble.

When he saw that everyone had managed to duck the ricocheting fragments, which littered the blacktop like a spilled truckload of ice chunks, he ran over and hopped down off the roadside to check on Cassie. Wah So had picked her up and was dusting her off; he motioned for Turner to set her chair back on firm ground so he could carry her to it.

"You guys all right?" Turner asked. When they both nodded, he gave Wah So's shoulder a squeeze. "That was fast thinking, buddy. Bless your heart." Wah So shrugged.

While they got Cassie situated in her chair again, Turner noticed Crowe and the monks gravitating into a knot at the far side of the road, looking down at a piece of the debris. As he walked over, keeping an eye cast uneasily toward the sky, he remembered the brief flash of gypsy-like color at the heart of the glass meteor and had a sinking premonition what he would find.

He was right. Even before the monks widened their circle to admit him, he could see beyond their legs the crumpled body among the shards of glass. Its limbs were extended at unnatural angles by the force of the impact, and a riot of bright flimsy scarves stood out from the edges of the shape like paint splattered at high velocity.

He didn't have to look at the girl's face, obscured from his direction by the shiny silk outline of the two perfect pillow-shaped breasts, to know whose it would be. Gayle Crosby. A Gayle still eighteen and red-cheeked and beautiful, redolent with the sweetness of possibility.

Crowe was kneeling now, fingering one of the fragments with a professional detachment as if critiquing a rival's skill at creating fake matter. Judging from the look he gave Turner, he was highly impressed with what he saw. "If I didn't know better," he began, "I'd say this was rea . . ." Turner glared him into silence.

"Guys?" Turner called to the monks, "Don't worry. It's not a person. She's not real. Okay? It's just something the realm's made to scare us with." As he spoke, the rich scent of patchouli wafted toward him on an unfelt breeze and he swallowed hard before he could speak again. "Come on, we need to keep moving. Just look the other way, and try not to think about it."

Cassie had wheeled silently to his side, a torn kudzu leaf trapped in the back of her hair the only sign of her involuntary dive into the underbrush. For what she'd just been through, she looked surprisingly settled and unconcerned. As for Turner, the near-miss had jolted his reflexes into combat readiness; his perceptions seemed heightened twelve-fold. The threatening sky became the worst enemy of the moment, and he felt his voice assume the old no-nonsense cadences of command.

"We need cover," he said, as the monks and Crowe reluctantly turned from the scene of the made-to-order tragedy. He motioned toward the right-hand side of the road, up ahead where a sheer cliff of rock overhung slightly the roadside ditch for a hundred yards or so—a shield, however slim, from any other projectiles that might come from overhead. "And we need to stay spread out, so we don't make as big a target. James? Show them patrol formation. How much space to leave. We've only got about half a mile to go, but I don't want to take any chances. Move it. Hurry."

He felt the old familiar grid of threat and reaction impose itself over his thinking, as cleanly as if it had been only yesterday, not twenty years, since he'd commanded men in the field. Without asking, he took the handles of Cassie's chair and began pushing her briskly toward the overhang. "I'll walk point," he told her. "James'll be second man, and you'll stay back in the middle of the line where it's safest . . ."

"Turner?"

"Just keep about a fifteen-foot distance from the next person, in front and behind. No closer, understand?"

"*Turner.*"

"What?" In the sudden windless silence he could hear his heartbeat in his ears.

"I don't like what's going on, here," Cassie said. "We all need to huddle a minute, and talk."

Huddle? Talk? He felt if he didn't keep moving, he'd jump right out of his skin. He tried to hide his irritation.

"Cass wants a conference, fellas," he shouted to Crowe and the running monks. "Everybody circle up." The wheelchair accelerated forward, out of his grasp; he saw Cassie's taut arms whipping at the wheelgrips in controlled fury, two blurs of pure intent toward the safety of the cliff.

When she got there, James and the monks squatted around her in a semicircle. Turner was too hyper to stay still; he paced along the row and glanced toward both ends of the highway, alert for catastrophe, but tried not to let his gaze touch for long on the colorful spot in the middle of the glass debris.

"Look, I don't want to hurt anybody's feelings," Cassie began, in a tone of controlled anger. "But this is starting to feel like a war movie, and that's not the way to go. We need to stay attuned to our *spirits*, here, and not get distracted by . . ."

"For God's sake, Cass," Turner erupted, interrupted, "they're *dropping* shit on us." The monks and Crowe looked mutely back and forth at each point of the interchange, like a crowd watching a tennis match. Turner knew it wasn't good to let troops see dissent in the upper ranks, but this one was already out of the bottle. "What are we supposed to do, lie down and draw a target around ourselves? You've never *been* in combat; you don't . . ."

"They can't hurt us," she said.

"The hell they can't. What about the . . ."

"They can't . . . hurt . . . *us*," she cut him off. "The two of us. Not at this stage."

"Says who? What do you mean?"

"Trust me."

Turner's exasperation level skyrocketed. "Well, shit a brick," he shouted, throwing his arms up hopelessly. "How come nobody *tells* me these things?"

For some reason Turner found his mind fastening around a totally unrelated subject. Namely, the sensation that he suddenly understood what had been subliminally signaling threat to him ever since they arrived at Zion Hill: a simple sound, or rather the lack of one. No birdsong. In ordinary circumstances the woods were full of it, subtly changing colors and harmonies with different weathers and slants of light, but overall so unceasing that it became a rich beneficent soundtrack to the day.

James Crowe cleared his throat. "Uh, let me get this straight," he said. "They can't do nothing to hurt you two guys, but . . ."

"*Physically*," Cassie amended. "Not until the Calling Out. Mentally, we're fair game."

"So the rest of us are kind of raw meat ready for the grill," Crowe said. "Physically, and every which way." Turner noticed a couple of the monks glancing around them, presumably looking for a grill.

"Right," Cassie acknowledged. "Which, in the meantime, is why . . ."

"Which is *exactly*," Turner broke in, "the reason I'm saying we need to spread . . ."

She raised her hand against the interruption and continued as levelly as if he hadn't spoken. " . . . is *why* . . . we have to make that rule work *for* us instead of against us. We need to be *closer*, not farther apart. Think about it. If we all hold hands, and stay as close together as we can, then everybody's protected because it's impossible for them to single one person out. Right?"

Turner had his mouth open to raise an objection, but one wouldn't quite gel. The idea had a bizarre logic, even if it was diametrically opposed to every field-combat teaching that had brought him through the war in, relatively speaking, one piece. At the very least, seeing their motley crew advance while holding hands like kindergartners on a field trip might disable the enemy with laughter for a bit.

He looked at all of the assembled and felt a pang of something that was midway between love and homesickness, and realized with wonder just how near home he was.

"Okay, I stand corrected on that point," he said. He went to stand by Cassie, rubbed her shoulders. "Everybody in a line, then," he directed. "Hold hands, and stay close . . ."

Turner looked both ways for traffic before leading the queue up onto the blacktop. When they were sufficiently bunched, they latched hands and set off down the long straight that preceded the final curve before home.

For some reason Turner had a fleeting thought of how they must look from on high, clustered and tentative in the eerie half light of the landscape: Cass was Dorothy and he was Tin Man and Lion and Scarecrow all rolled into one, a festival of coexistent weaknesses and fears.

BEYOND THE NEXT bend, the broad old four-square farmhouse of his childhood sat well back from the road, the same yellow bug-light in its porch fixture. Two guinea-hens perched on the arms of the wide wooden swing that hung from an oak limb at the yard's edge, motionless in the still, confined air. When the group drew closer the guineas began a rapid-fire clicking of alarm in their throats and finally launched themselves asqueal into the air, iridescent tails flashing, as they sought the safety of the oak limb above.

Turner felt a tugging at his sleeve. "Is what?" Beh Vah asked.

"Those are called guineas," Turner told him. "Kind of a distant cousin of the peacock. Sometimes they make a racket that sounds just like a person crying."

At that moment one of the birds demonstrated for them, sounding exactly like a woman in tears. Wah So, fascinated, mimicked the noise to perfection and gave it back to the guinea, which started its partner wailing too. The crying was so realistic that Turner could believe the old tale told on Mattie Sexton, just down the road, that after her son was killed in the war she went a little crazy one night with her shotgun and wiped out the whole guinea population of her farm.

Turner already had one foot on the whitewashed concrete steps leading up to the porch when he realized what a formidable barrier they made for Cassie. "Not very good access, huh?" he asked her. "We'll have to fix that, if we're here long." He bent over and held out his arms to her. "Upsy daisy. James, could you bring the chair up, bud?"

She clasped his neck and let his arms, one at the small of her back and the other at the bend of her knees, take her insubstantial weight. As Turner started up the steps with her, the clean bitterweed smell of her hair against his cheek, he was seized by a powerful old ghost of the heart: his recurring dream in high school, of carrying her over the threshold on their wedding day. For some reason the threshold dream was never a honeymoon suite on the beach, or some bright subdivision house nearer the city, but here. These steps.

"What?" Cassie whispered. "What is it?"

Turner was almost certain no catch in his breath had betrayed his flashback; more likely Cassie was gradually working her way back into the furnishings of his mind again, knowing what needed knowing.

"Homecoming," he said. "It's always been a little rough for me." Whether she believed him or not, she dispensed a quick kiss on his cheek and squeezed his neck a little tighter. Turner lowered her into the chair James had set up. The monks formed a reverent half-circle around him and Cassie, waiting for him to do the honor of knocking on the door.

When he did, a second ghost, nearly as strong, enfolded him. Show and tell, from grammar school. How many times had he knocked at this door, over the years, to display somebody he'd befriended out in the world? Boys at school. Then, Cass. His grandparents had a gift for making a person feel at home; anybody he ever brought to visit fell in love with them.

He even stopped by with Mick once, on the way to a fishing trip in the Keys. An unlikely matchup if ever there was one, Mick and Zion Hill, but by the time his grandmother laid out all her vegetables and cornbread on the table his legendary lips were telling them about the summers he spent on his Uncle Bartholomew's farm in Herefordshire. He even bet Turner a quid he still remembered how to milk a cow, and on the way back from demonstrating he asked so many relevant questions about tilling and land cover that Turner's grandfather was moved to ask him, "What line of work you say you're in?" Made Mick's day, to find somebody who honestly didn't know. "Way you handle a cow bag," his grandfather had said, "you ever need work they's plenty people around here'd put you on." In the intervening years Mick made myth of the day, telling it grander and more exuberantly every time.

Turner knocked. For the longest time no sound came from inside but the muffled hum of the big window fans. Ordinarily the front porch would be a riot of birdsong at this early hour. His grandfather had always loved sitting out here with a cup of stout black coffee, on mornings when there'd been rain in the night and the field was too wet to plow.

But now the two weathered rocking chairs were turned to face away from the yard, propped at an angle against the front wall of the house in what passed for a silent signal, out here in the country, that its occupants are away from home or otherwise indisposed to visitors.

Turner was readying to knock again when the door opened. His grandmother's face looked pale and haggard from lack of sleep, but her eyes lit up at the sight of him. She wiped her hands on her blue flowered apron and made for him with open arms, burying her head in his chest. As he held her he rubbed his chin against her thick head of hair, white as dandelion fluff. He had bent down a little so she could reach him, and when he straightened partway up she had so tight a hold her feet left the floor for a second.

"Y'all excuse me a minute," she said to the bystanders, her voice muffled by his shirt. "I've missed this old man." When she finally separated from him, her attention fell next on Cassie. She didn't seem at all surprised to see her there. *They are prepared*, Won Se had said.

"If you ain't a beautiful sight," Cordelia whispered. She looked from

Cassie to Turner and back again, and it was clear she referred to the sight of the two of them, together. "It's been too long," Cass acknowledged, and held out her arms to invite a solid neck-hug.

Cordelia stood back up and dabbed at her eyes with an apron corner before assessing Crowe and the monks. "Come in, come in," she said, motioning them past her. She patted James's arm. "You're the 'rithmetic man," she said. "I've heard about you." The smells of bacon frying and buttermilk dough met them as they walked down the entrance hall.

She looked suddenly concerned. "Thought you was bringing *six* preachers," she said to Turner. "I don't see but five."

Silence for a moment.

"Yes, ma'am. He got, uh, held up and can't come. It's a long story. I'll go into it later."

"Well, more biscuits for *us*, huh?" she said, winking at Cassie.

Turner knew the exact place in the kitchen where his grandfather would be, sitting in the old cane-bottomed straight chair nearest the window that looked out on his fields. There would be one unruly wisp of white hair sticking up from the crown of his head, and he'd be nursing a cup of black coffee, blowing on it to cool it. And Turner also knew that when he looked up at him from the cup, this time, there would be a new knowledge in his eyes, one that Turner had dreaded his whole life to see.

"Hey, here, folks," the big voice boomed out, undiminished, when they walked into the kitchen. He wore his green work shirt and the pants he called his farming pants, two patched rips along the right leg, and he set his steaming cup down to greet them.

Cassie was nearest him; he took one of her hands in both of his and kissed it, then held it against his cheek for a moment, his sad smile containing her whole history and his part in it.

Turner watched the eyes. His illness was there, but so deeply under his good cheer you'd have to know him to realize it. When he stood up and embraced Turner there was no decline in his strength at all; if anything his hold was tighter, as if he were trying to keep the world from receding from him any faster than it had to.

"Let me introduce y'all to some friends of mine," Turner said.

His grandfather looked sternly at the group. "Thought there was six preachers," he said.

"One got tied up, Jackson," his grandmother remarked from the stove, as if this were common knowledge.

Jackson held Turner's eye just long enough to verify there was more to the story than he was telling. The two of them had long ago discovered they were genetically incapable of telling each other a lie, however innocuous, with a straight face; and so they'd given up trying.

Jackson nodded at the wordless confirmation of Shy's defection, and looked out the window at the unnatural daylight. "Hate to hear that," he said. "This place needs all the praying it can get."

20

"AND WHAT ELSE?" Turner asked them, trying to find out all he could about how the realm had taken up residence in Zion Hill. James Crowe started passing the second pan of biscuits around the table; they were hot from the oven with a big dot of butter in the middle of each one.

"I think that's about it," Jackson said. God knows it was enough. Mr. Johnny was only the beginning. Wrecks, shootings, stabbings, break-ins, house fires, terrible illnesses. It was as if the whole place had been infiltrated by some cancer.

Turner watched his grandfather's eyes as he talked; as good a job as he was doing at going through the motions of living, the knowledge of his own ending was inside him and working like wildfire, growing even faster than the tumor must be. Now and again he would tenderly touch his side and then pull his hand away like a child violating some rule. Turner had to get him alone and talk, soon. But what do you say to somebody who's dying and knows it? In the war it wasn't a problem. No time for it.

"What am I forgetting?" Jackson put the question to Cordelia.

"The power?" she said.

"Electricity's been off and on, some," Jackson told Turner. "But it does that a lot, anyway. And the telephone's out, since . . . ?"

"Last night," Cordelia told Turner. "Right after I talked to you." Her eyes were still as bright and focused as a bird's. Either the news from the doctor hadn't fully soaked in yet, or else, as Turner suspected, she was better at hiding her inner self.

"Have you reported it to the phone company?" he asked. Ever the straight man.

Cassie shot him a look. "I'd think the whole town's phones would be out," she said, turning to Cordelia. "Right?"

She nodded. "They say they've got their computers working on it, but they're stumped. They can't find nothing wrong in the lines." Turner pictured a crew of well-scrubbed young technicians in neckties, intent on some far-off computer screen, blithely performing vector analysis or whatever on the offending phone-lines' printouts. What if they knew the truth? *It's all part of the realm's dog-and-pony show, guys. The real thing has come to town*. Would their worksheets have space to list Armageddon as an anomaly?

The big biscuit pan had made the rounds of the table and came last to Lu Weh. He raked the remaining three off onto his plate with one hand, while with the other he kept tossing down link sausages like they were Tootsie Rolls.

Turner had been surprised, in the beginning, to discover that there were even more varieties of Buddhists than of Protestants. While there were a number of vegetarian sects, Drepung wasn't among them. Though Louie hadn't done any transiting in a while now, he apparently wanted to have plenty of nourishment in reserve for the imminent time of testing.

"Try these strawberry preserves on 'em, hon," Cordelia said to him, but by the time the jar got passed down to him all three biscuits had already bitten the dust. She got up quickly to put the next pan of them in the stove. She'd never failed to keep pace with biscuit demand yet, but Louie was giving her a run for her money.

Turner's appetite had waned; there was just too much churning in him. He got up and walked to the big window that looked out on the fields. Farther back sat Johnny Patterson's house and barn. Cars came and went, their headlights on in the artificial darkness, as word spread through town about what had happened. Neighbors would be bringing food, condolences, promises of prayer.

"So there was no reason, that they knew of?" Turner asked. "Mr. Johnny, I mean. He wasn't in trouble, or sick, or anything."

"Not that anybody'd heard," Cordelia said. "I talked to him . . . when, Jackson? Monday. He stopped to bring us some extra squash he had. He was just regular old Johnny, then."

Turner already knew the answer to what he was about to ask. But he put on his best salesman's face anyway and walked to the table, where he put his arms lightly around his grandmother's neck and kissed the top of her hair.

"Listen," he said. "This would be a real good time, I think, for y'all to go to Aunt Helen's for a while. She's got the whole back end of that big lake house just going to waste. You could take your fishing stuff. Get you a little change of scenery. James could drive you and be back in . . . what, an hour?

Just till this thing blows over, some. Your car still works, doesn't it?"

He expected a polite demurral and some good-natured explanation about no place being like home. But instead Jackson and Cordelia shot each other incredulous looks that had somehow a great quantity of anger in them, and that was when Turner knew for the first time that Won Se was right. They *did* know, at least at some level, what was at stake here, and they were battened down for the duration.

"So, what do you say?" Turner smiled at them, futilely pressing his case.

"That wouldn't be right," Jackson said. The four words were the only enforcer of discipline he had needed for Turner, his whole life. Never laid a hand on him, or needed to.

Turner was framing in his mind some last-ditch argument and deciding whether it was even worth trying when a knock came from the back door. Because there was no doorbell at the front, friends knew to come to their back porch, nearest the kitchen, if you wanted to make sure they heard you.

Cordelia, at the stove to check on the biscuits, wiped her hands on a dishcloth and went to the door. She reached for the knob but the darkness outside gave her second thoughts at just the moment that Turner, coming up behind her, laid a restraining hand on her shoulder.

"Who is it?" she called loudly.

"John T. Patterson the Third, ma'am," a familiar voice rumbled back. "What you got for breakfast?"

"Oh, sweet Lord God," Cordelia whispered, and turned her stricken face on Turner for guidance. The knocking came again, louder. Turner sensed a flurry of motion at the table and looked to see Cassie gesturing at him wildly, shaking her head. Except for the ticking of the stove, the room was silent.

"It's all right, hon," the voice beyond the door said. "It's me."

Before Cordelia's mind could overrule her, her heart went into her hands and flung the door open. Johnny's bony frame stepped quickly in out of the dark bringing a draft of warm air, a baseball cap pulled low on his forehead and the trademark sprig of hay held in his corner teeth.

"How's it going, Mr. Jackson?" he said, raising a hand in the direction of the table. His eyes, unnaturally bright in the shadow of his cap bill, fell on Turner then. "Well, if it ain't the prodigal come back," he said. "How you doing, bud?"

He held out his hand to Turner and after a second's hesitation Turner shook it. Ice. The hand was like ice.

"Listen, don't let me interrupt y'all's breakfast," he said. He walked over toward Jackson, who had his napkin to his mouth, his eyes beginning to glisten. "I just come to mooch something off'n you, podner," the figure told him. "You're not going to be using your old twelve-gauge the next couple days, are you?"

A catch of breath in Cordelia's throat. Jackson dabbed with the napkin at his eyes. "Johnny," he said, in a voice almost obliterated by sorrow, "I . . ."

"That's all right, don't get up," the figure said. "I know right where you keep it." He broke toward the hallway with such speed it was as if time were stroboscoping; he was here, then there, then over there, with no intervening movements to link them. The hand Turner put out to catch his shoulder caught only emptiness.

"Don't worry 'bout shells," the figure said over its shoulder. "I got plenty shells." It dug in its pocket and held up a handful of the packed red casings.

"Don't let him . . ." a voice said. Cassie.

Turner ran, and when the figure easily outdistanced him he made a flying tackle, but he only collided with the hallway door that was slammed in his way. He rattled the knob but the door wouldn't budge; it wasn't locked, but jammed in place somehow.

They all could hear his footsteps rampaging through the rooms of the house with supernatural speed. In seconds the door opened back of its own accord and the figure strode through, the gun at its waist, swinging in a wide arc of aim.

"Get down!" Turner shouted at everybody. "Get out of his way!"

"Whooo-*eeee*!!!" the figure cackled joyfully, advancing on the table of people. "You better hustle yo' ass, you little mothers . . ."

They hit the floor resoundingly; James dived to embrace Cassie and rolled with her under the table, putting himself foremost toward the gun. Bah Tow and Se Hon dragged Jackson and Cordelia down almost as quickly, in a flurry of arms. China bowls shattered on the floor.

Turner marked seconds, crouched ready to leap when the gun hit the furthermost point in its arc, but before it did the figure stopped its advance and the barrel sank limply. "Aw," it said sorrowfully, "I's just having a little funning with y'all. You know I wouldn't hurt nobody. Tell 'em, Jackson. I wouldn't kick a flea's hind end, would I?"

Silence; Turner was tensed to jump if the gun started to raise again.

"Well, I gotta be going," the figure said. Then suddenly, gap-in-time quick with no intervening stages, it spun the barrel until the end was lodged in its mouth, bright eyes looking out at them comically from the shadow of the cap. The long skinny arm barely reached the trigger with its thumb.

When Turner jumped to slap the arm away, the explosion of the trigger's release rocked the room, a fountain of red and glistening bluish-gray against the ceiling and walls, reverberating away to Cordelia's scream.

But rather than collapsing, the figure stayed upright despite the foaming stump of neck where the head had been. "Much obliged," its throat growled, as it handed the gun gently to Turner. A familiar loping stride carried the bloody shape out the door and down the back steps.

The shotgun's barrel burnt Turner's hand. He flung it toward the carpet of the hallway and ran to lock the door. With his back against it, him breathing for what seemed the first time in minutes, he had a full view of the dark carnage that blotched the blue wallpaper. He had half expected the stains to turn to oily smoke and disappear by now, the way the realm's other illusions had when their work was finished, but the rules must be different for the end-game. The patches of blood remained, slowly blackening.

He said toward the table, "Everybody just, ah, stay put for a minute, please, until I can, uh . . ." but when he wet two dishtowels and began with them on one wall the drying blood only spread and the magnitude of the task hit him; it would take hours, not minutes.

He threw the towels in the sink, then kicked the broken china aside and helped his grandparents up.

In late afternoon by the clock, still twilight by the sky, his grandfather felt like sitting up again and Turner went out with him onto the screened side porch, just the two of them, to sit in the swing and talk.

Since the ocean and the fog had appeared, obliterating the familiar hillside, the temperature had dropped a good twenty degrees. The wind off the gulf of water had such a moist chill to it that Turner went back inside and got an afghan from the closet for Jackson to put around his shoulders. The electricity had been off for nearly two hours. Cordelia found some kerosene lamps, and Turner lit one of them and brought it out.

The ocean hadn't appeared gradually, a rising of water, but had suddenly just been there, eclipsing the old landscape of hills and pines in a single thought, when they looked out the window during lunch. They believed they could see an occasional gull wheel by, far out in the fog, but in the dim half-light it was hard to say for sure.

Now, as the waves lapped at the base of the porch and moths dabbed at the screen where the lamp sat, Turner had the odd sensation he was in the beach house they'd vacationed at when he was little. But it only took a look at his grandfather's hunched shape, the defeated eyes, to dispel that notion and to fix him firmly again in this place and time.

The bright advice that had been on the tip of his tongue to say when he first sat down, that doctors don't know everything and that he might yet outlive them all, seemed fake as carnival jewelry now. He was glad he hadn't said it. The moment needed to stay clean, unadorned.

"I know there's not any need," his grandfather finally broke the silence, "to ask you to see after Cordelia. I know you'll do that." By a seeming effort he kept his eyes on the waves and the fog, not on Turner, as if it were the beginning of a speech he'd memorized and any distraction might make him lose his place.

"You know I will," Turner said, when the silence loomed again.

From inside the front room of the house, the little battery-powered radio crackled out the regular evening news of the world: sound-bites of distress and accusation and grief, into which the random localized tragedies of Zion Hill figured not at all. Muffled by the wall, the agitated voices sounded like bees in a jar. Cassie and Cordelia were going through the closets for blankets and pillows, working out everybody's sleeping arrangements.

"I'm sorry," Jackson said, "for not telling you where she was, all that time. It hurt me, but I had to do it for my girl."

Cassie had been Jackson's "girl" ever since the first day Turner brought her home after school. She spoke his same forthright language, could debate politics and theology with him for hours on end, could win an argument and get his goat and make him like it. It was a measure of their closeness that not even her resignation from the Baptist Church had come between them for long, though by silent agreement the topic was off limits for discussion.

Once in the nightmare weeks following the accident, during a late-night emotional free-for-all over Jackson's adhering to her wishes to keep her whereabouts secret, Turner had accused him of loving Cass more than his own kin; he'd also, incredibly, said he wished Jackson dead for it, a shameful blot on his history that reared up regularly to haunt him, despite all the times he'd apologized.

"I had . . . hopes," Jackson went on, "of you being able to understand and forgive me, but I know that was too much to expect. Loving a woman is . . ." His eyebrows flexed in concentration, but what he was trying to express eluded him. "I'm saying I'd have been the same way as you, in your shoes."

"Nothing to forgive," Turner said. "You went by your heart, and that's the best anybody can do." From the other room he heard Cass and his grandmother sharing a laugh, apparently over some relic of his boyhood they'd found in a closet, because Cordelia followed up with a tale from her archival memory about one of his exploits in the cowboy-and-Indian wars that had won him a broken arm. *Soldier in training*, Turner thought bitterly. *We all were.* But the rueful reflection was overcome by their quiet, healing laughter, and he thought, *What a gift women have. The world crumbling, hell's got your house number, and still there's time for a good memory, time to smooth the wrinkles from a pillowcase.*

"Turner," Jackson said, "do you need anything?" For this part he looked Turner straight in the eye, so as to test his answer for truth.

The words registered slowly. *Need . . . anything.* It was so like the man, his own last days ticking inside him like a bomb and him still trying to find out what's needed by the people he loves so he can supply it if he's able. Turner pictured the profits from his last four concert tours piling up in such profusion the CPA firm had to hire two more people just to help count them. Not to mention enough stocks and T-bills from past successes to stuff a mattress with. He pictured the house he owned free and clear, worth a good half-mil, same for the condo in the Keys. He pictured the LearJet on call. All of this superimposed onto the waiting face of a man who'd been a dirt-scratch farmer his whole life, and who was willing to hand him over the proceeds now if he asked for them.

Do you need anything?

Yes. Some wisdom about this whole mess. My old life. Some peace.

"No," Turner said. "I appreciate it, but I've got everything I need." He had thought he could handle this exchange in a businesslike way, Jackson never being one for sentiment or emotional frou-frou, but now he heard his voice get away from him and he knew the hot rush of water behind his eyes would escape next.

He took his grandfather's crusty hand and patted it. "Really. I don't need a thing."

Jackson nodded slowly, and then turned his gaze out to the dark ocean again. He cleared his throat. "If I wasn't to get another chance," he said, "I want you to know that I appreciate you."

Turner felt the dam behind his eyes break, and he was glad Jackson was looking away.

"I mean I don't just love you because you're my blood," he went on. "I appreciate the kind of man you are. You're not a drunkard or a rounder, and you're as good as your word. A feller can't do much better than that, in this life."

Turner waited until he was sure he had his voice under control to say, "I appreciate *you*. You're the kind of man I've always wanted to be."

Jackson still looked out into the dark, but there was enough light from the lamp for Turner to see the wet streak descending from the corner of his eye. His old dry hand went up angrily to scrub it away. "I was hoping to not get emotional about this thing," he said. "I hate to get your mind all distracted, when you've got so much to do."

"We'll take the night watch in shifts, okay?" Turner said. He took off his wristwatch and handed it to James, who sat on one of the row of pallets that Cassie and Cordelia had laid out for them in the living room. The place had the look of a Cub Scout sleep-over party. "James will do the first hour, and then we'll go straight down the line. Just wake up the person next to you when your shift is over."

Cassie had made it clear to them that it wasn't her choice to take Turner's room, the one huge soft bed. But Cordelia had insisted that a lady needs her privacy, and wouldn't hear any arguments in the case.

"Remember," Turner told them, "we've got some measure of protection here, because of the way the rules are set up. Apparently, these . . . creations aren't allowed to force their way into the house. They only come in if we let them. So don't open any door or window, for *any* reason. Period. Everybody got that?"

He wandered to the window as he talked, and pulled back the curtain to see out. Not long after sundown, the ocean had begun receding and had left in its place a dark red desert, with shape-shifting mesas along all the horizons in the moonlight. Atop one of the mesas, the distant shape of a coyote howled.

"The same for going outside," Turner went on. "*Don't.* Stay in. Okay? Don't let them lure you out. No matter what kind of show they put on, just tell yourself it's not real." As he said it, his mind's eye saw the stains on the kitchen ceiling, resistant to an hour's scrubbing with PineSol and Comet. Maybe "not real" was a poor choice of words. "If you see or hear anything that bothers you a lot," he amended, "come wake me up. All right?

"Look, all of this will pass. It's just our testing. Keep telling yourself that. We might have a long way to go. But we'll do well." He had counted, all along, on being able to hear that familiar encouragement from Won Se's own mouth by long distance, as their testing wore on, had counted on being able to ask the great man's advice. He should have known the realm wouldn't allow it, would kill the phones. Cassie, likewise, was unable to visit Won Se's mind. Some great wall of interference prevented it, mind-static in the stratosphere.

Cassie's chair glided into the doorway from the hall. She wore a long blue nightshirt Cordelia had found for her, with a teddy bear appliqué at the neck. A glass of milk sat between her knees.

"Any questions, before we turn in?" Turner asked the group. "Anybody have something they want to say?"

Cassie raised her hand. "Motion from the floor," she said. "You guys get some sleep, and let me take the night watch."

A clatter of protesting voices met the proposition, but she waved them away. "Really, I insist," she said. "Sleep is something I can take or leave. I got a year's worth, last night alone." She wheeled over and put her hands on Turner's shoulders. He started to argue the point again, but she put a finger to his lips and kissed the top of his head.

"Look, you drove all night. Trust your second in command, here, Hope. I double, triple insist. And another thing . . . your old room's so full of you I couldn't get to sleep in it if I wanted to. It's like a museum of your mind. Why don't you take it?"

"Full of me? You're making this up," Turner said.

"I'd swear on a Bible. You know it's your favorite place in the world. I think there's power, there. And goodness knows you need all of it you can get."

The motion passed by acclamation of the group, over Turner's protests. "Get on with it," Cassie said, pointing down the hall. "We're wasting time."

"Anybody mentions to my grandmother I kicked Cassie out of my room's in big trouble, okay?" Turner told them as he went.

Whatever lingering guilt Turner felt was assuaged when he sank into the giant goose-down mattress of his childhood. He sensed sleep coming for him fast, less in the fashion of a sandman than a mugger.

In the dark hall, a loose floor-plank creaked. A footstep. The dim red illumination cast by the landscape outside the window showed a yellow monk's robe paused at the door, the face above it in shadow.

"Yeah?" Turner said. The nervous throat-clearing as the figure approached told him it was Beh Vah. He knelt beside the bed.

"I have, uh, not remembered," he said, "to tell you my thanks. For when the traitor was saying so many ugliness of me, and you never believed."

Turner felt a twinge in the region of his conscience. He *had* believed the worst. Or come damned close.

"Don't mention it," he said.

Beaver hung his head, perplexed. "Have I wronged you . . . by speaking of it?"

"No, no. 'Don't mention it' just means, uh . . . no big deal."

Further incomprehension.

"It means you're welcome," Turner said. Beaver breathed relief and stood to go, then hesitated.

"I am too much tempted by the world," he said. "That much is true. But I am fighting . . . to hear only the song."

Turner reached to squeeze his hand. "Bless your heart," he said. "That's a battle we all fight, buddy." Beaver went resolutely down the hall, his foot chiming the errant floor board in his passing.

As Turner felt sleep settling on him again, he could have sworn the warm air blowing through the immobile window fan smelled of the same night-blooming jasmine that had grown underneath the window when he was in high school, even though his last look outside had shown intact the barren, Mars-red desert stretching for miles.

He heard the water pipes in the old house's walls rumble. That would be his grandmother, on schedule, getting his grandfather a glass of water to take his pain medication with.

The last thing he saw before he shut his eyes was Cassie's silhouette, gliding silently past the moonlit window at the far end of the hall. Cassie, night watchman, making her rounds. Somehow it filled him with a peace all out of proportion to what he knew they would face the next day and the next day and the next, just as he'd felt protected at base camp in the jungle, when he'd wake up at night and see the lone sentry walking back and forth in front of the gray barracks windows.

As he gratefully let sleep subdue him, he was thinking *And the morning and the evening were the first day.*

21

DAYLIGHT WOKE Turner. He surfaced to consciousness so slowly, fresh from some pleasant place, that he felt moved to turn over and doze for a few more minutes and see if he could catch the thread of the dream again.

But then reality seized his heart with what the day held, and he jumped awake with a shock like falling into icy water.

Daylight.

He vaulted out of bed and ran to the window to see if the surrounding desert of the night before had undergone any change while he'd slept. The blades of the big fan hummed at low speed; the electricity was back on. A good sign. And when he pulled aside the curtain above it he saw that the desert had disappeared. The land was transformed into Zion Hill again, on a perfect summer day. The back yard was a sloping embroidery of pinks and greens: mimosa and cherry and dogwood, all in the fullest of bloom and thronged by fat yellow bees. The window fan drew in the scents of all the blossoms, air that promised a hot day even though the sun was just up.

But perversely, the immaculate scene instilled in him an even greater dread than the desolate landscapes of the previous day. Something fishy, here—the realm trying to lure them out? He'd best be on his guard.

As he went to check on Cassie and the guys he noticed his graduation cap and tassel hanging on the bedpost. Cassie must have found it somewhere during her rounds and hung it there for him.

In the hallway he smelled breakfast cooking. When he got to the living room, with the sun streaming through its lace curtains, the floor was emptied of sleeping-pallets. Had everybody gotten up before him and packed them away? His room was next to the closet the pallets came from; he must have been dead to the world if the commotion of *that* hadn't stirred him. Contrary to popular expectation, monks weren't the quietest people in the world.

Then he saw the door. The front door stood wide open to the sunshine, a big red wasp dabbing lazily at the door jamb.

Turner's neck flushed with anger. He lunged for the knob and slammed it. God . . . *damn* it, hadn't he told them? Hadn't he been specific? A little sunshine and they think everything's hunky-dory; don't they know the realm cuts no slack for carelessness? Might as well hang a frigging sign out, Demons Welcome. Shit. He threw the deadbolt closed so hard his hand stung.

He stomped off for the kitchen, intent on calling a conference just out of hearing range of his grandparents and chewing serious ass. All we've been through, and let a stupid mistake sink us? Damn. Use your heads a little, for Christ's sake.

But the kitchen was empty too, except for his grandmother at the stove with her back to him, frying bacon. The door to the back porch stood wide open, wafting slightly in the breeze. *What the hell . . .*

"Where's . . ." Turner shouted, but when Cordelia turned to face him the rest of the question froze in his throat.

She was middle-aged.

He clamped his eyes tight and opened them again, but the result was the same. Her stooped back was straightened, her face barely wrinkled, the jet black hair of her part-Cherokee ancestry just beginning to be flecked with gray.

God in heaven. How?

"Hey, sleepyhead," she said. "Jackson's in the garden. Do you need something?"

He couldn't speak.

She turned back around to tend the bacon. "He thought he'd go ahead and weed the corn before the heat got so bad," she said, laying the strips on a paper towel to drain.

All Turner could think to do was run. Back in his room, he locked the door and stood with his back against it, panting. *What in hell . . .*

Then, for the first time, he took in his reflection in the dresser's mirror, framed by the bedposts and black cap and gold tassel.

He was eighteen years old, and on his lip was the little slice of mustache he started in his senior year and finally gave up on because it stayed raggedy-looking, would never completely fill in like he wanted it to.

Eighteen, and he was . . .

Pinching himself, to be sure he was awake. Touching himself. His pounding heart, his arms, his legs. He even looked inside the front of his sagging pajama pants. All there, all real.

All young.

He sat on the edge of the bed where he could see himself in the mirror. The real world kept sifting over him like invisible snow, fixing him where he was, obliterating the place he had been in his dream.

What a dream. What one hell of a bad dream that had been. A couple of pieces of it were still vivid in his mind, outrageous stuff. But even those were fading fast, losing their shapes and edges as irreparably as a ruined watercolor.

A distant whistling came to him from the direction of the field. The tune "Amazing Grace," strong and on-key, each beat of it matched by the sound of a garden hoe slicing dirt.

The smells of bacon and brewing coffee filled the room, and he heard the clatter of Cordelia's biscuit pan coming out of the oven. Turner realized he was starving. He took a deep breath and let it out and it turned into a laugh. A relieved laugh. What a hell of a dream he'd had. Hell of a dream. His grandparents had been in it, he recalled dimly. And some monks? Priests? Something.

Cass had been in it, too. She was sick, or hurt, or . . . Somehow it had been his fault. Sad, stupid dream. He made himself concentrate on the here and now, force the cobwebs out of his mind. Crazy, though, how real it had seemed.

He pawed through his dresser drawers for some cutoffs and a T–shirt and put them on. But just as he was unlocking his door to go eat, a sharp rain of gravel hit his windowpane.

Only one person that could be. He went to the window and pulled aside the curtain and looked down, and there she was. Cass, wedged between two hedges, holding up a handful of wildflowers she'd picked for him in the woods—her ivory skin fluorescing in the bright sunshine, more than three-dimensional, against her favorite floppy black sweater hanging low off one shoulder, and her black leotard. Her hair pulled back, a daisy pinned above one ear.

God, what a woman. What a face. She motioned for him to come outside.

He headed for the door.

Breakfast could wait.

"THINK ABOUT something, for me?" Cassie asked.

They lay on their backs, heads touching, on a broad, flat rock that overhung the valley. It was level as a table, warm in the sun, and high enough that when you were lying down you could see nothing but sky and clouds. It was a place tailor-made for official pronouncements; it was the rock where they'd pledged to go steady, the rock where they'd promised to marry after they graduated.

As Cassie talked she plucked petals from her cache of flowers with a nervous efficiency, her hands alive with something she couldn't bring herself to say.

"Let me clear my head, first," Turner said. He rolled over and, upside-down to her, put kisses first on her forehead and then her closed eyelids, pacing himself before he got to her incendiary licorice mouth. He'd wanted to tell her about the wild dream, and the fact that she'd been in it, but it had receded so quickly in his memory that he couldn't frame any one part that did it justice. Hell with it. Maybe it'd come back to him.

He took a long time with her mouth, relishing its endless variability, always a bountiful half-second ahead of what his needed. But this time something wasn't right; her heart was not in it. Finally her hands, bitter with daisy scent, went to his face and lifted it away from hers.

"This is important," she said.

"This is, too," Turner joked, and went for her mouth again, but the finality with which she pushed him away this time stung him like nettles.

She sat up and started angrily digging in the pocket of her sweater. She yanked out a sheaf of green and fanned it open in front of his eyes. Hundred-dollar bills, at least a dozen of them.

He didn't have to ask what it was. It would be her half of their nest egg, part from baby-sitting money and part from the Savings Bonds her grandparents gave her every birthday, toward college. They hadn't broken the news yet that they'd use the money to get married instead, set up housekeeping that fall before the draft took him off for basic.

"Why'd you get it in cash?" he said. "That's dangerous."

She didn't speak, just started shaking her head. First in small motions, then more violently. She was between him and the sun, and her movements kept stabbing his eyes with daggers of light. He felt suddenly queasy with foreboding, had the weirdest sensation there was something very important, some life-or-death thing, he'd been remiss in, had forgotten to do. But what . . . ?

"I can't do it," Cassie said. "I don't know a lot, but I know what I can do and what I can't, and I can't."

"Can't *what*?"

This enraged her past all reason; the tears cascaded as she shrieked into his face: "Can't sit at home and WAIT FOR YOU TO DIE!!!" The force of her own voice startled her. She turned and looked down across the valley toward his house, afraid that the words had carried that far. At the middle of the green tapestry, a white speck worked its way patiently down rows of corn. She daubed at her eyes with the heel of her hand, hard enough to bruise them, and when she looked at Turner again, her voice was lowered. "Don't you watch the news on television?"

"Look," he said. This was old ground between them, old ground. "Nobody *wants* the war to be happening, it's just that . . ."

She laid the bills in her lap and put both her fists to her ears, shaking her head again. "I don't want to hear it," she said. "I don't want to hear it."

Turner failed to see the point of this whole exercise. He gently took her wrists and eased her hands down so she could hear him. "For God's sake, Cass," he pleaded, trying hard to moderate his voice. "It's not like we had a choice. *Bam*, my number comes up, it's the Army or go to jail. I mean, what am I going to do? Move to Canada?"

A sudden light in her eyes, expectant. Turner looked at her and looked at the stack of bills and it all came to clear to him.

The sick, sinking feeling again. What was happening to him? What was clawing at his mind from inside?

His distress must have shown in his face right off, because she immediately started trying to bolster her case, her hands gripping his like someone in danger of drowning.

"Robert's sister lives in Montreal. You remember. Karen? The guy she married got transferred up there. She's got a good job at the library, and they could put us up while we . . ."

Turner was swept by a strong wave of *deja vu*. He felt they'd had this conversation before, though he knew they hadn't. Why, then, did it seem so familiar? Had he made it up in his mind? Had his subconscious seen all this coming before he did?

"You know we couldn't live in a place like that," he said.

Cassie's mouth a grim line. "Why not?"

"It's *blue* up there," he said.

"What do you mean?"

"Look on the map, at school. How could you live in a place where everything's blue?"

She sighed and rolled her eyes in the forbearing way she'd learned, for times when he tried to take the edge off her anger by making a joke. But she did appear to brighten, a little. Turner felt the wave of paralyzing nausea start to recede. Hell, maybe he just needed some breakfast.

"Would you at least *talk* to Karen?" she offered.

He laid back down on the rock, making a pillow of his hands. To the south, toward Birmingham, a jetliner's big vapor trail was dissolving against the hard blue sky. Cassie leaned over him, waiting for his answer, and projectiles of painful sunlight bombarded him again from the edges of her silhouette.

He was suddenly afraid that he might faint. What had he heard, somewhere, about the dangers of flashing light? *Epilepsy.* Right. Hadn't their science teacher mentioned, once, that pulses of light in a certain rhythm—the sun through slats of a fence, a blinking strobe light at a concert—could trigger a seizure in someone who was prone to it? No, ridiculous. Surely the problem started younger, and he'd never . . . not once . . . felt this kind of . . .

He rolled desperately away from the light, turned onto his stomach and raised himself on his elbows, trying to bring the world back into focus again. Everything in his field of vision seemed doubled, overlapping itself faintly out of register, with an indistinct corona of red or blue around the mismatch. Everything in this haze of turmoil except . . . Cassie. Strange. Only Cassie was distinct and whole. He had a fleeting thought that this had something to do with the dream, the wild dream, but his memory of it was as featureless as the skin of a balloon, no crevice where a recollection could dig in.

Cassie was whole. Maybe if he concentrated on Cassie. He stared hard at her black-leotarded legs and pale feet, tried to ignore the turbulent grain of the rock underneath. He took hold of her ankle, ran his fingers across it. It was hot from the sun, and smooth as ivory. She laid her hand on his. The world seemed gradually to settle itself, give up its doubleness.

"Turner!" a voice from somewhere said, small and urgent. He could have sworn it was Cassie's voice, but it had seemed to come from the direction of the trees.

"What?" he asked her.

"I didn't say anything."

"I thought I heard . . ." But then he blinked hard, and the odd feeling of vertigo went away as suddenly as it had come.

"Don't change the subject," she said. "Would you *talk* to Karen, at least?"

For long seconds he lay looking up at her, basking in the return of his equilibrium. Strange, strange morning.

"*Would* you?" she said. It would be a small concession, he thought, for some peace. He shrugged. "Okay, I'll talk to her."

Even this grudging agreement overjoyed her. She opened her arms and fell on top of him, bills and brochure scattering across the rock. Her mouth fastened on his with such urgency that it brought little flickers of pain where their teeth and lips collided. Turner's hands went to her temples to pry himself a little breathing room.

MEANWHILE AT THE EDGE of the rock Beh Vah cried out at the sight of the great beast's gargoyle mouth lowering itself over Turner's head, his arms going up weakly to protect himself as he stayed looking remarkably unconcerned. "Can he not *see*?" Beh Vah said to Cassie, beside him, and knelt to bury his face in her shoulder and shut out the awful scene.

She embraced his skinny chest and shook her head. "It's like he's caught in another reality," she told him. "He thinks it's *me* he's with."

From their vantage, the space that Turner and the indistinct dark beast occupied seemed the only stationary matter in the whole nightmare panorama, the intersecting point of two vast planes of turbulence—the earthmost one a welling of mica-like particles of pure luminous silver, and pressing down upon it a black churning sky that appeared as an ocean of disembodied wings, spasming as they collided with some invisible barrier not yet broached and then rebounding upward into a broad curving sluice of twilight wave—all overprinted onto the barren redrock desert that had encompassed them since last evening, existing in its own spell of spectral half-light. At the opposite edge of the rock James Crowe and the other monks milled around with their heads hung in defeat after trying vainly to grab hold of Turner, get his attention. Repeatedly, their hands had gone through him and the scabrous hide of the beast as uselessly as through smoke.

Beh Vah's face lit with an idea. He said to Cassie, "Can you speak his mind? Speak . . . *to* his mind, I mean."

She shook her head. "I've been trying. The barrier's back. Some kind of membrane, or . . . it's worse than any I've ever felt. I can't tell if I'm getting through at all." She looked toward the ever-darkening double sky. Wisps of black fluff separated from the wings in their frantic motion and sifted slowly toward the ground, passing through Beaver and herself as if they were ghosts. In her mind she ran through a checklist of possible courses of action, a very short list, and then ran through it again.

One option was Louie. Was it possible for him to transit into the realm's reality? A long shot, and dangerous, and time was ticking. Even if he could manage it, he was the frailest of all of them and would be no match for the beast. She glanced again at the grotesque embrace out on the rock, and came to a decision.

"James!" she called out resignedly, and motioned him over.

"Yeah?"

When his eyes met hers, they both knew what was next. "I guess it's supervention time," Cassie said.

James looked at the ground. "You understand," he said, "that we might not have one left."

"Yes. Turner told me."

"And that we won't know . . ."

" . . . know until we try," she finished impatiently. "Right."

The guilt was clearly etched on his face. "I guess what I'm saying, Cap'n, uh, pardon that . . . *Cassie*, is that I haven't always made the smartest use of them, up to now. So are we really sure, before we use the last one, that this is as bad as it's going to get?"

Cassie took another look at what was transpiring on the rock. Not a long look. When she turned back around, her face was his answer.

James took out his calculator and then did something she'd never seen him do before. He crossed himself. As he started entering the numbers, he glanced up and noticed Cassie's perplexity.

"Couldn't hurt," he explained, and went back to his equations.

As he furrowed his forehead and punched numbers, Cassie averted her eyes from the vortex by looking across the valley toward the old homeplace, where the transparent green garden superimposed itself onto the empty landscape of rock and sand.

She could see four figures in the field now—the young Jackson and the young Cordelia, who had just brought Jackson out a fresh jug of ice water, and their present-day selves watching from the shade of a tree. Cassie had been forced to lie to them to keep them from coming to the rock in fear for

Turner, telling them it was no big deal, just a minor setback.

The younger, healthy Jackson and Cordelia had been bustling about the house that morning when they woke up, like two plays accidentally cast on the same stage; the phantom couple had been oblivious to all attempts at talk, no sign on their faces that they shared another reality's space.

If only the reverse had been true—Cassie would be a long time remembering the look on Jackson's face as he watched his middle-aged self give the other Cordelia a bear-hug at the stove before clomping down the back steps in his work boots to hoe the garden.

As James hurriedly finished the long equation and put his calculator away, the aperture in the air around the beast and Turner widened slightly, the vortex of blackness spooling ever more violently against the white sparkling second-air. The wheeling wings were rapidly growing bodies, which screamed when they took shape with what sounded like human voices.

James looked heavenward with tremendous concentration, making sure he'd stored the full path of the equation in his cranium, and then clamped his head in both hands, eyes shut, to concentrate on activating it.

Cassie realized she was holding her breath, and looked around and saw that the monks were doing the same, chewing on thumbs or knuckles to help the effort.

They watched the scene on the rock for evidence the equation's will was being inserted into the machinery of the world.

And watched. And watched.

James held his concentration posture far longer than any realistic hope required, afraid to open his eyes and see what the monks and Cassie already saw, that absolutely nothing had changed.

When he finally looked, the realization sat heavy on his face. "I was afraid of that," he said. "I'm sorry. I guess we blew 'em both in Yazoo City, gettin' Louie . . ."

Lu Weh, standing nearby, lifted his head and looked guiltily at Crowe and Cassie.

"Which was not your *fault*, of course," James rushed to put in. "Little sucker just bifurcated on me, and . . . I mean, when you assume a set is non-recursive, it stands to reason that . . ." He stopped, sensing a massive indifference to the technical details that had brought them to this sad state.

Lu Weh suddenly knelt in front of Cassie, his aging knees emitting two loud pops as he did so, and with great deliberateness took hold of both her hands. "I must try," he said, "to go there." He glanced over his shoulder at the wheeling, deafening crows. "I have done it . . . before." His forehead wrinkled in confusion. "I think," he amended. Out on the rock, Turner's teenaged self kept up its earnest conversation with the beast as the realm boiled behind them, ready to enter the world.

Cassie, obviously pained, looked at James for his reaction. "I don't see we got much choice, girl," he said quietly.

Cassie sighed and squeezed Lu Weh's hands as tightly as she could. "Louie . . ." She bit her lip as she studied the array of scars and scabs on his face and hands, souvenirs of past transits. "Don't . . . I repeat, *don't* . . . fight any demons on their turf, okay? Don't mix it up with them. I think that if Turner could just . . . *see* you for a few seconds, it might remind him . . ."

He nodded enthusiastically. "I will do well," he said, and got up to prepare himself for the transit. Because there was a lady present he ran quickly downhill to the protection of a big pine tree to make his attempt, so he could retrieve his robe in privacy when he transited back, naked.

"Be careful, Louie!" Cassie called after him.

For the second time that day, James Crowe did something highly unmathematical. He crossed his fingers. Both hands.

Ever since the moment Turner had gently pried Cassie's face away from their long, urgent kiss, she'd worn an exalted, beatific smile—the happiest he had seen her in months. Every fiber of logic he possessed told him to leave well enough alone. *Live for today*, as the peace-and-love song lyrics were admonishing him the whole summer from his transistor radio.

But some part of his mind couldn't let it go, kept worrying at it like a puppy with a rag doll.

"I just can't see spending the rest of my life that far away from home," he said, and the way her smile disintegrated told him the outcome of this would not be good.

"It won't *be* for the rest of your life," Cassie said. "Anybody with half a mind knows this war's insane. A year or two, at the most, and *everybody*'ll see that. They won't hold it against the people who didn't go. Then we can come back and visit."

She must have seen the way he flinched at the word "visit," because she said, "I mean, surely you don't see living *here* the rest of your life." Her eyebrows raised, as if this notion were obviously barbaric.

He could see clearly now where this was headed, unless he dropped it and changed the subject, but he felt incapable of doing that. He was seeing the outcome of it the way you see a car wreck happening, in slowed-down time, knowing how to prevent it but powerless to make the two drivers make the right moves fast enough. Except he could. Still could.

No.

"I *do* see living here," he said. "I take it you don't?"

She snorted an incredulous little laugh. "Life's too short," she said.

"What kind of place do you want to live in?" he asked. The doomed slow-motion cars growing nearer, nearer. They *had* said all of this before, he was sure of it. But when? In a dream?

"I don't know," she said. "The coast sounds nice. It sounds really free."

That would be the west coast. He noticed, again, the daisy in her hair. It should have tipped him off. She'd been doing that a lot since the simpy-assed song first came on the radio, about people in San Francisco wearing flowers in their hair.

"Nothing's free," he heard himself say. "You pay for everything, one way or another."

She looked at him for a long time.

"Let's go to California together," Turner said. "Let's go and see it, before I have to leave."

She looked down.

"We've got the money," he said.

He heard a hiccup of breath in the roof of Cassie's mouth; she was holding in a cry. She rubbed angrily at her eyes. "I don't *want* California with you," she shouted. "I want a wedding night at Niagara Falls. I want that more than anything. Why can't you give me that?"

The wreck drawing closer now, all motion unbearably slowed.

Why can't you give me that?

He put his hands to his face and smelled her scent on them, the cinnamony bath soap and the bitterness of the flowers.

"Because once you start running, you can't stop," he said. "It gets to be the way you live." He swallowed hard. "You deserve better than that."

When he uncovered his face she was surprisingly dry-eyed. She was looking, not at him, but at the point in the west where the sun would set that evening. She took a deep breath and methodically gathered up the bills spread out on the sandstone, made them into a roll and stuck it in the waistband of her leotard.

Still time, Turner was thinking. Still time to say some astute, coherent sentence that would keep it all from crashing down. But he hadn't any idea what that would be.

Cassie stood up. "Well, now we know," she said, through a wan smile. She held out her hand for him to pull himself up.

Before he could take it, a flash of movement caught his eye in the sky just above her, a transparent smudge of golden-brown that hovered there, wavering, then materialized into a swarm of particles that became the shape of a naked man, plummeting toward Cassie's back in midair.

"Look out!" Turner shouted to her, but at that moment the old bad dream of the night before came back to him with full clarity. Not a dream. Louie. *Not* a dream.

The air exploded with stinking black wings as Lu Weh's feet slammed into Cassie's back, propelling her head-first toward Turner. But as his arms went up to stop her from falling, her clothes and then her skin shredded violently away to expose the sudden bulk of the beast beneath, whose forward motion toppled Turner backwards, spread-eagle onto the rock. The impact made his skull resound with garish-colored light.

When it echoed away and his vision began to return, the horrible screeching that had occupied all the air seemed changed into a perverse lullaby, and despite an excruciating weight on his chest the sound washed over him with waves of well-being that carried him backwards and backwards into himself, away from the punishing pinpoint of light that was his vision.

Turner, a distorted voice said from behind him, within him, the direction of his sweet numbing fall, and only when the volume and pitch of the voice, the real Cassie's voice, swelled to become *Turner!* a buzzsaw of annoyance more painful than his eyesight *Don't pass out God not now don't* did he manage to slow, by great effort, his billowing inward descent toward peace and force himself outward again to surface toward the stabbing light stabbing stabbing light, surface through the entire breadth and depth of the dream-not-a-dream that suddenly opened out in his memory: the evil cloud, the conflagrations, the numbing miles on the road, sweet evening prayers, the inscrutable face of Chai Lo, the acid tang of betrayal, the soothing nectar of Cassie's proffered orange, horns of tugboats, his grandfather's defeated eyes, the red sand-grains of destruction . . . upward and upward through the past year and a half toward black screaming light until his eyes suddenly opened on wall-to-wall nightmare.

The skewed gargoyle face was inches above his, too near for his eyes to focus on, and its sweat and hot rotten breath overwhelmed him, worse than any corpse-rot from his war years. When he tried to turn his head and gasp air, the stink of the wings met him, lesser of two evils, feathers brushing at his cheek, talons tangling his hair. His body tingled, felt half-numb, as if his legs and arms had been asleep.

Cass! he said without speaking. *Where are you*?

Right here, her voice answered. *We're all here*. He looked to both sides of the rock and saw no one but Lu Weh, struggling to get to his feet after the shakeup of his collision.

Then where am I? Turner asked. *In the past?*

I don't know, Cassie's voice said. *It's . . .* He missed the next few words as the connection faded, like a distant station on an old radio at night. In the interim he cautiously shifted position in an attempt to get the feeling back into his arms. But when he tensed one arm to brace himself with, in preparation for making a roundhouse swing with the other to try and dislodge the beast from his chest, Cassie's voice within the back of his brain buzzed *No! Don't fight them on their terms. They just draw strength from it.*

Turner shifted himself by millimeters, tried to breathe around the awful weight.

What, then? he asked her, in his mind. *What do I do?*

I keep losing you, Cassie said. *Stay with me. Please keep the connection going. Please . . .* As her voice faded again, Turner saw a blur of movement past the edge of the grotesque, unfocused face above him. It was Lu Weh, galloping toward the beast with a look of terrified indignation, his hands balled together into one big fist which he raised above his head like a club. At the last moment he made a little leap into the air for extra momentum and brought the fist down with all his weight onto the region of the beast that would have been its neck, had it had one.

Turner expected to feel only a slight tremor conveyed through the beast's dark bulk by the ineffectual blow, but instead a blinding pain slammed the base of his own skull and ricocheted inside his already-aching head like a pinball in a machine. "God*damn* it," he said. "What was—? *Stop*, Louie. Get back. Get away."

But Lu Weh had already mounted another onslaught, this time striking at the middle of the beast's broad back. Pain radiated out from Turner's own vertebrae in the exact spot, cutting into his breath. This time when he cried out it brought Lu Weh up short. He backed away, looking confused.

"You're hurting *me*," Turner told him. "It's . . ." The realization of what he had just said left him speechless.

I was afraid of this, Cassie's voice said, barely audible as the signal re-emerged from behind some interdimensional mountain. *Just . . . just . . . rebuke it, and get away, any way you can. Get back to the house, to your room. The real battle is . . .*

The last of the thought was lost to the screeching of wings.

Rebuke. Rebuke. Yes. Lesson Three, Fourth Level . . . or was it Lesson Four, Third Level? During his training at Drepung he'd considered himself a none-too-shabby rebuker, but Drepung seemed an eternity ago, now.

Damn it, Turner. Think. *I rebuke you . . . as . . .*

Yes. "I rebuke you," he shouted into the terrible face, "as a demon of the realm. And I order you . . ." The great hooded eyes blinked with mild interest, and the mouth let slip a drool of viscous saliva that fell hotly on Turner's cheek. " . . . and I order you to say whose will you are working in the world at this moment."

The wide scaly upper lip, cleft nearly to the nostrils, spread open in a wet parody of a grin. But the voice that came out of it was clearly human.

"Captain Turner, sir. Serial number four, one, six, seven, two, four, five, four, five, sir." Not just a human voice, but clearly Turner's own. The grin spread wider.

Turner, seething, gritted his teeth. "You're a fucking liar," he said, and with a rage that bypassed conscious thought he convulsed and swung a stiffened arm repeatedly against the beast's face until the pain of it in his own head overcame him and he stopped.

Then two things happened. The crushing weight immediately fled his chest, and all light ceased. He tried to sit up, but the force his arms exerted against the grit of the rock was doubled and redoubled against the softest inner parts of his brain, the screech of audio feedback gone tactile, a profligate barrage of stimulation, and only when he hurriedly tried to lie back down for relief did he realize that the rock was gone and he was in motion, had been the whole time, a trajectory he had no part in determining.

He couldn't even discern whether he was rising or falling *Cass? Cass, can you hear me?* until he saw at a great distance on either side of him clusters of phosphorescent particles that flared and expired in stately lambent slow motion against what he now saw was a night sky of scudding dim clouds, lit from underneath in frequent bursts as if by rose-colored lightning. Underneath, which meant *he* was underneath, was on his back, was falling *Cassie?*

and by the time the dark vegetation of the hillside loomed at the edges of his vision he already knew from the pungent air—the unmistakable scent of ox shit and stagnant water and spent incendiary shells—exactly where he was, and when. The night. *The* night.

As he settled onto the damp vines, soft as a caress against his back, he was certain of one other thing: he was not alone. He knew it outside of any reasoning or thought, the way when he was a child he would sit up suddenly out of a deep sleep, coldly aware of his mother or father in the bedroom doorway watching him.

Cassie?

As he sat up and breathed deeply of the jungle air the voices began, soft and echoing as if through a filter of remote dead time, men shouting in confusion against the thud and crack of exploding projectiles. But in the place where he listened hardest, the inside of his mind, there was no voice at all. No Cassie. He was on his own.

He tried to stand and survey the small knoll, but all the strength left his legs and he sat back down hard. He was as tired as if he'd walked partway around the world. There was no sign of anyone, anything, in the space of vines around him, but the foreboding sense of some companion in the dark grew so much more assured that his skin prickled with it, his ears rang with anticipation of a voice.

A tiny puff of air grazed his left ear and he slapped at it, thinking it was an insect, before he smelled the corpse-breath of the beast. He sprang to his knees and turned in a quick circle, but the knoll was still empty.

This time when the voice came it was half animal and half his own. *I have loved you so long . . .*

This was so outrageous it froze him in place for several seconds; in brighter circumstances he might have laughed.

Don't deny me, the voice said, from some place simultaneously within and without. *You've made me such a warm nest in you, all these years.*

An invisible moist mouth pressed against his right cheek, and he felt the wetly whorled folds of the nose and lips slide downward toward his neck. He jerked away and struck at the place in the air where the head would have been, simultaneously wincing against the imminent pain in his own head, but hit nothing. "Go back to hell!" Turner shouted, but he felt a twinge of something directly behind his heart, some small leverage so totally unexpected that it startled him, sapped the strength from his hands.

Put on a good show, to tell your friends about. Our secret is safe with me.

The pandemonium of voices and shells increased in the valley below, and Turner gritted his teeth against the small mutiny inside him. "You *live* on lies," he said. "You stink with them."

The unseen beast made a soft clucking of tongue, a parent chiding a child, and Turner smelled the breath from it. *That one sounded a bit more half-hearted, don't you think? You've got to deny me* three *times before the cock crows. Come on, a little more feeling and I'll be on my way . . .*

Turner fell silent, sensing some trap in the taunt. He put his hands to his ears to block out the carnage of the ambush below, and fought off the sickening urge to look down, to see if he could find himself in the scene. But he could still hear, with perfect clarity, the beast as it began singing.

I can tell you now the time, it sang, a perfect parody of his grandfather's voice on the bass line of an old gospel hymn, *I can take you to the place . . .*

I can show you the tree it said, in a changed, girlish voice, *where we first made love.*

Turner felt his hands shake. Tree of his nightmares, tree he'd banished, drank it away pilled it away willed it away lo these many years, and here it was public knowledge.

Not really a tree but a sort of overgrown hedge common to the provinces around Tre Chinh. Black-green and with ornate foliage, an especially tall one dominated the ridge above the pastureland where his unit's first real slaughter took place—the ridge he climbed afterward to wait for the med-evac copter, sweat stinging his eyes and the copper smell of blood and spent cartridge smoke still in his nostrils.

Somewhere very near this same hillside, alone under the sky, he had tied a makeshift piece of gauze around the bleeding furrow a stray bullet had opened in his left forearm, clean as the stroke of a filleting knife, and then for reasons unknown to him had shaken both fists at the sky and screamed, or bellowed, a long exultant howl that seemed to come from some throat other than his own.

He frightened himself, and as much as he tried to explain it away as a cry celebratory of pure survival, or of bringing his men through a fight without getting any of them killed, in his heart of hearts he knew it was more. That was when he looked up and saw the tree, and its vivid shape became imprinted in his memory as the icon of that moment, that revelation.

Whatever part of himself the howl had come from, he worked from that moment to permanently mute it, pen it in. He had failed only once, on the night that was transpiring now in the valley below; his pride and rage and pumped-up overconfidence had maneuvered his unit into a fight they had no business taking on, and seven of his men, best men, had paid the price.

The beast's hot breath flared against his neck once more, and the unseen mouth brushed his cheek, then his chin. Turner recoiled and jerked away. "You bastard," he said. "I never let you out again. Not once. Not one time."

But such a nest, the voice cooed. *Such a warm, warm nest.*

It took all Turner's will to hold his arms at his side, to keep from striking out. Don't fight them on their terms, Cassie had said. They just draw strength from it.

In his misery Turner tried to picture this all as a dream or a vision, the kind the old prophets had, and thus to wake up, but he couldn't find a single seam of escape in its logic; it felt as real as life.

Just rebuke it and get away, any way you can, Cassie had warned. The real battle is . . .

Is what? Still to come? God, help . . .

"I . . . rebuke you," Turner began again, but he was interrupted by powerful rough arms hauling him into the air and flipping him with frightening ease onto his stomach; midair his hands slipped from his ears and they became filled by the cacophony of destruction from the valley. As he fell forward onto the sodden vines, his elbows took the brunt of the weight, impaling themselves inches deep in the decaying earth.

If you won't let me out, the voice growled above the clamor, *then let me in*. Coarse hands, the width of tank-treads, ripped at Turner's shirt-tail and yanked his belt away. One fastened on the waistband of his pants and yanked with such force that his elbows dragged and cut two long ruts in the dirt before the fabric relented and he felt cool air on his ass and thighs.

Jesus, no.

You know Cap'n wants it. Such a warm, warm nest . . .

Turner was exploding with the urge to fight. To the death, even though he knew he'd be receiving, not just giving, each blow. As he tried to wrench away, shouting "I rebuke you . . ." he caught sight of a soft yellowish glow beyond the smoke of the battlefield. Impossible.

But there. On the next hill sat his grandparents' farmhouse, shuttered against the night—its yellow bug-light a beacon, the only unmoving point of light in the entire landscape. So near, so far. *Get away, any way you can . . .*

"Say whose will you're working," Turner gasped, struggling as the heel of the rough hand stroked the length of his spine. "*Say . . .*"

Take too long to say 'em all, sweet Cap'n, the voice growled. *There's seven of 'em wantin' this . . .*

Seven. His throat tightened, a lump that wouldn't go up or down. "That's a lie," he whispered around it.

Call-l-l-l out their na-a-ames, the voice crooned, a sick parody of the old Carole King song. *They'll come running . . .* A distended cackle of a laugh, as the unseen hands tugged his thighs apart.

Seven.

"Hodges!" Turner shouted, with all the breath in him. "Help me!"

If you had asked him beforehand, he would have said that he didn't remember all their names, that he had erased them from his conscious mind by sheer will, along with the whole awful night, as a valiant attempt to stay sane. But once the first man's nineteen-year-old face popped into his mind and the unbidden name crossed his lips, the others were waiting alongside in straight rank, just as they always had been.

"Nix! Stevens! Jazeuski!" Each name took a whole lung's worth of air; the mortar fire below was growing louder and more intense by the minute, and at times he despaired of being heard over their pink blasts of light.

"Parker! Watkins! . . ." The voice behind him hushed, and the huge hands that held him had paused in their work, expectantly or from fright, he couldn't tell.

"O'Neal!" The instant he called the seventh name the hillside came alive with running footsteps, boots ripping through the dense vines.

Cap'n? You hit?

Hodges' face was the first to appear, ghost-white under its helmet in the wavering pink light of the explosions, a black slash of soot under each eye. Except for the very real carbine he carried, he could have been an overgrown kid out for Halloween. *Just a kid,* Turner thought. *A damned kid.* Why hadn't he known it, at the time? Because he'd been a kid himself.

"Jug . . ." Turner managed to get out, as the other running figures kept arriving, out of breath, their faces death-pale. Hodges' nickname had been short for Jughead, because wherever you saw him, latrine or PX or out in the boonies laying concertina wire, he always had an Archie comic book sticking out of his pocket. Damned kids. All of them. But every one as good a soldier as ever drew breath. "Jug, listen, I need . . ." His voice balked. Could they see the beast, or would they think he was crazy?

"He's hit, man," Jazeuski said, and flung his carbine to the ground as he knelt beside Turner and began taking out bandages from his medic's kit.

"No," Turner said. "No, it's . . ." But to his amazement he found he could turn freely onto his back, could sit up; the mocking voice and the pressure of the hands seemed like a bad dream, fled into the dark air. Except that when he reached to pull his jeans up from his knees they weren't jeans but fatigue pants, and Jazz was already taking a penknife to the fabric, peeling it back to expose a thumb-sized hole in the flesh of his thigh that was gushing dark blood in heartbeat spurts.

"What's the verdict, Jazz?" a voice said.

Watkins, it would be. Giant black man, naked to the waist. Good South Alabama boy, jive-talker, could see in the dark and hear a gnat breathe. All matter, all sound, shrank and expanded with Turner's pulse; the rifle fire resounded like drum solos in a concert hall. A fine mist of rain sifted down, cool on his face. He reached to touch his leg near the wound, but it was numb, felt like somebody else's leg. Numb. He thought of Cassie and her legs, a lifetime away.

"Shee-it," Jazz said, mocking Watkins' jive, "missed his jools a good foe, five ainches. Cap'n's finer'n frog hair. Aintcha, main?" The firm hand moved Turner's exploring fingers away; he could hear the gauze and bandages being taped into place. A hand touched his brow, whose hand he couldn't tell, and it came back to him in a flood how much he'd loved these men. But not enough, not enough to keep him from . . .

"You gone make it fine, fine," Jazz kept repeating like a spell. "Got you a little vial of good stuff, for when the feeling comes back in that sucker." An explosion from the direction of the battle lit the hillside like daylight and just as quickly was gone, leaching the color from things and leaving an afterglow like a pen-and-ink drawing in Turner's brain.

He heard a murmured conversation nearby.

He lost much?

Hell, yeah. We've got to get him to the house.

They must have thought they were out of earshot; a contention started, fear and dread in the whispers.

That's half a kilo past the fuckin' perimeter. They'll slice us up like a ham, out there.

Yeah, well how far in the shit did the Cap'n go for your sorry ass that day?

Quit the fuck arguing, get y'ponchos out. We ain't got no time.

This had to be a dream, *had* to. Turner bit hard on his knuckle, saw stars as his teeth neared the bone. Real. Felt real. He was being lifted onto the makeshift stretcher of damp ponchos, the old familiar smell of the raw rubber near his face.

Gone move fast, main, you brace y'self, awright?

Them running, Turner on his back in their midst, jostled and that leg still wholly numb. As his head dipped backwards he could see the upside-down phalanx the front men made, running with their carbines at the ready—the slow fireworks from the treetops in his eyes, the explosions like a great beast choking—until even with eyes shut he could tell by the pressure in his undead leg that they were running uphill with him. Then a sudden halt, all blood forced to his head.

Hump-tee shit, he heard Watkins say in awe, under his breath. *They everwhere.*

Turner opened his eyes and saw beyond the silhouettes of branches the upside-down front of his grandparents' house. A light fog had risen, and he felt the moisture of it condense on his top lip where his warm breath hit. The numbness had left his leg; it was beginning to throb all up through his middle, a swollen displaced heartbeat. His head felt light and spongy, sang the beginnings of off-key harp notes to him whenever he tried to shift position.

Just before the soldiers who were carrying him lowered him on the ponchos to the ground, Watkins and another man in front silently crouched down to survey the scene and for a moment unblocked Turner's view. The familiar yellow glow of the front yard was ringed around with dark threatening shapes, made indistinct enough by the mist and his inverted viewpoint that he couldn't tell whether the ragged swatches of black that twitched at the height of their heads were their own wings, or those of great birds that shared their shoulders.

The men around Turner grew so still and quiet that he could hear their breathing, ragged from the long running climb. The particular rankness of their sweat, soldier sweat, took him more clearly back in memory than he cared to go, reminded him how after months in the field you could assay the close stink of yourself and others with a chemist's precision—how many parts the lack of bathing, how many parts pure fear. This concentrate was high in fear.

"Maybe they ain't as thick at the back side," a voice whispered. Stevens. Gangly redhead with the voice that had never dropped from a child's high register. Damned kids.

In what felt dangerously like the beginning of the slippery slope of delirium Turner heard other voices joining these, echoing in the tunnel of time—the boys in his class at the old grammar school, whispering as they looked over the redrock barricade, planning their attack.

The convoluted pain of it all made his mind cry out in desperation *Cassie* but what resounded back was worse than silence, was pulses of sound that became patches of light and dark, a picture show larger than life, Cassie at eighteen pulling away in the lumbering old Dodge toward what he could see clearly now was the edge of the world, him stupidly two steps behind reality as he chased after her too late; the car revving past Zion Hill's single stop sign and beginning its slow plunge into the chasm of nothingness *Cassie* until his racing mind was yanked back as the men lifted him urgently in the swag of the ponchos, all of them running again, the phosphorlike moon a sudden white hole in the dark rain clouds *Shit shit shit, main, don't need no fuckin' moon* a tracer shell of pain until Turner shut his eyes and tried to pray it away, the slap of tree limbs and the rip of vines as the running men jostled him up what he could tell from the bullfrog sounds of the pond was the hill at the back of the house.

The blowing clouds dimmed the moon from a phosphor eye to a dim indentation of white in the gloom. Then all motion stopped. The men's silence told Turner they weren't liking what they saw. Finally Watkins was the one who let out the sigh for them all, an exhalation from someone much older than his nineteen years.

Just get back to your room, Cass had said. *Any way you can. Don't fight them . . .*

The chorus of bullfrog voices shimmered in Turner's brain, made colors when he shut his eyes. The numbness was receding from his leg, rings of fire spreading outward from the site of the wound.

One fo' the money, Watkins was murmuring, *two fo' the show. You gotcha runnin' shoes on, Jughaid?* Turner could hear the near-soundless inventory the men's hands were making of their carbines, their packs, their grenades, before they charged; a soldier's rosary.

Any way you can . . .

Turner grabbed the arm of the man nearest him. "Wait," he said, in a harsh whisper. "Listen. Don't . . ." He was thinking *don't die again* but realized it was insane to say it; weren't they already dead? They didn't look dead, sound dead. Despite the cool air, he was soaked with sweat. "I-I can make it from here. I'm steadier, really. Just find me something for a crutch, and I can . . ."

That's bullshit, Cap'n. Just hang on . . .

"No, listen. What if this is all in my mind? What if I could change it, by . . . by—" He saw Watkins and Jazz, above him, exchange a knowing look; Jazz made finger motions in a circle at his own temple, mouthed *Crazy; it's the shock.*

"The fuck I'm crazy," Turner hissed. He tried to roll sideways and set his good leg on the ground; the men hiked the ponchos higher to prevent it. Watkins got down in his face, wild-eyed. *You listen, main. Anybody that coulda blinked his mind and kept this goddamn war from happening, and didn't do it, a piece o' his ass is mine, you hear me? That ain't you, Cap'n. You just lay back and joy the ride.*

Then they were running uphill tumbling him side to side in the sharp chatter of rifle fire and the *wump* of grenades; he heard men cry out and fall *get there* but the ones carrying him didn't stumble *any way you can* and when they finally slowed he saw, in the burst of emergent moonlight, the white-framed window of his room, upside down above him like the face of a lover.

In the sudden pall of unexpected silence Watkins and Jazz hastily set the conveyance of ponchos down and, all the while breathing hard and looking over their shoulders, helped him to stand on his good leg.

You got his weight? Watkins grunted, and when Jazz gave the nod Watkins slid from underneath Turner's armpit and ran to the window. He tried to reach the frame to raise it, but the ground sloped off at this end of the house and his arms weren't long enough. He looked around frantically for something to stand on saying *Shit shit shit they be hearin' they be comin'* before he found an open barrel of rainwater and turned it over, wincing at even the mild noise the splash made. Turner realized he heard no other movement on the hillside, saw past Jazz's shoulder no other shapes but the two of them standing.

"Where . . . where are the others?" he said brokenly, "Did . . . ?" But he knew they'd all gone down.

Hush now, sir. We got to get you in.

Watkins was setting the inverted barrel against the wall of the house when the rumble of footfalls and squawk of voices began in the grove of dogwoods to the east. The black giant gave a quick look toward the sound and hoisted the barrel above his head instead, slamming it again and again through the splintering glass, his strong back a dark chrysalis of wetness in the moonlight.

Jazz was urging Turner toward the window, standing in for his bad leg as they ran and hopped, ran and hopped, until arms like logs were lifting him by the waist and pushing him headfirst through the battered window frame *Watch out now* his good leg getting traction on Jazz's bent back as the explosions began *Gone hurt like hell when you land* a sliver of glass biting into his shoulder and the whole wall of the house becoming indistinct and shifting and then a wet pearl white, undulant as some valve of viscera admitting him as he tried to say over his shoulder "Listen . . ." but Watkins having none of it *Nothin' you ain't done for us a many time.* That was his last glimpse of their faces, as the momentum carried him forward through the tightening aperture and the sky and trees behind him ignited into a wall of volcanic light. He somersaulted face-first onto the fragrant mustiness of the carpet and then held his breath until the rest of himself hit down, the slam of pain shutting out all other light, all other sound.

22

IN EQUAL PARTS dream and delirium Turner walked for hours through a darkened house, which resembled his grandparents' house except that it had become in his absence, as though he had been gone for decades, both a deserted ruin and illimitably more spread out. Room after crumbling room concatenated randomly around a central roofless yard, into which he kept dead-ending from different directions as he searched for . . . what?

Whatever he sought was urgently needed, that much he knew; the outcome of something momentous depended on it. But whenever he seemed on the verge of remembering what the object was, he would be distracted by familiar small sounds of life from the room just beyond whichever room he was searching in, his grandfather's cough or Cassie's laughter or his grandmother stirring a pot on the stove or some earnest mumbled disputation by James and the monks over a principle of physics.

But each time he took hold of a rust-pocked doorknob and opened it into the next room he found it empty, except for an occasional dove flapping in the dilapidated rafters, where the perpetual twilight showed through holes in the roof, or a squirrel skittering across a floor strewn with dried leaves.

His sense of urgency was increasing to the point of panic, doors opening onto other doors, doors revealing tunnels of doors, until he was frozen in his tracks by the sudden grace of a vision—an image flashed into his mind of a small closet he was certain existed somewhere in the interior of the house, a closet he hadn't seen or thought about since childhood. Whatever he needed was surely to be found there, though he couldn't have said how he knew, and his mind's eye showed him the long forgotten route to it, a glowing comet trail of pure intent superimposed onto the maze of halls and rooms.

The closet was exactly where he remembered it. The narrow door—

black and varnished, and with a fluted glass knob—was incongruously vivid against its dusty surroundings, and the faint cedarish scent of furniture polish gave the impression it had somehow escaped the general decline, over time, that the rest of the house had undergone.

Turner took hold of the knob. It was like ice, but the act of touching it seemed to complete a circuit that was almost electrical; a multitude of distant voices competed for attention in his mind, rising and fading like the signals on the old crystal radio set he'd built from a kit when he was eleven. He let go of the knob for a second, and though it left an invisible residue of iciness on his palm, the confusion of voices immediately hushed.

No time to figure all this out. He grabbed the knob again, resuming the connection to the voices, and twisted hard. But though he heard the latch-finger click free of the jamb, the door resisted opening, seemingly by the sheer pressure of the air, as if the closet housed the force of a considerable vacuum that resisted violation. His whole strength, applied with both hands now, made the door budge by less than the thickness, he judged, of skin.

He let go of the knob and took a step backwards to catch his breath, looking around the room for something to pry with, but seeing nothing except drifts of dry leaves in the corners. In the absence of clocks, the magnified sound of his heartbeat reminded him how relentlessly the time was passing, thum, *tick*, thum, *tick*, thum, and he enlarged his search for a pry bar, but when he had scanned three more rooms without seeing anything that could be pressed into service, he looked in exasperation to the ruined ceiling and saw, near an outer wall, a cross-beam that had nearly come loose from its joist, the free end attached by only a splinter.

By boosting himself onto the window sill he was able to make a lunge and wrench the plank loose, thum, *tick*, thum, *tick*, and run back to the closet with it, where he wedged one end under the knob and used the jamb as a fulcrum.

As he applied his weight steadily the mysterious seal began to give way, with a great groaning and creaking of wood. He could see, around the edges of the door frame, a brilliant ruby-colored light, intense as the beam of a laser; when the door finally blew open, rattling its hinges and slamming the wall as if by the force of a frigid blast, he had to shield his eyes from the overpowering brightness.

As his vision slowly adjusted, he saw that the source of the light was . . . now, this was strange. So totally strange that for the first time he stopped and considered that this surely must be a dream. He willed himself to wake up, but nothing happened. And when he edged his hands from in front of his eyes again, what he had seen was implacably there.

Suspended from the ceiling of the cramped closet was a gigantic crystal of mica or glass, easily the size of a man. The core of it boiled with molten red light, painful to the eyes, but at the same time its surface reflected, in inverted form, the closet door frame and the great ruined house and his own perplexed face. As he watched, the crystal's bulk rocked back and forth by millimeters on its glasslike cord with a sound like a half-imagined wind chime in a mournful minor key, though there was nothing visible that it struck to create the music.

Turner discovered that he had sunk gradually to a kneeling position, spellbound by the laserlike color and the plaintiveness of the chimes. But the real shock came when he happened to glance away from the crystal, toward the dim rooms of the house, and saw that they were no longer there, had been replaced by a panorama of the same barren red desert of a day ago—had it been only a day, or was his mind playing tricks?

The relationship of days to months, to years, to all things linear, shifted inside him like a kaleidoscope, and he realized with an intuitive leap that the desert and its shifting shapes had been merely projections of the crystal's brilliant light all along, the concept of a child's finger-silhouettes on a flashlighted wall raised to the thousandth power, a world given color and depth and scent and menace by the strange inner life of the glass.

But the fascination of watching the barren night landscape, a world with its own weather, own predators, own cloud-shadows, and knowing that it all arose from this flinty heart of light, began to pale as he remembered he'd gone to the closet hunting some weapon or defense against whatever terrible ordeal would soon befall him and this was surely of no help.

Before he could shut the door and resume his lonely search, though, he had an overwhelming urge to lay his hand, if for only a second, against the huge crystal's glassy skin. The urge was more than curiosity, almost as if something about the crystal, something inside it, called out to him, some eerie kinship of elements exerting its tidal pull beyond the range of thought.

Still kneeling, though it felt to him now more from reverence than from his earlier weakness, he reached out his hand toward the brilliant light, steeling himself against the expectation of either severe cold or heat.

But before he could touch it, an invisible hand seized his wrist. He jerked backwards, a cry caught in his throat, but still the hand held on.

Except that now, instead of exerting force, it was patting his arm soothingly, lovingly, and he rose through the recognized touch up into the world again:

The familiar ceiling of his old room, its faded wallpaper brushed by morning sunlight, the slow-tossed green of tree limbs outside the window. The window, whole and unbroken. Had the soldiers been a dream, too? They'd seemed so real . . .

As his vision sharpened he saw that it was Cassie who held his arm, sitting beside the bed in her wheelchair, one of a crowd of concerned faces looking down at him—his grandparents and James Crowe and Beh Vah and Lu Weh and Wah So and Se Hon and Bah Tow, their expressions intensely expectant, waiting for him to speak.

"Hey," was all he could manage; his larynx felt dry and creaky from disuse. The simple sign of life appeared to cheer them immensely, though—they breathed relief and Beaver clapped his hands, while Turner's grandmother wiped a tear from behind her bifocals. Outside, a gust of wind shook the green limbs and sent fresh combinations of light and shadow cascading across the comforting ceiling.

"So, where are we?" Turner asked. He saw James and Cassie exchange a distressed glance.

She patted his arm. "In your bedroom," she said softly, obviously fearing for either his eyesight or his memory.

All the dammed-up feelings of the past day's struggle erupted out of him, strangely, in a belly laugh that was so full he got choked on it, and he could see Cassie mentally adding his sanity to her list of concerns. His grandmother brought him a glass of water, and with several slow sips he got his breath back.

"I know where I am," he said. "I *mean*, where are we with the realm? I must have blanked out. What day is it?"

"It's Tuesday, Cap'n," Crowe said. "Funniest goddamn th— . . . uh, sorry." He made obeisance toward Turner's grandparents for the gaffe of language. "Funniest *thing*, we lost a day in there, someway. You just up and disappeared from the rock, and when we got back here the sun was coming up again. The radio and everything says it's the next day." He shrugged.

It suddenly dawned on Turner that he was hearing bird song from the front yard, and smelling the sweet-shrub bush that grew by the porch steps. That meant the door was open. Shit, shit. He sat up in a panic.

"There's nobody on watch!" he said. "James, lock the front door. Hurry. Louie, you watch the back until I can . . ."

This time it was Cassie's turn to laugh—gently, as she reached over to hug him. "It's over, Turner," she whispered. "It's all over."

The people around the bed took this as their signal to give him and Cassie some privacy while she filled him in on the details. His grandmother, ever insistent on regular mealtimes regardless of what universal clock went haywire, gave notice that breakfast would be served in fifteen minutes.

"You didn't see it end?" Cassie asked, when they were alone. "I thought you knew."

Turner shook his head.

"It was beautiful," she said. "Everything from the realm turned into this . . . kind of smoke, and the wind just carried it away. The desert, and the beast, and the wings, and . . . all of a sudden the world looked so clean it . . . sparkled . . ." Her voice broke, and she laid her head on his chest until she got her composure back.

"And their younger selves?" he asked her.

She didn't comprehend at first.

"My grandparents, the young ones," he said. "Did they turn into smoke, too?"

Cassie lowered her head sadly and nodded. "It's all over," she said again.

Over, Turner thought. It sounded as strange as a word from some unknown language. *Over.*

Cassie raised up on one arm and looked at him, stroked his hand. "And just to show you how selfish the old ex-Hope is," she said, with a wry smile, "all I could think about was, what I'd give to be hearing the music. What was . . ." Her voice almost breaking, then reining itself in. "What was it like?"

Turner knew he looked blank. "What music?"

Cassie was incredulous. "When the world realigned," she said. "'The music so much purer than music that it can never have a name' . . . ?"

As Turner remembered, he pictured Won Se's face telling him, that first night, amid the dripping water and torchlight in the silence of the oracle room: *He hears what no other human is privileged to hear. What leaks out into the stillness from the core of the core is a music so much purer than music that it can never have a name. And then he receives . . .*

He thought back to the night just past, the strange night out of time, and the great flash of light and sound as Watkins and Jazz pushed him through the shattered window. He had heard . . . the explosions, and himself crying out as the bad leg touched down, and . . .

Shit. Had he drowned out the purest, purest music with his own loud mouth, or . . . ? No, wait. *Can never have a name.* Hadn't there been . . . ? Yes. Just before the blast, a long grace note of silence and then a sound like the whole sky taking a breath . . . surely he hadn't imagined that.

Cassie's face was so reverently expectant he hated to disappoint her. "It's hard to talk about," he said. She looked a little let down, but nodded her understanding and squeezed his hand.

"Listen, about the other," she said, and as she looked out the window for a long time before continuing, Turner remembered the rest of Won Se's speech and knew what she was going to ask. *And then he receives his deepest heart's desire.*

Damn, how could he have forgotten something so important? All these months, his deepest heart's desire had been to have the whole thing over with, and get on with his life. But now the enormity of the thought chilled his blood. What could he choose?

At that moment his grandfather's spirited whistling came to him through the walls of the house, as in childhood. Either the medicine had leveled his pain off, or he was caught up in the celebration of the day. Turner realized that he could, with one sentence, ask to banish the tumor and have it be done, and the thought swept through him like some fragrance so sweet it made him giddy. But then his eyes fell on Cassie's limp blue-jeaned legs, and the depth of his dilemma robbed him of speech.

The possibilities were endless. Could he will her accident never to have happened, will her legs whole? Could he look through books for some dread disease and will all future generations to be rid of it? Yes, he could. He could . . . Jesus. Jesus Christ. He had a small glimpse, then, of how immobilizing it would be, to be God. Too many choices is no choice at all, is a heart in hell.

He said to Cassie, "I'm not sure if I can do this."

Cassie looked puzzled. "You don't *have* to do anything. It's already done."

"It is?"

"It's not a wish, it's a desire," she said. "You can't pick your heart's desire, it just . . . *is.* I just wanted to say that I know, and that it's all right."

And it was then that he knew what he had chosen without choosing.

"Does *he* know?" Turner asked her.

"He knows."

Amazing. The amazing grace of a good, honest man being able to work his land again. For however many more years God would spare him. Amazing, amazing grace.

The thought and the whistled song were still in Turner's mind as he bathed before breakfast, amazed too by the grace of being so relatively pain-free after the ordeal of the day and night before, so distant now that they almost seemed not to have happened. Until, drying himself, he saw the huge white scar, vaguely oval but with points like a star, on the leg that Jazz had bandaged so hurriedly, and so well.

BESIDES ALL THE other good things that morning was, it was a festival of smells, too. The smell of fried homemade sausage and buttermilk biscuits had barely started to dissipate when Cordelia hung her long-sequestered laundry out to dry in the sun; the sheets and pillowcases billowed and popped in the wind like sails, filling the hillside with the delicate tang of bleach.

Out back, the resinous scent of fresh pine lumber flourished where Turner hammered a makeshift ramp into place alongside the porch steps so Cassie could come and go in her chair, explore the yard and the woods.

Beh Vah and Bah Tow had found one of Turner's old basketballs in a side shed, and even an air pump and needle to inflate it with. The ball held air remarkably well, giving off the odor of dry-rot and warm rubber as the two monks played a creditable game of one-on-one at the rusted hoop still nailed to the side of the barn.

Bah Tow showed a great deal of finesse with the game, while Beh Vah operated on grit and desire alone, and at one point their competition grew so heated that Cordelia came out and canceled the contest because the red dust they raised was blowing dangerously near her wet laundry. But Jackson followed close behind her with a long garden hose and misted down the troublesome patch of dirt so they could continue. He winked at Beaver and Bartow as he went back inside, and when he made sure Cordelia wasn't looking he did a pantomime for them of her nervous hands that had them weak with laughter.

Meanwhile James had retrieved their van from the cemetery—cranked the first time, he reported, and ran like a top—and was out in the front driveway with it now, Turtle Waxing it with some rags Cordelia found for him in the closet.

The monks had gotten their instruments from the van, first thing; Se Hon and Wah So and Lu Weh sat just uphill in the edge of the trees, playing a horn and flute and cymbal trio on some ancient song Turner had never heard, but which sounded like a hymn of celebration.

Turner looked up from his hammering to see Cassie at the top of the ramp in her chair, drying a plate with a dish towel. "Ready or not," she said.

"It's ready," Turner said. "Try it."

She looked dubious, but she laid her plate and towel aside and inspected more closely the place where the ramp joined the floor.

"It's smooth as silk," Turner chided her.

She still looked dubious.

"Okay, so the slope's a little steeper than I'd like," he said. "I ran out of lumber. Just keep the brake partly on, and you'll be all right."

He squatted at the bottom of the ramp with his arms out, like a father coaxing a kid down a playground slide. Cassie wheeled forward slowly, holding her tongue in the corner of her mouth for concentration in just the little-girl way that made his heart do a backflip, until she hit the angle of the slope and picked up steam.

She let out a squeal when she bucked onto the level grass. He grabbed her by the waist and their foreheads lightly konked.

"Just a tad more brake, next time," he said.

"I love it."

"Want to take a look around, while you're out? Go down to the lake?"

Cordelia called from the window. "Hon? Telephone."

"Coming," Turner shouted, and said to Cassie, "Maybe it's Won Se."

They'd tried to call Drepung a dozen times since the banishment of the realm, but Nohr Bu's number rang and rang without an answer. Strange. Out of order, maybe? The operator promised him she'd file a repair request with headquarters in Katmandu and mark it "rush." That way, she related proudly, the expedition might set out as early as the following week. Cassie hadn't fared any better with the telepathic equivalent; she blamed her failure to reach Won Se on some dislocation of force fields from all the trauma in the world of late. Turner suspected she had just strained her faculties during the struggle on the rock and needed some time to mend them.

But as he trotted up the wooden ramp to the porch, Cordelia called out to Turner, "Not you, hon. It's for Cassie." He stopped and looked around at Cass, who was rolling herself toward the ramp with an enigmatic smile.

"It's some . . . *news*man," Cordelia added. "Clotfield, I think he said?"

Cassie winced, as if some secret had been spoiled. "Coming," she shouted, and began whipping her wheels energetically toward the ramp.

"*Zot*feld?" Turner called to Cordelia. "*USA Today?*"

"That's it."

He looked questioningly at Cassie. She kept wheeling, avoided his eyes. He hopped down and grabbed the back handles of the chair, helped push her up the ramp. "Why would Zotfeld be calling *you*?" Turner asked.

Cassie dodged the question. "It was going to be a surprise," she said. "Just trust me on this, all right?"

The house was still cool from the night; the windows across the front side didn't take the sun until afternoon. Once Cassie was on level flooring she gathered her own speed and quickly reached the small alcove where the phone was, leaving Turner walking fast to catch up. A breeze of cherry blossom blew through the alcove's window.

She picked up the receiver, but as she put it to her ear she noticed that Turner had followed. She lowered it and glared at him, mouthing the words "*Trust . . . me.*"

"Let me have him when you're through," Turner said, and shuffled off down the hall, a little miffed. He leaned against the doorway to the living room, breathing the fragrant air and trying to picture what his life would be in the weeks to come. He'd have to get the monks back home to Drepung, of course, and say his good-byes to Won Se. Surely Cassie and James would want to go along, and maybe even his grandparents, if they felt up to the rigors of the high altitude after the strain they'd been through.

But when he tried to cast his mind past that trip and his return, tried to picture himself resuming his old life—juggling phone calls and haggling with agents and running to catch LearJets—his powers of imagination somehow ground to a halt. He couldn't think that far ahead, right now; his insides felt too raw, too weary and hollowed out, to climb back into the pressure cooker right away. Why rush it? he argued with himself. He had healing to do. He had Cassie. No hurry. No big deal.

He heard Cassie's muffled voice down the hall, laughing at something Zotfeld was saying, and it was at that moment he noticed a flash of movement within the darkened living room, which he'd thought was empty. Someone on the couch. An arm that he recognized as his grandfather's went out to the small green pill bottle which Turner now spotted for the first time on the coffee table. The hand missed, knocked the bottle over, had to feel around for it.

Turner started toward the room to help him, but then decided not to intrude on his privacy. He watched as his grandfather's hands got the cap off, took a pill out, started to replace the cap, and after some hesitation shook out a second pill.

Turner knew from reading the label that these weren't souped-up aspirin; they were heavy stuff. He must still be in a lot of pain. Maybe your heart's desire isn't granted instantly, Turner thought. Maybe it takes a while. He wished he had quizzed Won Se further on this aspect, wished he could talk to him now.

He was startled by a finger poking him in the back. "Your turn," Cassie said, motioning toward the phone. She noticed his face. "What's wrong?" she said.

"Nothing."

He picked up the phone. "Paul? Turner. Listen, bud, I just wanted to tell you how much we appreciated the article. You said some mighty nice things about us, and it helped more than you know."

"Ah," Zotfeld said, "I just call 'em as I see 'em. So how are you feeling, guy? Not for publication, of course. Just asking."

Turner chuckled. "I'm a happy man, Paul. You can quote me."

"That's good, that's good. And the guys? How are they?"

Turner heard laughter and clapping from the yard. He pulled aside the curtain and saw that Cassie had joined the basketball contingent in a game of shoot-till-you-miss and had just sunk a one-hander from the foul line, to the unlikely accompaniment of the celebratory trio of flute, trumpet, and cymbal.

"They're doing fine, Paul. Just great."

"Oh, yeah. Have to be. Have to be. Hey, by the way . . . I love your friend's idea. I wish *I'd* thought of it."

"Idea?"

"Right. The concert. Fantastic concept, really. I don't know who this gal is, but she's got some heavy-duty contacts in the industry. I mean, doors are *opening*, fella. My bosses jumped at the chance to be a sponsor, so it looks like our next step is . . ."

"Whoa, Paul, whoa," Turner interrupted. "You're getting ahead of me, here. A sponsor for . . . ?"

An embarrassed silence on the New York end of the line. "Uh, I hope I'm not jumping the gun or anything," Zotfeld said. He added hopefully, "The *concert*?"

Turner had always hated appearing ignorant in conversation, and as a result often pretended to understand things he didn't. A weakness, especially in business, but what the hell. "Oh, *that*," he said, gritting his teeth. "Sure." Out in the yard Cassie's lyrical one-hander finally missed the hoop, and as she rolled away from the foul line to give her place up to Bartow, she glanced toward the house with an expression of concern.

"I didn't mention this part to Cass," Paul said shyly, "until I saw how you felt about it, but I think I've got us a great name for the show. You ready? Okay. 'Celebrate . . . Peace.' Huh? What do you think? Not the same ring as Woodstock, maybe, but I think it'll fly."

"It's a good name," Turner hedged. "It's just that . . ."

"Hey, we don't have to decide this minute," Paul said. "I know you're busy getting things ready, so I'll let Cassie fill you in on all the latest. What a gal, huh? Can't wait to meet her. Can't wait." He cleared his throat. "By the way, Turner—I, uh-h-h . . ." The way Paul stretched the word out, it sounded as if he were debating with himself whether to broach some touchy topic.

"I, uh . . . *know*," he said finally.

Turner waited for elaboration. When none seemed forthcoming, he asked, "Know *what*, Paul?"

"Everything. Or pretty much."

Turner sighed. "Everything about *what*?"

"About what you guys have been doing," Zotfeld said, in a confidential tone. "Look, I happened to run across a scholar at State U., here. You'd probably know his name. He says that in the fifteenth century, out of all the big monasteries, Drepung was considered the, uh . . . *oracular* monastery. The oracle. Emperors thought it could predict the future. Are you aware of all that?"

The back of Turner's neck prickled. "Sure, I've read about it," he said, as coolly as he could manage.

"Uh-huh, uh-huh," Paul said. "Well, this guy claims there's a legend in that part of the world, that once every . . . every generation or so, there's this huge battle between good and evil, and the monastery chooses a, uh, non-monk to be the main warrior, and then helps him fight it, while the world hangs in the balance."

"Mm-hmm," Turner said, "I've heard that old story. Very interesting."

A long space of silence.

"Turner . . . it's *not* a legend, is it?"

"What makes you say that?"

An incredulous huff of laughter. "Why do I *say* that? Look, I'm standing here, late last night, in a newsroom that's a, a, *hub* of communications for the civilized *world*, I mean, wire services galore, news pouring into our computers from around the globe, and for once . . . *once* . . . it looks like we might be turning the corner. The world, I mean. My . . . *God*, Turner! Communism's dying, dictatorships are falling like dominoes, and then I look down at my notes on this 'legend' thing, and all of a sudden it hits me. It's *not* coincidence, is it? You can level with me, guy. I promise it's confidential until we, uh . . . we figure out how best to . . . present it, and you can have a voice in that. But the world . . . needs . . . to know. I really think it could change some things, big-time. Help the process along."

The rush of words had seemed like a roman candle that was now fizzling out. The phone line was silent for long seconds. Turner could hear, from up on the hillside, the musical trio coming to the crescendo of its peace hymn, before Zotfeld prompted, "So, what do you say?"

Inside Turner, his promoter's instinct grappled with his higher self over the question of Drepung getting its fair credit for helping vanquish the realm. But his higher self got a good half-nelson on its counterpart, and momentarily had the upper hand. He had visions of videocams and movie lights invading the sanctity of the War Room. Yak-butter tea concessions outside. Monk quiz shows. Lifestyles of the poor and spiritual.

No.

"Paul, I'm very grateful for all you've done to help us, but I hope you understand this is something I'm . . . just not in a position to talk about, right now."

"But if I could just . . ." Paul began, so fast the words sputtered, but he caught himself and calmed down. "Well, think about it. It'll keep. Just so I have the exclusive. I mean, you and I can talk about it more when I'm down for the show. All right?"

"Sure thing."

"Great, great. Say, Turner . . . you still there?"

"Yep."

"Hey, if I could just talk to their main guy over there, the bishop or whatever . . . you know, I can be pretty persuasive in a one-on-one."

"I know. You're a sweetheart, Paul."

"Just a try. That's all I'm asking, just set me up."

Turner pictured an imaginary set-to in the garden, Zotfeld versus Won Se, and had to grin. The world wasn't ready.

"I'll talk to him," Turner said.

In truth, he wished he could.

"Well," Zotfeld said, "if you change your mind and . . . Wait. I hear them, don't I?"

Turner realized that the closing phrases of the trio's song were swelling in volume until they could be heard through the phone receiver.

"Yep. They're keeping in practice."

"God, they're beautiful. Hey, I'm gone. Peace, man."

"Same to you, Paul."

As he hung up the phone the last note of the song echoed away, tangible as a butterfly in the bright air of the yard. Suddenly, unaccountably, he had a vision of gelled spotlights sweeping against a night sky, TV cameras gliding across a stage as the applause of the crowd builds and the monks step meekly into the light with their instruments. His anger over Cassie's intended surprise began to dissipate, and deep in his blood a ghost of the old adrenaline rush roused itself.

A show. A *real* show, with first-rate lighting and a first-rate set, and an audience of millions. Didn't the guys deserve it? Hell, didn't the world? And couldn't Drepung put the profits to good use, maybe return its sad patched-up cubbyhole of a library to some semblance of its old glory? Turner's brain sizzled with the possibilities, and he felt his resolve of only a few minutes ago—to take a long hiatus before hitting the grind again—begin fading like a bad dream. His tired heart leaped up like a fire-horse at the bell.

A show. A first-rate show. Bless Cassie for thinking of it. Sure, it would be hard work, but if they swung into high gear right now, preparing, and if luck was with them, all the pieces might come together in as little as a month. Say six weeks, to be safe.

A real show. Hell, yes.

"*SATURDAY*?" TURNER'S voice boomed across the lake, scaring off a school of minnows that had surfaced beneath the dock to nibble at the biscuit crumbs Cassie was scattering for them. "*This* Saturday? You're joking. That's crazy."

"Look," Cassie said wearily, "all I did was raise the idea. Just to feel everybody out, see if there was any interest before I mentioned it to you. But it snowballed. It's got a life of its own. What can we do?"

"Well . . . *un*-snowball it, I guess," he stammered. "If it's so hot, surely it'll keep for a month or two, till we get back on our feet."

She raised one eyebrow. "You're a *promoter* and you're saying that?

Look, the article really made waves. It's got everybody curious. For a week, that might last. But a month? No way. You know that."

Turner spotted a pebble near his feet on the planks of the dock, picked it up and threw it hard across the water. It sank with an ineffectual *plook*.

"And another thing," Cassie said, sensing the momentum was on her side. "Has it never just royally . . . *pissed* you off that the stupid Book of Rules keeps the Hope from doing anything to help Drepung? And even the *former* Hope, for God's sake. Anything material to help, personally, I mean. Don't you resent that?"

"Sure I do," he said, "but . . ."

"So this is our *chance*," she said, folding up the empty biscuit sack and reaching to take both his hands. "Not a cent leaves my bank account, or yours. It's all third-party. I'm sure Won Se won't have any trouble with that. Think of the library."

"But think of the logistics. Think about how exhausted we all are. Even if we left for New York tomorrow, we'd still be cutting it close, by the time you figure rehearsals and . . ."

Cassie's face lit up triumphantly. "Ah! That's the beauty of it," she said. "It wouldn't *be* in New York. It would be here."

Turner wasn't sure he'd heard her right. "Here? In Birmingham, you mean?"

"No, *here*. As in, right here." She held out her arms. "Would that hillside make a great amphitheater, or what? And if you're worried about crowd control, or any of that, don't be. It wouldn't get out of hand. We'd have the best man in the business working on that . . . well, the best since *you* got out, anyway. Think of the guys. Don't we owe them this much?"

In his heart his knew she was right.

"Another problem," he said. "Zotfeld knows. About the Calling Out. Or believes he does."

Cassie shrugged. "He's a little weird, but I think his heart's in the right place. Don't you?" Turner stared across the water. "And anyway," she said, "what can we do about it? It's not like we can just . . . blot out the fact that it ever happened."

Turner found himself staring at the hillside, picturing the layout of the stage. Cassie seemed to read his mind, because she smiled.

23

IN THE HOURS BEFORE dawn on Saturday, the wide storm front moving east out of Mississippi bore down on the prow-shaped west face of Sand Mountain. At the very center of the swath of storms, a dense knot of hailstones, bigger than marbles, got funnelled into the huge limestone notch at the top of the mountain's prow—named Henderson's Gap, for the man who homesteaded the west face back before the War Between the States.

In minutes the hailstorm, illuminated by its own vivid lightning, was raking the level tomato fields that are the plateau's sustenance and spilling the blood of the big Lucky Beefhearts onto the black sandy dirt. The next week's issue of the *Sand Mountain Reporter* would quote farmers as saying that one-third to one-half of that crop, second of the year, was lost to market, although housewives in the vicinity hurried to salvage the damaged ones for canning as puree, which would make fine soups and stews the next winter.

Meanwhile the mountain's prow effectively split the main storm front in two, as it had done for thousands of years without any prompting, causing the northernmost half of the front—the part with the worst winds—to veer off toward Huntsville where it would down several power lines but cause no reported injuries. The orphaned south front, its fury mostly drained, was angled in the direction of Jasper and Parrish and Bessemer.

By the time it reached Zion Hill, where it found Turner sitting on his grandparents' back porch in the dark, too hyper to sleep, its torrent had decreased to a soft summer shower that caressed the old tin roof like a wide, wet hand, a homecoming music that helped to calm him down. Ever since he was a child, rain on tin had been for him the most peaceful sound on earth.

He shut his eyes for a minute to see if he could doze, but a creak of the floorboards brought him up straight. Silver spokes eased to his side, and Cassie's hand went to the back of his neck.

"Can't sleep?" she said, whispering it because Jackson and Cordelia's bedroom shared a wall with the porch.

Turner shook his head. Suddenly he smelled peanuts, mixed with the soft ozone scent of the rain. He watched as Cassie held up a sandwich she was eating, silhouetting it against the outside porch-eave lamp so she could see to tear it evenly in two. Her fingers worked gracefully but with no-nonsense precision, and when she was done she handed him half. He took a bite. Peanut butter and banana, his childhood favorite. "This is good," he said, around the bite. "Most people don't put enough peanut butter."

"Stick with me, babe," she said cheerfully, but he could tell from her voice there was something on her mind.

"What's wrong?"

"Nothing. I just tried to call Won Se again, and there's no answer. It bothers me, a little. But I guess if anything were wrong, he'd try to reach me. I think I can . . . *receive* okay, I just can't send very well right now."

"I tried to call him, too," Turner said. The cellular phone, with its steady amber eye, stood on the floor by his feet. "Don't I remember that they have a big festival, or something, when all this is over? Maybe that's where everybody is."

Cassie mumbled that it was possible, and added, "I'd like to see Won Se's face when he hears he can have the library restored."

Turner didn't comment. His own turn of mind was a great deal more melancholy; he still dwelt on having to see Won Se's face when they told him about Chai Lo's defection. Or did he know somehow, had he suspected all along?

Far across the valley, at the headland of Mrs. Sexton's pastures, a row of tall spotlights showed the silver eighteen-wheelers circled like a wagon train. At their center the portable stage was an anthill of activity, roadies clambering over the mountain of sound equipment to cover it with black plastic against the rain. Gas generators spluttered and droned like muffled chain saws; the actual power mains wouldn't be laid until mid-morning.

Cassie finished off the last of her sandwich, and with her other hand reached to pat Turner's stomach through his T-shirt.

"Butterflies?"

He nodded, took up her hand and kissed it. "The good kind," he said. "There's two kinds, and you learn them. This is the good kind."

They sat and listened to the rain a while. When Cassie broke the silence it was to say, "Listen, I hate to spoil the moment, here, but there's something you need to know."

Turner laid his head back on the seat of the swing. "Which is . . . ?"

"I'm worried about James. He's not one to let on, much, but he's taking it really hard."

"Taking what?"

"You know. Screwing up the equations. Wasting his best shots before you could use them." She sighed. "I found him packing last night. He was going to leave without even saying goodbye to anybody. Said he felt like a failure."

"It's not all his *fault*. And besides, it's water under the bridge by now . . ."

"I know, I know. I told him. We talked for a long time. But I think it would mean more coming from you."

"I'll talk to him tomorrow." He glanced at the luminous dial of his watch. "God, is it already Saturday? I'll talk to him *today*, I mean."

Cassie laid her head on his shoulder. "Good." The rain stayed steady on the roof, a soft chaotic percussion no human musician could duplicate, though a section of the monks' Mountain Fennel movement came very close. "This is so peaceful," Cassie said. Her small head burrowed more solidly into his neck.

He rehearsed in his mind what he would say to the world that night in the two minutes, forty seconds the producers had allotted him—very generously, they pointed out, considering what commercial time was selling at—for an introduction to the music and dance. He and Cassie and the guys had discussed it at length, and at one point he'd been inclined to start off talking about the Buddha himself, just lay the whole shining shining path out for them in miniature.

But for the last little while, though, he was coming around more to her perspective, namely that the path was a pretty heavy trip to lay on a typical member of the TV audience from out of the blue as he's raising his pizza slice to his mouth and yelling at his kids, and therefore the all-men-are-brothers approach might be a better first step to gain their confidence.

A gust of wind carried a fine, cool mist of rain through the screen wire and across their faces. "Brotherhood might be the way to start it," he said to Cassie. "What do you think?"

After waiting nearly half a minute for her response, he said, "Cass?"

A faint snore escaped her lips.

"Good," Turner said. He grinned in the darkness, looking at the far-off lights. "I think so, too."

". . . AND NOW, ladies and gentlemen, the sacred . . ."

But at this point the applause for Turner's brief opening speech about the world's newfound sense of brotherhood became an ovation; the noise swelled until it drowned him out, and the tiny producer in his hidden earphone buzzed *Hold up, hold up. Camera three panning the crowd, Four's ready to take it at the midpoint, an-n-n-d take it, Four. Good, good. Turner, when the reaction crests, I'll give you a countdown of five seconds. Stand by . . .*

A dozen spotlights, gelled blue for peace, raked the crowd from the high scaffoldings at the perimeter of the field. It was shoulder-to-shoulder people, extending as far back as the lights let him see. Even the high hummock of grass all the way at the horizon, where the satellite truck was parked, was lined with standing shapes silhouetted against the Milky Way, hands clapping vigorously above their heads. When Turner took advantage of the pause to inhale a deep, deep breath, it was cherry blossoms and the hickory smoke of far-off campfires. What a sweet night.

An-n-d five . . . four . . .

He glanced toward the edge of the stage, where Jackson and Cordelia and James and Cassie and Paul Zotfeld sat in folding chairs underneath the platform for Camera Four. They were all clapping and smiling, and by the shape of her mouth Cassie was shouting something, but he couldn't hear her for the roar of the crowd. Zotfeld stopped applauding long enough to give Turner two thumbs up, very high.

The earphone: *Now-w-w take it . . .*

"Thank you for that. Thank you. Ladies and gentlemen, it gives me great pleasure . . ." He could see himself on the small monitor at the footlights, his white suit an insignificant dot against the giant Tibetan tapestry behind him. " . . . to bring to you, this evening, the music of peace. The sacred music and dance of Tibet, as performed for centuries at the monastery of Drepung."

The brilliant arc light on his face was extinguished. As he walked off the darkened stage, soft blue footlights began brightening to illuminate the interleaved panels that made up the tapestry, its gold threads gleaming against a field of ochre and red. From unseen valves in the flooring, soft gray florets of smoke rose silently off of dry ice—an uncanny imitation, Turner thought, of the low-lying fog that drifted across Drepung's grounds from the nearby lakes this time of year.

There was a faint hum of motors and gears; the panels revolved, as effortlessly as a butterfly's wings, to make passageways the monks walked through into the soft light and the hushed expectation of the crowd. Their instruments were at the ready and they played as they came. Not the low, chaotic blatting of a world in distress, but the bright and fragile pirouetting of peace—the same song they'd played under the shade trees the morning after the realm was vanquished.

Lu Weh and Beh Vah took the lead on their cymbals, and Se Hon's stubby flute wove in and out of the cycle to a rhythm almost like a Viennese waltz, or a lullaby; the flute had never been his main instrument until Chai Lo's departure forced the change, but he'd made the transition seamlessly, Turner thought. Only after Se Hon's melody had established the solid thread of safety and surety did Bah Tow's and Wah So's long bass horns speak at all, and even then in playful dark half-notes, embroidered against the gladness of the tune in the shimmering way of leaf-shadows in a dappled shade.

James Crowe had high-fives for Turner as he came offstage into the wings; his mood seemed much improved after the long talk they'd had. Turner sat on the floor in front of Cassie, took out his earpiece, and laid his head back against her knees. Her hands began working the tension out of his neck. The last of Turner's stomach-butterflies flitted away, the anticipation over. It was happening now, and it was good.

Out on stage, the big low horns had given up their modest counterpoint to the clean crystalline melody and their owners had laid them aside; Se Hon and Wah So were thus freed to begin a whirling dance of celebration that resembled nothing so much as children let loose from a stuffy schoolroom prison into the freedom of a playground as big as the world.

From where Turner sat he could see every one of the nine large cameras, silently pistoning up and down on their hydraulic platforms in a ballet as precise as the dancers' was unconstrained. The red lights on the camera fronts, alternating to show which one was live at the moment, blinked on and off with a hypnotic rhythm, like lightning bugs he'd chased on this same hill.

Unable to see a program monitor, he got caught up in watching each camera's light go live and then off, trying to reconstruct what images were going out on the air. What finally drew his attention from this was some small disturbance out in the mass of the crowd, a flurry so quiet and minute that only his promoter's instinct let him know of it.

He looked out and saw an isolated spasm of violence, like water eddying around a rock—several people striking and stabbing at the person in the center, whose arms were around his head for protection but in vain. Turner scanned the edges of the crowd to see if a security man had spotted this yet, and he was about to get on his phone and report it when he saw a similar eddy of violence farther back, and then another one. The only difference with these was that the people doing most of the hitting wore police blue.

A sick feeling overcame him as he felt behind his chair for the portable phone. The grainy film footage of the Altamont concerts came back from memory—the chaos, the scuffles, the knifed body going down as its blood sprayed a girl's white lace miniskirt. Satan's birthday party. Not here. Please, not here.

He was so involved in trying to find his phone that although he was sitting with a plain view of the dark skyline he was not the first to see the encroaching black wing blot out the Milky Way and fill the whole curve of the world.

By the time he heard the frightened shouts and saw hands all pointing in the same direction, the wing's other half showed and the whole fearsome shape bore down on the hillside with a cry as loud as the roar of a warplane. It buzzed the crest of the hill, brushing the satellite dish and scattering the row of onlookers who had frozen in panic when they looked behind them and saw it coming.

Turner bounded across the stage toward his microphone. A stagehand near him who was wearing a headset, still mesmerized by the music, grabbed his elbow and told him he was walking into camera range, but Turner pushed him aside.

A quick glance uphill showed squadrons of black wings on the horizon, still distant but gradually swelling to blot out the stars. The monks' music faltered as Turner ran through the thick of the players, shouting at them to run backstage. As he grabbed the microphone from its stand, a whole phalanx of stagehands and grips were running toward him, sure he'd lost his mind. The great squeal of feedback, magnified in their headsets, slowed them for a second as they grimaced and tore the sets off; this gave Turner time to say to the crowd, "Everyone exit, please. Downhill, to your right. Toward the trees." His amplified voice echoed off the surrounding hills; screams began in the crowd. "No running, please. No need to run. Just exit immediately, walking. Downhill to the right. Everything's going to be okay. Keep moving, keep . . ."

The largest of the stagehands was almost on him now, arms poised to get a scissor-lock on his neck. Turner quickly tossed the microphone at him and his reflex made him grab it, giving Turner the fraction of a second he needed to duck the other converging men and run back toward where his people were. The cameramen all sat dazed, pointing their lenses by instinct at the nearest thing moving.

By now the wings were close enough to block out the field's farthest spotlights. One wingtip, with a resilience like steel, grazed a light tower and sent it crashing in a pinwheel of blue electricity as the roadies on its platform slid down the scaffolding supports like a firehouse pole, no time to find the handholds. The flapping black shape, silhouetted now against the night sky, carried in its talons a struggling bundle that Turner realized was a child. His heart rose in his throat.

A wave of screams swept the crowd, and the explosion of blue light helped Turner locate the monks and his grandparents and Cassie and James, huddled behind a tall amplifier. "This way," he shouted to them above the continuing squeals of feedback, and motioned with his head toward the trees. "That little shelf of rock by the creek. There's room for us all under there."

But when he looked toward the exit he hesitated. The crowd below the edge of the stage was in a full-blown panic now, pushing and knocking one another down. Policemen were firing pistols into the air, to no effect. Turner heard a grinding of metal and saw that the mob's surge had torn the single loading ramp's bolts loose at the joist. No rolling for Cassie.

He remembered a set of metal steps at the back side, where the electrical hookup was. Less crowded, there. He turned his back to Cassie and squatted. "Hop on," he said. "Grab my neck." His arms made stirrups for her pliant legs, and he jostled her a time or two to get her weight balanced.

"Mattie's barn is closer," his grandfather said. He was wincing, and had both hands pressed to the spot in his side. No wonder Turner's heart's desire hadn't changed a damned thing; the realm was just catching its breath. What an idiot he'd been.

"Okay, we'll try it," Turner told him. "Everybody stay close together."

A frightened shout came from James Crowe: "Look out!"

The hanging tier of lights over the stage was suddenly blotted out by blackness as a giant wing rammed the louvered Tibetan tapestries, toppling them in all directions with a ripping of cloth and metal. Cassie gasped and mashed her forehead into Turner's neck. The cameraman nearest the destruction dove off his platform head-first, but the camera stood intact, its red light still glowing. The huge wings became tangled in the web of lighting grids, and the bird gave an angry shriek as the big quartz bulbs of the grid exploded like popcorn. The rear of the stage was black as pitch.

"Hold the rails tight," Turner shouted to Cordelia and Jackson, at the front of the line. "Feel your way." The bird shrieked louder, and when it freed itself with a ripping of chains the whole web of girders came down through the curtains at exactly the spot where Cassie and Turner, last ones down the steps, had stood seconds before.

But when Turner's racing feet left the solid aluminum of the bottom step and hit the soft clay soil of the hillside, slickened further by that morning's constant rains, he scrambled valiantly to keep his balance and lost. Cassie, astride his back, clutched his neck harder and squealed out as they began to go over.

To his despair the top-heavy weight of him fell as cleanly forward as a cord of wood through the chaotic screaming air, and the one stiffened arm that went out automatically to break their fall skidded ineffectually aside through the slick clay and freed his breastbone to take the full brunt of the ground.

He held his breath instinctually as it struck him—in the confusion of falling the ground seemed to strike *him*—with the force of a broadened projectile, and in the instant that he clenched his eyelids shut, the pain the color of a bruise behind them, he felt Cassie's arms release him and felt, simultaneously, the paralysis of a moment ago command his whole chest. He was a stricken child on a playground again, unable to tell anyone he'd stopped breathing and might die there.

Cass? his mind called out, trying vainly to make his lungs do likewise, *Cass, you all right?* and though he got control enough of his arms to bring his hands shoulder-high, into push-up position, they refused to do more than give him scant leverage to raise his face out of the mud and wet weeds.

As he did, he had two vivid presentiments: that he was suddenly alone, and that when his vision fully returned, all light would have fled from the hillside.

Both of these proved to be true.

24

WHEN HE OPENED his eyes, he could tell no difference from them being shut except for the slightest kiss of barometric coolness against his eyeballs' surface; the total absence of light, blackness solid as cold soot, triggered the old dark terror that had ambushed him in the office building's hallways. Was he unconscious? Dreaming? Or jerked again by the realm into some nether-land between?

He pictured his folks and Cass and James and the monks and Paul, with hell busting loose around them on the night hillside, and he wondered whether they were seeing *him* at this moment or whether he'd once again slipped through a hole in their world, and hoped they would know to forget him and go on, would know that finding shelter was the most . . .

No. Following all his thousand trains of thought at that moment could only lead to confusion and madness, he knew; his one hope lay in living the here and now, wherever the hell *here* was. He sat up in the blackness and rubbed his palms in slow circles across the unseen ground—drier now, and feeling more of sand than clay—so as to keep his bearings about up and down and sideways in the absence of any visual input. He tried every mental technique he had learned at the feet of Won Se for heavy-duty centering, for serious settling, for banishing the panic and readying his best self to do what needed to be done.

He sensed, before he saw it, the reality that began assembling itself around him, pieces growing inward from every until-then-absent horizon with a gradualness more protracted than sunrise, and the more it impinged on the core of nothingness that immediately surrounded him the more his heart sank, because the slanting red shadows were clearly forming the same barren, nocturnal desert that had supplanted the regular world on his first evening back at Zion Hill.

As the dry multifarious winds of the forsaken place began raking his skin, bringing a rush of smells—yeast and decay and an odd animal odor that seemed built around the acid in urine—and the howls and barks of unseen creatures, he took in the crazily rearing towers of rock in the distance, crabbed-looking as crippled hands, and thought *Damn.*

For a moment he had an absurd vision of the realm as some outsized, infernal schoolroom, with lessons you had to repeat and repeat until you got them right or died trying—hadn't he been here already, hadn't he gotten past this desert, for God's sake? Back to square one.

He got up slowly and dusted off his hands, smelling on them the trace of something acrid as stinging nettles, and for some unaccountable reason he called out, "Hello?"

. . . low, low, low, his cry echoed back to him, but except for the briefest lull in the sinister discourse of the far-off animals there was no answer.

In the distance he saw a series of gnarled stone towers, and as he walked toward them he kept glancing over his shoulder, so strong was the sensation of another presence, but nothing showed itself. The distance to the towers seemed strangely altered as he walked it, changing in a way that he could not have explained, except maybe to James Crowe. It was as if his distance-sense assessed it through both ends of a telescope at once, so that he reached the rock both later and sooner than he had anticipated; he somehow grasped that time as he had known it was no longer operational in this place, could not be depended on. Eons could pass in the space of air between two quick finger snaps, and yet a single breath could take decades.

He was so weighted down by this idea that he leaned back against one of the towers of rock to think it through. When his hands came away with a thin, moist film like machine oil, or blood—impossible to tell its color in the red dimness—he smelled of them and determined the film to be the source of the ever-present odor of decay. He was visited by a sudden flashback to the chaos he had so recently left, everything that he loved in full reckless flight, and he felt suddenly more alone and more bereft of hope than at any time in his memory.

He slumped until he was sitting on the ground and tried again to feel Cassie in his mind, had been trying subconsciously ever since the sudden separation, but he couldn't find the barest trace of her and in desperation he let the effort go. The moment he did, though, the sense of someone near him grew so heightened that he recoiled from it, physically, expecting the touch of an unseen hand on his face or neck.

"Hello?" he said, barely more than a whisper.

No answer, except that the churning light at the far horizon took on a slightly different aspect; it still churned, but now its random maelstrom of red shadows seemed to be inwardly coalescing toward some form, like the time-lapse photographs that show a flower blooming.

Turner watched, hypnotized by the sky's strange kinetic logic, as one huge patch of shadow, roughly eye-shaped, was joined by a corresponding one at the same height nearby. The void between them became delineated vertically by a line that could have been a nose. As the whole face took on form and dimensionality it became vaguely recognizable, but it was not until the shut eyes slowly opened—pupils trained on Turner with the directness of radar, an expression of ineffable sorrow—that he let his mind believe what it knew.

Chai Lo.

Turner and the projection confronted each other wordlessly for minutes, centuries, until the familiar heavy-lidded eyes finally blinked. The red clouds pulsed faintly and a dry wind swept the mesa, cool on Turner's face with a sound that could have been a sigh.

"Greetings," the monk's countenance said, via the wind, and though the actual vast mouth was hidden by the curve of the earth Turner could tell from the bunched creases at the corners of the great eyes that Shy was smiling sadly.

The effect was so lifelike, so characteristic of the old-days Shy, his gruff best confidant and the long-suffering dorm parent to their frail, straggling troupe, that Turner overcame his initial shock and spoke to him:

So this is a fringe benefit of going over, huh? You get to fuck with the Hope. Twist the knife a little bit.

The quantity of sheer rage in his voice made it strident and trembly, surprising him on an issue he thought he'd made peace with. Except not *voice*, exactly; though he'd intended to speak, the words seemed to come instead from the core of his mind, the same spot touched by the balm of Cassie's mind when it visited, and there was no echo in the air. Was this new connection, this short-circuit, what was keeping her out?

The effect of his words on the looming half-countenance was as immediate as a blow. The great eyes sagged at the corners, the forehead between them growing so blank it could have let planets, comets, show through but for the obscuring clouds, and Turner knew that the sad conciliatory smile down below had vanished utterly. He even found himself beginning to regret the next thing he said, or thought, but the impulse that propelled it seemed past his control:

How much do they pay, up front? Just curious. I bet it beats the piss out of thirty pieces of silver.

Long seconds passed before Chai Lo's voice said softly, inside Turner, *You are saying this to get hatred out, or do you truly desire to know?*

Turner truly desired. Thought he did, and at the presence of the thought Chai Lo answered sadly, *No silver. No riches of any kind. No lustfulness. No famousness.*

Turner considered this. *You lied, then,* he said. *When you accused Beaver, you were lying about the Chojung . . .*

The face nodded slowly. *You would not have believed the truth,* he said. Turner thought he heard in the voice a flicker of the old Chai—his dry humor, his taste for the ironic—and for an instant, despite himself, he felt a tug of sympathy.

What did they offer you? Turner asked.

The eye-corners slowly bunched with the wrinkles of a smile again. *In a word? Peace,* he said, in a tone that savored its own irony.

Peace, Turner repeated, and Chai Lo's eyes, staring as if at some long-vanished inner scene, let the answer stand. *And you didn't get it.*

The vast head moved slowly side-to-side, indicating "no." Far off, an animal howled.

Where am I? Turner asked him. *Where are* you?

Evidence of the wry smile again. *In this peace,* he said, with mock irritation, raising one eyebrow the slightest degree, his old invitation to debate which Turner recognized from long, headlight-weary nights in the van when the other monks were dozing or in prayer. *I in my peace, you in yours.*

No, Turner insisted, *I mean where is this* place . . . *?* Even while asking, he was impatient with himself for letting this goddamned turncoat engage him in word games; what did it *matter* where he was, or why? He needed to be figuring how to get back to Zion Hill, where all hell was again breaking loose.

In truth, he'd expected better of the realm, had been prepared for them to trot out their finest Grand Guignol horrors for his testing and edification, dragons and ogres and walls of flame. He hadn't expected to keep being dropped off helplessly into other dimensions like an unwanted mongrel puppy forced to find its way home.

He was all set to ignore the huge ruminative face and strike off in search of some cleft or crease through which he might see the real world again, but just as he turned, Chai Lo's unexpected straight answer cut through him from the back like a cold wind:

Do you not recognize your prison? Your own heart?

The denial was at the very roof of his mouth, ready to be spoken, as he entertained the stray thought of wondering whether he appeared at the bleak horizon of Chai Lo's dimension the same as Shy appeared in his—a disembodied half-face of a moon—when he remembered with painful vividness the fleeting dream of the week before. The closet at the heart of the great ruined house, the strange red crystal that was the source of the surrounding desolation.

Impossible. Hadn't he trained to exhaustion in the dim Drepung classrooms, mastering the discernment of inner illusions from outer ones? And yet, Chai Lo's words somehow circumvented all his defenses of logic and touched him at his very core . . . *your prison, your own heart* . . . the way a suddenly indisputable truth will do, sensed by his bones and blood at a speed greater than conscious thought.

The huge heavy-lidded eyes at the horizon averted themselves from seeing the reaction their pronouncement had caused, which made Turner wonder if it were some point of perverse courtesy among torturers. He found himself sunk to a sitting position again, his head in his hands in a kind of trance, watching himself walk with fearful deliberation through the vast forlorn house of the dream toward the icy closet where the crystal rotated, giving off its sad, barren music.

The house, he suddenly knew, represented his life.

The closet (he thought, as the first tears came), his heart.

And the crystal . . .

No. The crystal was the one odd jigsaw-puzzle piece.

The crystal. The source, the seed, of this whole stinking red wasteland. No way, he thought, drying his eyes on his forearms, could this shit be emanating from his own heart. True, he might have been and done a lot of things he was none too proud of, but hadn't he always tried in his heart to do right, be better, serve the good? He *knew* he had. He . . .

A disturbance, real or imagined, pulled him up sharply from the ordeal of his thoughts. He heard, as if at a great distance, the pandemonium of the hillside he had shortly left—the screams, the crashing glass, the groaning of metal.

But when he looked up he saw the dark landscape around him unchanged, except that on the horizon Chai Lo's formerly averted eyes had become intent upon him again, their expression a curious mixture of distance and solicitude.

We must talk, Tur-ner, the air said. Turner ignored him, tried hard to concentrate on the other reality.

What transpired then was a long soft aching of telescoped time, in which the sounds of the distant chaos grew more distinct and the shapes of it solidified enough to become recognizable. The quavery complexion of the air eventually congealed into the form of the exact hillside he had so recently (was it recently?) left, the aftermath of the realm's onslaught obvious everywhere around him in the toppled towers, the fleeing remnants of the crowd, the huge half-seen wings sporadically oaring through the thickened upper reaches of the night sky.

Because Turner was looking about so anxiously for Cassie and the others he didn't at first comprehend that the transformation of the landscape was only partial.

All the familiar features of the gnarled red desert remained in place, showing dimly through the not-quite-solid scene of Zion Hill in much the way one snapshot accidentally double-exposes onto another.

His only relief from the confusion seemed to lie in imagining one of the two planes opaque and whole, and blocking out the other as best he could. He stood and focused with all his might on making Zion Hill the real one, and though it required a dreadful expenditure of mental energy it seemed to be working, because for the first time he was able to fasten his attention on a single face at a time in the droves of running shapes around him.

Just uphill, a knot of bodies that had been huddled for protection in the lee of a broad, squat satellite truck scattered toward him like leaves in a windstorm, and in a second he saw the cause, the squadron of house-sized wings that grazed the tip of the hill before colliding with the truck's roof and bouncing it onto its side, the umbilical cord of electricity ripping loose in a hail of sparks.

There is a legend, Chai Lo's voice began ponderously, seemingly oblivious to the chaos around Turner, *that your own people have preserved, which tells of . . .*

Go to hell, Turner's mind shouted. He was able to mostly shut out Chai's droning sky-voice by concentrating desperately, as he ran, on the remembered sounds of whippoorwills after a rainstorm, the sweet grass of the pasturelands as he'd walk to Cassie's house, Saturdays, through the brilliant morning dew; the spot of ground in the confluence of two hollows where you could pause on a windless-enough prayer meeting night and hear music from both churches at once, the black and the white, *Res-cue the per-r-r-rishing* and *'Way down in my bo-o-ones*; until in the act of willing it to life he had a flash of intuition as to where Cassie and the others might have gone. His churning head showed him a memory of Mattie Sexton's old barn, across the hills a half mile, maybe less, from the spot where the big stage had been set up. *Mattie's barn is closer*, his grandfather had said.

Turner ran on through the turbulent crowd, dodging other runners and occasional automobiles, the panicked drivers wrenching at their steering wheels as the rear tires only dug themselves deeper into the damp clay. When he reached the ridge where the land dropped off in a scoop-shaped hollow of scrub pines he looked hard for the old footpath that led to the Sexton barn.

It was difficult to see; he was at the outmost fringe of light cast from the stage area, where more bulbs were crashing and expiring by the second, and the ridge itself had been outlined for safety with tall aluminum stakes joined by orange tape like an accident scene. Even when he shaded his eyes from the far-off glare he couldn't make out the beginning of the trail.

His ambivalence worked its way into his vision as well, so that when he was on the verge of ducking under the tape and letting his feet take pot luck in the dark undergrowth, his lapse of concentration allowed the hated desert to take form again. The harsh red plain was reborn first around the spot where he stood, and soon enlarged to extend across the valley like a ruined, translucent lake, growing more substantial each second until he knew if he was to leap off into the valley he had to do it . . .

Now, clenching his jaw hard to overcome the reflexive fear of falling face-first against the hard phantom ground, he felt the sand open to admit him like the barest crust of powder before its surface splintered into unreality again.

To his amazement his feet found and followed the vanished woods trail down in the darkness by memory alone, but he had the sure sense that if he stopped and looked over his shoulder he would look straight into the traitor's face again, and whatever crazy legend Chai Lo had been babbling about would resume itself in his mind.

He didn't look back, only ran harder, down, down, as his confidence increased, so energized by the cool night-scents of pine needles and honeysuckle that for a moment he thought he could actually see the textures of the trees and grasses around him in the near-total darkness and . . . no, he really *could* see them; he took it to be a gift of moonlight that had popped suddenly through the low-lying clouds, until he noticed the warm flickering quality of the light.

He looked behind him and saw, at the skyline of the hilltop where he would have expected Chai Lo's expansive gaze, a violent pyre of flame whipping soundlessly at the higher darkness as sirens and, he was sure, gunshots began echoing from the area around it.

It hurt his heart that he couldn't stop any of this, couldn't change it—had other Hopes, in other times, figured ways to head things off before they got this bad?—but he tried to keep his thoughts fixed on finding the people he loved, a goal specific enough to keep him from being jerked back to the stinking desert and the hateful droning of Chai's voice.

He turned and ran with renewed purpose, and with a prayer on his lips that they were all safe.

The flames from the hilltop brightened his overgrown path, so that when it crossed an ankle-deep stream of water and then forked in two, he hesitated for only a moment before seeing that the weeds along the fork that bore west, his right, were subtly flattened and smoothed in that direction as if by the action of some great comb, and he knew it was from the years of passage by Mrs. Sexton's cows heading home to the barn at night.

The right-hand path led down a steep hill, then quickly up another, and though at this distance the light from the fire was much less intense he could see, to his joy, the lopsided shape of the old barn, black against the sky in the company of several tall oak trees.

The sloped earth around the barn was bare of grass, and slickened enough from rain and probably cowshit that he lost traction in it and stumbled, landing on his hands in the muck. But before he could curse it he saw, all around him in the dimness, skeins of slewed footprints, human ones, leading upward toward the barn door, and the rejoicing he felt was almost like a note of music caught in his throat.

It wasn't until he grabbed the old rope door-handle and pulled the door back groaning on its hinges and saw their terrified faces, in the backspilling glow of a flashlight that Paul Zotfeld hurriedly aimed toward him, that he realized he should have knocked, or at least announced his presence before barging in.

But the realization was quickly lost in his joy at seeing them all whole and alive and upright (mostly; his grandfather was stretched out on a pallet of loose hay they'd raked together for him, his head in Cordelia's lap), and he ran toward Cassie, who, bereft of her chair, was sitting with her back against a creosote support pole.

The first he knew something was wrong was when their frightened expressions didn't alter at all, even as he rushed into plain view and the flashlight beam outlined his face. He froze where he stood.

"Who's there?" Cassie shouted, barely containing the panic in her voice. Was she blind? Had something happened to . . .

"It was just the wind blowing the door open," Paul offered hopefully.

Then Turner saw, in his confusion, that Paul and Cassie weren't even looking at him, though the flashlight was still full-bore on his face. None of the others were, either; their eyes followed the beam instead toward the big wooden door which displayed only the quivering soft circle of the handheld light and, impossibly, no shadow of himself whatsoever.

"I thought I . . ." James Crowe said.

"Be quiet," Cassie cut him off, raising her hand. "Everybody be very quiet a minute." She held her breath, Turner saw, and cocked her head forward at an angle for maximum listening, so that her tangled hair hid much of her face. He heard his own heart beating, imagined he could hear hers.

"Cass," he whispered, and took a step toward her, intending to touch her shoulder. But she shrank back from the sound of his footstep on the sawdust, and looked wide-eyed at the spot where he stood.

"Something's in here," she said. "I can hear it."

"Cass, it's me . . ."

In desperation, reasoning more with his heart than his head, he went down on one knee by the post Cassie sat against and reached to take firm hold of both her hands, certain that it was only a matter of getting her attention, making her take note of whatever strange in-between dimensional status he was occupying at the time.

But instead, all these things happened in a seeming flash of the off-kilter elastical time that plagued him in the other place: his hands didn't come to rest on Cassie's hands at all, but rather went through them as if passing through smoke; and though he was obviously invisible to her the transition of a part of himself through herself disturbed enough of her neurons to set off some primal alarm in her brain.

He saw the immediate instinct flash through her, even after all these years of paralysis, to jump to her feet, but its frantic motion died at her waist and, reverberating back upward, served only to destabilize her balance against the post so that she fell away from him in a flurry of arms, a cry caught in her throat.

Bah Tow and Se Hon, who were nearest her, jumped to her aid, looking worriedly in all directions and attempting to step between her and whatever invisible menace had agitated her. But it was clear from the randomness of their glances of concern that they had no fix on his position at all, not even the inchoate sounds from him that Cassie had seemed to be sensing before he tried to touch her.

Turner was dreamily aware of everyone in the barn scattering from their places like a flurry of birds at the disturbance, even his grandfather raising up on one arm to see what was happening. At that point, though, Beh Vah leapt from the peripheral darkness like some avenging angel, holding an ancient manure-shovel above his head like a cudgel.

His rescue of Turner with the sacred brass horn must have given him a taste of the adrenaline rush that comes from solving crises through non-meditative means; whether the direction he swung it now was pure chance, or whether he sensed the position of Cassie's tormentor, the down-and-sideways swing was surprisingly true. Only by dropping quickly to his knees was Turner able to avoid being caught on the shoulder.

But as he glanced up in preparation for ducking another blow, he was struck by the absurdity of what he'd just done. Smoke was smoke, after all. Shouldn't matter as trivial as wood and steel pass cleanly through him with no effect?

Before he could test his premise, though, the shovel's second swing came from his blind side and it was too late to do anything but raise his arms to block the brunt of the blow.

Though the flat of the shovel-blade did pass through his head, the iron was so charged with Beaver's rage at the threat to Cassie that the metal seemed nearly sentient, the sheer intent of its wielder vaulting the molecular canyon between Turner's dimension and its own.

The force of the blade jolted him sideways and raked every hundredth or thousandth atom with a white-hot pain, suffusing his vision with violent auroras of purplish-red light that streaked downward and carried with them his consciousness, so that he was only remotely aware of hitting the sawdust as he fell.

25

A LEGEND OF A man who is given immortality, Chai Lo's huge patient face was saying, his melancholic tone as even as before, as if the events of the past ten minutes hadn't happened, had been a mere hiccup in the broad continuum of time; *but at the cost of his spirit being imprisoned in some remote place . . . a lighthouse, or . . . I can't recall.*

Turner lay in the cold powdery sand, his head propped against the base of one of the gnarled towers of rock; he considered standing, but it would have required more energy than he could summon at the moment.

At the pause in Chai Lo's speech, the monk's inscrutable sad gaze broke from his own and lifted to take in the dark horizon behind him. *His only hope of escape*, Chai Lo went on, *was to find someone who would take his place, there.*

The huge heavy-lidded eyes moved slowly from the far horizon down to Turner, with an expression that seemed to be equal parts overwhelming regret and a touching, incongruous, tenderness.

I am sad to say, the voice went on, sighing, *that is where we stand.*

Turner still felt dazed from his rapid displacement. He looked around the bleak landscape for the least transparent trace of Zion Hill, but saw only sand and red rock. He thought he had been paying attention to Chai Lo's words, but when the voice stopped he found he was unable to make sense of what had been said.

I don't know what you mean, he heard his mind say.

Chai blinked patiently and said, *Only one of us can leave this place.*

Turner considered this.

It is none of . . . Chai began, and paused, considering. *How to say, none of my . . .* doing, *that you and I be so linked, Tur-ner. But since it is done, we had best, ah . . . proceed.*

Turner's temper flared at this. *You're not making a damned bit of sense, Chai*, he snapped. *I was in the very middle of the Calling Out, and if you're the one who keeps jerking me out of it to tell me fairy tales, you're going to have the realm to deal with. Just look in the Books of Chojung, about the penalties for anybody who interferes with . . .*

His outburst caused the slightest change in the complexion of the sky. At the mention of violating the Chojung, Chai Lo looked keenly wounded, as if it were an insult to some remaining remnant of his former holiness. But when he finally spoke, his hurt was replaced by a barely-contained anger:

Don't quote the sacred books to me, *you infidel. You . . . you . . . Chinese in a bull shop. Open your blind eyes. This* is *the Calling Out. What do you think I have been saying?*

The idea was so preposterous that Turner rejected it out of hand, but when his mind cast around for an explanation that made more sense, the net came up empty. With a shocked methodicalness he began to perform the inner ritual that tested for the presence of a demon of untruth. Each test, clear as the ringing of a small glass bell, said no.

Chai Lo's eyes softened somewhat. *I did not ask to become the agent of this*, he said, with a sincerity that Turner never thought to doubt.

Turner offered weakly, *But you said before . . . this was some kind of* prison, *that it was my own . . . heart? That's not what I'm supposed to be doing. That's something new. I'm supposed to be back there fighting for . . .*

Chai looked down with what seemed boundless patience, goodwill, regret.

Nothing new, he said softly. *Same prison for you, always.*

The hell you say. I'd never seen *this place before. And you won't let me talk to any of my people. That's not the way Won Se said it would . . .*

But he suddenly saw in his mind's eye the enigmatic torch-lit face of Won Se in the Drepung basement, answering his naive questions that first evening:

"What will I have to fight?"

"What you most fear. Made worse than in your worst nightmare."

"But what do I fight it *with*?"

"With something you do not have."

Do not have.

Same prison for you, always.

The realization closed around his throat like a gentle hand.

Chai Lo, apparently sensing this new acceptance, intoned, *In Book Six, Lesson Twenty-Eight*, and went on like a minister choosing his text, *we are told, ' . . . so fear you the final day, when you who have labored in such fond disguise shall find your concealing mask rent twain, your true face manifest to all the suns of all the skies . . .'*

Turner had never claimed to be a scholar, but the line sounded so familiar he was certain he'd heard Won Se quote it to the monks on lesson days. And though the exact meaning had always eluded him, some part of him must have grasped its chilling nature, because the remainder spoke itself to him now as clearly as the primal rhymes indigenous to childhood, each word a half-thought ahead of Chai Lo's, their echo resonating in his mind:

'. . . and the tarnish of your impertinent path made plain, so that the merest child by slightest glance knows what the ages know but have forborne to say, till now; the remedy shining as flung stars outside your grasp, your prodigal heart weeping, brought at last to bay.'

Into the immense silence that settled when Chai Lo had finished, Turner asked, *What was* my *fond disguise?*

He pictured all his sins and faults working alive like an anthill in concealment—from causing deaths and pain beyond enumerating in the war, down to the mundane everyday crimes of negligence and omission. But he was unable to imagine which particular one the realm would consider supreme now, to shame him with.

The great eyes let the whole cosmos breathe one time before they answered, straightforwardly and without compunction: *Your fond disguise was acting as if you had loved anyone. You never loved.*

Turner made his mind play the answer back, to be sure he hadn't understood it wrong.

Never *loved?* Bullshit. The prospect was so absurd it made him laugh out loud, until outrage began to kick in. Never loved? Loved too *much*, would be more like it. Ruin half his frigging *life* for love, would be more like it. If Zion Hill Baptist's own version of a devil's hell had nothing worse in store for him than those first weeks alone after Cassie high-tailed it out West—sleepless airless nights of desperation with every stray sound, even the tree-frogs, mocking his misery, *so free out here*, mocking his stupidity for letting her go—then it would be a hell of a hell indeed.

His rage swelled like flames catching in a wind. Never *loved?* What about his mother and father, God rest them; if he hadn't loved *them*, why in hell had the twin black rectangles of their fresh grave-holes loomed just beneath his consciousness for so many years after the accident that waking to his own screams was a regular occurrence? And what about his grandparents? Did *that* love count for nothing, too? Sure, he'd showed his ass with them over the business about Cassie not wanting to see him, but wasn't that just a case of love *versus* love? And hadn't he tried his damnedest to make it up to them over the years? And did they lack for anything if he knew about it, didn't he call every week no matter how busy he was or what godforsaken part of the world his business took to him to, piece-of-shit telephones and screwy time zones no object, for Christ's sake? And what about . . .

About . . .

He was framing a coherent argument to voice to Chai Lo, about how ludicrous the charge was, but Chai's response showed he had already heard.

Are we talking about love, or your selfish pain? You seem to confuse the two.

I'm talking about . . . look, play your damned little word games, Turner said. *I know what I know.*

Chai Lo said *I admire your deviousness. Even* she *is fooled.*

She? Cassie?

A chill, damp wind sprang up, and intensified until Turner had to turn his back to it, shielding his eyes from the waves of grit it propelled across the landscape. It made a desolate sound in the limitless flat space, like a giant's breath blown across the mouth of a jar. Even with his eyes shut, he sensed some of the light going out of the world, and when he made blinders of his hands and looked up he saw the red-edged clouds scudding away one by one, revealing a depth of blackness so black it seemed polished to a gloss.

Let us begin, he heard Chai Lo say, with an odd formality. When he looked toward the part of the sky where the face had been, it was gone.

At that instant he felt the same sensation that he had on the airport runway, the first time Cassie had spoken directly into his mind: a whirlwind roar of murderous static, a tempest so loud it became visual, galaxy-shapes pinwheeling out of control, wildly throwing out colors and textures of violation and loss. But almost immediately, as then, the aural blitzkrieg gave way to the certainty, not altogether unpleasant, that he wasn't alone inside his skin.

Chai?

He was answered only by a diminishing of the external wind, and by an unbidden memory: the bittersweet note of adrenaline and dread that was struck inside him the days of basic training, when he would step into the small box drawn with lime on the training field grass and raise his padded pugil-stick, gripped life-tight in both his hands, to tap his opponent's stick. A salute, and their signal to begin.

Chai? What are we doing? I don't know what to . . .

The other entity's loss of patience exploded across his brain as a sleetstorm of coarse static, shards of purple and red as sharp as fish-hooks. *Fool! How many times must it be said? You have a mind. Use it. Don't trifle with me.*

Turner objected weakly, *I don't under—*

Love her . . . if you can, is your testing, the voice said, through what sounded like gritted teeth. *If you can do this, then I will remain in this place. If you cannot, then you remain, and I am free.* And in a more placatory tone he added, *I did not choose this.*

Love . . . Cassie? Turner said. *But I always have . . .*

The pain storm erased his voice. *Your . . .* true *. . . face manifest!!!* Chai roared, and Turner felt his heart's last defense against the truth cave in, the hot tears disgorge from a depth of wretchedness he had not known he contained.

It's a trick, his mind protested. *It doesn't make sense. Why would the realm give a shit whether anybody loves, or who they love?*

Enough, Chai Lo said.

But what does it matter to them? Turner pressed him.

The realm has a great thirst for worthy adversaries.

I don't understand . . .

You will be shown, if you prevail.

But . . .

ENOUGH!!!

Turner felt suddenly wrenched loose from his moorings in the material world, loose from all particularities of up, down, before, after, and into a void which came increasingly to seem cylinder-shaped and violently spinning, a centrifuge pressing him fiercely against its outward wall.

Then sunlight. Sunlight halfway across the world suddenly, blessedly, falling in a long slow soft healing arc, languorously prismatic in the blue uplifted morning air, across the cool roof of the temple of his want, the aged San Francisco brownstone facade still splotched with the dampness of night. Curtains gypsy-colored at all its windows, delectably unguarded as children's eyes, red yellow black white precious in his sight. Him going dreamfooted up the ancient cawing stairs to find her bang bang bang and nothing bang and nothing but the senile old man babbling toward the skyblue door with the single silver star and bang bang and nothing nothing

Nothing but him waiting praying eyes on the brownstone temple front until he prays her there still his world his oxygen and her heldback tears freed showering like blessings onto his parched want his fossil bakedblack soul unlimbering and hallelujah healed him rising to follow her hand to the lofty room and no

No

No respite from the stench of the defilement there the threads of the carpet the paint-flaked sills screeching it pinks of her castdown eyes swimming with it was war again war *guy I'm living with reminds me so much of you* and how many more for her none like nothing like himself goddamned how many more *reminds me* how HOW reminds *HOW?* could she see smell these ruins of what they could have had and feel anything of him nothing of him here but other other other how many other how

Are you stoned?

the familiar tragic downward plunge now effortless out of his hands already done the lines he speaks decided for him by the thundering immensity of his chokedback love the course of his life already decided except

Except that something like strong wings beats in him, a fluttering of spirit along the wedges of his back like a long-caged being who has scented the light and swells toward freedom.

Chai? he says.

The motion stops.

The scene before him freezes, and the knowledge is glacial in him of all he stands to lose. Yet no other outcome is possible, no path but from here to here. The object of his love at last before him, but her betrayal making warbones of rage assemble inside him until he becomes aware that something has stayed Chai's preparation for escape. What?

In this brief caesura of time Turner searches even more desperately the corroded circuits of his heart for other possible endings to the sordid passion play but only a single other looms, deeper and broader and more fearsome as his eyes avoid her face and alight instead on the cerulean starfield, her curtain of stars, *their* stars. As he watches, it becomes the terrifying painting on their Sunday School wall: a crucified Christ with Crayola-bright wounds against godforsaken midnight dark with piercing stars, and he thinks he could do this for her sake. Could have his hands pegged lovetight to the cross's wood by replicas in sharpened iron of each of her how many lovers, his white want forever defiled but him willing for her sake her sake a life of this with her.

The escaping mass of flesh inside his flesh remains stilled by his offer of selfless sacrifice, a sacrifice he is so willing to make that Chai's question when it comes is almost drowned out by his own thrumming heart; Chai's voice a loving touch, the words like a hand cooling a fever

You have chosen, then?

The scene before him still frozen, Turner's heart is on the threshold of assent when the blueskystars commence quivering in his vision through no doing of his own, as if some interfering wave of energy is at large in the room. But it has no sound to trace it by, no source that he can discern, and he is ready to dismiss it as an aberration of the realm and commit to the answer, commit his life, love her the way he should have done before.

Until he hears the song. Faint, but so distinct . . .

Imagine me 'n you . . .

a sound as sheer as raindrops on a sheet of mica, sound he thinks at first is from a radio left on, turned low, but when he sees the face of her bedside radio dark and unpowered (the half-filled bottles of pills on the table, white powdered mirror, cigarette butts with no lipstick, nails in his heart)

'n you 'n me . . .

he casts around for other sources of the song and, failing, grasps that the words are directionless, lodged inside his deepest mind by the will of . . . who?

Chai growing impatient, obviously not hearing the song, the least edge of steel now in his repeated soft question *You have chosen, then?*

And the song with no music, just urgent voice, not the whole song but the one phrase ending each time and repeating with quickening exigency and him realizing the one place he has not looked for it is in the eyes before him, Cassie's ruined eyes. When he looks at her he knows by their intensity, the galaxies of light contained behind the ruin, that the voice is hers and meant for him.

Imagine me . . .

And for the first time of the thousand times he's heard it he hears the words a different way, Imagine me *in* you and you *in* me, and though he doesn't know why (wind whipping the sunbright curtain of stars beyond) the fact that he's heard makes her greengold eyes kindle like emeralds lit from within, saying *Yes.*

You have chosen then? Chai demands to know.

Turner hesitating on what the words of the song might mean, might have to do with eyes, with stars, with anything.

Until, out of the vast awful void of possibilities comes a grace-gift and he thinks *eyes.*

He is filled then with a curiosity more intense than lust, to know what *her* eyes see, what the world looks like to her, what it looked like back then. What *he* looked like to her eyes. Unthinkable to him, suddenly, that he had never wondered this.

. . . talking about love or about your selfish pain you seem to confuse the two . . .

The fact that he wonders it now begins quaking everything, the curtain of wild sun reverberating off the fabric of time until she is two, the two one image, her broken her unbroken combined, and always eyes her eyes the constant

You have chosen, then?

No, Turner answers, I'm trying *this* now . . . trying . . . heart coming down off the cross to live behind her greengold eyes for once in time

Imagine me . . .

the effort requiring such exertion of heart, mind, imagination that for a moment he sees the monks too, arrayed around her in the light-troubled room as they were in the darkened barn, transparent but gradually solidifying, the present and the past as one one one

One last chance which he takes by seizing softly his own whole prodigal will and willing it to hover in the temple sanctum light behind her eyes, closing his own so as better to see

CHOOSE!!!

himself seen through her inflamed wet eyes, the officious drab green of his dress uniform a blight in the room of sun, his raw scalp through buzzed-away hair, pale face self-righteous with all he's seen and survived. Furious at the world for being the world, furious at her for being her, no room for another life in his eyes, himself so under siege his hands could rise at any point and strike her

No, NO! his heart shouts. Not true!

but the evidence clearly there, the quivering of his hands making and unmaking fists. Still no fear in her, just grief and a terrifying want of him, her pride so ravaged by his refusal to say the simple word *stay* that drove her here so far from home and famished for him, finding pieces of him in other eyes other hands, illusory but too late to undo too late . . .

He undoes his fists and holds his hands out to her, his only offering, the world a distant ringing of temple bells, the bright room drawing into the dark ascendant barn, the here and now a roar of poised silence as he becomes real to her and the people around her, his name in everyone's throat about to be spoken and Cassie of the now and real not clenching at his hands but rather offering her own hands spread free

spiders

and the touching of their fingers a wellspring of two visions

himself herself

join

become

one thought whole thought bountiful thought . . .

The company of the others in the barn moving to greet him but stopping instinctively now at the boundaries of the unseen circle enclosing him and Cassie in the sawdust. For the space of a breath the barn is quiet as thought.

Then comes a noise like a grinding collision of metal on metal, destruction bred in a medium of thunder—the clashing and unclashing of titanic gearwheels heard at so great a remove that the sound might have come from the cosmos' very core; the torque of the dissension deepens and swells until its vibration spreads upward in a quaking wave through Turner's feet, legs, chest, but when he looks to the others' faces for answer it's plain they aren't hearing it.

Only himself, hearing it. And then he knows.

The cataclysm, having reached its crescendo, began echoing away, the silence settling like a soft web. He listened for the next he was sure to hear, the music so much purer than music that it can never have a name, and felt the balm of knowing that his deepest heart's desire was at that moment being interjected among the paths of atoms, inserted into the workings of the world.

But what he heard instead was a cry of such pain and desperation that it tore at his heart, all the more because it came from deep within himself.

He knew then that it was Chai surrendering to the outcome of the struggle, his one chance for freedom ended. And though his fate was short of death, Turner had never heard more plaintive death-throes in all his jungle nightmares. Fierce spasms wracked the region of his back where, so shortly before, the restless presence had been ready to ascend. Then the disturbance gradually lessened to an expiring ghost of itself, small soundless whimpers of resistance coming farther and farther apart until Turner could envision Chai Lo disappearing into whatever private void was to be his fate.

But at the final instant the Other revived again, the same surprising superhuman last gasp whose memory would always live in Turner's thumbs after his first kill, hand-to-hand.

This time the wrenching was so violent he felt himself lose his balance and topple backwards, stunned, the warm stamp of Cassie's fingertips still fresh on his own. The commotion of running bodies, their hands extended to help him up, distracted him for a moment from the clouded shadow-shape that had materialized, he saw now, in the air just above him.

The shape rapidly heightened and broadened, still the consistency of smoke but definitely bearing the outraged weeping face of Chai Lo. Then, just as rapidly, the cloud transformed itself into flesh, actual and opaque, its surfaces working alive with dark electricity.

Most fearsome of all was the look in his eyes of absolute intent, coldly businesslike and unalloyed by any empathy or restraint—a look Turner recognized at once, having so many times faced enemies one on one as each made a last stand for his own small life.

Chai's manifestation had been so sudden as to have the effect of paralyzing everyone present with disbelief for crucial seconds, time in which the dark-encrusted shape looked frantically around for some weapon other than his bare hands.

A broad old pitchfork stood against a creosote post nearby, half hidden by bales of hay. Chai's shaking hands seized on it like a drowning man grabbing a thrown rope. He spun in the close pungent dimness with an almost supernatural speed and gained a choked grip on the handle just above the wide-spaced iron tines. The metal became immediately imbued with his own crackling darkness, and he lunged with it toward Turner's half-prone self.

Nearest the charging shape were James Crowe and Lu Weh, and though they managed to shake off their astonishment in time to dive and block him, Louie ahold of his leg and James Crowe shouldering hard into his lowermost clenched arm, the impediment they represented was only enough to slow Chai's inevitable deadly fall, not stop him.

Turner's body jerked fiercely to roll itself free of the prongs' urgent downward arc, even while his mind maintained sufficient detachment to realize the effort would not be enough, not quite enough, the virulent intent behind the fork even now adjusting its course by degrees in midfall toward his heart that swelled with a disengagement as crystalline as grief.

The clamor and confusion of the other monks rushing to his aid, powered by a high keening scream he realized was his grandmother's, seemed to take centuries of this truncated time. The only swift thing in his whole field of view was a sudden streak the color of goldenrod whose full-voiced yell identified it as Beh Vah, the shovel so recently used against the menace of an unseen Turner now held aloft and beginning its downward swing toward the grappling mass of men with Chai at its center.

Despite the pandemonium Turner saw, sensed, knew, that the avenging shovel's aim on Chai Lo's skull was true, exquisitely true.

Was. Would have been.

But at the very last instant the small yellow-sock-clad foot, planted so righteously on the floor of the barn at the precise point for maximum momentum of his crude weapon, encountered a surface of loose sawdust which hid a hole in the ground beneath it.

His ankle thus entrapped, not only did the shovel fall short of its mark, harmlessly grazing Chai's right ribcage, but Beh Vah's achieved speed was now turned against him, twisting him half around toward Turner, a look of confoundment on his face.

A cry scalded Turner's throat—"Beaver! *No!!!*"—as the boy toppled toward him, his arms waving for balance. His weight, when it hit Turner's chest, was not painful at all, but rather like a child's, or a woman playful in passion. But even as Turner struggled

"No-o-o!!!"

to roll with the awkward embrace of the frail mass scant inches right or left he could see beyond the trembling saffron shoulder the rocketing black tines, end-on and inescapable.

Turner, straining to his utmost but knowing in his skin it was too late, closed his eyes. When the thrust came it wasn't a thrust at first, but a dull explosion against his shoulders like a block in football. The shock transmitted two small daggers of pain into either side of his right breast. He felt the layer of muscle just under the skin separate to admit the tines. His eyes flew open and he cried out as one of the points chipped into a rib and then withdrew.

James and Lu Weh stepped suddenly back in surprise as the shape of Chai Lo, seconds before so vivid in its electrical darkness, seemed slowly to implode upon itself and crumple forward, with a sound like infinite sadness made aural across dimensions, until all that remained was an insubstantial husk, compressed and blackened as a burnt rag that a wind could carry away, his long imprisonment begun.

Meanwhile all the tension went instantly out of Beh Vah, who had taken the brunt of the impaling; his small head sank forward and came to rest against Turner's cheek. He'd made no sound but a startled intake of air.

Simultaneous with the warm rush of the boy's blood across Turner's midsection he felt half-delirious, seemed ministered to by a hundred hands. They helped roll Beh Vah off of him, and laid the still form on its back in the sawdust and straw like a child they were trying not to waken. The shouts had transformed into weeping.

Turner knelt and, for some inexplicable reason, felt the need to touch Beh Vah's forehead. When he reached toward it, the stabbing pain of his own wounds seized his arm; he drew it slowly back, nursing it against the patches of blood on his shirt, and used his other hand. He was aware of Paul somewhere shouting into the portable phone for an ambulance. He started to tell him it was no use, but he let it go.

Beaver's skin was warm as life. His mouth, which had been slightly open as if in preparation to speak, was gradually closing in resignation. The violent abstraction of red across the front of his robe darkened slowly as it dried into the air.

Turner felt Cassie enter his mind an instant before he felt her arms close around him from behind. The probing of her consciousness stung him, like a fingertip in a raw wound. So much. So much, he'd seen. She seemed to sense this and withdrew, to wait for healing.

Lu Weh, obedient to some ancient protocol as eldest, sat down beside Beaver's still form and took its hand. The remaining monks efficiently arrayed themselves around him on the ground, hands linked, and they began with one voice a somber prayer that was, Turner divined, equal parts grief and thanksgiving, at having come this far.

Soon his grandparents joined their circle, and Paul and James, each praying in his own way to his own source of comfort.

Turner couldn't bring himself to join them. A seemingly bottomless well of hot hate and bitterness had begun rising in him, like bilge in a leaking boat, at the appalling and immense injustice of it all.

And awash in the vile tide were a thousand barbed indictments of himself, *if only, if only*, and at least as many memories of Beh Vah in happier times—sprinting late into a sober gathering of monks with his hair still wet from a swim in the lake, or cartwheeling across a boundless Kansas lawn on the afternoon the dark cloud had first come—all of which unfortunately kept being eclipsed, would always be, by the scene in the accursed motel room, Chai's accusations and the scrap of towel and Beaver's tearful *Det det det* and Turner, to his shame, half believing the worst.

None of which he was able to voice to Cassie now, his throat tightening in refusal each time he tried, her soft listening spirit as absent from his mind as life from a mausoleum—one more grief in a hierarchy of griefs which he could not bear to address.

"It's over," she whispered in his ear, as if finality were the only comfort that existed outside prayer. Around them, the circle of subdued voices were finishing the ritual conversations with their higher powers and, interspersed with much sighing and blowing of noses and patting of shoulders and hands, turned to one another to express, however haltingly, the ineffable sorrow that they felt.

What Turner said to Cassie at this point shamed him when he heard his tone, petulant as a spoiled child and irrelevant to all that had just transpired:

"Won Se said there'd be music, if we won. I don't hear any damned music."

. . . music so much sweeter than music . . .

Cassie breathed against his neck.

"I hear it," she said. "Listen . . ."

Turner strained his ears but did not, and only when he *quit* straining did he become aware that the hellish cacophonies from the surrounding hillsides had all ceased, the riots of cries and explosions and fatal sirens and the screeching of distant wings all superseded by a vast canyon of holy silence, the barn and themselves safe in the lee at the very center of its enveloping bowl.

From a corner came a cow's measured stamping and low complaint. From the circle around Turner came the voices of the people he loved, individual and irreplaceable—his grandfather's rasping baritone underpinning all the other sound, his grandmother's crisp tenor like stars sprinkled above it. His own and Cassie's separate quiet breathing.

. . . so much sweeter than music that it can never have a name . . .

"I hear it," he said.

26

AT FOUR THE NEXT morning, the trucks were all still in the yard. Turner pulled aside the curtain of the living room window and saw the long row of cream-colored satellite dishes still bordering the moonlit front lawn like an occupying army.

The reporters had at least had the courtesy to quit knocking on the door after one a.m. But they still milled in the yard with their cameramen and technicians, drinking coffee from styrofoam cups in the islands of halogen light where they did their hourly standup reports, gesturing somberly back toward the house as they spoke.

"I don't get it," Turner said to Cassie. "What the hell could they want now?"

She shook her head.

It was Zotfeld who answered, from the far corner of the room where he paced the floor, nervously taking off his glasses to polish them every few minutes as though forgetting he'd just done so.

"They want statements," he said. He sounded embarrassed, apologetic for his breed.

"I *gave* them a goddamned statement," Turner said. "They think something's changed in, what, three hours?"

The air smelled of candle oil and incense, and the soft cadences of a prayer in Tibetan drifted occasionally from Turner's old bedroom where the monks held their vigil around Beh Vah, waiting for dawn and the ceremony.

"Television's ravenous," Zotfeld said, walking into the light of the door. Without his glasses his small naked eyes showed the ordeal the night had been; he looked crazed, desperate for solace. "They'll be updating for days, unless something else breaks. An earthquake, or if the president gets shot."

They pondered this in silence.

Zotfeld said, "Listen. If there's anything I can do . . ."

Finally Cassie wheeled over to him. "Paul," she said, "have you ever wanted to be a press secretary?"

He hurriedly put his glasses on and looked at her in bewilderment. "Have I . . . *what*? Uh, not that I know of. Why do you ask?"

"We're going to slip out back in an hour or so, and we'll need some privacy. Could you distract them for us? Go out and give them a rehash, whatever. Make something up."

He took a minute to think, paced one circuit of the room wringing his hands before stopping to nod at her. "Yeah. I guess I can do that."

She patted his arm. "Wonderful. We owe you one, Paul."

Pots rattled in the kitchen, cupboard doors closed. Turner went to see who was there, though he should have guessed.

Cordelia, starting breakfast. Her hands were white with biscuit flour. "It's a long walk up there," she explained. "Y'all need to eat first."

He started to object but thought better of it, and just nodded. Jackson sat in the old cane-bottom chair by the window, holding his coffee cup in both hands and looking out at the dark. He had his work clothes on.

"I found what-all things I could," Jackson said. "See if you think they'll do." He blew on his coffee and looked up at Turner. "I'm going with you."

"You don't have to," Turner said. "You need to get your strength back first."

"I've got it back," he said. "I want to."

Turner went over to examine the tools laid out by the back door on a burlap sack. Two hatchets, a small one and a bigger one. Several long knives, most with teeth. Their wooden handles were a blotched mahogany color, stained that way from long years of butchering hogs and goats. A wave of fear rose up through Turner, not just at what they had to do, but something older, darker. The times he had watched animals go down, the bleat and the bright necklace of blood.

He forced the fear downward. "These'll do fine," he said. He patted Jackson on the shoulder. The black sky out the window was lightening the least perceptible bit, rotating slowly toward dawn.

He walked through the dark hallway and stood at the door of the candle-lit bedroom. Soft prayer went on without ceasing, and fine skeins of smoke from the incense moved throughout the room like something with life, with intelligence; one would drift sideways toward a flame and then, caught in the upward vortex of heat, turn itself inside out and become the shape of a flower, or a hawk, or a woman's hair, before returning to featurelessness and drifting off toward the slowly brightening window. Even with the scattered fresh flowers that surrounded him, Beh Vah's shape looked impossibly small on the big white bedspread.

Turner had earlier asked Lu Weh's advice, him having a seniority of sorts, on whether the sky burial shouldn't wait and take place back in Tibet, Beh Vah's home. The concept had seemed strange and frivolous to Louie. "Is only one sky," he answered, and the other monks, when it was put to a vote, agreed.

"Cap'n?" a voice whispered. James Crowe, behind him in the hall. "I need to see you."

They went to the back porch and sat in the swing. By the reflected light from the kitchen window, Turner could see that Crowe's eyes were wet. His face looked to be in torment, as if something were crushing the life out of him from inside.

Twice Crowe opened his mouth to begin, but words failed him. He put his head down in his hands. "I messed up, Cap'n. I messed up bad."

"How? What do you mean?"

"You know that time when I . . . and it wouldn't . . . I mean, I just now . . ."

James made himself get a breath and start again. "I just now did the numbers again, from when . . . the last time I tried the supervention, and there wasn't one? And I figured I'd used up two, when it bifurcated?"

"Right," Turner said.

"Well, I . . ." His fist pounded the arm of the swing. "God*damn* it. I messed up again. I got in a hurry. It *wasn't* used up, it was the *numbers* wrong. The place in the function where I needed the two primes, I . . ."

"Wait, wait," Turner said. "Let me get this. You're saying you *do* have one left, after all?"

Crowe nodded sadly.

The wild hope that flashed through Turner then must have shown in his eyes, because Crowe immediately put a damper on it.

"A supervention can't raise no one, Cap'n," he said, gesturing toward the far bedroom with his head. "Can't but Jesus do that, and they killed him. See, the thing is, though . . ."

He choked again, and this time his fist took its frustration out on himself, hitting his leg so hard the swing shook. "Damn it, I could have stopped it *happening*. That's the part that eats at me."

"But you don't *know* that," Turner said. "Maybe you could, maybe you couldn't. Sometimes a thing's meant to be. Don't torment yourself." He looked out at the nascent gray sky. "We all could do that, all the time, if we let ourselves. Who *wouldn't* want the whole thing to do over again? But what's the good of dwelling on it?"

Crowe sat in silence a minute before he whispered, "Lord, I loved that little booger."

"I did too, James."

Cordelia was calling them to the kitchen.

THE SUN CAME up a pure platinum white, and the air over the rock was so bright it was blinding. Se Hon and Wah So carried the rolled sheet between them, one holding the head and the other the feet, and when they laid it down and folded it back, several of the flowers inside fell out, violently colorful against the dull sandstone.

In his golden nakedness, anointed throughout the night with oils and herbs, Beh Vah looked like something made of fine, burnished wood. His eyelashes, always as long and black as a girl's, seemed to have grown even more in death. The wounds across the front of his chest where the fork had exited seemed in this exaggerated bleach of light a row of harmless scratches, made absurdly small by the emollients of the night.

The light intensified as the sun raised in almost visible increments. It burned Turner's eyes, made them water. When his mind wandered back from staring at Beh Vah, he noticed, almost with a start, the burlap bag that Jackson had lowered to the ground alongside Cassie's chair.

What needed doing seemed foreign as the moon. The one burial ceremony he'd helped with at Drepung had been done in a swirl of purifying snow, and the man had been very old, in pain until the last, his joints obscenely gnarled by arthritis, so that dissembling him seemed almost a kindness. Turner saw the falling snow again, Won Se's chiding stare, at him and at the unused knife. *You loved him, too.*

But this was different. This was . . .

Turner cleared his throat. "Who's done this?" he said, and when he heard his tone of voice it sounded as if he were accusing them of the death. "Who's done this . . . *before*, I mean?" he amended.

Amazingly, none of the monks had. Lu Weh and Bah Tow had each witnessed one, they said, but it was long ago when they were children and they had stood off to the side throughout, knowing their place.

When Jackson spoke it was in his new, strengthened voice. "I've, uh . . . you know." He hated to say *butchered hogs.* "I guess it's a little the same." With his thumb he carefully flicked away the single drop of wetness at the outer corner of his eye.

"Turner," Cassie said. There was an urgency in her voice and she held her hand half up, her eyes shut tight in concentration. "There's . . . something. Won Se is . . . it's too garbled to make out exactly, but it's him."

Turner knelt by her chair, waited for more. After long seconds there was a sudden brisk unease in the layer of air around them. It shimmered and then grew hollow and the familiar tweak of sound was heard, at the place on the stone where Won Se materialized.

He wore a somber expression and, as the discipline of the travel required, was totally naked. He blinked, allowing his atoms to acclimate to their new state, and when he looked around him and saw Cassie he covered his crotch with his hands and nodded politely.

The monks were all on him in a bunch, hugging and slapping, but he couldn't give them his full attention. He scanned the ground around him, and when his eye fell on the burlap sack he walked over to it, hands still strategically in place, and whispered in Jackson's ear.

Jackson nodded, then squatted down and emptied the sack of its implements. He used one of them, a good serrated knife, to coax two holes in the seam of the burlap. He handed it up to Won Se, who thanked him and faced the other way with calm gentility while he put his legs through the holes and wadded the excess of the sack at his waist, a coarse brown diaper.

This done, he faced the group again and held out his arms. Cassie wheeled to him first, and they whispered to each other in Tibetan while they hugged. Turner introduced him to James and Jackson, and then received his own hug, long and firm and wordless, before Won Se made the rounds of the monks again, and said a few words to each one.

Then Won Se went to the place where Beh Vah lay. He knelt beside him with visible difficulty, because of the stiffness in his knees. He touched Beaver's hair first, then held one of his shoulders for what seemed a minute or more, all the while saying something in a low voice that Turner couldn't hear because a warm steady wind had sprung up from the west, the direction of storms, though there wasn't a cloud in the sky.

Finally Won Se looked up at the group and said, with the authority of someone long practiced at presiding, "We may begin."

Jackson handed the implements around; Cassie wheeled herself as close to the sheet as she could and asked for Turner and James to each take hold under her arm and set her down with them on the rock. When Jackson passed the tools, she took one.

As they set to work, the only person who still stood back was James Crowe. With the knife in his hand he squinted toward the sun, his face struggling with itself. But when he looked down toward the work, Won Se gave him the briefest of glances, the same one Turner remembered from years before, at his first sky burial.

You loved him, too.

And James Crowe, reading Won Se's meaning, knelt down and began.

"I remember," Won Se said, "once, when he was nine, he . . ."

And that was the way the morning passed, stories back and forth. When it came Lu Weh's turn he told about the day when Beaver, playing hooky from his prayers, got chased by a villager's stray goat in the gardens. Won Se threw back his head and laughed—a clean, ringing laugh—and when Turner shut his eyes he could half believe he was back in the big stone dining room on festival day, listening to stories in the endless yellow sunshine.

27

AT DAWN THE airport in Atlanta was covered by a layer of gauzy gray cloud, but the old airliner soon rose above it and before long the view out the windows was pure blue sky, horizon to horizon, and the blue-green Atlantic below.

Turner had gotten window seats for all the monks, as he'd done on the flight over. Now, as then, they sat with their foreheads against the glass, hypnotized by the immensity of the world.

His own attention was on the infinite number of ways Cassie's fingers could interleave with his own on the chrome armrest.

"Feels strange," she said, after a while. "Like coming home to a place I've never been."

"It *is* home," he told her. "You'll love it. Once you get used to the air being thinner. You just *think* you've seen stars, until you see them from the mountain."

A tug on his sleeve. James Crowe, from across the aisle. "Cap'n?" He wore a look of amusement, and pointed toward the front of the plane.

A line of people was forming, each of them holding a notebook or a napkin and waiting their turn for an autograph; the line began with Lu Weh in the frontmost seat and was working gradually toward Turner and the other monks. Lu Weh glanced back at Turner in tolerant confusion before resuming signing his name and shaking hands with the row of admirers.

"Oh, Lord," Turner said. "I keep forgetting they're celebrities now."

Cassie laid her head on his shoulder. "The power of television," she said. "Oh, well. It'll be over for them soon. They're almost home. I know it's hell on their meditation, when people won't leave them alone."

THE WHOLE DRIVE out to Drepung from Lhasa the monks got more and more excitable, anticipating the familiar landscape, until they were bouncing and singing in the back of the station wagon like kids on the way to camp. It lifted Turner's heart, because they hadn't felt like singing in weeks; but now even James joined in on the chorus of a song he knew, and while Turner was absentmindedly trying to figure out what else was different about the song, the fact struck him like a fist in the stomach that what he was hearing was the absence of Beh Vah's clean, reverent tenor.

For the first time during the trip he was almost glad his grandparents had backed out on their plans to come along. He missed them, but he was not in need of any more emotional baggage to deal with right now.

"Is it like you thought?" he asked Cassie, referring to the land—all blue sky and black volcanic stone and crystalline lakes, desolate as some uninhabited planet except for rare surprising sprinklings of yellow or blue wildflowers along the roadside and an occasional small pasture of beige grass where yaks grazed. "I forget, though," he said. "You've seen it through Won Se for so long."

"His eyesight's not that good," Cassie said. "I had some idea. But this is wonderful."

Their route led up, always up, for nearly two hours, the paved roads having long disappeared and the station wagon's tires leaving a cloud of gray dust in their wake. Twice he topped a rise and swerved to miss yaks standing in the road. He had to keep swallowing to let his ears pop as the air thinned.

The countryside was looking increasingly familiar when Se Hon leaned up front, between songs, and pointed out a side road that led to the community where his parents lived. Around the next curve the jagged horizon began to even out; on either side of the road were identical blue lakes, with slender white waterfowl swimming in the sunlight.

A lump rose in Turner's throat when he remembered how the lakes had looked in cold moonlight with fog rising off them when he would walk back to Drepung after a midnight ramble, the stars so bright they almost gave off warmth.

Over the next rise was the monastery. He wanted to prepare Cassie for the sight, but his throat wouldn't cooperate and he settled instead for squeezing her hand.

The top row of windows showed themselves first: glaring diamonds in the lowering sun, set into the craggy tan stone of the masonry. As they approached the crest of the rise, story after story of the huge rambling building was gradually revealed, and the gardens at its base, and the curving stone steps cut into the sheer hillside, at the bottom of which sat . . .

"Oh, shit," Turner said. "No."

A forest of white trucks with satellite dishes ringed the base of the steps, and as he got closer Turner could make out the milling reporters with their ever-present styrofoam coffee cups.

"Shit, shit, shit." He turned to the back seats. "Guys, get down, please. Just crouch low for a minute."

He gunned the gas and kept going, past the turn to the monastery, until the road rose and dipped again and the big gleaming dishes no longer showed in the rear view mirror. He slowed then, and drove downhill into the village, deep in thought. Nobody spoke until he pulled over into the side yard of Nohr Bu's market and cut the motor.

"How could they have known we were coming?" Cassie said to the windshield.

Turner shook his head. "Contacts. Spies. Hell, it's their business to know. I should have . . ." But the thought trailed off there. He couldn't think of what he should have done differently.

A young woman in a dress of yak hide came out of the market with a bundle of groceries under her arm, leading a child who gnawed at a long stick of red candy. But they faded in Turner's sight as he imagined the scene back at the monastery. Reporters and producers roaming the halls of the great stone building asking endless questions and pointing out oddities to one another, flashing quartz spotlights into the midst of evening prayers to raise the light level enough for video. No locks or fences to keep them out. Even if there were, the monks would be too polite to use them. And this contingent from the world would be only the beginning.

Turner leaned his forehead against the steering wheel and thought, or prayed, for a long time. When he finally looked up, he said, "James."

"Yes, Cap'n?"

"Blot it out."

"Beg pardon, Cap'n?"

"All the things we did. Blot them out of everybody's memories, please. Everybody's but ours. Like you did for Louie, that time. Use your last supervention to blot it all out."

James pondered this doubtfully.

"I don't know if that's good," Cassie said to Turner. "If the world forgets . . ."

"They'll forget anyway," he said. "Eventually. People always have. Their hearts get lazy, and things go back to the way they were. That's why they keep needing Hopes."

"It could happen *sooner*, though, couldn't it? If we just let it all disappear?"

She looked out the side window in the direction that they had come, at the hill the monastery lay beyond. She must have been picturing the same incursions of the television hordes that he had pictured, just now, because when she looked at him again most of the resistance had gone out of her face.

"What else can we do?" Turner asked. Nobody answered; not Cassie, or James, or the monks.

Finally Cassie sighed. Then she nodded, and looked out the window again.

Nohr Bu came out the door of his shop carrying a broom. The apron he wore was stained across the belly. After he finished sweeping the stone front stoop he stood for a minute, looking up at the weather. He never noticed the station wagon, and by the time James Crowe began punching numbers into his calculator Nohr Bu had gone back inside.

The only person in the world who noticed when the car and the gravel around it began pulsating in colors like neon was the little boy with his mother, far down the path to the village by now, when he chanced to look back over his shoulder. Living alongside a community of holy men day to day, men whose spiritual exploits were often far more colorful than this, he paid the phenomenon no more notice than he would a passing bird.

By the time James Crowe's deed was finished and the thunderclap of light radiated out into the world, the boy's attention had returned to his diminishing stick of candy. The two walking shapes grew very small and disappeared over the top of a hill.

On the drive back up to the monastery the monks began a new song, but it was one that only they knew. When the huge old stone building came in sight again, with the fringe of incongruous white dish-trucks at its base, Cassie said quietly, "It all needs to be written down, at least."

Turner asked, "What does?"

"*This*," she said, her voice breaking. "All of this. It can't just be like it never happened."

Turner shook his head. "Who'd believe it? It'd never sell. Too many holes."

"Holes?"

"Weird stuff. Coincidences."

"Like what?"

"Well, just for starters, two Hopes from the same little town in Alabama? Nobody'd believe that."

"You might be surprised," she said, ever the optimist.

Turner parked at the base of the steps, and several of the men milling around the satellite trucks began walking over.

He squeezed Cassie's knee. "It's something to think about," he said.

The first reporter to the car was a middle-aged man in a khaki shirt and matching beret. He nodded to Turner and touched the edge of his cap.

"Afternoon, sah," he said, in a British accent. "We're, er . . . a bit lost, I suppose." The men behind him had sheepish grins. He went on, "I don't know what happened, really. I suppose we were looking for, er . . ."

He turned to the crowd for prompting. "Beijing," a man with a coffee cup said, with shaky assurance. "You know. Where they're having the . . ."

James Crowe hopped out of the car to take charge. "Student unrest," he supplied. "Sure."

The crowd of reporters nodded eagerly.

"Lord, have mercy," Crowe said, with his best public-relations smile. "You fellows are way, *way* off . . ."

He got out a piece of paper and started drawing them a map.

THE DINING HALL that night was a festival of candles, more quavering orange dots of yak-butter light than Turner had ever seen in one place before. A huge tarpaulin of a tapestry, gods and demons and unknowable symbols ornate with fine gold thread, was retrieved from some dark recess of the basement and hung to cover almost the whole western wall of the big stone room.

There were homecoming prayers and homecoming speeches and homecoming toasts with small stone cups of the frothy, honey-tasting drink that had six different names, depending on who praised it. At midnight the festivities were still going strong; the newer initiates to the order, especially, were so invigorated by the nightlong respite from their ancient routine of sleep and meditation and prayer that they were almost manic with insight and love. From time to time Turner would glance down the long stone table and see Lu Weh or Wah So or Se Hon or Bah Tow disappear completely inside a knot of well-wishers, awash in hugs and questions and laughter.

Somewhere around eleven-thirty James Crowe had excused himself to go check out a theory that suddenly crystallized for him after his third cup of the six-named drink; namely that the geometry of the ancient building's architecture, with its circular promenades and their spoke-like corridors connecting in a different pattern on each floor, was not the random assemblage it seemed but rather was based on an inverse factoring of the cosines of phases of the moon.

As the night wore on, the sounds and smells and flickering motions of the room seemed to Turner to rise in level gradually upward from the floor like an incoming tide of invisible heart-balm, and he finally sank back on his bench and gave himself up to it and spent long minutes studying the way the countless small flames could reflect from the back of Cassie's eyes.

It was the kind of moment, rarer than any eclipse, when the only temporal connection required by the soul is the loose intertwining of two people's index fingers, lighter than any butterfly, no words required at all.

How long the moment endured he couldn't say, but it was broken at last by a small robed arm encircling his neck and another encircling Cassie's and the insubstantial weight of Won Se's chin with its honey-smelling breath settling onto the tops of their heads as he drew them together.

When the embrace finally ended and Won Se sat down on the stone bench beside them, arranging his besieged bones carefully on the yak-skin pillow one of the younger initiates provided, Turner felt so peaceful and complete and free of worldly concerns that he was startled to hear his own voice ask:

"When will it all happen again?"

Won Se, far from being dismayed at the question—as Turner expected—seemed almost to welcome it, as if it were the natural thing for a Hope to ask. He said, "Do you want to see?"

Turner did and he didn't, especially not in the afterglow of so sublime a celebration, but when he looked at Cassie her eagerness broke the tie vote inside himself.

They followed Won Se down darkened corridors and through the central hall where a lone monk sat alongside a candle, his head bowed in unceasing prayer.

When they reached the torchlit entrance to the steep basement stairs Turner leaned down so that Cassie, in her chair, could grab around his neck, and he picked her up.

After the clamor of the big dining room, the growing silence as they descended flight after flight of steps was especially intense. He could hear Cassie's breathing and his own and Won Se's, puffing slightly from the exertion. Age was catching up with him. He was noticeably more feeble than the last time Turner went down these steps with him, years—no, God, only months—ago.

When the stairs ended and the wall opened out into the smoke-scented immensity of the War Room, it was quiet in the way only vast repositories of human activity can be upon abandonment—a factory on a holiday, or an auditorium at midnight after the janitors have gone. The only sound besides their own breathing and footsteps was an occasional cooing of doves from the long silver cage. The tined rods at its base that had made such discordant music before were stilled now, and there wasn't a single gap in the row of birds.

Likewise the tall map of the world, with its abandoned stepladder, showed only the barest scattering of red. The battered green teletype machine sat motionless, and the forest of abacus rods had their ivory counters set almost entirely against the floor.

As they passed the long curving wall surrounding the mandala chamber, cool air washed over them like a blessing. At the narrow entranceway Turner had to turn partly sideways to wedge himself and Cassie through. Inside, under the great diffused sourceless light, the sand-grain replica of the world with its delicate blues and greens and browns stretched out placidly beyond the stone railing, the former anthills of violent red reduced to mere specks.

No one had spoken the whole journey, and still didn't, as Won Se led them around the circumference of the room to the ascending steps cut into the face of the wall. They climbed through the dark to the small observatory room, where the soft reflected light showed a pair of woven-cane chairs set beside the turret of brass lenses as if in anticipation of his and Cassie's coming. Turner lowered her into one, sat down in the other, and Won Se set about adjusting the webwork of dials and levers and gears on the underside of the machine.

As he did, Turner noticed the soft dots of light inside the eyepieces go dark, and then light again, then dark, the pace increasing through sunup and sundown until they became a flickering stroboscope of passing time. As the rate kept accelerating the flicker became too rapid for the eye to discern, and the old lenses held solid gray light again.

Gears deep in the machinery gnashed, and as they slowed and became silent Won Se got up from underneath and positioned himself at one of the eyepieces, where he made fine adjustments to another set of dials and levers while he watched the scene inside. He stepped back from the turret and swung out two of its counterweighted arms so that Turner and Cassie both had a lens to look through.

Turner swallowed hard, listening to the distant drip of water somewhere within the underground walls, and wished fervently he hadn't brought the whole thing up. Most days, the rawness that had settled over him after the Calling Out was receding, but at other times—such as now—he wanted only to shut himself in a quiet room and spend weeks, months, just letting the whole event sink in; no more facts, please, no new information, no more food for thought.

But since he'd come this far with it, he felt obligated to look. He steeled himself, ready for the worst imaginable gore, and leaned down until his forehead rested against the cold brass of the lens rim. He felt the assembly vibrate once as Cassie did the same. He turned the ring and adjusted the focus to his vision, his heart pounding.

What came into view, though, wasn't continents or armies or disasters, but a small playground within some green city park. At the center of the frame a girl of eight or nine, with dark unruly hair, ran and played with a small white dog in summer sunshine.

Turner watched for a long time before he turned to Won Se and said, "I don't, uh . . . this must be something else."

Won Se smiled patiently and reached into the gear assembly again, where he grasped a knob and clicked it a half-turn to the right. "Now, better," he said.

When Turner looked again, the magnification of the scene had been increased so that only the young girl's face showed. Which served to confuse him even more, because close up he could see that, except for the long hair and delicacy of features, she looked a great deal like himself at that age. A sister he might have had.

Turner was saying, "I still don't see . . ." when suddenly he *did* see, an instant before Won Se explained:

"The Hope."

While this registered, Won Se's arm settled across Turner's shoulders, as insubstantial as a child's. "She has her mother's eyes," Won Se said, and when the face inside the frame turned fully front and the eyes showed best, they were indisputably the identical lineage of green and gold.

Turner heard Cassie's sudden soft expulsion of surprise, midway between laughter and a sob. Her hand found his and fastened around it, so hard that it hurt.

Why should the realm care who I love?, he remembered asking.

And Chai Lo's ready answer, *It thirsts for worthy adversaries; you will be shown, if you prevail.*

Turner got up from the machine to stand facing Cassie's chair and hold her, but she was so reluctant to give up the magical view inside the ancient brass cylinder that she brought his hand up to her face instead, rubbed it slowly across her lips and her dampened cheek. From where he stood he could see the twin dots of moving colored light that the lenses projected deep into her pupils, a fascination that seemed capable of occupying her for hours.

"There is . . . more," Won Se interjected gently, and moved a step toward the portion of the gear assembly that would carry the image forward in time.

Cassie, though still not taking her eyes away, shook her head.

"This is enough for now," she told him. "Thank you."

At that moment the sound of running feet echoed beyond the walls of the chamber, and a voice called Won Se's name. The figure who bounded up the stone stairs had to lean against the wall to catch his breath before he could speak. He was a young monk, barely old enough to be shaving, new to the monastery since Turner had been there last.

When he got control of his breathing he stammered out to Won Se in Tibetan, "It's . . . he's . . . the gate . . ."

Turner's first thought was that some tragedy had struck, or that James Crowe's calculations of that afternoon were flawed and droves of reporters had returned with a vengeance. But then he saw that what he'd taken for fear on the boy's face was actually excitement.

"Slowly," Won Se was saying. "Talk slowly."

When the boy spoke more calmly it was a phrase of Tibetan that Turner had never heard before. Part of it had the sense of *over* or *again*, Turner wasn't sure which, and something about *take form* or *in body*. Whatever, the news clearly transfixed Won Se. His skinny old throat swallowed hard, and he glanced at the ceiling for a second to collect himself before he could speak.

"We must go quickly," he said.

The stiffness that had hindered Won Se's descent of the long stairs fled him altogether in the excitement of the moment. Turner, with Cassie in his arms, had to trot the whole way back, up the countless stairs, to keep up with him and the young messenger. He was badly winded by the time they reached the central hall. A large crowd had gathered, all encircled about something or someone in the center, and there was a great clamor of talk.

He put Cassie in her chair and they followed Won Se as he parted the crowd back, whispering instructions to one monk or another. In seconds the talk had hushed and the crowd all sat on the stone floor, their hands clasped in front of them as reverently as prayer.

Revealed at the center of the circle was a small, frightened boy—five years old, six at most—looking apprehensively around the huge candle-lit room.

In the sudden total silence Won Se approached the child with the slow grace of ceremony and knelt in front of him, his ancient knees popping as he did so.

He looked into the youngster's eyes for long seconds, then put his hands on either side of the small head and kissed him gently, longingly almost, on the forehead, before sitting down in the circle of other men. This seemed to calm the child somewhat. He looked toward his feet and breathed deeply, then clasped his hands at the level of his chest, in prayer.

Won Se said loudly in Tibetan, "In whose name do you come to us?"

The child answered something, but his soft voice was lost in the hollow acoustics of the chamber.

"Say again," Won Se said sternly.

"Lim . . . Rhya," he replied, with a growing assurance.

Something tugged in the back of Turner's mind, pieces fitting beyond any conscious thought.

"Do you affirm you are the vessel of this great holy man's spirit?"

"I do," the boy said.

Won Se instructed, "Say when his wisdom entered you."

"Day thirty of the Onchu month."

The pieces in Turner's mind fell suddenly together with a force like an electric shock. July. The day Beh Vah died.

Lim Rhya.

At this, Won Se stood and announced quietly, "We may begin." He walked around the circle until he came to Cassie, leaned down and kissed her forehead. When Won Se sat down, she rolled her chair up to the child in the center as naturally as if the ceremony had been rehearsed for weeks.

She asked him, in Tibetan, to recite Lim Rhya's Trilogy of Spirit and Flesh, and he began in a halting voice that picked up strength as it went:

"If the spirit . . . is . . . within the flesh . . . and the flesh within a larger spirit, then . . ."

So that by the time he finished expounding on the principle and its application to the trials of daily living and Cassie thanked him and wheeled back to her place, Turner already knew from some older and deeper knowledge that she would kiss his own forehead next and he would walk up to face the child and ask to know Lim Rhya's Twelve Tests of Right Action.

The whole way up to the front he felt as if he were walking in a dream, the colors and smells and rustlings of the big reverberant room all amplified to an unnatural intensity, the way they are in paintings of historical scenes.

When he knelt at the child's feet his long ungainly frame still put him a head taller than the boy standing, and forced the youngster to crane his small neck back in order to look Turner in the eye. So instead he chose to sit akimbo on the stone floor, which put him directly on the level of the boy's tiny, solemn face.

"What are the Twelve Tests of Right Action?" he asked in Tibetan, and the child responded as casually as if he'd invented them:

"One. Does it cause harm to any sentient being? Two. If I were the recipient of the action and not its doer, could I look upon the doer and feel rightly dealt with? Three. Is the action . . ."

And so on, flawlessly and fluently, never taking his large dark eyes, the color of pecan shells in his flushed golden face, away from Turner's eyes.

But when the recitation was finished and Turner thanked him and started to stand, a small hand grabbed his wrist.

"Sir?" the boy asked in Tibetan, in a whisper.

"Yes," Turner said. The boy looked anxiously from side to side, as if in fear he was violating protocol.

He whispered, "What is . . . 'lizards'"?

When Turner found his voice he looked into the dark eyes and said, "It's a long story, buddy." And then, in Tibetan, "We'll talk later, okay?"

The child nodded and looked around the room for his next questioner, whom Turner somehow knew would be Se Hon.

After Se Hon came Bah Tow, and then Lu Weh. And on and on that way, till day.

About the Author

Carroll Dale Short, a native of Shanghi, Alabama, has worked as a teacher, newspaper editor, advertising photographer, magazine writer, layout designer, video producer, radio D.J., and corporate communications consultant. His fiction and non-fiction have appeared in *Redbook, Roanoke Review, The New York Times, Newsweek, American Lawyer, USA Today*, and other periodicals. He received *Redbook* magazine's "Outstanding Young Writer in America" prize in 1977. He lives in Birmingham with his wife, Mary.